I0600261

THE MYTH OF ROMANTIC LOVE: A STORY

Olivia Eielson

The Myth of Romantic Love: A Story
Copyright © 2024 Olivia Eielson

All rights reserved. No part of this book may be reproduced in any form
or by any electronic or mechanical means, including information storage
and retrieval systems, without permission in writing from the publisher,
except by a reviewer who may quote brief passages in a review.

Published by Lebendig Press
ISBN 979-8-9925245-0-5

Printed in the United States of America

"L'on n'aime bien qu'une seule fois: c'est la première. Les amours qui suivent sont moins involontaires."

La Bruyere

In loving memory of Jack Burki and Carson Jeffries.

PREFACE

How simple it was in the 1970s. On one side stood thin-lipped white men, dropping napalm on Vietnamese villagers so that elections could be won in America. On the other side stood everyone young, whether in body or spirit. We marched through the streets, chanting *power to the people* and *make love, not war!* Enough bombing, killing, torturing. We wanted freedom, peace, and we wanted equality – for everyone, not just white males.

We 1950s girls could grow up to be nurses or secretaries or school teachers; but everyone knew that real success meant catching a man and becoming Mrs. SomeoneElse. Identity? From then on our name would simply be a category word: wife, mother, grandmother.

Time for change: independence, based on money we had earned and could do with as we chose. Freedom to dress comfortably, so that we could walk, run, breathe. Wild improper colors, if we liked. Feathers! Rags! And when at last the pill came along, we could have sex as freely as men: no fear of getting pregnant and dying in an illegal abortion, or cutting off our future in a shotgun marriage. Syphilis seemed a thing of the past, and AIDS was unknown. In 1972, the first issue of *Ms.* magazine came out, with a picture of Superwoman on the cover. We could do anything, couldn't we?

Except the question was there: If we weren't the old definition of woman – helpless, silly, though useful to others in kitchen, bed, and nursery – then what were we? Did we really want to be like men? We didn't want the lives we'd seen our mothers living, and no one wanted to be like men over thirty (age after which, the saying was, you might as well be dead). And love? Between whom? Surely between equals – whoever and whatever they were. A revolution had begun, but it was hard to know just what to do with it.

1976

W hat on earth are you doing, Louise?" her mother cried out over the telephone. "Leaving Andrew? What's wrong with him? And you want to become a painter? Oh, Louise! What about your Ph.D.?"

There was a short pause while the phone was transferred to her father. "I hope you know what you're doing," he said dryly. "Sounds pretty crazy to me, but it's your life. Just don't expect any help from us, you know. Here's Mother," and the phone was silent for a moment.

"Louise," her mother began tentatively, "you haven't done anything you can't undo, have you?"

"Mother, there's no reason to put off anything – we've tried everything. You know – talking things through, different kinds of therapy –"

"Therapy! Louise, that's ridiculous. Everyone goes through difficult times in a marriage. You just have to keep trying."

Louise was silent for a moment, thinking of the endless dinners when Andrew told her she did not smile enough, or she smiled too much; or stonily silent himself, demanded that she be entertaining; his resentment if she left the apartment at night without him; the sensation of living in a small apartment with someone who did not want her there.

3

"I've been trying for so long, Mother. I don't have any more trying left in me."

There was a pause as her mother considered. "Well, Andrew is just reserved. He's a lawyer, and an Easterner. You have to make some allowances, Louise. Besides, how will you support yourself?"

Louise gave a short laugh. "Well, it isn't as if Andrew had been supporting me! We split everything down to the penny – and I always paid the penny, even though his income was four times more than mine. Next quarter I'll be teaching again, and my Ph.D. will be formally awarded in June. So then I'll just find a part-time job. It'll all be okay. You don't have to worry."

"Well, darling, I don't approve. I think it's very foolish. You do so well in school; and as for painting" – she paused a moment here to give emphasis – "I'm not sure you have enough talent."

Pause again.

"As for Andrew, well, I think maybe we'd better talk to you later. Goodbye, dear."

"Goodbye," she said, her defenses momentarily crushed. But she knew that even if she could think of her defenses, they would not seem like reasons to her parents. There was no way she could win them over. She hung up the phone and paused for a moment, her hand still on the receiver. What had her mother said? "Not enough talent"? Maybe, maybe she was throwing her life away: career, husband, secure future. But all right. Take the worst case, she thought melodramatically. She would just live alone for the rest of her life and paint. So what if it was bad painting? But, part of her retorted angrily, it wasn't bad painting. And it was her choice.

Absorbed in this crossfire of selves, she wandered back to her study and closed the door. She needed to think. But the sun porch, which had once seemed so light-filled and open, now felt cramped. She sat down at her desk, shutting her eyes for a moment. Back in Minnesota her parents were probably talking now, angrily shaking their heads. It wasn't that they had really liked Andrew, with his Harvard airs; but they did like the story about their daughter and her lawyer husband, who would soon be teaching at some prestigious university or other. Now she had stepped outside that story, into a sort of void – though there was room in that void for shame, embarrassment, and the fear of having a daughter in need of money.

She had sat at her desk only a moment when she heard the phone ringing again out in the hallway. Soon Andrew's voice, stiffly polite, announced through the closed door: "Telephone, Louise."

She got up slowly, reluctantly. What if it was her parents, eager to tell her again that she was making a terrible mistake? When she got out into the hallway, Andrew was hovering by the telephone, needlessly holding it, the awkward stiffness of his body a reproach. Wasn't he doing his duty, going to all this trouble to make sure she received the call? She looked at him as she approached, but his eyes did not meet hers. Swiveling his body around like a remote-controlled robot, he disappeared into his bedroom-study and closed the door.

"Hello?" she snapped into the telephone.

"Hello?" The voice was high and piping. "Louise Borgstrum? My name is Sylvia Schwartz. You left a message for me about sharing my apartment? Can you come down here this afternoon, maybe around three o'clock, and talk things over?"

"Oh yes," Louise answered, trying to make her voice sound more agreeable. "I have the address. I'll be there. Thanks a lot. Bye."

She hurried back to the safety of her room, and sat down at her desk. In front of her were books and papers for a new course she would be teaching, her parting shot in graduate school, a course in Women's Studies – a new field, which she and others had fought to establish. She called her course – provocatively, she hoped – "The Myth of Romantic Love." It was all about trying to solve puzzles, including, for her, the puzzle of her marriage. Yes, she had been lonely, coming across the continent to graduate school, knowing almost no one in Berkeley. She had been lonely for years before, too, at a first teaching job in Boston. So when she met Andrew, his head bobbing a little madly above the crowd at a Berkeley party full of strangers, he seemed interesting. Or maybe he was interesting because he seemed interested in her. And then, later, when she saw him naked, she could not help thinking that he did look sort of like Apollo, his pale marble smoothness perfectly proportioned, an educated god she could talk to, a god with a fine erection headed her way. But how could she have actually fallen for him? Certainly he had given her warnings, told her he had "problems," that he had already been in therapy some fourteen years.

When, one evening at her place, he had fallen on one knee before her, imploring her to "save" him, she had been astounded. What to make of it? But ultimately she had been seduced. Andrew was helpless, frozen in a sheet of ice. If she loved him, she could melt the ice, free him to live. Only after they were married had she come to realize that the ills formed a wall around him, impossible to penetrate. He was too fragile to be touched, and too sensitive to bear the brute energy which, he implied, she so inconsiderately exuded. It was very well for her to be intelligent, he said; he wanted an intelligent wife. But as for her doing things, and especially finishing her thesis before he finished his – well, that smacked of competition, unseemly in a wife, and damned irritating.

In their last therapy session together, she had cried, "But I love you!" Andrew had looked at her, his face set hard, angry. "Why do you keep making these demands on me?"

"Demands?" she echoed. "You did love me. You even said so."

"I thought I could. I was wrong." There was a little triumph behind the impassivity of his eyes.

She sighed. She had thought about all this, gone through three kinds of therapy with Andrew, filled pages in her journal. Enough. She forced her attention towards the papers before her. She had more than an hour of good working time before three o'clock.

* * *

The farther you go down the hill in Berkeley, the poorer the neighborhoods become. Starting in midtown, Louise had coasted on her bicycle for nearly fifteen minutes before she found the house. It looked shabby, and was somewhat isolated. The only real neighbor was a faded white house to the south. Across the street stood the Berkeley city equipment repair yard, closed and deserted now, Sunday afternoon.

She chained her bicycle to a tree and checked the notice she had taken from the co-op bulletin board. Yes, this was it: the right address, a place to share, cheap, an upper flat. After ringing the bell she stood a long moment before the windowless door. Extra plywood had been nailed over the original wood, making the entrance blank and, presumably, impenetrable. From behind the door, still closed, a voice called out: "Who is it?"

"Louise Borgstrum, to see the flat that's for rent, to share. I'm looking for Sylvia Schwartz."

"Oh yes," the voice said, and Louise heard the rattle of a chain and then the snap of the deadbolt before the door opened.

"Hello," Louise repeated, "I'm Louise Borgstrum."

The woman looked up at her with shrewd eyes, set in an appealing, childlike face.

"Mmm. Nice to meet you," but Sylvia's voice trailed downward as she spoke, making the formulaic words sound doubtful. "Come on in. I have the whole upstairs here."

The stairwell was dark, but when they emerged at the top there was sudden light from the large windows, which looked into the green boughs of trees. When they came to the kitchen, painted an intense orange color, Louise could not resist smiling. The style for psychedelic colors had pretty much passed by now.

"Wow," she said, hoping it had not been Sylvia who chose the paint. Sylvia nodded. "Yeah, I agree. It was that way when I moved in. You want a cup of tea?" Already she was turning up the fire under a tea kettle as Louise sat down at the kitchen table, aware that she was under inspection. Once again, as with Andrew, she was the suppliant. *Accept me, please accept me.*

"You have some kind of income?" Sylvia asked, turning around from the stove and seating herself across the table from Louise.

"Yes, I'll be teaching up on campus, starting in a few weeks."

Sylvia raised her eyebrows. "You teach? On campus?"

"Well, it's the last time I can, actually. They'll officially award my Ph.D. in June, and after that they won't hire me. They have to pay a Ph.D., but graduate students – like me, for now – are cheap labor. Even so, it'll pay better than being a teaching assistant, and I can easily save some money. After that, I'll get a part-time job of some kind. Don't worry, I can type, so I'm always employable."

Sylvia smiled. "Yeah, well, temp work is always there, but – with a Ph.D.?"

"I guess it does sound odd, but what I've decided is that I want to spend my time painting, not teaching."

Louise listened to her own voice telling this fact. She sounded calm, as if people regularly spent years getting a Ph.D. and then ditched all that work in order to live the uncertain, precarious life of a painter.

She went on. "Nearly all my life I've been split between painting and books. So all the time I've been studying literature and teaching it, I've been painting on the side. What I want to do now is switch that around."

"Hmmm," Sylvia considered, mulling it over. Louise watched carefully. If Sylvia thought her decision was wrong, if she came down on the side of the solid job and money and respectability, then it might be hard to live with her. It was hard enough to live with her parents' disapproval, to say nothing of her own self-doubts.

"You're brave," Sylvia finally said, looking at Louise with a new directness.

"Well," Louise replied, relieved, and more eager now to explain herself, "I asked myself how I'd feel when I got old and looked back on my life, and I'd been teaching the whole time. I knew I'd feel as if I'd missed the boat, almost as if I'd wasted my life by not doing what I really wanted to do more than anything. Not teaching English, but painting – doing it. Even if it turns out to be bad art, I still have to do it."

Sylvia nodded. "Yeah. I like that. I can understand that."

The tea kettle began to whistle, and Sylvia stood up again, turning to the stove. "What kind of tea?" she asked.

"Anything herbal," Louise replied.

"So why do you want to move down here?" Sylvia continued, her small hands busy with the tea-making. Everything about her was small and gently rounded, even her shoulders, which bent forward slightly, as if carrying some long-accustomed weight.

"I'm splitting from my husband," Louise said, feeling more reluctant now to talk. The breakup of her marriage seemed like a serious failure, something to be ashamed of.

"Ooh," Sylvia said, eyebrows cocked again as she poured out their tea. "Isn't this kind of a hard time for you? I mean, I bet you're not feeling too good. I mean, mightn't it be better for you to live alone for a while?"

Louise reached for the warm cup of tea. "Well, I can't afford a high rent, and sixty dollars a month is really reasonable. And I think I'm okay. I am upset, it's true, and it's hard, but – I think it's okay. We've been – or I've been – thinking about splitting up for a long time now. And then suddenly I knew that the time had come to actually do it. Or even, that I had to do it to survive."

She paused, wondering whether she had to explain more. Did she have to tell Sylvia about the whole tangle of things where she and Andrew had lost their way? Revisit the confusion and pain and endless analysis of it all? Just thinking of it again made her tired.

Sylvia seemed not to notice Louise's hesitations. "Well, the truth is, my boyfriend was living here until last month. We just broke up and frankly I'm not feeling so happy myself – and I don't really want to share the apartment, but I need the money. So," and she paused slightly, forcing herself, "obviously you could have half the kitchen space and all that. Since we're probably both not so good right now, maybe we'd get along as roommates. We both need some quiet time to recover."

As Louise walked out the door half an hour later, she congratulated herself. Sylvia seemed fine, and with such low rent she would not have to spend very much of her time earning money to support herself. She liked this neighborhood, too, with its lack of middle-class pretensions. Down here she would not have to be the correct graduate student, the proper wife, the good daughter. In the absence of old pressures, maybe she could learn to follow Nietzsche's admonition: "Become who you are!"

Across the street, unchaining her bicycle, she paused to admire the house with its uneven brown paint, and the weeds that crowded up to the sidewalk, tall and thick as wheat, untidy, irrepressible. She was eager to move in.

* * *

It was work riding uphill again, back to the apartment where she would have to face Andrew. Hoping to get to her room without being noticed, she tiptoed up the stairs. As she passed Andrew's room, however, the door was open, inviting her to look in. From the comparatively dark hallway, his light-filled room

looked like a stage. In the middle sat Andrew, his back to her,
ostensibly absorbed in study; but his body spoke. The high-held
shoulders and rigidly bowed head, with its pale hair plastered to
the scalp, all seemed to announce that he heard her, that he
suffered because of her, particularly and universally. She scurried
through the living room and into her sun porch, closing the door
behind her, protection against the silent recriminations Andrew
was sending out like the smell of mildew through the apartment.

Tonight at dinner she would have to tell him that she would
leave soon, that she had a place. She felt ecstatic, and terrified.
Soon she would be absolutely alone again; but she would also be
free. In three months, her teaching done, she would have
unlimited time for painting. She was reaching out for what she
wanted, and getting it. She felt as if she were stepping off a cliff in
the dark: exciting, this airy leap into the unknown, but also rather
frightening.

* * *

Moving was surprisingly easy. Andrew went out of town.
She hired a mover to take her few heavy belongings. The
only bad moment was when the mover, his giant hands tossing
her desk up in the air as if it were a big pillow, paused and looked
at her with kindly curiosity.

"Why you moving?" he asked. "Everyone needs someone, you
know."

Complication tied her tongue. It would be too much to
explain, in response to his simple statement, that yes she did need
someone, that she did not understand why Andrew hid from her
and drove her out; that she had tried, too long, to win him; and

that at last she thought it was better to live alone with her need, accept need as her partner, a known quantity, and one that would not turn her away.

* * *

H er room at Sylvia's was quite large, with plenty of room for her old upright piano. She especially needed the piano now; it provided a way for her feelings to push out of her fingers, out of her system for a while. It was Bach's thirteenth two-part invention that drew her most; but she played it not in the cool detached mathematical style she thought was probably correct, but in a floridly passionate way, each hand picking up the theme in turn as if to rescue it from oblivion, nostalgia and grief already present even as the part was being played. Then came the complications, the two hands corresponding, repeating one another's beauty at slightly different moments, and sometimes fighting, the melody straining and kicking and being ground into fragments. Then at the end it came back whole again, just long enough to flaunt itself, to remind her how beautiful it was, before it disappeared and was gone.

Music, painting, reading, and, for now, teaching: her ideal life, but it was a very quiet one. While she did continue to see old acquaintances on campus, she gradually realized that she had no good friends there, no one with whom she was really intimate. She had encapsulated herself with Andrew, who resented any life she had outside their apartment; and it had been convenient enough for her, too, as she concentrated on her thesis. Now, she found that her only real contact was with the people in her Reichian therapy group, her ersatz family. Even though it was temporary, a concoction, and one she paid money to be part of, still she welcomed the warm hugs before and after their sessions. It was the only place where she could be entirely herself, as the others were too, accepted and safe even though all defenses were let down.

But therapy met only every other week. Now, every morning, she woke at Sylvia's, an hour or two before she had finished her sleep, visited by sadness. Her room was painted a deep royal blue, with a pale blue-violet ceiling. They were the colors of her childhood winters, the colors of snow just after the sun has gone down and the temperature is ten below. She stared at it, immersed in isolation, failure, and fear. She could not foresee any change. She had given everything she had to her marriage with Andrew, but it hadn't been enough.

* * *

Louise looked out at the circle of young women in the classroom. They were quiet, looking at her with attentive eyes.

"The assumption at the heart of this course is that there *is* a myth of romantic love, or myths plural, stories we've absorbed, often without realizing it, sets of hopes and assumptions that may be damaging to us, insofar as we want equality in love as well as in the rest of life. Even though the basic idea of romantic love was a late medieval European development, I've chosen to start earlier in time, with *Medea*, because women have always loved and nearly always been at a big disadvantage in love. You've just read *Medea*. Would you say she is strong? In our current way of thinking, could you say she was a feminist?"

Everyone seemed to have an answer.

A woman with long dark hair leaned forward, eager to speak. "Yes, she was so strong. And she knew magic. If it hadn't been for her, Jason never would have gotten the Golden Fleece."

Her neighbor turned to face her. "But how could she have loved Jason so much? He was a creep. He just used her. For him she betrayed her father and killed her brother. So what did he do for her? He betrayed her by going for a younger woman – a king's daughter, someone with new power to give him."

A third student leaned forward. Well, but she gets back at him, she kills the new woman – love that beautiful robe that wrapped her in flame! – and kills their kids and then gets in her chariot and flies away into the sky!"

"Yeah, really great – kill your brother and your own children and this other woman, all for this man who I would agree is a major creep. All he does is order people around. He doesn't get it until the end that Medea could be any way equal to him, and when he does get that, he calls her a barbarian. I mean, she can't be civilized and like a 'real' woman should be, and still be power-ful and equal – or really, stronger than he is."

"Yes, and he says that about her sexual energy, too, did you get that? It sounds as if she really liked sex and he says oh yes, I know you're not a modest right woman. To him a real woman doesn't have any sexual love or sexual pleasure – just men do."

"Let me ask a question," Louise broke in. "Which character would you rather be?"

They looked at her, startled.

"I know it's a tragedy," Louise conceded. "Everyone is da-maged – beyond repair. Plato says 'the god is in the lover.' Medea loves Jason; Jason loves only power – only himself."

"Right," another student put in. "Power is as good as sex to him. Medea would've been better off if she'd never seen Jason."

Louise pressed on guiltily, knowing she was protecting herself now, her own choice. "Yes, in a way. She could have stayed at home, never have really loved anyone. But why is the play named for her, not Jason?"

Again the class was briefly silent. Finally someone wise-cracked, "So it's better to love and have the guy fuck you over because at least you can say you loved someone?"

"And this is power?" another woman added in a sarcastic tone.

* * *

After class, Louise lingered outside in the sunshine, thinking. She had begun seeing two new men, both very young – twenty-five and twenty-six, some ten years younger than herself. She knew she was pushing things, trying too desperately to disprove the violet ceiling of her room, to show that men could be attracted to her, that she need not live alone forever. But these two? The carpenter was still half in love with his old girlfriend, who had broken off the relationship; and he had begun to show a disconcerting penchant for sex that pretended a forcing against her will. It made her uneasy, and brought to the surface an old and deep ambivalence about sex and being a woman: sex was an invasion, a being taken-over. The fact that she liked this seemed, at best, undignified. Full human beings – or was it just men? – were supposed to take, not be taken. Yet she was a chooser, too; and she found that when sex turned to a pretend-rape, it became irrelevant, as if someone else, some cardboard stereotype, had

been put in her place. As for the carpenter, he seemed to be playing a role, himself. Underneath, she suspected, he was uncertain,
and quite possibly also affectionate, though he could not let her
see that.

At least it was better than the engineer with his permanent
smile, who offered no sex at all. The smile, those teeth: he was a
closed gate. And she needed to be invited in, warm body to body.
Neither of these two new men could fill the emptiness which had
gathered in her, and the deep anxiety.

* * *

W hat makes Heathcliff such a memorable character?"
Louise asked her class.

"Tall, dark, and handsome," one student quipped, grinning.

"Well, he's free, he's strong, he's outside the bounds – kind of
like Medea in that way. Sexy, if you like the type."

"Yeah," another student put in, kicking off her sandals
impatiently, "that's the myth all right, the wild powerful male.
Heathcliff's so attractive because he hasn't been tamed, and
Catherine hasn't either. They both belong outside in the wind
and weather, out on the moors where there's no one else, and they
can be free. But Isabella – she's a good girl, she's an indoors girl,
she's tame. So to her, Heathcliff has all the strength and stuff she
lacks. Actually she put Heathcliff on a pedestal. Bad move! She
just lies down in front of him like a big insect. Yuck, so he stamps
her out. Catherine's the only one with the primal force, like
Heathcliff."

"I think their love for each other is just a kind of excuse,
actually," said an older woman who usually sat silent, listening.

"It's the same as with Tristan and Isolde. Each is like a symbol to the other of some vastness they want union with. Sex is a way of touching that vaster realm, but it's confusing because they may think for a while that sex is really it, and not see that it's this bigger thing – which maybe they can only get to by death."

Louise nodded. "When Tristan and Isolde first drank the love potion, they both thought it was poison. Love and death are linked from the very beginning."

A freckled young student shook her long hair impatiently. "But how does this relate to us? Come on, if I go looking for love, I'm sure not looking for death. That's just too much."

"Well, some women like to be swept off their feet, I think," another woman replied. "To be kind of wiped out, taken into someone else's world. It's like that old saying, that in marriage two people become one, and that one is the man. It's like death for the woman – but I don't know if that's true for the man. He gets sex, someone to cook for him, a sidekick. Back to power again, not love."

"But what about love as just a kind of, well, a closeness between people?" a small shy woman asked timidly, looking up from her desk. "Not like Heathcliff or these self-absorbed egoists like Jason, but something more simple, like two people who really understand each other and love each other, and no one has more power than the other one, they're just together in this really close way?"

"Pooh!" her neighbor answered. "That's practically impossible in a patriarchal society. Men are too used to having power, they don't even notice how superior they feel, they just take it for granted. Probably they can't even get it up unless they feel superior, so women help them – or they do if they want sex, or even just a relationship. That's the problem – women get rewarded for acting dumb, and wearing heels and stuff so they're all, like, helpless. I mean, you can get lifetime support for doing that, men love it! The kind of equality you're talking about is impossible."

"Or boring," another student put in.

"Or unromantic," a third woman added in an arch tone of voice.

The class laughed, but a little uncomfortably.

Louise looked around the circle of students. "If the things we've been describing in *Medea* and *Wuthering Heights*, and what we've been talking about in our own experiences, if all that is part of a myth of romantic love, then what does it mean to try to leave this myth behind? Do we automatically step into something called 'reality'?"

There was a brief silence, until the shy student mumbled, "Like, that feminism, or being a strong independent woman, is just another myth? I mean, not any truer than that old stuff?"

"Who cares?" another interjected, "It's better for us."

"But some women still like the old roles."

"Sure, but it's just a question of where it leads to. It's fun in the beginning, but who wants to just be everyone's servant, a person with no mind of her own?"

"Can someone be happy being like that, being second-class, not being free?"

"Maybe," Louise said, reluctant. "That gets us into the question of what freedom is, and what happiness is, which are way more than we can tackle here. In Shakespeare's *King Lear*, when Lear is weak and powerless, wandering around half-mad in rags out in the freezing rain, he encounters a loyal subject, Kent, who says to him, 'You have that in your countenance which I would fain call master.' And in the play, Kent was fine and strong, this was loyalty, it was completely admirable, and it held the entire social system in place. For us, now, the old male-female system is very much in question, and as women we have choices that probably our mothers didn't have. In a way this is harder: we have to think, and decide. We can try to define ourselves, and our lives, and do it without that many models, either."

The older woman cocked her head to one side, and laughed. "We're always assuming here that we have to have a man – or a woman – a partner for life. But what if that's not really the way life works? Is anything permanent? Do we just want a sort of place to hide?"

She seemed about to go on, but the classroom door opened and closed; there were students out in the hallway, waiting for the next class. Looking at the clock, Louise gathered up her books and papers. It was time to end the discussion. An hour was too short for this eager class.

* * *

It was Saturday, and Sylvia was in the kitchen with Louise, making breakfast.

"Are you going to the library today?" Sylvia asked, putting the kettle back on the stove with fresh water for Louise.

"Thanks," Louise muttered, not quite awake yet. "Oh, no, the course finished last week and I'm done reading the student papers. I'm free!"

"Wonderful. So what are you going to do?"

"Paint, I guess," Louise responded, feeling fear creep into her belly.

"I have to say, you don't look that enthusiastic," Sylvia commented.

"I don't know if I can paint. I mean, I've done a lot already, but never full time. What if I don't know what to paint? No ideas? Or I get stuck somehow?"

"I think you worry a lot," Sylvia said, sipping her coffee and looking a little amused. "Besides, how are you going to have time to paint? You're seeing all these men. How do you keep track of them?"

"I don't," Louise spoke ruefully, conscious of using a pat answer to skim over her disappointments. The carpenter had gone back to his old girlfriend, and the engineer had simply disappeared, his fixed smile, like the teeth of the Cheshire cat, the last to fade from view.

"Well," she went on, "the two young ones are gone. Too young. Or I'm too old. Or something."

"Isn't there another one, too, a new one?" Sylvia asked, persistently and a little irritatingly amused.

"Yes. He's the only one with absolutely no education and no ambition, but also no games, just a kind of simple animal warmth."

"But it can't last, can it? Won't you get bored?"

Louise paused, picturing Charles at his apartment, slouching in the bedroom doorway, slim-hipped, broad-shouldered, Stanley Kowalski without the meanness, coming in to the shadowy room where she lay waiting, the dinner he had cooked for them just leftovers in the kitchen, something for the roaches, nothing she had to worry about.

"Well," she admitted to Sylvia, "we have run out of things to talk about. And he's going to get a roommate next week, and she – it is a she – has herpes. So I figure that pretty soon Charles is going to have herpes."

Sylvia raised her eyebrows. "Herpes – that's this new thing people are getting? Like itchy pimples?"

"Very itchy pimples, and painful, I hear. Crotch and mouth."

"God. And if you get it, you have it for life?"

"Right. But it isn't fatal or anything. So, they cured syphilis. Maybe they'll find something for herpes too."

"Hmmm," Sylvia ruminated. "So is this the end of free love? We have to worry about disease again? And so for Charles . . ."

"Right. No more Charles for me."

"Hey, your tea water is boiling," Sylvia pointed out. "I got you out a cup already. Sit down."

Louise let these things happen, and warmed her hands at the cup. It was good to sit in the kitchen with Sylvia and drink tea.

* * *

She had forgotten how much she loved the smell of oil paints and turpentine. Even when she left her room, she could sniff it on her hands, under her fingernails, a secret pleasure. She began also to attend life-drawing classes, determined to build her craft from the foundation up, properly. She was making a life, creating someone who might eventually dare name herself "painter." An independent person, who could live without a man. Maybe even something like the person her students had thought her to be.

And soon Christmas would be coming. She could go home to Minnesota, sleep in her old single bed in the upstairs room where the familiar windows looked out into elm branches, their dark brown angles outlined in snow. By now her parents would surely have forgiven her for leaving Andrew, and for not pursuing a university teaching career. She would be surrounded by comfort and warmth, go ice skating on the lake, make crispy buttery Christmas cookies, see old high school friends.

This thought helped her through the summer, as she woke up daily to the painting, rushing at her work in order to make progress before her savings ran out, fighting through the difficulties in front of the easel in the silent apartment. Although Christmas was the only landmark on her calendar, there would be others, later.

It was early December when her mother's letter arrived:

Dear Louise,

Daddy has been very sick. He was in the hospital for several days and is now at home. He is out of all danger but still very weak. You can't imagine how frightening all this has been. Maybe if you had still been with Andrew I would have written you, but I hated to worry you when you are without him. As it happens, this year your sister can come be with us at Christmas, along with Swede and all three children. It will fill up the house, and I'm afraid it will be as many people as Daddy can handle, weak as he is. There just won't be any place to put another person, and you have so many friends out there in Berkeley, I know you will have a fine Christmas holiday with them. We will be thinking of you on Christmas.

*Your presents are in the mail to you. Let me know if they arrive
safely.*

    Love,

    Mother

Louise carefully put the letter down on her desk. It wasn't
possible. No room for her in the house? At home? At Christmas
time? Now of all times in her entire life, when she so badly needed
to be there? She burst into tears, pounding the desktop with the
heel of one hand.

A moment later she felt a hand on her shoulder. It was Sylvia.

"Sylvia! My parents don't want me to come for Christmas! My
father's been sick – but it's really that my sister's coming," she
sobbed, "and she's taking up all the space! My properly married
sister," she added, "my acceptable sister. And I have to be alone at
Christmas!"

Sylvia stroked her head and arm for a moment, and then said
softly, "I'll be here, you know. Jews don't celebrate Christmas."

"Oh Sylvia!" Louise sniffed. Suddenly Christmas looked a
little less important. After all, more than ten percent of the
population didn't even celebrate it.

"We could have a nice dinner here on that day," Sylvia went
on.

Louise lifted her head, wiping at her eyes with the backs of her
thumbs. "Oh. Yes. We could. Oh," it occurred to her, "there's
someone I think you would like, Deirdre, and she can't afford to
go all the way back to North Carolina for Christmas with her
family. I'll invite her too."

It began to take shape in her mind. "We'll have turkey, okay?"

"Sure, I love turkey," Sylvia laughed.

"Yes, we always have turkey." Louise stopped suddenly, the pain rising in her throat again at the thought of being excluded from home on Christmas. She pulled in a deep breath. With enough effort she could forget about the family who should have been part of her celebration. They were absent, very absent. Sylvia was here, and so was Deirdre, someone who might become a real friend. She had to look forward, look at what was possible.

On Christmas Eve, Sylvia went over to her new boyfriend's place. She would be with Harvey until late afternoon the next day. Louise was alone in the apartment. The high windows leaked cold air; it seemed impossible to keep the apartment warm. Standing by the wall heater, Louise drank some brandy and decided to open the presents from her parents. The sound of ripping paper and popping string echoed in the empty house. She let the wrappings fall on the cracked black linoleum floor, not caring to be neat. Her mother had sent her two shirts and a dress – from both parents, really, but her father had probably never seen the things themselves – only the bills.

She tried on the shirts. They were very pretty, but too small. Her mother had probably found them on sale. Maybe they would look all right under a sweater. She tried on the dress. It, too, was at least a size too small. How could her mother not know her size after all this time? Struggling out of the dress, she inspected the seams and construction. If she cut it off below the waist, and incorporated the cut-off material in the side and arm seams, she could enlarge the whole thing to the point where it might be wearable. The lovely complicated blues in the pattern lent themselves well to the project; the changes, drastic though they were, might not be all that visible when she was done. She could have a shirt out of it – more useful, anyway, than a dress, since she mostly wore jeans.

She began pinning, and set up her portable sewing machine. Cutting and sewing, trying on, altering – she worked obsessively. It was long past midnight when she finished. The dress was now a shirt. It fit and she could wear it – though her mother would probably never recognize her gift now.

But she was finished, she had passed Christmas Eve, the one time absolutely alone. Too tired to think, she crept under the bedcovers, piling them high above her, making a warm cave. Tomorrow, with all the cooking she had planned, would pass easily. Christmas would be over, like a bad cold.

* * *

Deirdre arrived in a flurry of brightly colored woolens. "Ahh," she said, "it smells good!"

"You should see Louise cook," Sylvia joked. "She used every pan in the whole house! You know any bag ladies we can invite? I'm telling you, there's food!"

And there was. Louise had cooked enough to fill and overfill Christmas day: turkey, its skin dark gold with butter basting; yams roasted with walnuts, butter, dark brown sugar, plus a little bourbon; and a simple old-fashioned stuffing.

Deirdre swirled lightly around the kitchen. "This is new, isn't it?" She pointed to a painting on the wall and paused, studying it.

Louise didn't reply, held by the usual mix of feelings she had when someone looked at one of her paintings: childish delight at her work being actually seen; shyness at opening her world to another person; fear that what she had done wasn't good enough. "It's a little hippie-psychedelic, maybe," she ventured. The painting showed an ocean, represented by snaky bands of blues, greens, and purples, with someone advancing into it, about thigh-high. "But I want to just do whatever comes out, and not censor."

"Yeah. I like the colors," Deirdre said.

"It's not such a cheerful painting," Sylvia put in.

"No, but you wouldn't want it to be." Deirdre peered more closely at the canvas.

Pleased and embarrassed, Louise deflected attention: "Let's eat!" she said, gesturing towards the table, set with the best remnants of wedding presents given to her and Andrew, six years earlier.

"It looks beautiful," Deirdre said, sitting down at her place, looking at the napkins and tableware.

"It pays to get married," Louise replied dryly.

"I don't know." Sylvia sat down too. "I've done it twice. A lot of heartache, and no stuff for the kitchen. How'd you get any, Louise?"

"Well, we never bought anything together, so no problem there, and the wedding presents we divided by whose friends or family had given us what. Since his family and friends were all skinflints like Andrew, I got just about everything in the way of kitchen stuff. And I'd paid exactly half of all our expenses – food, rent, movies –"

"Excuse me," Sylvia broke in, "but isn't that sort of dumb? I mean, didn't Andrew have lots of money? Lots more than you? Why shouldn't he pay?"

"Because then I would have had to do things to make up for it

– the usual stuff women have always done when they were sup-
ported by a husband, like all the housework, shopping, laundry,
social life – not to mention having to ask if I want to buy myself
something."

"Hmm. This all seems too . . ." Sylvia paused, looking for a
tactful word.

"Mercantile?" Deirdre put in.

"Yeah. Like where's the love? Shouldn't everything be more
simple?"

"Should be, should really be, but hasn't really been," Deirdre
said. "So now we're renegotiating."

"Oh. Yeah." Sylvia looked at her plate. "How about some of
that turkey, Louise?"

Louise had carved a lavish amount of turkey while they spoke.

"You know how to do that!" Deirdre exclaimed, eyeing the
pile of meat.

"Well, how hard can it be?" Sylvia responded. "I mean it's
pretty obvious. You just start cutting. Life is so much easier
without a man. Who needs them?"

"Well, you have Harvey," Louise pointed out.

"Yeah, Harvey," Sylvia allowed. "But it's not that exciting.
He's smart, but . . ." she smiled ruefully.

Louise looked at Deirdre. "Let's see now: Bill, George, and
who's the other one?"

"Damion."

"You're, like, sleeping around?" Sylvia asked.

"Well, we used to call it that. Free love, right?" Deirdre passed
around the bowl of wild rice. "But we're all really free. Bill's more
attached to Joanna, but I go over to his place sometimes and spend

the night, when I'm not too involved working on my thesis. And I don't even know who else George sees."

"You mean sleeps with?" Sylvia interposed.

"Yes." Deirdre smiled easily. "And Damion is in a commune. So is his girlfriend Diana, but I think they rotate on a system."

"God," Sylvia exclaimed. "Sex on a schedule. So who does the cooking in the commune?"

"Oh, everyone," Deirdre said. "Well, maybe the women more because they like to take care of the children."

"They like to," Sylvia repeated in a slightly mocking voice. "Don't the men like to?"

"Well," Deirdre said, spearing a yam, "you know, the commune children are loved by everyone. It's probably much better for them. Not the little box of the nuclear family. These kids are growing up free. And would you want kids to grow up the way you did?"

"God, no. I couldn't breathe. I mean, my parents loved me but it was like jail. I got out as soon as I could. I got out actually by getting married – that's how desperate I was." Sylvia laughed. "So is it better to grow up in a commune? With people coming and going? Maybe."

"Everything's new," Louise commented, as uncertain as Sylvia.

"So we're all like this person in your painting," Deirdre said. "Venturing into a new ocean."

"The ocean of love!" Sylvia giggled, wineglass a little unsteady in her hand.

"Let's hope!" Louise replied, lifting her glass in a mock toast.

* * *

Winter and spring passed. Louise took temporary typing jobs, and painted in between. She did not need to work more than about seven days a month to keep ahead of the low rent and a vegetarian diet. She still had some savings from teaching, but those she kept in reserve. A new woman-owned gallery sprang up, and gave Louise a one-woman show. Only a few things sold, but for now that was almost irrelevant. She was being shown; someone thought she could paint. She worked on steadily through the summer, increasingly contented with her life. She would not have said she was "free of men," because she did not reject the idea of a man. It was simply that life had come to seem all right as it was.

Then on the street one day she caught sight of Herbert, a friend from her undergraduate days. Like Louise, Herbert led a sort of Berkeley dropout existence, though in his case there were no material uncertainties, no lack of fine furniture and fine whiskey, and no fear of old age spent in unprovided poverty. He was from a wealthy family, and had married a fiercely capable woman also from a wealthy family. At first Louise had feared for Herbert's safety; he was soft, dreamy, given to vague thoughts of Plato over a stiff drink. He had a delicate Celtic whimsy which she thought Elizabeth might destroy. In fact, after eight years of marriage, it was Elizabeth who was tamed, by Herbert's absolute dependence on her. If they were to eat, she had to provide. If they had to live somewhere, she house-hunted and did the moving. Somehow she had managed to get a Ph.D. in linguistics while caring for Herbert, but these two absolutely absorbing careers had exhausted her, and she was no longer a threat to anyone.

"Herbert, how nice to see you!" Louise called out, but then immediately tried to modulate her tone. He was the kind of Easterner who never shows surprise or excitement, these being noisy evidence of lack of travel, education, and the long view on things.

"Do you like this new fish place?" she continued, noticing the little white box he carried.

"Louise, nice to see you. Yes, we've gotten rather addicted to sushi. It's quite beautiful, don't you think? I'm just going over to the park to meet Michel. We'll have a game of chess, I think."

"Oh well, I won't keep you. But let me know if you have a free moment sometime. It would be nice to get together for a cup of coffee. I'm in the phone book, still under my old name."

And that was all, until a few weeks later when Herbert phoned to invite her to dinner at their house. "A small gathering," he said, "food and wine – and a good cigar, too, if you're so inclined." Louise smiled. Cigar smoking made her dizzy, but she was glad of the invitation. It was a long time since she had been to a party. She wanted to rub elbows with people, maybe get a little high so that the hard casings around her and the others might crumble and allow a few hours of contact.

When she arrived at Herbert and Elizabeth's house, she found the drinking well begun. The other five guests seemed much in need of alcohol to thaw them, and Louise was not slow to join in. They had a long time for drinking and talking, while Elizabeth stayed in the kitchen all by herself, refusing help, making dinner for nearly two hours.

Louise picked a pale blond woman as someone likely to be interesting for a long talk. She was from New Hampshire, and said she had taken many years to adjust to California. "My parents still don't understand," she said. "They think it's a sort of corrupted garden of Eden – Eden plus continual orgy, maybe. My neighbors got a hot tub. I haven't dared write home about that yet. But in fact," she said, folding herself into the crack of the chair, "it's nothing very scandalous." This piqued Louise's curiosity. No one she knew had, or dreamed of having, a hot tub; that required owning land and having money.

"They really have a hot tub? And you've been in it? What's it like?"

"Well, I only went in when it was all other women – just a few other women, actually. And it's very dark, because it's outside, of course, in among trees and away from the house lights. You can't see anything," she assured Louise. "It's very relaxing, very serene."

Louise wanted to ask if people wore swimming suits or were naked together, but wasn't sure how to put it to Peggy, who was clutching her beige shawl around her bony shoulders, pale blue eyes peering out sharply over her glass of bourbon.

"Is there some sort of etiquette or ritual that goes with it?" Louise tried.

"Not really. They just open up their tub to the close neighbors every other Friday night. If you're curious and want to see what it's like, you could go with me next Friday."

This was a casual offer, not entirely intended to be taken up, but Louise seized the chance. "Friday? I would love to do it, if you think it's all right. I've been curious about these mysterious hot tubs for a long time."

* * *

F eeling a little shy, she went to Peggy's house the following
Friday. A babysitter answered the door, and Louise sat with
her on the living room couch, watching TV a long time before
Peggy finally appeared. She looked thinly elegant in her shorts,
her towel slung over her shoulder, her long blond hair swinging
rather severely across the blue shirt. Very eastern, Louise thought,
and a little superior. Then she caught herself. Perhaps that was
not fair. After all, she too was thin, and, if she got enough sun,
blond. She was also considerably taller than Peggy. But Peggy had
the confidence. Inside Louise's fashionably correct woman's body
there were still remnants of the skinny girl of thirteen who had
shot up to five feet ten and wished, in vain, that she could be
invisible.

She tried to start a conversation, but had no luck. It was like
trying to start a fire with three matches and wet logs. Gradually,
as they walked along the silent wooded street, Louise realized that
Peggy was totally stoned. She would have an introduction to the
neighbors, but no company.

"Here," Peggy said shortly, as they turned off the road. Louise
looked with astonishment. This would not be a quiet or private
initiation to the hot tub: the house, which stood just above them,
was generating light and noise like a small power station. It must
be filled with people. But maybe, Louise thought, Peggy had been
so stoned on her previous visits that to her the place had seemed
absolutely serene; maybe she had not deliberately misled Louise
at all.

As they entered the front door, a tall freckled man came and shook hands with them, a practiced host. Louise was not sure he actually saw either of them, and yet, five minutes later, all three were undressing together in one of the bedrooms, preparing to go into the hot tub. Louise looked at her host from the corner of her eye, curious. Pleasant body, face not easy to read just now. He paid no attention to her – and in any case, there must be a wife somewhere too. She had to remember to stick to her agenda: she would just see what a hot tub was like.

Her first impression was simply that it was crowded, almost shoulder to shoulder. Both men and women gave her a quick look-over as she clambered in, but only general shapes could be seen, as it was reasonably dark, under trees and with evening coming on. Everyone seemed to be about the same age – around thirty or thirty-five – and somehow the men all appeared professional in some way. It was amazing how they managed to radiate this sense even while naked in a tub of hot water.

"Joke time," one of them called out. "Whoever tells the best joke – or should it be the worst? – goes to the middle and gets massaged by everyone."

Louise's breath constricted. She both longed to go to the center, longed to be touched and stroked, and feared this exposure of herself to strangers. So she held back while the jokes began, and the first teller, a man, got pushed to the center. Both women and men massaged him. It was hard to say just what was happening, with most of the hands – and bodies – hidden under water, and the noise of the laughing and splashing. One woman and then another got massaged. Louise began to realize that her chance was slipping by her. Very soon the group would grow bored with this game, and she would never get to be massaged. Yet telling a joke was an exposure, too, a risk; she did not feel as witty as these people, nor as sophisticated. At last, desperate, she thought of an old joke, the first and last even mildly dirty joke she had ever heard, knowing it was so corny that it would not even be measured against the others, about a baseball player who found it difficult to run because he had so many balls on him. It was enough to get some groans, and a push into the center for the worst joke so far. Hands frighteningly, miraculously, came out of the dark water, but they acted with a reassuring nonchalance. This was old hat to them. None of the hands went too far; there was a politeness even here, under water; invisible rules had followed these people though they had thrown off their clothes and climbed into the tub together in the semi-dark. Some hands were gentle; some were self-importantly brusque and businesslike; the host's were vigorous, but without much relation to her. He might as easily have been stroking a table top. At last it was clear that her turn was over and reluctantly she surrendered her position. No more hands came up out of the dark to touch her. No one else took her place in the center. The conversation began to lose energy; beginnings were tentatively made, but no one took them up. A few people got out. Someone started passing around a bottle of wine.

"That's it," her neighbor said approvingly. "Drink up. It's a decent red. Won't leave any hangover. You can go to the office tomorrow at the crack of dawn and start preparing your briefs – no headaches at all. You are a lawyer, I suppose, like everyone else here?"

"What do you mean, Robert," called out a woman from across the tub. "Some of us are engaged in higher pursuits – cooking, for instance." As she spoke she pulled herself up so that she was sitting on the edge of the tub, ostensibly to cool herself. The attention of the men swiveled around to the pale, barely-visible forms of her body. A few of the men sat up on the edge of the tub, too. "Hot, hot," they said, leaning towards the woman.

She laughed. "Now you," she said, swishing water with her foot towards the host, "being a scientist – that's more like being an artist, I think. And then Concha's not a lawyer, either."

A voice rang out behind Louise. "Do I hear my name?" A small, slim, squarely-built woman, who carried herself erect as an athlete, stepped into the tub, clearly meaning to focus the attention in her direction.

It was Louise's moment to leave the field. She stepped out, feeling sure that her retreating rear end was covered, so to speak, by the newcomer's arrival. Soon she was safe behind the towel again. Her neighbor in the tub had stepped out also.

"It's time for the sauna, don't you think? Here, I'll show you the way."

That sounded attractive enough, and Louise followed him into the house. "My wife is probably already in there," he added as a safety precaution, signaling his state.

What a relief, to have this gift: an escort, a guide who charmingly prevented her from being alone, led her to an activity which would not demand cocktail conversation, and yet as an announced married man, made no claims on her. Wrapped in a big towel, she walked with him boldly through the living room, which was crowded with talking people, and down a set of stairs into what looked like an enlarged closet, very dark and very hot. Against one wall was a double-decker platform. Someone was lying quietly on the top deck. Louise and her companion sat on the bottom.

"What do you do in a sauna?" she asked, trying to make some connection with this stranger, to feel more at ease. "Should we be pouring water over ourselves, or flagellating each other with birch boughs?"

"No, no, just sit down and relax," came a woman's voice from overhead. "You don't have to do anything. That's the pleasure of it, after a horrible week's work and all that competitive small talk and one-upping out there. Just sit down and let the heat sink into your bones."

"Well," the man said, "a little massage never hurts, either. Would you care for my beautiful back?" he asked, beginning to swing around so Louise could reach his back. But this was a little too close in for her, conscious now of being in a small dark space, naked, with someone she scarcely knew.

"No, actually I prefer feet," she answered. "Give me a foot here. You'll see, it's very relaxing." She liked feet. They seemed to her like unappreciated hands, Cinderellas, and in spite of pounding on the ground every day, quite sensitive.

As he put his feet up near her, the sauna door opened, sending a blinding light into the room. Louise could just make out a tall male figure as the door closed again. "Well, who have we here?" the man laughed, without seeming to expect an answer.

"There's just space here," came the voice overhead. "Come on up."

He was up instantly, though Louise could not tell how in the darkness. She continued with her massage, appreciating each toe, quietly communing with this big stiff foot.

The sauna door opened again and the figure of a woman, fully dressed, appeared outlined against the light.

"Hal?" she said, "it's time to go home. You know we promised the babysitter, and it's getting so late . . ." She trailed off, but her words were as much command as question. The door closed without waiting for a reply, and the owner of the foot stood up.

"Nice massage," he said, "my foot's a new man." As he turned to leave, he suddenly reached down and brushed Louise between the legs. She was so surprised that she didn't say anything at all as the door opened and closed again and he was gone. She did not know what to think. Maybe he had thought she was giving him a come-on with the foot massage. One side of her cried out indignantly at this liberty he had taken with her. And yet it was only a passing gesture, and obviously it had been meant as a sort of compliment. He seemed to have said she was attractive, sexy, a woman.

She lay down full length on the empty bench. On the bench above her the woman and man were softly talking and laughing, with longish pauses between sentences. Perhaps ten minutes of this went by, and Louise began to feel that she might not be welcome there. Tentatively she spoke, testing: "What do you suppose the temperature is in here?"

"We keep it fairly cool, as saunas go," the man replied, "about 115 or so."

It seemed hard to speak again, to send a brave column of words out into the darkness, where these two others were indifferent to her or perhaps even impatient, wanting her to leave. At last she stood up, feeling her way in the dark, saying as explanation, "It's just a little cool for me, I guess."

But as her hand moved along the edge of the upper shelf, it was touched by another hand. Small but strong, it moved along her arm with a sensitivity and tenderness that she had never known in a man. Another hand touched her face, smoothing her hair back. She stood there transfixed a moment, uncertain whether to run away or remain. These hands were not impersonal; they were touching her very differently from the way of those hands in the hot tub, those polite, decorous, casual hands. And they were different from the hand of the man who had just left, with his cavalier liberty. These hands reaching out of the darkness now really touched her, they promised something like intimacy, something almost like love. These were, moreover, a woman's hands, there was no mistaking that. No man would have touched her with this delicacy, this unutterably sweet knowledge which slipped past her defenses so easily. This hand knew her already, registered her flesh without surprise, without preconceptions, immediately – her own kind.

Louise stood immobile for a moment, uncertain. Did she dare stay? Instantly she knew she would. She had wanted contact for so long; now it came in this unorthodox, even shocking way; but she wanted it.

Although she could see nothing in the darkness, it seemed that the other two descended quickly from their upper berth. Almost immediately she felt another pair of hands caressing her, masculine hands, seeking an outcome to this joining, possession. Louise turned to them both, united them in her arms, and found that somehow she was the center of this strange beast with three backs. The hot darkness swallowed them up, as they came close and closer to each. When at last they emerged on the other side, they were shaken, spent, but not quite as alone again. Then they lay a long time together, their hands on one another, huddling together, speaking little. Louise refused to think. She did not want to break the spell, subject this dream-sequence to the possible disapproval of her waking, analytical mind.

The door opened once more, letting in a draft of cold air, and revealing the black outline of a woman in an elegant, clinging gown. "Philip, is that you?" she said. "Everyone has gone. Come on out to the hot tub. I'll meet you there in a minute." The door closed again.

Philip and the other woman got up slowly, reluctant to leave, and oddly shy. One of them turned the lights up and Louise saw the tall freckled man with whom she had first undressed for the hot tub, and a plump young woman she had not noticed before. The woman left quickly, but Louise lingered, lying on the bench.

"I suppose you do this sort of thing all the time?" she asked, trying to get her bearings a little.

Philip leaned in the doorway, looking ill at ease now that the light was turned on. "Well, you could say that, in a way," he said. He looked at her for a moment. "Well, no, not really." He paused, and then evaded: "I don't remember seeing you here before."

"It was my first time in all respects," Louise answered. "I've never made love to two total strangers before, in or out of a sauna. But it seemed like the right thing to do." She laughed, hearing her own words. "Well, not exactly what I was taught in nursery school as the 'right thing to do'!"

Philip shook his head and left. She lay there a few minutes longer, and he appeared again in the doorway, wearing a robe. "Are you all right?" he asked. "Maybe you feel –" and he paused, "I don't know what your experience has been."

"Yes, yes, it's all right," Louise reassured him. She shook her head, wonderingly. "Three people reaching out for one another – yes, I can't help thinking it was right."

He was silent, still looking at her in the weak light of the sauna. Becoming self-conscious, she changed her tone, becoming more social and distant. "I certainly never expected this kind of thing – not ever, and especially not tonight. I was told it would be a small group of women going into a hot tub off in a dark corner of someone's lawn." She laughed. "But I'm not sure Peggy was the best guide. I guess your Friday night parties are all like this?"

"Well, I actually never have done anything like this before," he said. That didn't quite convince, but then it didn't seem to matter. Louise found that she still did not care to analyze. Philip went out to the hot tub and in a while she followed him there. Two women were already in the tub with Philip: his wife, Concha, and someone introduced to Louise now, with a little smile, as Grace.

It was clear that Philip was uncertain where to place himself in the hot tub. Louise felt him pulled towards herself and Grace, but holding himself carefully in a neutral spot between the poles. All three were silent: Concha was talking. And she talked well, very well, about her reading. They heard about Margaret Mead's childhood and about World War II and the bomb decision; no one else could speak. She cast a net of sounds and well-ordered ideas over them, silencing them, and slowly pulling Philip back into her orbit. It was strange to see him move, gradually, closer to her, as she and Grace were neutralized. When a break came in the talk – it could not be called a conversation – the two outsiders excused themselves and returned to dress in the house.

"God that woman is beautiful," Grace said. "Those blue eyes set in the Spanish face! Or is it Aztec? With those high cheek-bones – talk about exotic! And so little – what do you think, five feet two?"

"I guess," Louise said laconically.

"And brilliant," Grace went on. "I didn't feel as if I could say anything up to her standards."

"Well, she didn't give you a chance. You would have needed a battering ram to break into that monologue." Then ashamed, Louise added, "But she does talk well. Extremely well."

Grace glanced at her in the mirror, and then grinned. "You know what day it is? It's April first – April Fools!" They both exploded in laughter, and, still smiling, passed by the hot tub, calling their goodnights as if mere polite acquaintances, nothing more.

Louise, seeing Philip and Concha together there in the hot tub, felt strongly that he was married, unavailable. She shook off her desire to see him again, to have some continuation. And she could feel the connection with Grace loosening. She could not imagine phoning her up later. Grace had given her an experience of lovemaking more tender and delicate than any she had ever known; but Louise was conscious that for her the excitement was with the man, and this man was not free. He had wandered, briefly, in the allowed context of the party; but she had seen him roped, tied, and thrown afterwards by his wife. He was not free.

Safely back in her old Datsun station wagon, she drove slowly down through the maze of narrow streets, through the tree-crowded pseudo-countryside of the hills, with the expensive homes engineered into the steep wooded slopes, half hidden by great oaks and pine and eucalyptus, down, down, watching the trees recede and grow sparse, the streets widen, the buildings come up to view on either side, bare and angular, down into the noisier, smoggier flatlands, the world she had chosen when she chose to paint rather than teach. She sighed, coasting through the empty late-night streets, and smiled. It was amusing to move from one world to the other; it made her feel free of both. The amber blinking stoplights did not slow her down, and she rolled smoothly home and into her narrow single bed. Tomorrow she would wake to painting.

* * *

She did paint, but to the accompaniment of a noisy inner debate. It was, after all, hard to say which was the worst aspect of what she had done. Sex with a married man was immoral by the old standards, but by the new? He was a free agent, and had made his decision, with no prior encouragement from her. And she knew that couples were "swinging," changing sexual partners. She had heard of orgies – middle-class orgies. But involvement with a married man was foolish. It was practically proverbial that the woman would get hurt sooner or later. And was it a feminist thing to do, to help a man betray his wife? But maybe the wife was doing the same thing; maybe they had an "open marriage."

She needed to tell Sylvia, but feared the part about having a sexual experience with a woman. In theory that was fine; but it could make Sylvia afraid that the simplicity of their woman-to-woman friendship, growing steadily stronger all the time, might not be taken for granted anymore.

It was several days before she could bring herself to speak. They were in the kitchen together, making dinner.

"You know, I had the most bizarre experience at the hot tub party Friday night," she began tentatively, watching Sylvia as she chopped vegetables in a big wooden bowl.

"So you did something bizarre, huh?" Sylvia replied obligingly, glancing up. "And so that means . . .?"

"Well, there was this man and this woman in the sauna," Louise began slowly. As Sylvia continued calmly chopping vegetables, Louise gained courage. Soon she had confessed the whole episode.

Sylvia threw the vegetables into the wok and sat down. "I'm amazed at your nerve, but I don't see what harm you could do. I mean, probably this new herpes thing isn't really a problem, not yet, anyway, but what about, I mean, what if . . .?"

"No, I'm safe, I think. It was the end of my period so chances are it's okay."

"I guess you're worried about his being married, but what do you know, I mean face it," and Sylvia's voice rose, shrill and girlish, laughing, "you really don't know anything about him. He could be doing this all the time, and his wife might be too. I don't think you should worry about him. But would you ever see him again?"

No – well, I guess not," Louise answered, looking out the window evasively. "I guess I shouldn't, but –"

"You wouldn't just phone him up, would you? What if his wife answered?" Sylvia snorted and got up to stir her vegetables.

"No – well, I guess not." It was hard to admit that she had actually called Peggy to get Philip's last name so she could phone him. "Well, I did think of it but then I decided to wait and see if he would call me. Then I wouldn't be interfering in his marriage. If he calls me, then it's his free decision."

"Hmm," Sylvia murmured. "So you want to see him?"

"Maybe," Louise said. But it was not easy to maintain this casual attitude. She could not forget the feeling on her skin, Philip's hands, and Grace encircling them both. And afterward, as the three of them rested, leaning against each other in the dark heat of the sauna, one of them had murmured, "Oh, I needed this so much." Louise couldn't remember now which one of them had said that; it seemed as if each one of them might have said it, was in fact saying it. The tenderness and the joy with which they had come together had seemed beyond sex, although sex had been its expression. Philip, she thought. Who was he, really?

Carefully, she did not throw out his phone number; equally carefully, she buried it at the bottom of a pile of loose papers she kept by the phone. Though she couldn't see it, every time she walked by the phone she was aware of this thing, hidden from view but radiating its presence powerfully. Once she checked to be sure it was still there and then, shamed, resolved to leave it alone.

It was almost a week before the phone rang for her. A sweetly reedy voice, a tenor: was her name Louise? Louise Borgstrum? Was she the woman at the hot tub party, the one in the sauna? It was Philip, who had found her name by asking Peggy.

Louise laughed when she heard that. "Peggy must be wondering! I called her too, to find out your last name. I was so tempted to call you –" Here she stopped, censoring the question about his being married. She did not want to introduce difficulties – not to him, not to herself. This was too delightful. She could find out what the situation was, and then make her decision.

They went swimming at the university pool: a neutral activity, and one that eliminated the need for long conversations. They were cheerful and polite with one another, swam vigorously, lay correctly on the stiff plastic-looking grass by the pool, each on a carefully separate towel.

The breeze was cool, and after a while Louise sat up, thinking that she would go back to the changing rooms and dress.

"You're cold!" Philip exclaimed, as if he had just learned of some great natural disaster. "Here," and he took his towel from beneath him and wrapped it around her.

"Oh, no, you need something to sit on," she protested. But Philip was not swayed. She felt enveloped by his attention and concern. He was not merely being polite.

"You still look cold," Philip said. "Let's get dressed. We can go up to my house and I'll get you something hot to drink."

She accepted the invitation gratefully, and with a strong curiosity which she refused to examine. Once they had arrived at the house, it seemed logical to go into the hot tub, where she could immerse in heat, get warm clear to the bone.

They undressed and got quickly into the hot-tub, avoiding obvious looks at one another's bodies. Now, in the afternoon light, Louise could see how beautifully the tub was set in the midst of oaks and lemony-smelling eucalyptus.

"This is wonderful," she said, gesturing around. "And so quiet. I suppose most people are still at work. But," she prodded, "what if your wife comes home early? Is my life in danger?"

He laughed rather hard, as if Louise had just made a good joke. She looked at him uneasily.

"Concha? Don't worry. She has a new lover every week. I'm just a convenience she likes to keep around the house. You know, 'Here's my expensive house, here's my career at the hospital, here's my husband, doesn't he fit in well with the furniture?' And she's gone out of town for a few days – supposedly on business."

Louise was so pleased with this answer that she turned her back on Philip, to hide her face. He came up behind her, close, and began to massage her neck.

"Are you feeling warmer?" he asked.

She smiled and turned around. To her surprise he backed up a step; he was scrupulously not taking advantage. In the leaf-filtered light his skin gleamed, translucently white under the freckles. She looked at it with mock seriousness. In a corny German accent she pronounced, "I belief, Mr. Brett, zat you haff some dreatful disseease, known as goosepumples. Zeez need treatment," and she moved closer as if to examine his skin, picking his arm out of the water.

Almost at the same moment he was kissing her neck; their arms slipped around one another, their naked bodies half pulled, half floated together in the water. A few minutes later they were racing through the cool air into the house, laughing. He pulled her down onto the soft rug before the fireplace; then they were in the loft, then on the floor by the TV, all over the house they made love, furiously, unable to stop until the afternoon had passed, it was dark outside, and exhaustion overcame them. They lay, sweaty, their bodies touching still all their length, and looked at one another in astonishment.

"My god," he said, "we've been doing this since early afternoon! And now it's past dinner time. I've never experienced anything like that. Our bodies just took over."

Louise nodded, her eyes fastened on his in the dim light, as their bodies also clung to one another. She did not know what to say. She felt overwhelmed, amazed, and also quiet, a deep inner quiet. She felt as if her whole body were smiling, and as if her face bore the smile of those archaic Greek statues which so puzzled art historians. Words were superfluous. It was enough simply to lie there, so close to this man, Philip, whose name was still unfamiliar on her tongue.

He ran his hand slowly over her hip and thigh. "Our bodies just took over," he repeated. His eyes tightened. "Has that ever happened to you before?"

Louise smiled broadly now, seeing him already jealous of her imagined past.

"No, never," she answered truthfully.

They lay there together a while longer. As their energies returned, however, so did their desire. They rolled together, and then rolled apart, groaning and laughing. They had to get up, gather their wits.

"Probably we should eat some dinner," Louise suggested. "We could go to my place," she added, not too enthusiastically. She had rice and beans at home: healthy, but not what she considered company fare.

"No, no, I want to take you out someplace," he insisted. Again she felt the warmth from him, as when he put his towel around her at the pool, a warm arm gathering her in.

They went to a small restaurant not too far away, Casa Carlos. While they read the menus, Philip shifted about on his chair, changing position every few minutes.

"Are you comfortable there?" Louise asked, wondering. Philip grinned, leaning across the table and taking her hand in his. "I can't believe this," he said, "not since high school have I had blue balls."

Louise was puzzled. "Blue balls? Hmm. I've heard of Blue Beard. Are you warning me not to go back to your castle with you tonight?"

"Maybe," he said, playing with her hand. "Did you notice this afternoon that I never came? Maybe you were too busy coming all over the place to notice! I was afraid you weren't protected. If you come back with me tonight," and here he wiggled his eyebrows with a flourish, "you better be protected!" Louise flushed, embarrassed. "Well, the truth is" – she paused, unable to say it for a moment, "the truth is, I wore my diaphragm today – I have to confess it."

"What?" He was incredulous. "You mean you knew all along what would happen? And you look so proper! Butter wouldn't melt in your mouth! Well, it's the quiet ones you have to look out for, I can see that." He laughed, amazed and teasing both. "So you really knew what would happen, and here I thought you were so innocent."

"But I didn't foresee what really happened. How could I possibly?" She shook her head, thinking back. "Still, I have to admit that after that first time I thought, wonder what it would be like if we had more time? And I wanted to try it – it's true. But I didn't know exactly what would happen. It was just in case."

"My god," he groaned, "here I thought it was all just a date to go swimming with this woman I . . ."

"You what?" she challenged. "How would you describe this woman? This woman you fucked sight unseen, practically un-introduced even, in a pitch-dark sauna? It wasn't exactly the most conventional introduction, I thought – though maybe that's how you meet lots of women? I'm not sure I believed you when you said it was the first time you'd ever done such a thing."

"No, I've never made love with two women in the sauna before, or any other time, either. And total strangers – you're shameless!"

"*I'm* shameless!" Louise cried. "And did you really think we'd just go swimming and that was all? After an introduction like that? Come on!"

"Well – I didn't make any plans, I just thought I'd make sure you were all right and didn't feel bad about what happened. Here I thought you were so innocent – and you even wore a diaphragm!" He widened his eyes in mock horror.

"It's true," and her hands tossed his lightly in the air, "I am, alas, no longer an innocent virgin. But aren't you glad?"

"My god, what have I gotten into?" he said, leaning back in his chair, laughing.

* * *

The next weekend was Easter; Monday was a holiday, and Philip's wife was to be out of town at a conference for three days. The house was theirs to play in. Their game was engrossing. They came up for air, as it were, at dinner time, and he took her to fancy places she had only heard of before. At dinner, too, they were gluttons, like starved people suddenly set in front of a banquet. Louise had not known so much need and desire was in her. He, too, could not hold back or be reserved. Both gave in, gratefully, to the intense tide which was sweeping them up. Lying in Philip's own bed, at his house – the bed he shared with Concha – Louise felt strange. She felt not so much an interloper as a tourist, here in a country meant for some other people – Philip and Concha, not Philip and Louise.

"I hate this furniture," he said. "She picked it out."

Louise looked at it: heavy dark pseudo-Spanish, clumsy and cheap looking. Something dishonest about it, she thought. But of course Concha would lack taste; she clearly did not see what she had in Philip – a gross error of perception.

"What about the window shades?" Louise asked, testing. They were brilliantly colored Marimekkos.

"I chose those," he said. "They're one of the few things in the house I really like. But none of that is important." He turned in the bed so that their eyes met. "If we loved each other – if she loved me – I wouldn't give a damn about the furniture."

Louise nodded. Softly she began to stroke his head. He seized her hand, pulling her to him.

"Louise, Louise, I can't believe you're real!" Then, suddenly again, he laughed, and half-lifted her out of the bed, over him. "You don't know! Before I met you I was going out with so many women I couldn't remember all their names. I had to write them down so I could say the right name to the one at lunch, and the one in the afternoon, and the one in the evening. I had a whole string of dates set up for this week, but I canceled them all. You don't leave anything for the others. God, I wish we had met back in college."

"You wouldn't have liked me," Louise replied, propping herself up on her elbow so she could look in his eyes. "Besides, I didn't want to marry and settle down. I wanted to be alone and suffer and wear black turtleneck sweaters so I could write poetry. I didn't think I could write poetry in a nice suburban house. And I wasn't very developed socially. I bet Concha really knew her way around socially."

Philip nodded. "That was part of what attracted me to her. Here I was, a poor boy from the Philly slums. Every single boy I knew from that time wound up in jail by the time he was fifteen – and there she was, the beautiful and cultured professor's daughter. It seemed as if she had everything – looks, intelligence, articulate, everything.

"Her father was an Anglo – blond and blue-eyed – and when he was young, he taught English literature at the university in Mexico City. Concha's mother was just a secretary there, but beautiful – a lot like Concha, in a way – and they got married. Then after a few years Concha was born, and then Concha's father got a teaching post at Stanford. But when they got up to Palo Alto, the Anglo father began to notice that the little Mexican wife was not very classy. I mean, she could read and write, and she's smart as a whip in her own way, but she's not really educated. And after Concha was born the mother got fat. And the father began to ignore her; he was ashamed of her. And she took it all out on Concha. She hated her, because it was after Concha was born that her father stopped loving her – and loved Concha instead. The father-daughter bit, except that Concha still could never quite measure up to please her dad.

"When she told me all this about herself I just felt sorry for her and wanted to take care of her. I didn't understand that it was like a kind of family curse, that Concha can't love anyone. It's like her mother – and her father too – inoculated her against love, against ever trusting anyone. Back when I met her, though, I only saw what she wanted me to see. To me she was like an ideal image, something to chase after, to achieve. Even her good looks – for years I really got off on the idea that every man in the room wanted her – and she was mine. Or so I thought. It turned out that I was the classic dumb husband." He tightened his arms around her, pulling her to him, as he spoke.

"While I was faithful, and thought that everything was okay and we had some sort of home life, a home together, she was sleeping with every man that came along. The one I finally found out about was a good friend of mine, too. Everyone else knew except me – one of those things. I couldn't believe it. I really loved her. But she told me awhile back that she only married me because it was senior year and everyone else was getting married, and I was the one around at the time. That's all. Just the least bad. Also I was Catholic. She cared about that. Isn't that funny? Religion but no love. She insisted on having this big church wedding. I hate that kind of thing. I should have known then, and broken it off, but I was too blind, too in love."

Louise was silent for a moment, thinking how Philip's and Concha's two sets of insecurities had locked them together, allowing a kind of current to flow. It must have seemed like life, power, what each needed; but for Philip, at least, it had also been subtly corroding. They were hooked up by the wrong parts – by their weaknesses, not by their strengths.

Propping up on her elbows again, she said only, "It's hard to imagine you starting out that way, I mean from the slums and all."

"Oh," he smiled, his eyes returning to look directly into hers, "all I said was 'dis' and 'dat' until I was eleven or so. Then we got prosperous and moved to Levittown. Ever heard of that place?"

"Isn't it the first tract housing place?"

"Yeah. That's it. No trees. Just ugly houses, all exactly alike. But to my parents it was a big move up, into respectability. And it did save me from winding up in jail like my old friends."

"Hmmm. But look at you now, in this beautiful house, a biophysicist, doing research at one of the best universities in the country. A real rags to riches story."

"Yeah, it looks good, doesn't it? But you can't imagine what it's like, being with someone you can't trust at all. One party night a friend and I – Hugh – we were standing outside, getting some fresh air after all the smoke and noise inside. And Hugh grabbed my arm and said 'Look!' and pointed in the bathroom window. It was all lit up, and there was Concha, screwing with some guy from the party. I don't know who he was, Hugh didn't know him either, and we didn't know whether we should go away and not look, or just watch. After a while we did leave and go back inside, and pretty soon out comes Concha, cool and collected, and later I told her what I'd seen. I didn't mention Hugh because I thought maybe that would embarrass her more. And do you know what she said? She denied the whole thing! But we both saw her. She never would admit it. And I wasn't accusing her. I mean, we were both getting it on plenty, and we both knew it was going on. But that she would go on denying it when she knew I'd seen her! She didn't give a damn whether she was up front with me or not. She probably got a kick out of lying to me, in fact. You can't imagine what it's like, living with someone you love, or once loved, who doesn't love you."

"Well, actually, though my case wasn't exactly like yours, I can imagine it, easily enough. I did it for most of the years of my marriage."

"What? You?" He seemed unable to believe it.

"Yes, I loved Andrew but he didn't love me. At least that's what he told me, time and again."

"God, how could you stand it? And you need love, you're like me, we almost can't survive without it."

"Mmm," she muttered in agreement, thinking. "You know, when you were telling me about Concha's mother, at first I was thinking she should have gone to school and gotten as educated as the father so he would have respected her. But when I think of Andrew and me, I think maybe that wouldn't have done her any good. He just would have resented her, and been afraid. Because sometimes I think that if I hadn't been in graduate school, and doing well, Andrew and I might still be together. There was probably no way Concha's mother could have won."

He broke in. "What? You were in graduate school?"

She smiled, aware of surprising him. "I have a Ph.D., actually. In Comparative Literature."

"But you're not supposed to have a Ph.D.! I thought you were just a hippie artist!"

"Well, that is all I am – a hippie artist who got a Ph.D."

"Oh no," he protested. "All right, now tell me, what else have you been hiding?"

She was bemused. "What difference does it make? I'd be the

same person with or without the degree. Does it make a difference to you?"

"Look at it this way. Now, be honest. Would you see me differently if I were a carpenter instead of a research scientist?"

"I'd see you differently, but it doesn't mean I'd like you more, or less – or at least I hope not. No, definitely not, come to think of it, since I went out with a carpenter last year."

"Hmph. Well you're different from me, then. I think it does make a difference. I even think you're wrong on this. A degree means something. You must think so too, or you wouldn't have gotten one. It takes something special to go after it. It's not just a casual thing. Well, don't worry, kid, I'm not like Andrew. I encouraged Concha – practically pushed her – to go back to graduate school in public health. She was only a nurse when I met her. Her parents didn't expect her to do much after college. After all, she was half Mexican! And a woman! And her mother's daughter. But I knew she was too smart; she had to do something with it. So now she's in hospital administration. Big bucks!"

Louise rolled a little away from him in bed. "Well, I see that you like achieving women! So now that you know I have Ph.D. you have to take me seriously, huh?" she said, rather hurt at the idea that he might not otherwise, without this external ornament and vindication of his feeling for her.

"What people do is important," he returned. "But look – until this moment I thought you were just an ordinary Berkeley type. Don't you think you're important to me? Come on, let's not argue," and he reached out for her, pulling her in close again. She could not resist. It seemed impossible for them to get close enough; constantly they were pulling and straining at one another, trying to put nerve on nerve and make the contact complete.

"Oh Lou," he groaned, "I need this so much! You can't imagine!"

She smiled at him. There was no need to say anything. Words seemed irrelevant, unnecessary.

The Beginning

This loving cuts like brandy
drunk to burn, chocolate crammed
by the pound and too much
pleasure pressured into pain
when we two meet, touch,
make time and space, balloons
blown up too far, explode.

On the bed, alone, I rest
and think of you, gone home
where your wife with her long brown hair
waits like Rapunzel for you to climb
that dark stairway to the tower
where you beg for the dry crust
and the bowl of stagnant water.

* * *

They started meeting for lunch. Louise came up hill by bicycle, and Philip walked down from campus. They met in midtown Berkeley, at a small restaurant which was set underground. Leaving the brilliant noonday light and the crowded sidewalk, they descended into a different world, dimly lit, quiet, elegant, private. There were white tablecloths, and cloth napkins, immaculate, that weighed on Louise's lap when she unfolded one. And there was wine. Philip chose the wines with a care which at first embarrassed Louise. Back home in the Midwest, no one drank wine, and even to prefer Scotch to bourbon was considered an affectation. Gradually, however, Louise realized that Philip knew something about wine, that his choices tasted good, better than any wines she had ever had. It was partly the social newcomer's studied sophistication, but it was also an aesthetic choice about the kind of life he wanted to lead.

Appearances mattered, too. She could see it in his clothes: the expensive silky shirts, in deep shades of blue or rust, perfect with his pale skin and reddish-brown hair, open at the neck to suggest the current right degree of casual masculinity; the closely-fitting slacks, so unlike the ragged blue jeans that lower Berkeleyans wore as a sign that they did not belong, disdained to belong, to the world of "the Establishment." And she could see that Philip cared how she looked. She spent some of her savings on better t-shirts, French ones in fine colors, and slacks rather than blue jeans. Still, she arrived from one world, lower Berkeley, and he from another: academic, established Berkeley. Her bicycle was tethered to a lamppost outside, waiting to return her to her chosen place.

Seated at a table, she could barely speak, just looking at him. Their hands were joined across the table. "Well, what have you got to say for yourself?" he laughed. "Too much sex makes the blood leave your head, you know. Is that why you're so quiet?"

In fact her head did seem empty of things to say. Philip's physical presence seemed to fill the space where thoughts usually were. And there was another factor, more shameful, cowardly: she was silent partly because she did not want to break the spell. What if she were to show herself too uninformed, or too far left politically, or too something or not enough of something else, and this drunken sense of unity would fade, and the intense current pulsing between them would be cut off? Yet the longer she remained silent, the less he would know her real self, and the more the relationship would risk being illusory, fragile, ending perhaps in angry disappointment.

Meanwhile, Philip had settled into his chair and was watching her. "God, there's so much I don't know about you, Louise. Wait, do you like salmon? They serve it with a wonderful bearnaise sauce here." She was instantly jealous of the times he had come here and enjoyed the wonderful bearnaise sauce without her. She wanted him to have no history before her, no existence worth mentioning. It should be like time B.C. and A.D: the past was unredeemed.

Disconcertingly, he seemed to read her thoughts. "I've been coming here for years, but none of that matters. You know that, don't you?" he asked earnestly, cupping her hands in his. "But wait a minute, probably you came here with that husband of yours – you probably even had a good time – damn you!"

The idea of eating out with Andrew made her laugh. "I'm afraid Andrew ate nothing but pills – six or seven at a sitting. Restaurant food, like life in general, didn't sit well on his stomach. Never fear. You have nothing to be jealous of."

"Yes I do – you married him, didn't you? And you loved him – you even said so. Damn! Why didn't we meet when we were young, twenty years ago."

"Oh yes, and we'd have, how many did you say, six kids? Eight? Ten? Ugh!" Then she remembered that Philip had a very real four-year-old boy. "Well, the one you have is probably nice. But we already figured out that we would have hated each other twenty years ago."

"God, you're so contrary," he said. "I've never known such a contrary woman." In his look he was kissing her again, though the table separated them. Not being in bed, they wolfed down the salmon and finished off the bottle of wine. The waitress hovered around them as they ate shamelessly. She was attracted by the scent of Philip's sexuality, which he gave off like an electric radiance, and by their happiness, which extended to her. She fed them, flirting with them, egging them on, heightening the tension.

Finally they struggled out of the dark cavern into the sunlight. Philip motioned towards her bicycle. "Do you have to go right away? We could walk up to campus and sit on the grass for a little while. I know a nice spot," and he wrinkled up his face with melodramatic suggestiveness.

"Too much!" she laughed, putting her arm through his.

"I love it, the way you're always touching me," he said. "Did you know that? It feels wonderful." They walked, arm clutched in arm, uphill onto campus, a sort of enchanted garden, completely separated from the noisy traffic-filled town. As they walked, Louise saw one of her thesis advisors coming towards them, a Swede who saw things from twenty cold distances. Suddenly she saw herself and Philip through his eyes: a somewhat gangly couple, walking in a daze, Philip in the unwrinkled slacks which announced his unfashionable desire to appear professional and of the world; she self-conscious and unsure. Somehow she had betrayed Svensson's monastic ideal of scholarship; she had fallen to being a mere woman, with a merely mortal man. Her parents' angry accusation – what was she doing with her life? – flashed into her mind.

"Whooph," she said, "there's one of my thesis advisors, Svensson. He's a wonderful person, he helped me a lot – but it gives me the heebie-jeebies to see him. I don't regret giving up the academic life for painting, but sometimes the uncertainty of it scares me." She looked desperately at the foliage and flowers, trying to think of something more pleasant.

"It amazes me that you had the courage to do it, Lou," Philip answered. This simple reassurance brought her back into their own world, where they set the values. Svensson passed by, giving his unreadable half smile, and they went on to a grassy, partially secluded spot near Philip's lab. There they sat, as if held in a spell, saying very little, hands touching, each body basking in the warmth of the other. Finally they got stiff as it began to get cooler, and Philip had, at last, to go to the lab. They could not see each other until the next day. He had to spend the night in that alien place, his home, with his child and with the enemy who still held him in her power.

When Louise got home she stood a long time in her room, getting her bearings again among these familiar things. Here was the portrait which was so much trouble, bound to dissatisfy the woman it portrayed because Louise's hand and eye, independent of conscious will, refused to paint Elizabeth the way she saw herself: beautiful, strong, successful. Instead the painting showed a sad and dissatisfied woman, strong but chained down. She had acquiesced in her chains, and that was the condition of the success she had. Louise knew she would not like this portrait, but every time she tried to paint what she thought Elizabeth saw, the likeness vanished.

Still, looking at her work renewed her sense of grounding. No matter what, she had that, she would be all right. And besides, she only had to wait until lunchtime the next day to see Philip.

* * *

They had a Saturday afternoon to themselves; Concha was working. Louise was especially glad to be out of the apartment, because Sylvia was in the process of moving into a bigger place, where Harvey could visit her every weekend without a third person – Louise – underfoot. The timing was good. Louise wanted space now for the same reason. One bedroom, the front one with the best light, would be her painting studio; the other, back bedroom would be strictly for desk work, piano, and sleeping. She luxuriated in the new sense of privacy and space. Though she would miss Sylvia, she would not lose touch with her; their friendship had become too strong for that.

Philip picked her up in his green VW bug in the early afternoon. The sunroof was open; he loved to expand upward and outward, and to feel the air and light come in on him directly. As usual, the electricity was strong between them, though they did not talk very much. He was smoking a cigarillo, blowing smoke out the sunroof with gusto. Though she did not like the smell of smoke, and did not want Philip to begin smoking – he had given it up before she met him – she had to admit to herself that Philip looked particularly sexy just now. Maybe it was brainwashing by too many cigarette ads, but she loved the way his long fingers held the cigarillo, and the hollow of his cheeks under the high cheekbones as he puffed. He was full of energetic relish, almost bouncing on the car seat as if the VW were a horse and he were posting, the elegant thin arch of his nose leading the way.

They went to Muir Woods, a large redwood preserve near San Francisco. Because it was a sunny Saturday, the place was crowded, and it was hard even to find a place in the parking lot.

"It's mobbed!" Louise exclaimed. "And they have the trees fenced off. I guess there are so many of us that we could destroy them." She didn't like her nature to seem quite so fragile, nor set behind fences with explanatory signs telling her what to think and feel. Philip had seen these groves many times, and had already memorized the signs. As Louise dutifully and irritably read, feeling she was meanwhile bypassing the trees themselves, Philip nudged her. Ahead of them were two whitehaired people, speaking French, and gesturing upwards.

"They don't have anything like this in France," Philip said. "Listen: What a wonderful language! And look at them. Maybe you and I will be like that." The woman and man leaned lightly against one another, arm in arm, as they gazed upwards towards the almost invisible point where the trees ended in the light. It seemed they had been together so long that they took this mutual support for granted. They looked upward in silence for a long moment, Louise and Philip silently regarding them in turn.

"Let's go farther in," Philip suggested. "Most people don't go more than a hundred yards here, and it's beautiful farther on. But you probably know all the paths – you've probably been on them hundreds of times with your hundreds of lovers."

"What imagination! You certainly worry a lot about my past, but in fact you're the one who had to keep track of his dates in a book so he wouldn't forget the name of the one at two o'clock or confuse her with the one at three-thirty."

"Don't be hard on me," he said. "It wasn't that much fun. A lot of beautiful bodies, but it takes more than that. I learned a few things, though. Do you know that some of them wanted me to be mean to them, hurt them – and I don't mean just a little pinch – really hurt them. It was the only way they could get off. It was hard to believe. I couldn't do it, and they lost interest. I disappointed them. I guess lots of men would give them that."

Louise was not sure how to respond. She had to believe that Philip was telling her the truth, unpalatable though it was. It was strange, too, to think that as a man, he might know more about women, in these sexual ways, than she herself did.

"Look," Philip said, "look at that one," pointing to an enormous redwood. "Probably makes you horny, doesn't it?"

"Crazy," she replied, crazy. You're fixated on size. All those jokes of yours about penis size – those are male jokes, did you know that? It never occurred to me to worry about it."

"Come on, tell the truth. You love a big one in you."

"That's not what I meant," she objected. "What attracts me in a man is something else – some combination of things: personality, build, the look in his eyes, intelligence. It's the whole thing put together that makes a man either boring or sexy to me."

"Hmmph. You didn't exactly wait to have an intelligent conversation with me when we first met."

"But do you think we'd be together now if that were all – if it was only sex?"

He raised his eyebrows thoughtfully. "What's it been: two months? Usually I figure six weeks is the most, so we've passed that point. But two months isn't very long, Lou. I think you only love my body, and you'll get tired of me. I'll have to keep you so exhausted you don't think of getting away," and he reached down and started rubbing the cloth over her clitoris as they walked. By this time there were no other people in sight, though the path was so well pounded down it seemed they could run into people at any time.

"Philip!" she gasped. "Stop! This is ridiculous!"

But he persisted. "I've got to keep you horny, it's my only chance," he said, smiling a mock-evil sidelong smile. "Damn!" she said, and in retaliation put her hand on him. Almost instantly she felt him grow erect, a soft-hard mound rising and pushing against her hand through the khaki cloth.

"What are you doing?" he exclaimed. "What if someone comes?"

"But that's just what I was saying. It's only fair!"

So they walked along, hastily pulling their hands away when they thought someone might be approaching. Pressure began to build.

"There's a nice little path," Louise said, pointing.

"Really? You want to make it in the woods? Evil woman! But it's not hidden enough."

They walked a little further. The light shining irregularly through the trees, the complexity of the foliage, the smells of pine, the varying sound of the stream at their side – all seemed to come in on Louise's senses directly, unfiltered, with overwhelming intensity. She wondered if it was like this to be on drugs.

"There, there's a place," he said, and they pulled one another off the path and ran up the hill to a thick grove of trees, where they could lie down together without anyone seeing them.

"Look, what about this?" he said, pointing to a relatively flat space under a tree. "Here, you be on top, I don't want you to be uncomfortable, and my clothes are older and don't matter." They fell on one another like starved dogs on a hunk of meat, laughing a little at the same time, incredulous.

Afterwards they rested. "I think you want to have a baby with me," he said. "You weren't wearing your diaphragm, were you?"

"Well, no," she admitted, "but it's right before my period; it's not supposed to be a fertile time."

"I'd like to see you swell up like a watermelon. Wouldn't you like that?"

"Swell up like a watermelon? Ugh. Besides, afterwards you get eighteen years of trouble while the watermelon grows up."

"But you liked it better this way," he pressed. "Wasn't it more exciting?"

"Maybe." It was possible. She did not like to hold back anything with Philip, she did not want any barriers. "But it just happened, really."

"We should have met when we were young. You'd have six kids by now." It seemed unnecessary to insist again that they would not have liked each other when they were younger, would not even have seen one another as possibilities.

They began to put themselves back together for return to the public world.

"Tell me more about what you were like back at age twenty or so," she said.

"I've told you some things. You want a lot, don't you?"

She considered a moment. "Not a lot, exactly, just –" she paused a moment, "just everything. I just want everything." It seemed the simplest statement that fit.

"That's right!" he roared, "You do! Damn you, you do! Can't I hold anything back?"

"Not if I have anything to say about it."

"Damn you, Borgstrum, where did you come from?"

He took her hand and they ran drunkenly down to the main path, now in deep shadow. As they walked back, bonded in silence, Louise wondered why she was not more concerned about the possibility of getting pregnant. What filled her mind instead was the realization that no other woman had wanted Philip as she did, with love, wanting all the parts, all the knowledge, every scrap. She felt his hand in hers, aware of him with tenderness. After twelve years of marriage he was coming to her as a sort of virgin – exactly as she came to him.

* * *

Virginal, but not alone. Louise had heard Philip mention his son Joseph, or Jo-Jo, many times. One afternoon, without warning, he simply drove with her to the daycare center. As she realized where they were going, her stomach tightened. She was about to be admitted into another, more intimate layer of Philip's life. Maybe it was clever of Philip not to warn her beforehand. This way she had no time to work up her anxiety, wonder what to do and say.

"Wait here," he told her, leaping out of the VW. "We'll be right down."

The daycare center was at the top of a small hill, up and back far enough that the sidewalk – and Louise – could not be seen by the people inside. She wondered if Philip was embarrassed to have her seen. They would know what Concha looked like, know that Louise was not the mother.

After a few minutes Philip appeared at the top of the stairs. A small boy raced ahead of him, down the stairs, and as Philip followed, beaming, the child catapulted himself into Louise's arms for a hug. All her shyness evaporated under this onslaught. She forgot that this being was half Philip and half enemy, that he tied Philip forever to Concha, that he was an encumbrance on Philip like an old unpayable debt. She was aware only of the small warm body, and her own delight.

From then on, Jo-Jo was with them quite often. The next time Louise met Philip at the running track, Jo-Jo met her first, screaming excitedly, "Dad, Dad, here's your girlfriend!"

Louise scooped him into her arms for another hug, delighted again.

"Look, a four-leaf clover," he cried, waving it before her. "A whole big patch of four-leaf clovers!"

"That's a lot of good luck," she replied, kneeling down to look, glad of this easy opening into his world. Before they could say much more, however, Philip was by her side, large, smelling slightly of sweat, exuding a masculine warmth which enveloped her. As she stood up, she could feel him pulled into her orbit as she had just been pulled into his. The sexual energy metamorphosed into words; they talked excitedly about running. Dimly, Louise was aware of a smaller, shriller voice trying to get their attention, drowned like the sound of a sparrow in the roar of a passing freight train.

Fighting for Jo-Jo, she managed to interject, "Jo-Jo just found a whole big patch of four-leaf clovers."

Philip looked briefly at the patch. "Sorrel, not clover," he pronounced. He ruffled Jo-Jo's hair affectionately. "Are you going to play here like a good boy while Daddy and Louise go running, and be sure not to walk out on the track and get in people's way?"

Jo-Jo nodded, and immediately piped up, unwilling to be left, "Look what else I found, Dad," and pulled Philip by the hand away from the track.

"Not now, Jo-Jo," Philip said, disengaging himself. "Ready?" he asked, turning to Louise.

And so they ran off together. When they came around again to the place where Jo-Jo played by the side of the track, he was busy and absorbed. Louise did not allow herself to wonder what her future place would be in Jo-Jo's life; that meant facing other questions she was not prepared to ask.

* * *

One afternoon Philip came down to her place. He sat in the kitchen and pulled her down to sit on his lap, his arms around her.

"Lou, Lou, what are we doing?" he asked. "What are we going to do? You know I love you. But now I have to go away. There's a conference in Puerto Rico, and then Concha wants to meet me the next week in Mexico, on the Yucatan. I don't see how I can get out of it, and I'll have to be away from you for two whole weeks. Will you be all right?" Louise began to cry, and thought she felt him stiffen in resistance.

"These things have to happen. It's just our situation," he pleaded. A chasm opened up before her, the prospect of being without Philip for two weeks. And while she would be alone, with full time to brood, he would be taken up by the scientific meeting, and then he would be with Concha, the talkative, amusing and beautiful rightful wife. Louise felt suddenly how weak her own position was, how illicit and uncertain. The old strict rules about marriage were dissolving, but where did she fit in? She could not help crying. Would he come back to her at all?

"Hey, hey," he said, stroking her hair. "It's only two weeks, and then I'll be back."

"It's just so hard. I feel so much on the outside of your life. Do you really love me?" she asked, frightened of the question and the possibility that the mere pressure of it could create a distance between them.

"God, you know I do," he said. "Come on now, let's get up. You know I love you – too much, damn you. Come on, get up. My legs can't take your weight any longer. For such a skinny thing, you weigh an awful lot."

"Well," she said, trying to swallow her tears, summoning her pride of independence, "I guess it's not the end of the world. I'll think of you at your meeting, exchanging papers and whatever you do there. I won't ask you what goes on at night, but just don't bring back any bizarre diseases. And as for your week with Concha," and she began to smile, "I hope you have a perfectly horrible time."

"Don't worry," he said morosely, "we always do on vacations. All that time alone together is fatal. It's all right at home. We hardly ever see each other there, and when we do, we can talk about what's happening – you know, groceries and babysitters and all that. But on vacation it's just us two, and it's awful. Guess it says something about this wonderful marriage of mine. I don't know, Louise – I don't know if I have the courage to leave her. I tried, two years ago, when my mother was dying. Concha didn't care, didn't help me at all. She told me it was too expensive to go visit my mother in those last months. Of course I went anyway, several times, but there was one time near the end when I wanted to go again, and I let Concha talk me out of it. I've always felt –" He shook his head, his eyes on the cracked linoleum floor. "Well, I should have had the guts to just go anyway, and I didn't. Then after Mother died I was supposed to go work at a lab in Europe for a few months. A week before we were set to leave, Concha announced she wouldn't go. Little did I know it was because she wanted to be alone with her lover! And I didn't get tenure – she blamed me for that. Everyone on my committee voted for me and I went off to Europe thinking it was okay, I had tenure, and then it was denied higher up because there were two of us up for it and there was only money for one, and the other guy was somebody's friend. And maybe it was because there had been a picture of me on the front page of the campus newspaper leading this march against the Vietnam War. The higher-ups thought it was inappropriate, but hell, I'm a free man, I have the right to protest. I don't know. But in the end, there I was, suddenly maybe without a future – I didn't know I'd have this research job I have now, work I love, my own lab, everything – but then I was just alone, stranded by myself on another continent, and finally someone told me about Concha, how she'd been having these affairs for a long time and everyone knew – except me, of course. I didn't know whether

I even wanted to live. I was working in this tiny town in Germany, and on weekends I'd drive to Paris. I'd go so fast, driving like a crazy man for hours, trying to get this stuff out of my system. It's a wonder I survived. Talk about losing the will to live."

As he spoke, he had turned his back to her, looking out the window. The words were coming out of him so fast that she wasn't sure he was aware any longer of her presence. He was reliving his old hurts, on a recording that played with furious energy. Louise did not try to move closer or touch him; he seemed as if behind a curtain of glass, in a past she could not change or help.

"When I got back I moved into an apartment and stayed there for a couple of months. It was terrible. I was no good by myself. I'll never know how you just left Andrew and went out by yourself. I envy you that. Concha phoned up and more or less asked me to move back – and I did. I shouldn't have. I could never trust her again. I could probably get over the way she was when my mother died – so cold and distant while I was hurting. And the tenure thing, too, blaming me and withdrawing as punishment for my failure, or supposed failure. But this affair – I thought we were married, you know, faithful, while she had all these lovers and this one that she was serious about, and she never let me know in any way. She just wanted me there for convenience, and she was laughing at me the whole time. A woman from work came to one of our hot tub parties and she told me later that when she walked in, she'd asked Concha where I was. Concha laughed and said, 'What do you mean? Do you really want to talk to *him*?' As if I was some kind of idiot and no one in their right senses would ever want to talk to me. That's the way it was. I guess that's why she wanted to have a baby. She thought that would tie me in for life."

Louise's ears were beginning to ring. Oddly, though Philip was telling her his innermost life, she felt excluded, forgotten in the outpouring. "What will you do with Jo-Jo while you're away?" she asked, trying to bring Philip back to a present they could share.

"Oh, Concha will send him down to his grandparents in Palo Alto. She has a good setup with them."

"Well, take a good book along to Mexico," Louise said, with a touch of malice. "And I'm sure Concha will have read up on the Yucatan and will be able to speak volumes – and volumes and volumes."

"Devil!" he said, turning around to her. "Promise you'll be here when I come back. I couldn't go if I thought you might not be here."

"This is my address, and I'll be here, right here, in two weeks, or two months as far as that goes. Never fear."

A few days later Louise drove Philip to the airport. It was a strange, wife-like action. He was dressed up as a man of the world, in a suit and tie, and carrying a briefcase loaded with papers – as well as a change of clothes, and a clipholder for the last burnt ends of the marijuana he expected to find in Puerto Rico. They were both nervous, afraid of the disproportionate weight anything they said might take on in the silence after parting, distorting echoes that might make reunion more difficult somehow.

Philip didn't speak until they were almost at the airport. "I don't know if I should tell you this, Louise," he said, "but a lot of the time when I'm away from you, I can feel you, your presence, the feel of your body wrapped around mine, your weight, your smell. It's as if you've imprinted yourself on me."

She nodded, and kissed him shyly on the cheek, aware of all the strangers around them. "Yes. I'm so glad you told me. It will make the next two weeks a lot easier."

* * *

The day of Philip's return, Louise went as usual to a life-drawing session. When she returned just before dinner time, she found in her mailbox a sheet of notebook paper:

Louise,

I am back and so much has happened. Since your car is gone I guess you might be away. God I hope not because I need you! I will keep trying this afternoon.

Love, Philip

Louise phoned his lab and office but there was no answer. Everyone had gone for the day, and she could not call Philip at home; he might as well be on another planet, once he was at home. Shaky but resolving to work, she ate a hasty dinner. The phone rang. It was Philip.

"Hi. Want to see a flick?"

"What?" she asked, puzzled. To be together in the evening was an impossible treat; he always had to be home then.

"I just split. Want to go to a movie?"

"You split? You mean –"

"Yes, I left Concha. Oh, Louise, I have so much to tell you! This has been the most terrible week you could imagine."

* * *

He picked her up in the familiar green VW. At first they did not speak, but simply held hands, with comic awkwardness shifting the gear stick together as they drove.

"You left Concha?" she asked, needing to hear it again.

"Yes, yes, it's all over. God I hope you do love me, Louise, I don't know what I'd do if you failed me now. We had it all out in Mexico. I hadn't intended to, but it was just hell being with her. I couldn't even talk to her, much less do anything in bed. Finally she began to push me, and that was it. I told her – in a general way. She knows there's someone else. She doesn't know who it is, but she knows the general picture. And we had it all out. She still wanted me to stay on, but I knew then I couldn't. All I wanted was to get back to Berkeley and be with you. Have you missed me? Do you – no, I won't press you –"

She interrupted. "Yes, yes, of course I love you, Philip, I love you, don't worry!"

"I kept thinking, what if I left and Louise wasn't there when I came back? And then I couldn't find you, you weren't home. It's just been hell."

He avoided looking at her, his face set stiffly looking forward into the traffic. "I wish I weren't so damn dependent. I have a feeling you're more independent. Look at you. You were fine all by yourself. When you left Andrew you didn't have anyone new to go to."

"Well, I wasn't exactly happy. I used to wake up two hours early every morning and look at that depressing violet ceiling, and cry. I wouldn't wish it on anyone."

"Yes, but you didn't go running back. And after a while you got happy again. You were happy when I met you."

"Yes, that's true, I was okay, I had my balance back again. But you will too. It just takes time."

"I'm staying at the Faculty Club – not with you, that would be too much. I've got to learn to be independent. Then we can be together by free choice, not because I can't be alone, can't live without you."

"Don't worry, don't worry," she said, stroking his arm and trying to soothe him. "We'll work it out."

They went to some French jungle movie. Louise never knew more about it than that. Through the whole picture Philip sat pressed against her. They were both semi-conscious, unable to think yet exactly what was going on. Afterwards, half-feverish, they drove to her place, and Philip spent the night.

Their love-making was strange. For the first time, there was a coldness in him; he was fantasizing that she had no power, was mere object, slave to his will. She had become too important: he was obliterating her. In the morning he did not stay for breakfast but went off to work, in a hurry to change and shave at the Faculty Club.

"I'll call you," he said over his shoulder as he went down the stairs. Louise felt uneasy as she watched him leave. He had never been cold with her before. What would happen to them with this new pressure – the pressure to make it, to justify the gigantic step he had taken with Concha, breaking off twelve years of married life? They had been happy when their relationship was separate from their ordinary lives, a forbidden secret garden. But what would it be like now?

She was so upset that she could not work well. To use the time, she went up to campus and applied for every half-time job listed there. That disposed of the morning but still she was unsettled, and unwilling to go back to her empty apartment. Overcoming shyness and pride, she phoned Philip at work.

"Oh Louise, I'm so glad you called. I couldn't reach you. Where have you been? I can't work. I can only think about us. Listen, I'm meeting Hugh, my old friend, at the museum at one o'clock. Can you come too?"

They met at the door. Philip glowed. "You can't imagine how happy I feel, to be here with the only two people I really care for. You can't imagine." He stationed himself between Hugh and Louise, glancing eagerly from one to the other. Hugh and Louise smiled, each curious about the other. Louise did not know what to say to him. All she could think of was that he had known Philip and Concha for many years, and that he must be judging her, comparing her with Concha.

Philip expanded over her like a mother hen. "And Louise being an artist, can guide us through this exhibit."

She blushed; she didn't feel like any kind of guide just then. The show consisted of life-size dummies, startlingly real-looking, but without any special interest for her. She knew that much could easily be said about lines between life and art, the breakdown of definitions, or questions of identity; but that kind of theorizing had never interested her very much. And in any case, her brain seemed to have shut down and she had no more words of any kind. Self-consciousness made her feelings and thoughts so mended, patched and tied up in long convoluted knots that she could do little but smile, while in her mind she phrased, criticized, and rephrased thoughts appropriate to the conversation a minute or two earlier, but now hopelessly irrelevant. Philip and Hugh kept up a kind of banter; they both liked the show, and seemed not to notice Louise's silence.

Out on the sidewalk, in the blinding sunlight, they said goodbye to Hugh. Louise was relieved. While he had seemed friendly, he was nonetheless a potential judge from Philip's other, foreign world.

"Shall I walk you to the lab?" she asked.

"Yes, come on, I'll show you my room at the Faculty Club on the way," he replied. "But no messing around, now! The place is full of respectable old farts. I don't want to be kicked out – not until I can find an apartment. The Faculty Club is damned expensive, but the idea of moving in with you would be all wrong. It would be that terrible dependence again, and I want to learn to be independent."

"Well, you can come for dinner tonight, can't you?"

He laughed. "I don't know. What kind of cook are you?"

"Who knows?" she shrugged. "I have beans a lot. Do you like desserts?"

"You know what I want for dessert."

* * *

But when he arrived he was beside himself.

"Concha phoned me at work. I feel terrible. She said she was raped. She asked this man back to the house for coffee or a drink – just a civilized kind of thing, she says – and he attacked her. She was all alone in the house and there was no one to help her. I'm so angry, I could kill this guy, I mean it. God, I don't know what to do. It's so terrible and she was crying –"

"It is terrible," Louise agreed quickly. "But it sounds as if she expects you to go back and rescue her. As if maybe it was all your fault for leaving. You were supposed to be there, right? It's all your fault."

"Yes, damn it, that is what she's saying. And I always fall for it. I always feel responsible for women – that's what that shrink told me and it's true. But it's so terrible. It's just lucky I'm not sure who this man is or I'd really kill him. Or get Hugh and a few of the guys together and we'd really teach him a lesson." He stared ahead of him, absorbed in the fantasy of getting at this man.

"I can't say I'm more pure than you," Louise began. "I've had the same kinds of revenge fantasies about imaginary rapists, just the idea of being threatened, or reading that it happened to someone in my neighborhood – any time I feel threatened. I mean, that's why I studied martial arts. But why is she calling you? What does she expect you to do?"

"She wanted me to come over," he answered. "I almost did, too, except that I couldn't stand the whole idea, somehow. But it's so horrible!" he repeated. "She phoned up Hugh, too, and he did go over. She was crying and all this shit."

"She doesn't have any women friends?" Louise asked.

"No, not really. She never has. Women have told me they tried to get close to her and couldn't." His eyes began to focus on things around them again; the spell was broken.

"Damn! Why did this have to happen! She knew it would make me feel guilty."

"Well, it probably was terrible, but I don't know if there's anything you can do, really, to help, short of moving in again and being her watchdog. She's smart; I'm sure she'll learn how to take care of herself."

"Looking out for number one always was her best act," he said. "I almost suspect the timing of this, frankly. But no, that's going too far. But what about you? Have you ever been through anything like that?"

"No, I've been in some tight situations but I always get out of them. By getting mad, actually. When I'm really mad I feel ready to fight to the death. I think men sense that. They always sort of backed off and went away."

He looked at her in surprise. "God, I can't believe I found a woman so much like me. I didn't think a woman could be like you. I'm just like that. But when I got mad at someone when Concha was with me, she would always get embarrassed and try to shush me down. Would you really stand by me?"

"Depends. If I agreed with you, I would."

"I can't believe it," he said, shaking his head. "Someone who would stand by me."

* * *

The next morning he did not leave so abruptly; and two days later, to Louise's surprise, he was ready to move in with her.

"Why not?" he said, aware that he needed to explain. "You tell me that the owner of your place wants to sell and you have to move out in a month or two."

She nodded.

"So," he continued, "it can't be a permanent thing, my living here. I'll start looking for a place of my own right away, but meantime, we might as well live together. We're together all the time anyway. And it's too depressing up there at the Faculty Club. Don't you want me down here?" He looked at her confidently.

She nodded again, smiling.

"So, Lou," he said, taking her hand, "we can enjoy playing man and wife. No guilt – and I can be independent later!" He grinned a little sheepishly.

By the third morning, the new situation seemed natural. She woke gradually, aware that it was not just the bedcovers that reflected warmth back to her, but Philip, nestled up close to her. She was not in her narrow single bed, under the purple ceiling, but in the painting room, full of the smell of linseed oil and turpentine, on the old sofa bed. As she wakened, Philip pulled her into his arms. They lay peacefully there for awhile, until Philip spoke.

"I dread going to the lab today, Lou. She's phoning me there now. She wants me to know I'm a monster and cruel and also stupid for leaving her. And she says she'll get more than half my income in the settlement, even though she earns more than I do! Can you believe that? Even though she earns more than I do! And she wants plenty starting right away. I have to get myself a lawyer. She wants my blood."

He was silent for a moment. Louise could feel his body grow tense. Once again he was lost in the struggle with Concha. She began to stroke his head, still holding him as he held her. Deep sobs shook his body.

"I know you loved her," Louise whispered. "It must be terrible to face her now as an enemy."

"I loved her too much, too much. I couldn't help it. I put her on a pedestal. I guess it wasn't fair, but I did. I thought she was so perfect. But don't worry, there'll be no going back to her this time. I was dying in that relationship, literally. I think I would have died in a few years. My will – whatever it is that makes a person want to live – was gradually getting blotted out. I don't know exactly what was happening to me. And I don't understand why her hold on me was so strong."

She held him closer again as he cried.

* * *

But they were not ready to enter paradise; only to play house there for a few weeks. Philip found an apartment of his own, and moved in. Louise loaned him some extra sheets and kitchenware; and to help her while she looked for a new apartment, he agreed to make room for her piano at his place. They both liked this tacit presence of hers in his bachelor stronghold.

It took Louise longer to find a new apartment because she could not pay as much rent, and nonetheless she was determined to find a view of the bay. She loved this thing Berkeley had to offer, its perfect location facing San Francisco, the Golden Gate Bridge, the mountains of Marin, the enormous expanse of water, cloud, and sky; it gave her spirit space. But as time grew short and still there was no bay view she could afford, she answered an ad for a cheap studio on a busy street.

The building was unusually ugly, utterly utilitarian, with a billboard on top. The street floor was taken up by a Berkeley mélange: a furniture store; a beauty salon patronized by elderly women with tightly curled blue hair; a community center offering advice on food stamps, jobs, and local therapies; and a massage parlor. What the respectable ladies from the beauty parlor made of the men slinking into the massage parlor, or the attractive young women who worked there, Louise could not figure out. All seemed to cohabit in peace.

As the building manager guided her through the fire-engine red halls, he muttered, "Well, might as well show you the one that opened up today. It's the same price, $141 a month," and let her in to a sun-filled third floor studio looking westward, out over the Golden Gate, and with no impediment from Palo Alto in the south to the San Rafael bridge in the north. She rented it on the spot.

She had not even moved in when she was offered one of the jobs she had applied for on campus nearly two months earlier. It was a half-time secretarial job at the law school. Walking in the park the next Sunday, she and Philip debated whether or not she should take it.

"Well kid, when you're hot you're hot," he teased. "First an apartment with a bay view, and now a job." He put his arm through hers. "The job isn't exactly glamorous, but you do need the money, from what you tell me. But half-time? $430 a month? You don't know me. I'm used to a high standard of living. If we ever live together, you'd have to make at least a thousand a month."

"But Philip," she began hesitantly, "I could never do that unless I gave up painting."

"Well, you could just take a full-time job for a year or so, make yourself indispensable and then tell them you want to work half-time. They'd practically have to let you do it."

"But a year is a long, long time. What if I died then? I'd have missed my chance. I'm not asking you to support me, you know. Just not to mind the way I choose to spend my time. Look at it this way: painting is work; it's just not paid work."

"Maybe you could teach," he said. "Why not?"

She fought off the tears. "Because teaching is as bad as painting, it's endless, at least for me. I could prepare day and night and still want to do more. I can't both teach and paint."

Apparently he heard the desperation in her voice; she had no more heart left to justify herself to this embodiment of the world's accusing voice.

"Well, after all, there's nothing wrong with this secretarial job at the law school. At least you'd have a steady income." He shrugged impatiently. "I can't worry about this now, Louise. You have to do what you want."

Exasperation saved her from her tears. Her eyes cleared and she silently resolved that she would, indeed, do what she wanted to do. To hell with the world – that vague entity which had mainly meant her parents, and now seemed also, painfully, to include Philip. But she might still win him over.

Disconcertingly, as if once more following her unspoken thoughts, he added, "Besides, how much do you expect me to do? Already I've changed my lifestyle completely. Look, here I am in blue jeans and this old blue jeans jacket. I look like a hippie. What more do you want?" and he gestured theatrically at his clothes.

She laughed. "I like your blue jeans, I have to admit – very sexy. But I notice you already had them. You must have hired someone to wear them to the point of such fashionable fadedness!"

His eyes rolled around sideways to look at her. He was smiling. "Devil! Devil!" he whispered. "What am I going to do with you?" and he grabbed her around the waist and pulled her towards him.

"You love to do it in public, don't you?" he said in a stage villain's voice. "In a park like this where people might come by and see you? Strangers watching you?"

He pulled her off into a grove of trees, away from the path, and they lay down together in the grass. Fiercely they made love, until exhausted, and their differences forgotten, they rested on the pine needles.

"I don't know why I can't keep my hands off you," he said. "You know what it is, all this sex, two or three times a day, even, it's death-fucking. It's against death somehow."

"You've said you felt as if you were dying in your marriage," she said slowly, feeling her way. "It does seem strange in a way, doing it so much we even make each other sore. Doesn't seem to go with the pure pleasure-principle."

"No. To feel alive, or maybe to get to the bone, the center of you – or of me, I don't know. When we're making it I can't tell if I'm in you or you're in me. Did you know that?"

She looked into his green eyes a while: she could look a long time. Finally she said, "To arrive in some final way? To know absolutely that we are together, that nothing can undo this closeness? And about death-fucking, in *Tristan und Isolde* –"

Philip broke in with a laugh. "Oh just look at you, Madame Philosophe! The professor lady. No one would ever guess what you're really like." Though he spoke, as so often, in hyperbole, she felt there was truth in what he said. Not just about the scholarly side; it was also, and more importantly, the side of her that painted, that expanded out into the light spaces of the bay view, that cast away security and took a chance. This was the side that was hidden to most people, a side that Louise herself kept hidden, her socially unacceptable essence. Philip alone saw it, encouraged and loved it.

* * *

He had to go away again, this time to Colorado – and this time by himself.

"It's a good conference, Lou, I can't miss it. I have to give a paper there, and I want to hear what other people are doing. Besides, it's at Keystone, it's a wonderful skiing area. Have you ever been there?"

She smiled. "Our lives have been sort of different," she answered. "I've only been skiing a few times. It's so expensive, and you have to go so far away to do it, and have all this equipment. It always seemed more practical to get my exercise some other way, like walking or bicycling."

He sighed. "You're so contrary. Well, you'd love it, but I can't afford to take you. It's actually two conferences back-to-back, and I figure on taking about ten days, including a couple of skiing days at the end."

"That's a long time," she said, looking out her apartment window. They were just finishing dinner. The sun had disappeared near the horizon, sinking into banks of fog which rolled like vast mounds of whipped cream over the Golden Gate Bridge and the mountains to the north.

"I know. I'm going to miss you – too much, damn it."

She thought ahead. She would miss Philip, but on the other hand, she would be able to get a lot of painting done, too.

"You don't look too sad, Borgstrum. I bet you won't miss me at all. You'll just be painting away down here. You won't even think of me."

"Oh, that's not true," she cried, moving to sit on his lap, putting her arms around him.

"Wait!" he commanded, moving one hand toward the window sill. With the wine bottle, he crushed a cockroach that had been moving along the ledge, attracted by the smell of dinner.

"Damn," Louise said. "This apartment is so wonderful, so perfect, really – my little paradise – and then it has to have cockroaches."

"It's not exactly high-class," Philip said. "I don't know how you can live here and seem happy about it, even."

"But look!" and she gestured out the window at the view.

"Yes, it's nice, you're right, you're right, you're always right."

"And maybe there are cockroaches in paradise," she went on. "So you remember to appreciate the paradisical aspects."

"Is that what Protestants think?" and he roared with laughter. "God, Borgstrum, what am I going to do without you in Colorado?"

* * *

That turned out to be a more serious question than Louise had anticipated. It was only about a week after Philip left that she received a long-distance phone call from him.

"Lou? I'm coming home. It's no fun being out on the slopes all by myself. I miss you too much. I hope you won't lose respect for me or something, but I just can't see staying out here and having a lousy time. So I'm coming home tomorrow, Oakland Airport, seven p.m. Can you meet me?"

"Of course! I'm glad you're coming!"

This was true. She would be very glad to see Philip. But it also worried her that he was coming home early. It was as if he didn't trust their relationship enough, didn't believe he was loved and not alone unless she was actually there to prove it. But he had to be able to be without her sometimes. She couldn't always be with him.

"See you tomorrow, Lou," Philip closed the conversation.

The next day, she took care to dress well – her good boots, jeans not too baggy, her leather jacket, a purple and magenta scarf – to welcome Philip at the airport, wanting to give him maximum pleasure.

When she saw him in the crowd, she ran to meet him, and he beamed. Then, after holding her to him a moment, he let her go. As they walked down the airport corridors, she sensed a distance in him. He held his body far away from hers, and would hardly answer her questions. Irritation and chagrin rose in her. She had looked forward to this meeting, to basking in his love. Now all she got was his anger – at himself for needing her too much, at her for seeming to have too much power over him. It was several weeks before he dared let go again.

* * *

To her surprise, Philip wanted to celebrate the Fourth of July. "I found a good place to go," he said, "a little town north of here. It should be small enough so we can feel part of everything, like an old-fashioned Fourth of July."

Ordinarily she did not like to drive several hours just for something as simple as fireworks, but Philip seemed very excited by the idea.

"I'd like to," she began, "but I did have a tentative plan to watch the fireworks here, with Sylvia."

"Bring her along, I'd like to meet her. It's high time I did, isn't it? She'll like it, a small town celebration."

"Well, she really wants to meet you, too. I'll talk to her about it."

On the morning of the Fourth, the three of them set out in Philip's green VW. Louise sat in the back, so that Sylvia and Philip would be able to hear each other without straining, and so Sylvia would not feel excluded from the two of them, the couple. Louise hung her arms around the backs of Sylvia's and Philip's seats, her nose nudging forward between the two in the front.

"How's your new place?" Louise asked.

"Fine, I can't complain, $125 and a bay view and Kensington, I mean, what more could I ask?"

Philip glanced over at her in surprise. "$125 for all that? I don't know how you two do it. No wonder people in the counter-culture look so happy all the time. All the good things, no worries –"

Sylvia's eyes and mouth opened wide. "You think I'm the counterculture? And Louise too? Boy, are you naïve! *Me?* A school teacher? Going back for a credential to work with the disabled? And Louise? *Counterculture?*" Sylvia snorted loudly.

Louise flinched. She wanted Sylvia and Philip to like each other. What if they fought?

"That's true, Sylvia, Louise is straight-arrow, she's practically a Lutheran at times! But I thought you lived in the Haight-Ashbury, a flower-child, the whole hippie bit."

"Well, for a while, sure, when I was young –"

"How old are you now? You look about nineteen. Nineteen and a half?"

Sylvia snorted again. "You think I look nineteen? Really? And how old are you, twenty-three?"

Philip guffawed.

Louise watched in amazement. She hadn't guessed that Sylvia's hands-on Brooklyn style would work so well with Philip's joking tough-boy Philadelphia neighborhood style.

"Hey, Lou, what's going on in the back seat?"

"Yeah," Sylvia chimed in, "why are you so quiet?"

"Oh, I'm just congratulating myself for having found you two."

"So you're happy?"

"Yes, I'm happy."

* * *

When it began to get dark, the three of them went out into the stubbly field where the fireworks were to be held. They lay down together and looked skyward. Showers of red, green, and brilliant golden light exploded almost directly over them as they lay safely together on the dark earth. The evening was cool, and Louise, sandwiched between Sylvia and Philip, felt the weight of them, felt their warmth pour into her from either side, thawing and soothing some anxious and frightened part of her that was still waiting for this, waiting a long time. How much would it take? Did everyone have this much need? Love – was it as evanescent as yesterday's dinner? Did she have to be fed again and again? But in this moment, she was complete.

* * *

P hilip had been lucky in his new apartment. It was set in the middle of a block, well off the street, surrounded by trees and garden spaces. He thought of it as the place where he would begin his new life. Louise loved the green of it, and the privacy. Now music added another pleasure, as Philip needed her to accompany him on her piano while he learned the tenor parts of Handel's *Messiah*; he had joined the university chorus and there would be a performance in a few months. Philip's voice, though not power-ful, was sweet and true, and they learned the music together as they went along.

One day he phoned up Louise while she was at work.

"Lou, I think my new social life is about to begin," he said, obviously pleased. "Can you come over to my place this Friday? I'm counting on you. We'll have a little party."

She raised her eyebrows. "A party? How many people?"

"Oh, nothing formal. Just Bill and Rachel. I've talked about them before. Rachel works with me, and Bill used to be one of my students – one of the best students I've had, actually. Now he's doing a post-doc with someone else in a related field. You'll like them both, don't worry. They're just going to drop by after dinner for awhile. I guess it's not really a party, but we'll have some wine, and maybe something to smoke, and probably play Monopoly or some dumb thing like that. Can you come over around five? I'm cooking, Lou, something good, don't worry."

"How can I refuse an offer like that? I'll be there," she pro-mised.

It was just getting dark when they had finished their steaks and potatoes and salad and wine. Louise felt almost too full, but it was luxurious. As they put the dishes in the sink, the doorbell rang.

"Pheelup?" came a high woman's voice, speaking with what seemed to be a French accent.

"Rachel! Bill! Come in, meet Louise," Philip greeted them.

The first to come in was Rachel. Louise smiled at her, but was not sure whether there was any response; Rachel's face was more or less hidden behind curtains of heavy blond hair that hung below her waist.

Louise shook hands with Bill, set at ease by his open, boyish smile.

"Well," Philip fussed over them, "sit down, let me offer you some wine before we challenge you to Monopoly."

Bill shook his head, grinning. "I don't know if Rachel will want any wine. We just had a little smoke –"

"What do you mean," came the high-edged voice from behind the hair, "of course I'd like some wine." She broke out into shrill giggles.

Bill rolled his eyes. "I think she's feeling it, though I don't know how she could get high, actually, on the one little puff she had."

More shrieks of laughter.

Philip leaned down towards her.

"Little Rachel, are you high?"

"Vat do you think, I am only five feet two," she said, at the same time removing her extremely high heels.

Louise noticed for the first time that Rachel was clad in short shorts, black fishnet stockings, and some sort of little bra, totally inadequate to her large breasts. The whole outfit – clothes Louise had seen hitherto only on hookers at tough street corners – had been partly camouflaged at first by the long hair.

"Little, but powerful," Bill laughed.

Soon they were sitting on the orange-swirled rug, playing Monopoly.

"Your turn," Philip said to Rachel.

"Oh, it ees?" she replied. "I don't understand how you do thees."

"Well, Rachel, you shake the dice," Bill said.

"Oh, yes-yes," she replied impatiently, taking up the dice.

"You'd never guess that Rachel has a graduate degree in chemistry, would you?" Philip commented, turning to Louise.

"You never would," Bill echoed, with some satisfaction.

"She does? You do?" Louise asked, trying to readjust her idea of Rachel.

"Yes, it is true," Rachel lisped, pulling one side of her hair away from her face just long enough for one heavily mascara'd eye to encounter Louise's surprised ones. The curtain fell again.

"She got her degree in Israel."

"No, France," Rachel pouted. Then, quickly, "No, Israel, that is right. Israel. I was working with my husband. He did all the research, really."

Philip and Bill came momentarily to attention.

"What?" Philip said.

"Yes, really, he did all the research, and I got the degree. He already had a Ph.D., so why not?"

"Why not?" Bill echoed; but his eyes met Philip's in consternation. Evidently Rachel had made a serious faux pas.

"Eeech!" Rachel cried, "I just bought Park Place! Isn't that good? I like the name." She giggled violently behind the hair, all the bare flesh shaking.

The two men leaned towards her.

"Little Rachel had a smoke, I think," Philip crooned.

More giggles.

"Whose turn is it?" Louise asked, but no one seemed to hear.

Louise did not see Rachel's eyes again that evening. All she saw was the body, shaking, and the heavy curtain of hair. There was no word Louise could say. The evening's mode was flirtation, and Louise was not good at playing this game competitively. So she sat watching, sipping her wine, bemused, wondering if Rachel had really gotten her husband to do her research for her, or whether that story was only a sort of red herring, like perhaps the shimmering veil of hair and the ostentatiously proffered body.

* * *

Although in theory Louise was the only woman now in Philip's life, Concha was still a powerful presence as divorce proceedings began.

"You know," he said one evening, as they sat after dinner in his new apartment, "Concha always was fierce on women's rights, and she lectured and badgered me until I felt good and guilty and really tried to change. I did change – a lot, actually. You think I'm a male chauvinist pig now, but you should have seen me before!"

Louise smiled, but at the same time it occurred to her that she might, after all, owe Concha something there.

"But she wanted it both ways. That's not fair. If you're going to be equal, okay, but then you have to give up the privileges. You can't be the poor little thing anymore that all the men have to run and help because you're so weak and frail. And she's about as weak and frail as an armored tank. Do you know what she wants in the divorce settlement? Everything! The house, the better car, and alimony! Plus a percentage of what I make every month, too, even though her salary will go up faster than mine, and I educated her, encouraged her."

The words poured out of Philip like steam from a hot car radiator.

"And you know what she wants now? She wants full custody of Jo-Jo, even though after Jo-Jo was born I was the one who got up in the middle of the night, changed him, fed him – loved him. She couldn't. I tried to supply enough love for both parents. I don't know if a child can be all right without a mother's love too, but maybe that's sexist. Love is love, and if that's all that matters, Jo-Jo will be all right. It's really important that I get joint custody. I want to have him at least half the time.

"And you know what else she wants? She wants to have lunch with me once a month! Can you believe it?"

"What for?" Louise asked, amazed.

"She says we need to talk about Jo-Jo, what school he should go to, talk about how he's developing, stuff like that. I don't know." He pursed his lips, frowning slightly. "I guess maybe we should. It's true, it's hard to talk over the phone, sometimes there's too much that needs to be settled. I can get a better idea of what she's up to this way."

He paused a moment, then laughed bitterly. "Ha! She's even got a new man. I feel sorry for him. But maybe he can handle her. He's older. From what she says, he's coming on strong."

"That was quick."

"Right, she has to have a man around. Not like you – she

couldn't be by herself for a year or two, she couldn't stand it. God I feel sorry for this guy. But maybe he's a bastard like her. Let's hope. If he's gotten her in bed by now he knows he won't get any action there. She didn't like it. Not with me, anyway. And later, when we were kind of, oh, swingers I guess you'd have to say, all the other men said the same thing: nothing in bed. No fun. Dull. Fizzle."

Louise was silent. It was not entirely surprising that a woman as coldly manipulative as Concha would be cold also in bed; nor was it surprising that men were disappointed. What shocked her was that the men had obviously discussed the sex amongst themselves afterward. For both sides it was just an exploit: for the men, scoring the best-looking woman and using her afterwards as a prurient joke, a way of affirming male superiority; for Concha, similarly, a way of asserting her power over men.

"Ugh," she said, "you led a grubby life with her."

He smiled, and stroked her hair. "Come on, admit it, you'd love to make it with a lot of different men."

She side-stepped. "This sounds too impersonal. Everyone was just using everyone else. It's sordid."

"So what? They all got what they wanted."

"But what do you talk about with Hugh, say, now?" The thought that Philip could be discussing their private sex life with other men made her flinch.

"Hugh? I don't know. I don't tell him everything now." He paused. "I've been getting the feeling he's telling Concha things about me, about my plans for the lawyer and the divorce. Sometimes I even wonder if he's getting it on with Concha – maybe even did a long time ago."

Louise raised her eyebrows, not knowing how to respond. Could Hugh be so treacherous?

Philip nodded and went on. "You don't realize how lonely it is, without a man friend I can really trust, the way you can trust Sylvia and Deirdre."

She thought for a moment. "Well, actually, when Andrew and I were splitting up, I suddenly realized I had no close women friends. There were some graduate school women, but we weren't really intimate. It was just about school. And I was horribly lonely, and resolved not to let that happen again, never just to rely on a single man in my life."

"Do tell!" Philip exclaimed. "So you wouldn't dare just be with me?"

"You wouldn't want me to be, would you? It would be a big responsibility! And what if I didn't have anyone to complain to about you?"

"Fiend!" he whispered melodramatically. "So do Sylvia and Deirdre know everything about me?" He sounded a little worried.

"Um, no, no, don't worry. It's – well, it's nothing disrespectful, put it like that."

"Huh. But what do you actually say?"

Louise hesitated. She had said more to Sylvia and Deirdre than Philip would probably like.

"Well, sometimes you kind of withdraw, without giving me any clue as to why, and it's subtle, so I think maybe it's my imagination because everything seems fine on the surface and yet I feel excluded somehow."

"That could happen, Lou, but it's too general a complaint for me to do anything about it now."

"I know, and I know Concha gets you mad at women in general. And I suppose the game she plays with men – it's probably a constant temptation to her, to be so exotic, so beautiful, to have that power."

"Could be," Philip laughed. "Is that what keeps you honest, Ms. Independence?"

Long after they had gone to bed, Louise lay awake, rigid, her back turned to Philip. How could he imply that she was homely? She knew she was not beautiful, she thought to herself, but she could at least be counted pretty. Besides, how could he, who claimed to love her, not see her in her best light?

After fifteen or twenty minutes of this, Louise had worked herself up into tears and fury. Pulling on her robe, she went down to the kitchen. She would be damned if she would lie in the same bed with him. He had better not just assume her presence, no matter what he said. Fiercely she picked up a book, trying to distract herself, not think about Philip, show she could do very well without him.

After a while she heard Philip's footsteps on the stairs leading from the loft. She wavered, glad to be recalled from this painful self-inflicted vigil, but then quickly firmed up her hurt and anger by a mental review of his insults.

Sleepily he came into the doorway, blinking at the bright kitchen light. "Babe, what's up? Are you cross or something? Did I say something?"

"Well, I don't know why you came down here, when I'm so ugly and –"

"Oh god, what did I say? Just because you're two years older than I am –"

"A year and a half!" she interrupted.

"Just because you're older and I call you an old bag sometimes that doesn't mean I don't love you"

"I'm not an old bag!" she shouted. "That's horrible! It's not loving at all. It's horrible!"

"Come on, you know I think you're good looking. And you have the most beautiful blue eyes in the world. Come on, I can't sleep without you, it's not the same. Seriously," and he came up close and held her head, looking into her eyes, "don't you know that I love you? That to me you're the most beautiful person on earth?"

Louise got up and kissed him, and they went back to bed.

* * *

Louise had liked being a teacher at the university. Although just a graduate student, she had taught freshman English as well as the Women's Studies course. There had been times when teaching was a heady experience, when Louise felt her own love of literature was being passed on: the gift she offered was being taken. Mixed with the altruistic pleasure was a sense of power, of having something worth giving, and being liked and respected for it. As for those students who seemed to go through her courses unmoved by anything but boredom and incomprehension, even they had to recognize her momentary importance in their lives, for they all wanted to pass.

Now, class, let us turn to the other end of the social scale, from learned ladies who read in five languages to that class which is presumed barely to read at all, beyond perhaps *Woman's Home*

Circle. I mean the secretaries. I mean Louise.

There is a section in *Paradise Lost* where Milton describes the fall of Mulciber – by whom Milton also means Vulcan, builder of palaces, plus of course Satan. This many-faced person was thrown by Jove

> *Sheer o'er the crystal battlements: from morn*
> *To noon he fell, from noon to dewy eve,*
> *A summer's day; and with the setting sun*
> *Dropped from the zenith like a falling star,*
> *On Lemnos the Aegean isle.*

We shove off with "sheer" and take a nose-dive down, but the fall is silky, light. Those battlements are crystal, and as Louise floats down she admires their diamondy refractions, their transparency and luminescence. She is falling vast distances, marked by a few stations in time, at each of which the verse tosses her up as if from a soft landing net, and flips her out into the next stage of fall. Everything takes place on a warm summer's day, she is falling through light, and the movement of air has a southern caress to it, like a warm bath that is not tepid or dull, but just exactly delightful. Then, having run out of space to fall free in, she arrives, blazing with light and warmth, "like a falling star."

But as she approaches material creation she also becomes aware of limitations, and fear; she has "dropped" – what a sodden word! Like a lump of earth, clunk. Satan, of course, lands in Hell, perhaps in a cloud of dry dust. He lies there awhile, bruised, flat on his back, gradually realizing that it is damned hot. At least, he thinks, it's nice and quiet without those choirs of souls running around singing elevated songs, eyes rolled piously upward. Too much worship of the spirit he finds tiresome. But still, the lower regions look awfully bleak.

What a wonderful thing a literary education is! Unfortunately, this cannot be discussed further here because room must be made for the secretary. Here she comes. There she goes. Did you see her? No? Well, she is very hard to see, actually, almost invisible, even though many of her kind dress with extreme care, to match the expensive office decors of which they are often a part. If you are a student you may be especially unlikely to see her; as a student, Louise herself had worn special blinders which, like solar devices tracking the sun, followed the line of sight to professors and that was all. As in the ditty about Boston, "land of the bean and the cod, where the Lowells speak only to Cabots, and the Cabots speak only to God," students saw only professors and professors often saw no one at all, their vision focused immeasurably higher than almost anything actually in sight.

And so Louise fell from professional woman to "girl," as in "my girl will do that for you"; from the lofty starlike status of near-professordom, she fell to the invisible limbo of secretarial staff. She had fallen about as far as it is possible to fall, in one step and within one closed realm, the university. It is true that there was a fine sense of adventure in taking that step. After all, Jove didn't kick her out; she jumped of her own volition, an extremely important point. On the other hand, since the desire to paint inexorably brought with it the likelihood of little money and low social status, Louise did feel somewhat kicked – or rather, perhaps, to change figure, bound to Fortune's wheel, which someone had given a big shove. But as Milton's Satan discovers, if you're happy in your work, even the lower regions may seem quite comfortable after a while. As she began to feel out the dark terrain of the law school, she discovered other souls, kindred to her; and some had hearts better developed than most she had found in the more ethereal regions.

Louise had her own quiet office in the library stacks, with a window looking out over trees and hills, and an extraordinary person to work for, who tried to abolish class distinctions wherever he went. The more he tried, of course, the more the lower classes appreciated him, which just reinforced the sense of class; but the attempt was noble, and completely sincere. So it could have been a lot worse. He conscientiously referred to Louise as "Doctor" Borgstrum; and her check, small but enough, came in every month. She had her security and independence.

Philip was delighted with that aspect of her job, knowing that she would not need to impose on him financially. As a full-time research scientist, of course, he made vastly more than Louise did as a half-time secretary. But he was making plans, and felt insecure.

"I built a little empire," he said, as they sat at an outdoor café near campus. A plate of bagels, cream cheese, and lox was in front of them, Philip working on it with gusto as they talked. "Man, was I lucky. I was living in this little house with a view, when I first came here, and the lady wanted to sell. All I had was $5,000 for a down payment, but the house only cost $30,000, so I did it."

Louise was struck by the absence of Concha from this story. They had been married, Concha had lived in that house with Philip and presumably shared in the decisions, and even, she was learning, had sometimes contributed to their income by nursing jobs. But Philip always spoke as if the decisions and actions had been all his own, as if no one had shared his life with him. Perhaps he felt no one had. Or had he egoistically ignored Concha's contributions?

"That was the luckiest thing I ever did. When I bought the new house two years ago, I sold the old one for $50,000. The new one cost $90,000, and already after a year it's worth around $140,000. Think of that! From $5,000 to $140,000, and I didn't have to do a thing. The timing was just right. But now – I don't know. If I can just get another down payment together, I can begin again. Concha shouldn't get more than half! If she's smart she'll stay in the house. That way she'll have everything – and not one bit of it did she earn!" Louise raised an eyebrow. "Well, unless you count the nursing jobs she did for a few years; but except for that I paid for everything – and now she gets it all!"

Once again it seemed as if Philip had just been released from ten years of solitary confinement. Suddenly in possession of a sympathetic listener, he poured things out with the pent-up energy of all that lonely time. His talking was a battering-ram, a weapon with which he fought for release from walls that no longer existed.

Louise had begun to feel too often invisible. She was not a wall, she silently objected, she was there, listening, and had some thoughts of her own. But there never seemed to be any room for these. Her self-confidence was melting, and with it her ability to string together a coherent thought and thrust it out into Philip's stream. She began to be angry as well as hurt, began to feel she'd be damned if she would say anything at all, since he evidently did not care to hear it. She watched the last lox, mounted on a white puff of cream cheese, disappear into Philip's mouth.

"What's on your mind, Lou?" he asked, chewing.

"Nothing much," she replied, withholding.

"I'm not so sure about that," he said, looking at her.

"Well, I've got to start talking more, is all. The trouble is, I'm not sure I have anything to say. It's very quiet, painting. I mean, there's lots of action, running back and forth to the canvas, or times of being stuck and thinking I can't do anything, and times when everything just flows and it's like dancing and I think I'm the greatest painter the world has ever seen – but that about says everything there is. I don't have these big dramas – a ruthless enemy I once loved, or thousands of dollars to win or lose. I just get on my bicycle, go to work, type a few things, come home, paint, and see you. It's a great life, but not much to talk about. But sometimes when you talk so much I feel left out, a sort of nonentity."

"I'm not sure that's something I can do anything about," Philip said thoughtfully. "I have to talk – you can't put restraints on me that way. But you talk a lot. You talk all the time. Why are you worried?"

That was not her perception of it, but without a tape recorder and a third person called in to arbitrate, the factual question could not easily be settled.

"I don't know. It's something I've got to work on," she replied, still feeling anxious.

"Well, it's certainly a change. The other one talked all the time. I could never get a word in."

"The other one," she considered. "Hmmph. Funny thought. But you do give the impression of someone who hasn't had a chance to talk for a long long time. I think that's one reason it's so hard to compete with you. But don't worry. I'll find a way of getting my two cents in."

She thought for a moment, found what interested her, and with a feeling of fear in her stomach, plunged in.

"You know, Philip, when I started out as a half-time secretary I was prejudiced myself about the kind of people who would take such a job, especially full time. But I'm gradually discovering that there are some very bright and interesting women at the law school, doing this secretary thing. For myself, I figure I'll get out of it after a while. But the others mostly won't, not because they aren't bright or able, but because they don't have any other job experience, and being a secretary robs you of self-confidence. You get told where to put every comma and so you fall asleep mentally and make a mistake here and there and you think, 'my god, I can't even do this job, the lowliest of the low, correctly or properly. It would be insane to try for anything more ambitious; I just hope they'll overlook my stupidity and allow me to stay on here as a secretary.' It's very sapping. If I didn't have a Ph.D. in a hard subject from a good school, I'd think of myself that same way – very depressing. In fact some days I have to remind myself about all that school work. Sometimes I actually need it when my boss refers to me as 'Doctor Borgstrum,' funny though that title sounds."

Philip's eyes were on some young women going past on the sidewalk. "Hmm," he said mischievously, "not bad! But it's really disgusting. I'm getting so I measure other women by you. If they aren't tall and blond I'm not interested any more. Those were all too short."

Louise laughed, but only as a preliminary to her serious business. "But Philip, did you hear what I was just saying before?"

"About the other secretaries? Sure, I heard it all, and it was interesting. I could repeat it all to you, about the way it takes away self-confidence. You see? I do listen to you. You're just too sensitive. I always listen to you, and I watch you, too. I know you better than you know yourself sometimes. Like your eyes following that man who just walked out of here. You were interested – don't deny it! You're not so pure yourself. But don't worry; I don't expect you to be pure. Just be yourself, but don't worry so much. I pay attention to you all the time – Doctor Borgstrum." He reached across the table and took her hand.

For the moment the struggle was moot; the warmth of Philip's hand made her feel included again. But she knew that later her struggle not to be invisible would have to be carried on. She wanted her words to be more than just isolated interludes in Philip's dominant flow. She wanted him to respond, to enter in imaginatively, to take part in her world as she tried to do with his.

* * *

It was Sunday morning. Philip had surprised her by getting up early, to go in to the lab. "I've got to change the culture that the cells are growing in. The cells go through different stages, always the same ones, in a sort of circular way, and I think there may be one stage where they're especially vulnerable to damage by an outside agent. Who knows, Lou, maybe we might find a way to protect cells. Who knows – one step in the cure for cancer! Don't worry – go back to sleep. I'll be home in an hour or two."

When he returned to the house and they had had breakfast, Philip was restless. "If I don't have anything to do on Sunday, I get bored or depressed or something, especially in the afternoon. I call it 'getting the Sundays,' like some kind of disease. Sundays are just too long and empty, even when I have to go in to the lab first."

So they put their bicycles on the rack of the green VW, and took off for San Francisco, fleeing the Sundays. They parked the car near the ferry building, and then bicycled slowly through the crowded streets of Fisherman's Wharf and on along the waterfront. Finally, huffing and puffing, they climbed the windy hill up to the Golden Gate Bridge. Already they could see the divide, the surf pounding the cement walls as it poured in from the Pacific, and on the other side the picture-book sailboats out on the bay, safe in the harbor.

The walkway on the bridge's outmost edge, the ocean side, was reserved for bicyclists. The cold wind sweeping in from the ocean was so powerful that they had to fight to steer their bicycles properly. On their left was the sea, vast, gleaming gray-gold, relentlessly pushing its vastness against the headlands' dark green. Somewhere in the middle of the bridge they stopped and got off their bicycles. Side by side they faced out into the wind, feeling utterly alone. Behind them cars rushed past, too intent on arrival elsewhere to disturb their world. Louise leaned against Philip and he pulled her in to him, close, and bent down to kiss her, enveloping her in his warmth. She could almost smell him, though it was the heavy salt of the ocean wind as much as the sharp salt of his body. Turning her face up to his, he was at that moment the essence of the male to her; and by the way he held her, she knew that for him, she was the essential woman. Suspended between the warm safety of the harbor and the endless cold power of the sea, they renewed their pledge, wordlessly, buffeted by the wind.

On my right, the stream of cars
rush closed metallic worlds
from the beginning to the end
anxious to begin another end
sea glimpsed like stabs
of light and fear between railings
closed more and more tightly by speed.
To the left, all space
lies between the spreading of the cliffs.
Tides push vastly in.
Sun and earth open.
Light everywhere, gold and gray.
I could cross this bridge
with you forever.

That night at dinner he once more reached across the table with both hands. "Have I told you lately that I love you?" he asked.

She shook her head, unable to speak, smiling.

"Then listen, Louise Borgstrum, I love you. You can never say that no one has loved you. This is it." His hands held hers, warm, firm.

Something like an enormous sadness welled up inside her, pressing tears out of her eyes.

"Hey, Lou, why are you crying?" he smiled. "I love you – does that make you cry?"

"It just hurts to be so happy," she whispered.

✳ ✳ ✳

It was a Friday and Philip came, as usual, to pick her up at her place. "For an old bag you look pretty good," he kidded her as they walked to the car. Damned if she would be put down, she retorted, "For a little kid you're not bad-looking yourself. Wonder what you'll be like when you grow up?"

"Watch out, Borgstrum, watch out," and he hit her lightly on the upper arm, the one form of semi-violence they had agreed each could exercise on the other. Usually it was Louise who hit Philip, after he had said or done something particularly out-rageous and irritating. He took it then as an admission that she could think of no good verbal response and so had to resort to the more primitive physical blow. For her part, however, she feared some of the retorts that came to her mind. They were too close to the bone, could expose him to himself so nakedly that he might not easily forgive.

"How about Chinese tonight?" she asked as they got into his car. This was unusual. Most often Philip suggested the restau-rant, partly because he knew which restaurants were good, and partly because he paid more often than Louise did.

Philip raised his eyebrows in surprise.

"Chinese? Well, I had it last night with Hugh, but if you really want to, I guess it doesn't matter."

She persisted, pleased that she was making herself heard. "It just sounds good tonight." Then, as an appeasement, she threw in, "Maybe they'll have the crab tonight, in that garlic sauce you like."

Philip laughed. "You don't have to convince me, Lou. If you want to go Chinese, that's where we'll go."

But when they got to the restaurant, it was full, with a forty-minute wait.

"How about Mexican?" Philip said. "I'm so hungry, I've got to get some food in me, and Mexican is always good."

She nodded. There was no point in making them both un-comfortable, just to prove her existence.

Philip raced the car through the early Friday evening traffic, pushing hard to make lights, passing slower cars, tailgating where he couldn't pass. He began to talk rapidly.

"You don't know how tired I get by Friday night. All week long the people in my group are at me, they can't seem to follow directions and work independently – except Georgiana, she's good – but all the rest, all they want is to stand around and bullshit, and they come in late and leave early. And they call in sick every time the weather's good. That's not ethical. Sick leave is for when you're sick, it's not vacation time, and they know it."

He shifted angrily, and made the VW engine roar as they took off from a stoplight. "And now Concha's got a lawyer. You know what she wants now? Besides full custody of Jo-Jo, besides the car and house and alimony, she actually thinks she can get my retirement pension – even though she'll have her own retirement! If she wins all that in court I swear I'll move. I'll leave the country, I'll go to France or New Zealand where she can't get a thing from me. It'd be worth it!"

"I see a parking space over there, on the right," was Louise's only reply, as they neared Casa Carlos. She could think of no reply appropriate to Philip's outburst.

"I'm sorry Lou, laying all this on you. Just bear with me. I just can't stand it sometimes. But I won't let her ruin my whole life."

They walked in silence to the restaurant, where they were quickly given a table. After studying the menu for a moment,

Philip leaned across the table to Louise.

"Can you hear anything here? We're so close to the kitchen, and the tables in this section are jammed so close together, I don't see how we can talk."

"It is noisy," Louise allowed cautiously.

Without waiting for her to say more, Philip motioned to the headwaiter.

"This table is so noisy I don't see how you can put anyone at it. We'd like something quieter. Otherwise we don't want to eat here."

The headwaiter raised an eyebrow, but Philip stood up, towering over him, fists clenched.

"We do have one other table free," the waiter said, and took them to another room.

It was much quieter there, and once again they studied their menus.

Louise shivered, aware that her whole body had become stiff with tension. She pulled her jacket back up over her shoulders, and wrapped her scarf around her neck.

Philip noticed. "Are you cold?"

"Yes, I don't know why. Probably food will fix me up." Philip looked up. Directly overhead there was an air conditioner, which seemed to be turned on. Once again he motioned to the head-waiter.

"Please turn off the air conditioner," he said. "We're freezing here."

"I'm very sorry sir, but we can't turn it off. Otherwise it would make the rest of the room too hot. It's only a fan, so you needn't be concerned. We almost never use it as an air conditioner."

"That's it," Philip snapped. "I've had enough. We're leaving. I've been coming here for years, but this is the last time."

He marched out, not allowing the waiter to reply. Louise did not demur: she really had been cold there, and maybes it was the fan. In any case, Philip did not seem reachable just then.

As they paused outside the restaurant, the headwaiter came out after them. "Sir, you do not understand. We must have the fan on. I'm sure that if you –"

Philip cut him off with a roar. "What do you mean I don't understand? First you put us at the noisiest table in the restaurant, where no one could possibly talk, and then you put us under a fan where it's freezing and no one should have to sit, because you want to pile more people in there and make more money off us no matter how uncomfortable it is. That's a lousy way to run a restaurant and I'm going to tell everyone I know to stay away. And if you don't get out of my sight, you'll be sorry," he added, lowering his head threateningly.

The waiter drew back slightly, but persisted. "You came late, sir, without reservations –"

Again Philip cut him off. "Without fucking reservations! What do you mean putting any human beings at those tables? This place has gone downhill! If you lie to me again I'm telling you –" and his body coiled as if he were about to hit the man. The waiter, pale and stiff, did not reply, disappearing quickly back into the restaurant.

"God! How can they treat people that way?" Philip shouted. "Come on, get in the car, we'll go to the pie place. We'll never go to Casa Carlos again."

Silently Louise got into the car with him, drawing her jacket and scarf ever more tightly around herself, embarrassed and troubled. She had known such anger was in Philip, but had not seen him let it out before, except in streams of talk aimed at no person present. She sat beside Philip anxiously now as they sped to this third restaurant. What if it, too, were full? How long could they go from place to place? Hunger and cold were taking over her body. And Philip? Was there a further breaking point for him, beyond blind anger at strangers? Would he ever aim such anger at her? She was not sure how she could handle that.

But the Elegant Pie had space. All their tables were equally homely and there was no problem choosing one. Under the even neon light they looked at menus once again.

"Think I'll have thistle pie," Louise ventured with a small smile, lifting her eyes over the menu top to see if she could find Philip's.

His eyes, surprised, changed from colorless dark marbles to their more usual variegated green.

"Rough evening, huh Lou?" he said, meeting her look fully before returning to his menu. "Thistle looks about right."

She smiled ruefully and took his hand across the table, admiring it as she held it – large, strong, beautifully shaped. "Nice," she commented.

"God, I love you Borgstrum," he muttered, taking her hand now in his. "Just bear with me. This stuff with Concha is getting me down. Sometimes I feel as if the whole world is rotten. If it weren't for you –" he broke off, shaking his head. "I'm getting too dependent on you, babe. It scares me. Look what Concha's doing to me. It's doing things to me, to my ability to trust. Just remember that I love you, all right? Bear with me, Lou."

He paused, and then went on. "You know, sometimes I wonder if you really exist," he began, a little hesitantly. "I was so miserable, dying in that house, living with this enemy, and then you sort of materialized out of nowhere. It's as if you could just disappear again the same way, as if you were just a spirit from the woods or just a dream, and I –" he broke off.

His expression was so intense that she felt frightened for him; but all she could do was to return his gaze, trusting that the powerful current running between them would, eventually, cleanse away anger, sadness, fear.

* * *

Philip's birthday came up soon afterward. Louise bought him a handmade bowl for his new apartment, and, on a gamble, strung him a necklace of beads. She picked out the beads carefully: deep umbers and reddish browns to go with his hair, with a few crimson ones put in here and there for his fiery, flamey brightness; green flowered beads for his green eyes, and one rose flowered bead for his translucently white skin. She contrived to measure his neck, and the gift fit perfectly. He did not take it off. Day and night, through swimming and showers and sleeping, no matter what else he wore, the necklace was always there, a secret sign between them, an amulet against the possibility of separation or loss.

* * *

Philip began running more regularly at the track, timing the laps, pushing himself. Although Louise could not keep up with Philip, she also improved, and it was not long before they

THE MYTH OF ROMANTIC LOVE

THE MYTH OF ROMANTIC LOVE

could run together on the trails which wound up the wooded hills behind campus. It was beautiful there and fairly secluded. They could talk freely as they ran; there was no one to overhear.

"You know," Philip said one day as they ran side by side, eyes facing ahead, "I'd like us to establish a schedule. On certain nights we should be apart, and really be apart those times, with no calling or surprise visits. Otherwise we could slide into a situation where it's not clear, and we're actually together all the time."

"I guess," Louise said, thinking it over, "I guess it's reasonable. And I really need to have more nights free for painting anyway. What kind of schedule do you have in mind?"

"About half the week free, say Mondays, Tuesdays, maybe some Wednesdays, Thursdays and maybe Fridays."

"What!" she responded with amazement. "Why not throw in Saturdays and Sundays too? I mean that would make it even simpler, wouldn't it? You could be *really* independent that way."

"Come on, Louise, you know there's a reason for us not living together. As I see it, living together is like being married. You have to be faithful because the other person is there all the time and, well, frankly, you couldn't bring someone home with you. And it's too early for me to be married again. That would be crazy. They say it takes at least two years after you break up before you can make a sane decision for a second marriage. Before then it's some kind of desperation, you're apt to be a little crazy still. Do you see what I mean?" he demanded.

She was silent for a moment, trying to absorb this. "You mean you want to see other women?" She could not keep the hurt and fear out of her voice.

"I don't know if I do or not, but if we're essentially living together I can't, I don't have any choice. I have to be free, Louise. I don't know what I'll be wanting to do. I've never been in this situation before. But Hugh was talking about bringing women over to my place in the afternoon, because he can't at home, because Hannah could walk in on them. He was talking about my place as this wild bachelor pad, and it's true, I am making it a neat place to live. And it is mine. I've got to be able to have privacy there. This schedule isn't so bad, after all. You'll still see me Saturday night and all day Sunday, and Sunday night. By Monday you'll be glad to go home anyway! And then we'll have Wednesday nights, in the middle of the week – or at least every other Wednesday night, or something like that."

"It sounds like dating again," she said, "the way you would with someone you didn't know very well. I don't know. It scares me. I know I can't hold you back. But from what I've seen, open relationships don't work that well. So much of our lives would be separate. Do you really feel a need to be with other women? You want your old schedule back, one woman at two o'clock, another at three, another after dinner, and then I'll be around for when you're tired? And Hugh – I think that's shitty. He *is* married – and he wants 'a wild bachelor pad' to screw other women in? It doesn't sound as if they have an open marriage, the way you and Concha had, because if they did, Hannah would know and would have agreed and there'd be no need to hide. So what's the difference – married or single? Does he love Hannah? Why does he stay married?"

"I don't know the answers to these things," Philip replied impatiently. "Sure, he loves Hannah. But he just wants to screw around sometimes."

Louise looked desperately at the live oaks, the bay trees, as if all this could somehow organize her thoughts for her. But she could think only one thing, and it was not what Philip wanted to hear.

"I would never want to be married to someone who thought it was okay to screw around at the same time, secretly, behind my back. It's a betrayal – a terrible emotional betrayal. Like whatever he feels like doing is okay, and Hannah's feelings don't count. He doesn't love Hannah – not in my idea of love."

Philip in turn was silent a moment. They had reached the top of the trail, and stood looking out at the view of the bay between the trees. Finally he put his hands on his hips. "I can't settle all this stuff about Hugh. What he does is his business. If I were married, I mean really married, not the way it was with Concha, or the way I thought it was, but a right marriage, I wouldn't screw around either. That's what marriage means, that's what I would want. But we aren't married, Lou. It's too soon. You can't force me. I don't know what I want. Maybe I do have to try out other things. I don't know. But I need the time now. I need the freedom."

Louise kept on looking ahead, out over the bay; she didn't want Philip to see the tears forming in her eyes. This was pride; and it was practicality. If she tried to curtail his movements he would not only take his freedom, but use it. He would have to, simply to prove that he was free.

"So you want to be by yourself Monday, Tuesday, maybe Wednesday, and Thursday, and Friday nights. I don't like it. I don't feel any need to run out and find other men, though maybe I should do that. I don't like being the only faithful one." She struggled, blinking back the tears. "All right. Of course I'm not going to push my company on you. You're free." Saying this felt like hari-kari, splitting her gut in order to be faithful to some idea.

They turned and started running down the hill.

"I'm not sure how we should handle it,' Philip continued. "Should we tell each other if we're seeing other people?"

"Yes, definitely," she said. "If you're going to do something, then at least be open about it. You said it was Concha's not telling you about her affairs that made it impossible for you to trust her anymore, and that it ruined the relationship."

"But this isn't the same – we aren't married," he pointed out.

"I know, I know, you're absolutely free. We don't ever have to see each other again." She trusted her feet to find the way; her eyes were clouded with unshed tears.

"I don't think we should tell each other unless something becomes important and a threat to our relationship," Philip said.

"Well, you're making your own rules, because I can't force you to tell me anything. And you can be sure you won't see me anytime except on schedule. It's not my style to hang around and spy, or to be where I'm not wanted. That's why I left Andrew."

She looked down the trail ahead, and took it, easily speeding ahead of Philip. Going downhill she could run faster than he could. Although she lacked Philip's muscle power, she had the ability to let the hill provide the impetus, while she simply placed her feet and let go. Maybe it was mean to leave Philip behind that way, but nonetheless it was satisfying. He could just see what it felt like.

When he caught up with her at the bottom, he was miffed. "I don't like it when you just take off like that. I didn't know what to think, whether you'd even be here at the bottom when I got here. If you don't like what I was saying, why don't you just tell me?"

"What good would that do? I'm not going to hold you back – I just told you that," she said, finally bursting into tears. "Do whatever you want! You're completely free!"

She waited by the car door, feeling at a disadvantage because it was his car and she had to wait for him to unlock it and let her in.

"You don't like it now," he said, getting in on his side, "but when you find you have more time to paint I bet you'll like it after all."

She had nothing to answer.

* * *

The next day she phoned Sylvia.

"He wants to see other women," she announced, without preface.

"What? Who? Philip? That doesn't seem possible. I thought he was so much in love. Madly in love. Like you."

"Yeah. I thought so too." Then, truth nudging her, Louise added, "I think he still is, actually. But he resents it. He didn't want to fall in love so soon. He wanted to play the free young bachelor-about-town for a while."

"But I thought he did that already. I mean –" Sylvia giggled at the thought – "while he was married. I mean while he was to-gether with his wife. You said they were both sleeping with lots of other people, and they even had these hot tub parties to bring in new bodies. So why does he want that again?"

"I think he only thinks he wants it. He thinks he should want it. It's like part of the definition of being a man, you know, a virile free independent spirit, all that shit."

"Hmm, you talk differently from before you met Philip, you know that?"

"You mean saying things like 'shit'?"

"Yeah. You used to be more, I don't know, more . . ."

"Restrained? Ladylike? It's true, but I like this change; it's the way I wanted to go. I need to get noisier, and Philip is forcing me to. It's either learn how to shout and stick my foot into a conversation – like kick my way into it – or never get to talk – which would mean the end of the relationship, because then I would start hating him. And I don't want to be ladylike anyway."

"Why? Don't you just love to be sweet and quiet and demure and wear little white gloves and –"

"Ha!" Louise shouted, "You know just what I mean!"

She could hear Sylvia give her snorting laugh into the telephone receiver at the other end. "But back to this business of seeing other women. You know what I think? I think maybe he really wants to be married, underneath you know, and that terrifies him. What do you think of that for a theory?"

"Funny you say that. I think it's possible. He says every once in awhile, just out of the blue, 'I'm not going to get married again, you know,' as if I were proposing! I don't care if we get married or not. But it's on his mind. Maybe – maybe the gentleman doth protest too much."

"It could be. And you know, he's not going to risk really losing you."

"I trust not." The thought of any lasting separation was too painful to think of.

Sylvia evidently heard the doubt and sadness in Louise's voice. "Don't worry. He just needs some time. And you're lucky – you've got your painting. And what's he going to do?"

Louise smiled. "I don't know. Get good and bored, I hope!"

"He's going to want to change back the schedule, I wouldn't be surprised. In the meantime, if you get depressed, call me, okay?"

"Okay." Louise smiled again. Philip could go hang himself. She was not alone in the world.

* * *

B ut it was not easy. At first she had long depressions every day on getting home from work. It was too much trouble to get the wall-bed down, so she simply lay on the floor, falling into a trance-like sleep for half an hour at a time, hoping that no cockroach would come her way. But gradually the weight in her life shifted back to painting, back into her own control, and out of Philip's hands. It was not vindictive; it was survival. And what he was losing, she reflected, was perhaps something she should never have given him in the first place.

* * *

A fter a time, Philip did seem to return to her. He began to want to see her on Friday nights as well. She was now reluctant; Friday nights were especially good for painting because she could stay up late, allowing a momentum that shorter times forbade. They settled on every other Friday night.

"I guess it's good for me to see Jo-Jo at times without you," he said. "That way he gets all the attention, and it's good for him. But a whole evening with a five-year-old isn't that exciting."

"Maybe you should bring along one of your other women," Louise sweetly suggested.

"What other women?" he growled. "I can't get interested in other women any more, damn you. I measure them all against you: you're the phenotype now. A woman has to be tall and blond and skinny before I'm even interested, and it helps if she's a painter with a Ph.D. What am I supposed to do?"

"Looks as if you're stuck with me," she observed.

"God help me," he said, actually somewhat glum about it.

They were sitting on his new orange and yellow Danish rug, in front of the TV set, in the process of finishing off some chocolate truffles Philip had gotten for dessert.

"These are wonderful, Philip," Louise said, licking her fingers greedily. "In fact, the whole dinner was. Good steaks, good potatoes, and salad, fantastic dessert – I like the wine, too." She couldn't resist: "You would make someone a great wife."

"Fuck you, Borgstrum," he said, laughing. He turned on the TV. It happened to be showing a Toyota ad that concluded, with a full singing chorus, "You asked for it, you got it, Toyota!"

"Agh, it's fate," Philip said. "I asked for it – I sure got it. What did you tell me they said in therapy? 'Be careful what you want – you might get it'? Oh god, how true!"

She pulled him over close to her, and they settled in for the movie. Soon Philip was sound asleep, lying warm and heavy against her. She did not disturb him, and after an hour or so, at a particularly loud commercial, he woke up.

"I didn't fall asleep, did I?" he asked, alarmed.

"Um, yes, I think so."

"Oh! What a terrible thing to do! You must have been bored. Are you mad at me? I've never done that before."

"Mad? No, of course not. It seemed so trusting and natural and relaxed. The movie isn't bad, and I didn't feel alone. Just because you were asleep, still you were here with me. Don't worry."

He shook his head. "You mean I don't always have to be on good behavior with you?"

"But there's nothing wrong with falling asleep. It's not as if I were a stranger you had to entertain all the time. And you know – I want all the parts of you, not just the parts you've decided are socially acceptable."

He looked at her for a long moment. His eyes were bright, but all he said, finally, was an amused, "Well, I asked for it, I got it all right."

Soon they found something else to do on the orange and yellow rug, and not long afterwards they were asleep, curled warmly around one another in the bedroom upstairs.

Growling, he loves me,
gristled beard-cheek turned
he thinks it's baby's pink
soft-bottomed, it is
and thrusting his need
in my direction
we perform love's algebra
making two minuses
oh really making them
to plus and problem solved,
gurgling he snarls

and goes to sleep
body arched around mine.

* * *

I t was Saturday at six, and Philip had come to pick her up. He stood waiting for her outside the locked apartment building door. As she came down the stairs and across the entry hall she could see him through the plate glass, slightly turned aside, slouching gracefully in his worn blue jeans jacket and the khaki jeans. As soon as she had opened the door and stepped outside, he pulled her in for a quick kiss, then pulled back to look her over appreciatively. "Hey, you look great." Then, embarrassed at showing appreciation, he added, "What happened?"

She flinched. Although he liked her new jersey tops and better slacks, he would still have preferred her to look more conventionally fashionable, wear tight-fitting – and uncomfortable – jeans, make-up, or even dresses and heels. Philip seemed only partly to understand that between feminism and the anti-establishment feeling following the Vietnam War, dresses and heels would have made her look like a visitor from Mars – a kind of zombie, willingly constricting her ability to breathe and walk, obedient to a money-hungry fashion industry. Louise felt comfortable and unencumbered in her clothes, and thought she looked all right in them.

But she did not want to lecture Philip on all this. "You wonder why I look okay? Oh, well, I felt I had to shine brightly to compete with that great light reflecting off your head," and she gestured towards the bald spot Philip tried to conceal beneath unnaturally combed-over hair.

"Don't be mean to me," he muttered, grinning, smoothing his hair back up over the bare scalp. "If you were going bald you'd be sorry too."

She laughed. "It's too much testosterone, I read that somewhere years ago."

"God, the longer I know you the faster I'll go bald. Do you think you're good for me?"

"Absolutely. Where do you want to go eat?" she asked, as they settled into the VW.

"How about pizza tonight? You never have to wait to get in, and it's right where all the movies are."

"Sounds good," Louise replied promptly. She did not want a repeat of the night they drove from restaurant to restaurant, while hunger and irritation loosened the chains of Philip's inner demons.

At the pizza place they both relaxed. A big pitcher of beer stood on the table; their pizza was ordered and being cooked.

"Want a green salad?" Philip asked. "You need the vitamins."

"That could be, but if it's all iceberg lettuce it's nutritionally worthless," she answered.

"Is that so?"

"So I've read."

"Smart-ass. But I believe you. And would you believe me if I said something like that?"

She looked at him for a brief moment in surprise before answering. "Of course – assuming you were serious."

He nodded. "I thought so. Concha would never listen to me. When she was pregnant with Jo-Jo, she wanted to be x-rayed, to see the fetus. There was nothing wrong, no need for an x-ray. I told her not to because x-rays on a fetus are serious, it increases the chances of childhood leukemia by a significant factor, it's well known, and goddamn it, I'm a biophysicist, I began in radiation physics, this is what I know about. And she went ahead and did it anyway. I was so shocked, I couldn't believe it. I still don't understand it. To endanger her own child – isn't there some instinct for mothers to protect their young? But what I said didn't make any difference to her."

Louise was shocked in turn. "It's hard to believe she would do such a thing. I mean, with her own child? I thought she was supposed to be so smart, but this sounds dumb, terribly dumb."

Philip slowly shook his head sideways, and leaned back in his chair, sipping his beer, melancholy.

Louise was not sure how to respond, and they were both silent for a moment, until the waitress came with the pizza.

"Eat up, kid, we have twenty minutes before the movie begins."

Twenty-five minutes later they were claiming the last seats in the movie theater, about five rows from the front.

"Good. I like to be close," Philip said. "You hold the seats while I go get some popcorn and Cokes."

She raised her eyebrows. The beer she had hastily finished off just ten minutes before still filled her stomach. But maybe she would need something, because the film, *Carrie*, was a horror film. She expected it to be unintentionally funny, camp, but still she might need some extra sustenance.

As the movie progressed, Louise pushed closer and closer to Philip, taken in by the people on the screen, the young girl with her budding sexuality, innocent, full of hope and life, and the repressive mother, afraid of the daughter's invisible power, trying to stop it, kill it; and the power inevitably, unstoppably coming out, twisted, furious, until anger at last took on an independent life and destroyed almost everyone in sight.

The story was absurd in its mechanics, but the feeling was believable. Louise and Philip, completely absorbed, gobbled popcorn and drank soft drinks as if fortifying themselves against the powers of darkness. Finally, their minds full of images they wanted to forget, they lurched out of the theater and stood on the curb edge for a moment, undecided.

"How about going to Edy's?" Philip suggested. Louise nodded. She needed to go somewhere to unwind, to think about the movie and demystify it by reasoning, talking, categorizing. And Edy's was safe, a world of ice cream and candy, pastel-colored stuffed animals and proper ladies.

By the time they had walked the few blocks to Edy's, Louise was feeling better.

"Phew," she said, watching Philip settle back into the pink Naugahyde booth. "That was some movie."

"Got you scared, huh?"

"Yes. And interested. I mean, why does it have such a grip – on so many people, too?"

"They like to be scared. It sends all the blood to their sexual organs," he said, wriggling his eyebrows.

"Oh Philip," Louise laughed, although feeling frustrated at Philip's way of referring everything to sex.

"Well, yes," she went on, "it was a sexual movie, I will admit, repression and all that. But I wonder about all these horror movies, with the most innocent and helpless-seeming people having this incredible power – and being possessed by it, too, they don't have any choice. Sex – maybe, maybe."

"Come on, Louise, that's the way we feel, that's the way it is. Did you choose to love me? You can't help yourself."

"Egoist," she retorted, conscientiously. "Yes, I know what you mean, but there's something else too, not just sexuality alone. It's this ability to make your thoughts come true. You know, you're pursued by this evil person and finally you let loose the full power of your mind on him and he just bursts into flame or the ceiling falls on him or something. It's as if you could remake the world the way you like it. Isn't there a part of you that feels as if your thoughts were omnipotent?"

"They are, my dear, they are," he burlesqued.

The waitress, clad in short pink, stood at their side.

"Chocolate sundae with walnuts on thin mint," Philip said.

"Chocolate sundae with marshmallow sauce over thin mint," Louise said.

The waitress looked carefully at Louise. "With marshmallow sauce too?" she asked.

"Yes."

"Anything else?"

"No, thank you."

The waitress walked slowly away, still scribbling on her pad.

"Pig, pig!" Philip cried. "How can you eat so much? I can't believe you're as bad as I am. Do you know, I'm sure my mother picked you out for me. Did I ever tell you my mother was a witch? No, really, she was – or she thought she was. You know she was born in a wild part of Ireland, in the west, where they still speak the old language, and she said she learned all kinds of things there

– the evil eye, and how to lean on somebody's house to bring a curse on it. She said she only used the power once, when someone really asked for it – and it worked."

"What about you? Did she ever teach you any of her witch knowledge?"

"Not really. It's too bad. It's all lost with her. She hardly ever said the things she really thought. My father didn't take to that. He liked to do all the talking."

Louise raised her eyebrows.

"You think I'm just the same? But I don't want to be. Aren't you feeling better about talking, Lou? You haven't complained for a while, anyway!"

"Well, I do think I'm getting better at breaking into the conversation. But I have to rebel at this idea of your mother sending me to you. I feel more independent than that. Still, I wish I could have met her."

Philip nodded. "She would have loved you. She never said anything against Concha, but I know she worried about it. She saw better than I did what Concha was really like."

"It must have been very hard for her," Louise mused. "From all you've said, she loved you so very much, and then to see you marry a woman who couldn't love you."

"Yes. Concha always looked down on my mother. Just the way her parents looked down on me. I guess they always thought I was lower class. And cold – they would never call me Philip. I didn't ask that they call me 'son' or anything like that, but you'd think they could say my name. But it was always 'Dr. Brett.' Hell, I've been to college, I've been to France, I can speak French, I read – I like all that, it's important, but with them I could just as well have been a complete clod. Concha wanted me to stay away from my parents. Well, my mother. I didn't want to see my father. He hated me as soon as I got old enough to challenge him. I left home at sixteen and put myself through college. He had two new convertibles – two! – and went to the fanciest places in town to eat, but he never gave me a nickel after age sixteen. Or earlier. I had to pay for my room and board after I was twelve or so."

"When he had money? It's hard to believe."

"You don't know him. He's completely selfish. We had our first break when I learned something in school that he didn't know, and it got into a confrontation and he wound up coming into my room and breaking up my furniture – he actually broke my chair and desk and threw everything around the room. That was the last time we ever had any kind of relationship. There was nothing after that."

The waitress brought their sundaes.

"Wow," Louise muttered, contemplating the mound of sauce and ice cream. She delicately touched its perfection with her spoon. "My father and I certainly have a love-hate relationship, with lots of hate, but it's still mainly good. We can't talk to each other, but there's a deep undercurrent. We understand each other at an intuitive level. We're irrational in the same peculiar way."

"You're so lucky," he said, dipping deep into the bright green of the thin mint. "Well, my mother really did love me, I think, but that was bad for me, too, because she was so dependent on me."

Louise reached over with her paper napkin to blot a drip of ice cream that had fallen on his sleeve.

"Yes, I know," Louise nodded, dealing with chocolate and marshmallow. He had told her this story several times.

"The shrink said I was taking care of Concha the same way I used to take care of my mother. My father would go off on long sales trips, and Mother would depend on me for company, to play cards or go to the movies. I had to entertain her completely, but when my father came back, she would put me to bed early and go off with him. I always felt so betrayed. A lot like with Concha, actually. I had to take care of her, but she was never there for me when I needed her – or any other time, when you get right down to it."

"Am I too dependent?" Louise asked, polishing off the maraschino cherry.

"Christ, you're too independent! You're a pain in the ass."

"To be frank, I'm not sure I can get up after all this food," she groaned. "I'll need your strong manly arm to waddle over to the cash register place. Maybe we could take a little walk?"

He didn't answer, but put on his jacket. By the time she got to the cash register, he had paid, and they went out.

"How about just walking a few blocks?" she asked.

"Okay, if you want to."

There was silence for a few minutes. The fog had come in, and it was cold. "Brr," she said, putting her hand under Philip's arm, and moving closer. There was no response. His body stayed rigid.

"What's going on over there?" she asked, peering up and around into his face.

He did not look at her, and it was a moment before he replied. "It's about Concha – I don't know. I felt she used me for a free ride. I was good for the money and what she could get out of me. Maybe that's why I'm sensitive about money. You always seem to expect me to pay. I feel as if you're taking me for granted. It's too easy.

Why should the man always pay for the woman? It's like being a prostitute, as if I were paying you for something, as if you weren't with me for anything but the money. It's not fair. It's not right."

She had the feeling of hearing out loud something which he had said many times before to himself in rehearsal.

"Have you been thinking this for a while?"

"It's been bothering me lately. I don't want to do it anymore. I want you to start paying your own way."

"Well, I guess we kind of slid into it. I felt as if you liked the sense of taking care of me, and I liked feeling taken care of. But also, you make so much more money than I do, it didn't seem so bad. I do pay sometimes, you know. I paid for the movie tonight, for instance."

"Yes, but all the food cost lots more. And as far as my making more money, you can't use that as an excuse. If you wanted to, you could get out and make a lot more money than you do now."

"Well," she said, her back up, "I could quit painting and sell my life for money, it's true. Yes, I would still be alive if I were working full-time, but only nominally. To me, my life doesn't have meaning without the painting."

"I know, I'm not very important in it," Philip muttered.

Their hands were by now thrust deep into their individual, separate pockets.

"What do you mean, you can't expect me to give up what's most important to me. I mean 'most important' in a special way. You know it doesn't cut you out."

"You're always painting – or you say you are."

"But it's only three nights or three and a half out of four – and you don't want me around those other nights."

"It's true, it's true, so I can see other women – teams of dancing girls. You leave me without a drop left over; you're insatiable. I BET you paint all the time."

"Philip, this is crazy, crazy."

Neither one said anything more. Stiffly they walked, got into the car; stiffly they went to his apartment and closed the door. Neither wanted to bend. Finally, getting into bed, Philip said, "Can't we end this? We should never go to bed angry. All I want is for you to pay your way. You don't have to go to work full-time for that. Don't you want to be a liberated woman? Don't worry, I know how important painting is to you, in fact, I think you need it. But can't you see how I feel? It's not fair if I always have to pay."

She relented. "Yes, of course, of course I don't want you to feel taken advantage of, or to doubt that I'm with you because I love you, not just because you can take me places. I really will start paying more. But I don't know if I can pay equally all the time. What if we share on the basis of percentages? At the same ratio as the ratio between your salary and mine?"

"But it's your choice not to earn much money," he protested.

"Well, say, at the ratio of your salary to double my salary – what I'd get if I worked full-time."

"I still earn more than twice what you'd make, even so. But maybe that's okay, it's more fair. It's really the principle of the thing as much as anything."

"Besides," she went on, "I'd never live this way if I didn't know you, restaurants and movies all the time –"

"You love it, Borgstrum, don't give me that!"

"Yes, I do," she admitted, "but still I probably wouldn't do it on my own. Well – okay, let's leave it at that: we pay two to one.

It's okay by me."

Philip looked a little sour, but he nodded. Louise, sure that he would not understand the rest of her thought, that he would fight and argue if she told him, kept silent her sense that he was getting the best of both worlds, pre- and post-feminist. On the one hand, she would pay a considerable portion of their joint expenses; on the other hand, since she was not able to pay her way entirely, she would still have the guilt and the subtle sense of being less important that go with being the taker, the receiver. He would automatically assume, and she would concede, the right to choose more often where they ate and what movies they saw. Any time they spent money together, he would have the advantage, while financially she felt the strain much more than he: $100 out of $430 each month looms much larger than $200 out of $2,000. And all the while he could enjoy a sense of superior generosity. Even if she worked full-time, she would not earn anything close to Philip's salary. Yet none of this would he notice, any more than he noticed the other advantages granted him from the moment he appeared, naked from his mother's womb, with a little penis attached.

* * *

The next week, Philip called her at work. "I know it's not one of our nights together, but my landlady wants me to go to a séance tonight, and I think you'd enjoy meeting her and seeing all this supernatural shit."

Louise was startled. "Oh – I was going to paint tonight," she began.

"Damn, you don't have to paint every night! You've got five

afternoons and three other nights free this week," Philip replied, with a mix of exasperation and laughter.

"A séance?" she repeated. "Seriously?"

"Yes, and it's serious. She's an intelligent woman, and she's doing it scientifically. Not everyone gets invited to these things Lou, but I think she likes me. There will be some real psychics there."

"Hmm, I've always wanted to go to a séance," she mused. "I guess this is my chance. Okay, I'll bicycle over after dinner."

The landlady's house was large and, by Berkeley standards, old – late nineteenth century. When Louise and Philip rang the bell, the door was opened by a woman of about seventy, who hid her great bulk in a shapeless black gown suggesting, simultaneously, the witch; the flirtatious, sophisticated woman of the world; and the severe dignity of a judge.

"Welcome, welcome," she said, encircling them both as they stepped into the house. "Philip, and is this Louise? Louise, they call me Euphony – an odd name, it means 'sweet sounds' in Greek – you can go right into the living room and sit down and be comfortable. We'll begin in a minute, as soon as Miss Caldwell arrives."

"Miss Caldwell is the psychic," Philip whispered as they went into the living room. There was a small group of people already there. They nodded stiffly as Louise and Philip came in and found seats, side by side on a couch.

Sunk in the deep well of the old couch, Louise looked around her. The other people did not look extraordinary in any way. No wild rolling eyeballs, no bizarre get-ups, not even the simple predominance of older women she had half expected. As she

looked, though, Louise found her eye baffled. Large mirrors had
been set, seemingly at random, amongst equally random-seeming
pieces of old furniture. In the fading light, forms were repeated at
odd angles, reflected first in one direction, then another. In the
center of all this was the circle of furniture on which they sat, an
island of order lit by an old standing lamp.

About ten minutes passed in silence. Then they heard the
front door open and shut, and Euphony came into the room with
a tiny white-haired woman: Miss Caldwell. Louise was surprised
by the guileless sweetness of the psychic's face. Miss Caldwell, at
least, must believe in the truth of her vocation.

Euphony took her place. "As some of you know, we are trying
to conduct a scientific séance. My son –" she gestured towards a
middle-aged man who had begun to fiddle with some machinery
in the corner – "will be recording everything, so that if someone
does speak to us from the beyond, we will have proof. We have
often seen things here, but so far we haven't been able to record
them, though we do have some very suggestive photographs."

She settled herself in her chair, draping the heavy black cloth
of her dress over her ankles. "The person I want to reach is my
husband, who died twenty-eight years ago. He was very interested
in things of the spirit, and I feel sure he is trying to reach us." She
paused long enough to look sharply at each member of the group,
making sure her audience was with her. "Now let us begin with a
moment of meditation."

Louise heard a tape recorder switch on in the corner. So this
woman was trying to reach her husband after twenty-eight years.
Was it possible she still missed him? They must have loved each
other the way she and Philip loved each other – though this was a

possibility Louise could entertain only intellectually. Emotionally she felt that no two people had ever experienced such intensity. As for Euphony, she did not seem the type to sit around and mope. She was too full of strength and vitality. Yet she had created this shadowy room specifically as a lure to this dead spirit; and in this lure she lived.

The séance was not a success. "We know the spirits are there," Euphony told them afterwards, as they stood politely eating ice cream and cookies around the great black dining room table. "One time my husband came right up behind the green chair and stood there for a full minute. We couldn't communicate with him, but we will, we will. We just have to keep trying."

"Quite a woman, hmm?" Philip asked Louise as they went to his apartment next door. "Too bad she's so old; I'd like her myself."

"I'm sure it's mutual," Louise replied. She could see that Euphony liked the energy which came in warm waves out of Philip's body. "But what do you think about all this?"

"I kind of believe it," he admitted. "She wasn't alone when she saw her husband, for instance. They all saw it. And there have been other things she's been telling me about, interesting things. How about you?"

"I tend to be skeptical, but maybe it's only because the thought of ghosts is too scary. When I'm alone in a dark room, I don't want to think someone else – without a body – could be there too."

That night they made love, as so often, past the point of exhaustion. Afterward, lying together in the dim light, Philip said in a low voice, "I swear my mother is in this room. Don't worry, she loves you, but she's here – I can feel it."

Louise did not answer, but tried to open her mind to this possible presence, to put aside her usual shield of disbelief and fear. As she did so, a sense of a third presence pressed in on her. She tried to picture a face, make it particular, something she could describe to Philip for confirmation. As she looked into the darkness, though, what she felt was a hostile angry presence. It was an older woman, but she could not make out any features.

"Philip! There's someone here, but she hates me! Hold on to me!" Louise clung to him in fear.

"Oh my god, Lou, I'll do my best. I think I feel it too. Who is it?"

They clutched one another in the tangled bed. Louise felt as if she and Philip had descended into a joint nightmare. Concentrating, she began to make out the features of her grandmother, who had once replied to a happy letter from Louise with the harsh comment that she should not let circumstances mislead her: life was "not a bowl of cherries." Now her contorted face looked down at her and Philip, naked together in this bed.

"It's my grandmother!" she whispered. "Why does she hate me?" But Louise knew why. She had disobeyed all her grandmother's precepts. She had left a marriage which was eroding her spirit; she had left a respectable career in order to do what she most deeply wanted; and now she was passionately in love with a man with whom she had sex while both were still technically married to others. No matter that both divorces were nearly complete, for she and Philip had no plans to marry; that was a question for the future. For now all that mattered was their love, a power which overruled every social propriety, every ordinary expectation. Louise's grandmother had put aside everything in order to fulfill her duties, acting on a different sort of love, based on self-sacrifice. No matter that she had had no choice, that "womanhood" and "self-sacrifice" were then defined as synonymous; no matter that countless others were now doing as Louise and Philip did. The anger was still there, the desire to see Louise punished. For it was not fair, it was not right that Louise could break every law laid down for proper female conduct, and be happy.

All night long she and Philip held close to one another in a feverlike half-dream, half-sleep, until at last it began to get light outside. Then, exhausted, they slid into an hour of real sleep before they had to get up and go to work.

They did not discuss the previous night. Louise was glad to shut the door on that experience. Perhaps it had only been a guilty projection: she and Philip, raised to believe in the moral code of her grandmother, had imagined this retribution, had visited this nightmare on themselves. But what if that angry presence had not been a mere projection? She felt she did not want her world filled with such beings. Perhaps there were such things as spirits and ghosts, but if so, she would wait until she died to find out. If she never allowed her mental eye to look in that direction again, maybe she would be spared more such sights.

* * *

Christmas was coming up soon, the first she and Philip would spend together. She did not even consider going back home for the holiday. Although she and her parents were gradually smoothing over the break following her split-up with Andrew, she had no desire to spend a difficult week or two trying to prove that she was, after all, the things her parents could approve and love.

Besides, Philip needed her. It was on Christmas Eve, three years earlier, that his mother had died, and he needed Louise to be with him on that sad anniversary. Jo-Jo was to spend Christmas with Concha and her parents. There was nothing to hold Philip in Berkeley for the holiday season, and no family to draw him to any other particular place.

After dinner one day in late October, he began to make plans. "I don't want to stay here and have a Christmas tree and all that shit. Besides, my apartment's too small for a tree, and so is yours. Let's escape the whole scene. How about going skiing? We could go to Utah – I've done it before, it's beautiful, you'll love it. Drive, otherwise we can't afford it. I can pay for the car costs, but you'll have to pay your own way for most of the rest of it. Let's say up to $500 each. Okay?"

She flinched. A lot of money – more than a whole month's salary for her. Still, she wanted to go. She had enough saved.

"Okay," she answered, beginning already to feel excited.

And so for ten days the two of them escaped Berkeley, with all its old habits and associations. All day long they skied, Louise on the easy slopes, Philip on the hard ones, meeting for sandwiches and hot tea at the hut on the slopes, nursing their tired muscles in a hot tub at night. Philip reveled in the competency of his body as he tested it each day on the steep mountain runs, and in the reassuring sense of luxury at night. He seemed to forget his uncertainties and anxieties about their relationship; he was as unconditionally loving as he had been during their first months together.

Once they returned to Berkeley, however, Philip grew preoccupied, worrying about Concha, the property and money she wanted from him in the divorce settlement, the endless confrontations at third hand through their respective lawyers, the feeling that he had an enemy constantly plotting pain for him, night and day looking for ways to undo him. He grew nervous and brooding. Under a surface of reason and coping he was angry: angry at Concha, angry at women, angry at Louise who was a woman from whom he could not turn away – a double anger. She got a horrible cold and retreated to the security of her bed for almost a week, coming out only when it seemed worse to be bored in bed than to deal with the bleak-looking January outside.

* * *

Philip found a real estate agent, Maxwell Gordon, recommended by his friends at the lab. "I've got to get that money from Concha," he said. "The real estate market is just about to rise again. This may be my last chance to get another house. I'll be damned if she gets to live in that beautiful house all her life and I have to spend the rest of my life in some miserable little apartment. She phoned up the other day, all sweetness and reason. That means she's hatching some kind of plot. I told her to put everything in writing and give it to my lawyer. I want full joint custody of Jo-Jo. This business of the mother always getting the power over the kid is ridiculous.

"There's a house Max has told me to go look at. We passed it last week and I thought it was too ugly, but he says we have to see the inside. Want to go take a look?"

They drove up to it. It was a big stucco house, painted an unfortunate orangey-flamingo color on the trim. It sat high on the hill, a little ungainly, though solid-looking enough. Walking inside, however, was a revelation. The entire space seemed filled with light; there was an old-fashioned grace everywhere. The living room and front bedroom had magnificent views of the bay. Walking through the upstairs, Louise lost count of the rooms. Space, elegance, simplicity, light: these reigned. It was the house, though neither Philip nor Louise dared say so: she because it was not her money and therefore not her decision; Philip because he did not know yet whether he could get together the down-payment. They walked out, trying to restrain their praises.

"There are an awful lot of rooms."

"Yes, but we could fill them."

"Twins?" she asked. "Quadruplets, maybe?"

"Well, one a year would probably do it."

But this was mere fantasy play. They were not ready even to live together yet.

"We should look at other places just to be sure," he said cautiously. They did. Nothing compared.

"You know what?" Philip said the next week. "They're asking $127,000 – I can't pay that. But Max said I should make an offer of $108,000, just to see. Maybe they might compromise. The house has been on the market for ten months. It's so big no one wants it, and there's no garage. They may be hungry for an offer and come down some on the price.

"So I talked to Concha. You know what she said? She said our old house is worth $120,000 so I should only get $15,000 for my share – we owe $90,000 on it. But it's worth at least $130,000 and more likely $140,000. God. I was so stupid to let her know I want this new house. Now she thinks she can get more out of me because I'm in a hurry and might have to take anything she cares to offer. I can't believe this woman! I tell you, Louise, if I could kill her and get away with it, I would. In fact sometimes I think I will anyway. A lifetime in prison would be worth it."

"Oh," she replied, angry herself, "that would be really great. I could visit you once a week, right? That would be wonderful for both of us. Not that I'm surprised you want to kill Concha – I mean she's doing everything she can to hurt you – but for heaven's sake, please don't talk that way. And you'll get the new house."

"We don't know that," he said gloomily. "She could win – don't forget that. I don't know if I've got the right lawyer. He may be too honest. It could keep him from imagining what Concha might do and she might catch us unprepared some way." He paused. "No, damn it! I'm going to win this! I'm as smart as she is, though she doesn't think so. I'll study law myself. I'll find out the angles and be prepared. And I'm going to find out about this child custody thing, too. She's not going to get Jo-Jo, all the money, my retirement pension, child support and alimony – she can't get everything! I'll move, damn it! You'd loved it in New Zealand, Lou."

"I bet. Philip, let's go get dinner. It's Sunday night. Let's go to Pedro's."

He looked surprised to be reminded of this simpler world, where the two of them could get into a car and drive to a familiar restaurant. Pedro's was a ritual now which they observed every Sunday evening.

"Yes," he said, "yes. I'm sorry, honey, but I can't help hating her. I really meant everything I said."

"I know." She did not say that his hatred was almost as obsessive as his love had been. But probably, she thought, it would pass – at least, it would if Concha did not succeed in wresting from Philip everything he had.

* * *

It was rainy spring weather. Deirdre was waiting for Louise inside the Café Med when Louise arrived, laughing a little at all the water dripping from her umbrella and raincoat.

Deirdre looked at her as she settled into her chair, putting down the cup of coffee she had gotten at the counter. "You look so healthy," she remarked. "You look great. Things must be going well."

"What!" Louise exclaimed. "Don't I look pale? Dull?"

"Not offhand," Deirdre smiled calmly. "You feel pale? What was the other word, insipid?"

"That'll do," Louise sighed. "I'm just a poor human being, you know, nothing like as important as, say, a house."

Deirdre raised her eyebrows in surprise. "You mean Philip is buying a house?"

"I'll say. It's all he can think about. Talk about involved. He eats house! He sleeps house! And," she shook her head, "he talks house. Oh, does he talk house. Did you know that life is measured in years to pay back mortgages, that interest rates are more important than breathing, that termite reports are more fascinating than pornographic novels?"

"My goodness, no, I didn't realize. Actually I thought the main drama of our century was whether or not I'd get my last thesis chapter done by Wednesday when my adviser says I have to get it to her or she'll resign from my committee. I don't know why this hasn't gotten into the newspapers. Guess it's just the media's regular bias toward the sensational, the cheap, what sells." Deirdre smiled a crooked, self-mocking smile.

"Oh Deirdre, you've weathered lots of deadlines. And your adviser wouldn't drop you."

"Dunno. But there are other thesis advisers to be found. Anyway, I think I can make it – if I stay up essentially every night between now and then."

Louise stroked Deirdre's hand sympathetically. "Well, you've made all the other deadlines."

"Almost all," Deirdre corrected her. "But tell me, if Philip is about to buy a house, how long until he's got the divorce finalized? Can he buy the house without knowing that?"

"Right, it's more or less done, and it does seem pretty certain that Concha will agree about the money. They just have to sign the papers, and Philip won't stop worrying until that's done."

"It's been a long haul," Deirdre observed. "A tough one. Maybe a lot less pressure on you, once Concha's out of the picture. But how about you – how's the painting going?"

"I just finished a watercolor of a great big building, almost a temple, with Greek columns, that looms up very high over a green landscape, kind of dwarfing everything else. And then there are some kind of skinny little people, locked into geometric pieces of the lawn, and they're bowing and groveling in front of the temple. Significant, huh?"

"Yeah," Deirdre grinned. "Significant. But what makes you so little in relation to this house?"

"Well, look, how can I compete with thousands of dollars' worth of stucco and wood? And I'm not even as old as it is!"

"How old is this house, then?"

"1896. I can't beat that. No competition at all."

"And is it prettier than you?"

"Definitely. I don't know how to describe it – light, full of light, you look out across the bay and see all three bridges, north to south, it's incredible. And I guess it was designed by a real architect, not just a builder, because somehow you just feel good when you walk into it. And the price is right – maybe because it's too big, or too many stairs out front, or maybe because the only garage would be a rented one across the street."

"And does he want you to live in it with him?"

"That's not clear. Partly, yes. And so he wanted me with him when he first looked at it. And if I'd hated it, I don't think he would have tried to buy it. Someday I guess I'm supposed to live in it. But not now. Right now it's supposed to be a bachelor castle. It's practically going to have a moat around it with special woman-eating crocodiles in it, to keep us dangerous creatures out – though with a special permit for dancing girls."

"Do you ever think about that course you taught, on what was it,' Deirdre paused tactfully. "Something about romantic love?"

"The myth of romantic love, Deirdre, the myth! Do you think I'm living out a myth? I mean a cultural invention?"

"Maybe. What's the myth, the tall dark handsome stranger who, um – let's see, is that the same one who comes riding up on a white horse? And sweeps you off your feet, and he's a prince and you're Cinderella and need rescuing – have I got the myth right?"

"I guess so. At least I'm definitely swept off my feet. Everything about him turns me on. I even love the way he seems so young, transparent like a little kid and then so male and sexy at the same time. But I feel as if I can keep my own identity – I'd never give up painting no matter what, and that's core. It seems as if he's the one who has to struggle hard to keep his identity. Well, he calls it his independence. He can't seem to hit the right balance where he can acknowledge his love and still be sure he exists separately too."

Deirdre gave a crooked smile. "Ah yes – relationships."

"George?" Louise asked. "Or Damion?"

"Umm, well, Bill is getting married to Joanna, and the commune broke up, so Damion is going to Colorado. He'll come back sometimes to see his baby, but Diana may go to Hawaii and take the baby with her."

Louise shook her head. "It seems as if after all the experimentation, the woman is still left holding the bag."

"The baby," Deirdre corrected. "Yes."

There was a pause as each woman studied her cup of coffee.

"Better to have a thesis to worry about," Louise commented.

"Maybe. But the political struggle is important. If we had universal day-care, Diana could have her baby and still have a job and make enough money so they don't have to be on welfare."

"Free love," Louise mused. "It sounds so good."

"Well, with contraceptives!" Deirdre laughed, and then went on. "As far as sharing George, I don't really mind. He's with his other woman more, but he comes over to my place about once a week. I like this. It's about right."

Louise laughed. "Maybe just a little is enough. If it's a freely-given little, anyway. With Andrew it was all withholding. Horrible. I could never go through that again." She sighed.

"How's the divorce going?"

"I had lunch with Andrew a while back. A beautiful sunny day. He had taken care of the divorce. He said the procedure in California was easy, and cheap. It's funny – our lunch was kind of nice. Maybe because there weren't any expectations – everything was over. We had a nice conversation, normal, both of us. I guess it wasn't necessarily an insult that he said I looked like Beethoven –"

Deirdre laughed. "Beethoven! What?"

"Well, I'd ridden my bike over to where we were meeting, and I guess my hair was a bit wild. Anyway, it was nice. I could almost remember why I'd ever liked Andrew. So at the end, out in the sun, we hugged – the only really warm thing Andrew ever knew how to do. And then as we were leaving and I was about to say goodbye, he stood there and said, 'God, I'm glad I'm not married to you.' Just that. I felt as if I'd been slapped. Just like Andrew. Bring me in with a little warmth, and then the knife in the ribs. Thank god it's over. I'm free – and for just $60!"

"Congratulations, Louise! Here's to freedom! And a final end to all that misery."

"And here's to a finished thesis – here's to your freedom too!" Louise put in.

The two women raised their coffee cups in a toast, smiling.

* * *

I t was April Fool's Day, 1978, exactly a year from the time they had met, when Philip closed the deal on the house. The final papers with Concha had been signed, he had his loan, and he had acquired his castle; but not, for now, a home. It was already occupied by a Danish family, who had been renting while the house was up for sale; Philip had agreed to let them stay on through the summer. With cold politeness they allowed Philip the front bedroom, but the rest of the house was clearly their territory. At mealtimes they were in the kitchen, and occupied the dining room. After dinner they were in the living room. The children and the au pair maid took up the spare bedrooms. Although no harsh words were spoken to Philip, it was made clear that he and Louise were barbarian invaders on the Danes' superior European intelligence.

Phillip's front bedroom, however, was so fine that it almost made up for exclusion from the rest of the house. The walls were lined with carved wooden bookcases, with locking glass doors. Window seats invited them to spend time gazing out at the views. Often when Louise came up the stairs in front of the house, she would see Philip sitting there in his bedroom, looking out. There was something wistful about it, even lonely. His hands were drawn up around his knees, his attitude one of pensive waiting, at odds with the cheerful energy he usually gave off around other people. For his birthday she made him a watercolor painting of the house, with his shadowy figure looking out the upstairs window.

* * *

The Danes finally moved out, and Philip was by himself in his new house. "It's pretty funny, Lou," he said, as they stood looking out the front window, enjoying the living room for the first time alone. "People think a man wouldn't want to live in a big house by himself. A woman – sure. But a man? Why can't we enjoy these things? I'd love it. But I can't afford it. I've got to get some people in to share. I'm going to choose carefully, so it'll be good, like family almost. We'll share dinners, and the cooking will be good – not just some shit thrown together out of a can. We'll live well, it will be civilized."

Louise remembered Philip's earlier talk about French salons, where people who knew each other well could meet for warm and lively conversation. She could not help thinking, though, of the supposed friends who had come to his hot tub parties, and Philip's pained puzzlement when they simply disappeared, evaporated like the steam itself. But she kept this thought to herself. Why shouldn't a shared house work? Maybe Philip could make a little utopia, with care and a bit of luck. The house was certainly beautiful enough.

Because the house was only a few blocks from the university, Philip had a lot of eager applicants. The first person he chose was a young woman with a boy the same age as Jo-Jo. "I think she's perfect," Philip said excitedly. "She's Irish – like my mother – can't be all bad! And she's supporting herself and her boy while she's finishing up her B.A. She's tough – she's really had to struggle. I admire that. She has grit. And charm, too – you'll see."

Louise was not entirely delighted by this, but she could well understand Philip's choosing Kathleen. She sounded dependable and stable, and her child would provide a companion for Jo-Jo, who on rainy days had asked too many times, "What should I do now?"

After Kathleen came another woman, not quite as young and pretty, but exuding motherly warmth and bringing with her a daughter just slightly younger than the two boys.

"It should be a good mix," Philip said. "Kathleen is a student, but at twenty-three she's seen a lot. Martha is older, and has a steady job. She's more like me, though she's a librarian and probably leans more towards the humanities than the sciences. But we still have one bedroom to fill, and I've got to do it soon. I can't afford to wait and keep paying all the house costs without help. I have almost nothing left over to fall back on. If anything serious goes wrong with the house, I'm finished. I'd have to sell it. Pray that the roof doesn't go, Lou. We need our third person by Friday. That's just three days from now. I'm really worried."

The next night, a young man came by to be interviewed for the third place. Louise had volunteered to make a communal dinner, and while she rushed around the kitchen, chopping onions and eggplant, she tried to talk to Bob. Certainly he was good-looking, tall, rosy-cheeked, about twenty years old, maybe too young, but very attractive. It was hard, however, to carry on a coherent conversation, between cooking and the fact that Bob seemed a little shy, and it was a relief when Jo-Jo came in to see what was for dinner. Bob took Jo-Jo on his lap and struck up a conversation, managing to be friendly without condescending or affecting to be a child himself. Louise liked that, and when Philip asked her opinion, she said that Bob seemed all right, judging by the little she had seen. Kathleen and Martha agreed.

"He's younger than I would have liked," Philip said, "but I can't help it. I need him now, he's here – and he'll do – I hope. Anyway, his father has agreed to pay for anything Bob leaves unpaid or damages, so we're safe. And this whole set-up should be great for the kids."

When Louise went to the first official house dinner, Philip was cooking. He wanted to set a high standard, and insisted on having more than one course. "It's the way the French do it," and there was no higher praise. Thus there was liver pâté with baguette, both locally made at a small French charcuterie. Then there was chicken cooked according to the latest recipe, served with rice; a salad; and fresh fruit for dessert. At each course Philip suffered the cook's dismay: the pâté should have been served a little colder; the chicken needed more spice; the fruit wasn't as ripe as it might have been; the wine was merely so-so; and he'd forgotten about coffee altogether. Still, it was a success. Kathleen and Martha were clearly impressed, and seemed to be planning their own menus. There was perhaps a little competition in the wind: it would not do to be surpassed by a man in the kitchen. Bob did not say much, but no serving platter left the table unpolished by him. Apparently it took a lot of food to fuel all that youthful meat and muscle. Later he became known as "the mouse," the mysterious agent by whom all odd bits and pieces put in the refrigerator disappeared overnight. There was no leftovers problem in Philip's house.

There was, however, one house member not chosen by Philip. Kathleen, who had the bedroom at the back of the house on the first floor, first mentioned the presence she felt at night, usually at the foot of her bed, but one time venturing to fiddle with the electric heater she sometimes put on. Then others mentioned the sound of someone going up and down the back stairs, always at night, invisibly. One night Louise and Philip, coming into the house when no one else was home, heard footsteps and a sound as of clothes rustling in movement, receding ahead of them up the front stairwell and along the dark upstairs hallway. Their hearts pounding, they followed the sounds, going into each room in turn, switching on all the lights, poking into closets, looking under beds. They found nothing, but the sounds had seemed too distinct to be doubted. Still, if there was a ghost, no one was seriously disturbed. It seemed content simply to be the unnamed fifth adult member of the household. Restlessly pacing the rooms and hallways, it was perhaps caught, tangled in some drama on this familiar stage, with a cast of people long since disassembled and dispersed.

* * *

Philip liked having the two extra children around. "It's lucky for them that they came here," he said. "Both Willy and Gloria need the discipline, and it's great for Jo-Jo to have friends. He'll probably have a better time here now than he does at his mother's."

It was definitely a help for three single parents. A rough schedule appeared. Philip took the children Friday nights, and Kathleen and Martha alternated Saturday nights and Sunday afternoons. The children seemed to be happy, and each parent got some free time.

As the year went on, however, Martha and Bob began to seem problematic. Martha was not well connected to the physical world.

Days or even weeks after she had cooked, they would find her unwashed cooking dishes stashed out of sight behind the refrigerator or under the sink. Her belongings went the same way, scattered through the house. Philip was neat, and while he could tolerate the rolls of dust which were gradually accumulating, the untidiness offended him.

Bob was more seriously alarming. He took difficult courses, did not study, and then was astounded to find that he was failing. Floundering scholastically, he applied – late – for a Rhodes Scholarship, phoning England and elsewhere to rally support. All he should really have had to do was send a photograph: if anyone ever looked like the Rhodes Scholar Incarnate, it was Bob. But his mind was not in the right place. His long-distance phone calls became more frequent, and more random. His cooking became more and more primitive: a bowl of cold noodles and a can of tomato sauce passed around on a plate. The can was at least opened, and this seemed to him evidence that he had tried.

He began to follow Kathleen around, until she was afraid to be alone with him in the house. Philip was not sure what to do. "How bad does it have to get before I kick him out?" he asked. "If he leaves now I could get stuck with hundreds of dollars' worth of phone bills. But what if he refuses to go? But no, he has to go. He has parents – and they must be used to taking care of him. And he's frightening Kathleen."

"And Martha, and even me sometimes too," Louise admitted.

"You too?" he said, startled. "Then that settles it. He has to go."

Philip could not sleep well for the entire month following his eviction notice to Bob. By the middle of the fourth week it seemed impossible that Bob could move out on time: he had too many things, and had done nothing they could see towards establishing a new place for himself. Philip grew so tense he could think of little else. "If I have to, I'll put all his stuff out on the sidewalk, and I don't care if it's raining, I'll do it," he swore. "He's got to get out. I'll call the police, I'll call the sheriff, I don't care who."

On the very last day, without a word to anyone, Bob began to move. He moved things out steadily all day, and nearly all night. His damage deposit covered his phone bills.

"Thank god he's gone!" Philip said the next day, as he and Louise ran along the trail above campus. "But you should see what's happening with the kids now. I'm worried about Gloria. She refuses to stick up for herself, and lets the boys do as they like and then goes screaming to Mommy. So then Mommy runs over and yells at the boys. It's disgusting. Gloria's bigger and taller than the boys are, and plenty strong. She could take care of herself, but she's learned how to be 'a little girl.' What a thing to see happen right under your nose. And she'll grow up that way and be one of those damned helpless women, preying on men to help her all the time and feeling superior at the same time because she wouldn't do anything so crude as to defend herself. And it's happening in my house!"

Louise had seen Gloria lately in shoes with heels too high for a five-year-old, shoes that pinched and warped her child's feet and had slippery bottoms so that she could not run or even walk fast. The boys were not interested in having her go along on their adventures because she couldn't keep up.

"Yes, I hate to see her wanting to make herself into a cripple. But it's the message too much of her world is sending her."

"It's not really good for Jo-Jo, but it's too late to think about all that now. We got Bob out; he was our only serious problem. Man, have I learned a lot in these months of house-sharing! Did I tell you I'm considering having a couple take Bob's place in the house? It would be a lot of people, one more than I really wanted, but they are exceptional. He's British, and is getting his Ph.D. in economics at San Francisco State. She's a musician, and has brains too. They may be too good to pass up."

On hearing this, Louise felt better about not living in the house. That would make five adults plus three children; and a musician would have to practice. It would be neither peaceful nor quiet.

"This should do a lot for our dinner conversations. They're both educated and sophisticated people. Kathleen is pretty and always nice, but she isn't really educated and doesn't have that much to say. Martha has read more and seen more, but she's too flaky. We need something like this new couple."

Louise did not argue, though she thought Philip very optimistic. Soon, however, it seemed that he had been right. Ilona and Jonathan were in fact well-educated, interesting to talk with, and responsible house-sharers. Once they moved in, the dust rolls began to disappear. Sweet-peas and petunias were planted outside. Stocking-up on household foods became more orderly. And Jonathan was also a runner, giving Philip a running companion now that he was going farther and faster than Louise.

It almost seemed that Philip had achieved his goal: a real household, something between family and friends, sharing dinners five nights a week, with good cooking and lively, relaxed conversation. For Philip, it was a step forward in his independence. For Louise, it meant that she could paint three or four nights each week without pressure from Philip for entertainment, and without fear that in the vacuum of his self-imposed independence from her, he would go find other women. Then when they did get together, he was not resentful of her having enjoyed her painting time. He, too, was having a good time.

* * *

B ut once the house situation seemed under control, Philip grew restless, needing something new to engage his spare energies. He considered returning to sailing, in earlier times his favorite sport. And he wanted Louise to do it with him.

"Come on, Lou," he coaxed her one afternoon as they sat in his living room. "You'll love it. It's beautiful out there on the water, with the mountains all around and the Golden Gate and the fresh wind blowing on you, and the waves –"

"Yes," she broke in, "that's just it, the waves. Remember, I did go out sailing with you one time, and do you remember what color I was when we reached Tiburon? Green! I hate it!"

She did not add that it bored her. Philip did the actual sailing; the crew merely drank beer and obeyed. She did not like being ordered around any more than she liked sitting in the cold wind being seasick and pretending to have fun.

"Besides," she went on, "you can find people to sail with. Bill likes it, and maybe Rachel too. And what about Jim, the man you're getting to know on campus? Didn't you say couples shouldn't always have to do the same things? Sort of in forced lockstep?"

"Mmm," he replied, thinking it over. "It's true I gave up everything that was mine when I married Concha. And now I do have music again, with the university chorus singing. But I need something more."

It was a few weeks before they found a joint project. Two friends of Philip's, Berkeley people with leanings towards the arts, began to teach disco dancing. Mimi and Victor were the only "beautiful people" Louise had ever met. Both were good-looking to begin with, and kept themselves in magnificent shape, she by swimming and he by his work as a carpenter. And they knew how to dress. Down to the parting of each hair, everything looked natural and yet was perfect. They never seemed ill at ease. They invited Philip and Louise to a demonstration; the two danced like trained performers, flawlessly, effortlessly, gracefully.

Philip was persuaded, and wanted Louise to learn disco with him. This was something she could not easily refuse. After all, why not? It didn't take more than one evening a week; she could assuage her guilt about not going sailing. And perhaps most important, Philip would want to go dancing on weekend evenings, and she did not want him taking along someone else, a more accomplished and accustomed partner.

The first lessons were trying. His ways of moving were not predictable to her; she could not sense, as she could with some men, how he would move, and they could not seem to achieve the wonderful coordination of two people moving in one free-flowing pattern. It almost seemed like a failure of the relationship, belying Philip's favorite boast that they were "absolutely alike." They went awkwardly and self-consciously through the motions, robots following a cookie-cutter outline, angry with one another for this failure, and embarrassed before the performances of Mimi and Victor.

After weeks of teeth-gritting work, however, they did learn the basic steps. Then Philip decided that Louise must purchase a disco outfit: an under-layer that was essentially a swimming suit, and a matching wrap-around skirt, in brilliant colors, the whole to be worn with exceedingly high heels. "I'll pay for it," he said. "You'd look great in it – and you really need it to go dancing. I mean, what else would you wear, if we went to a disco place?"

It was a good argument. She did own two dresses: one for summer and one for winter. The rest was blue jeans, proper slacks for work, and some shirts. Nothing wild, sexy, attention-getting, because she did not see herself that way. But Philip loved to shine and be the center of attention, and Louise had to be a fitting partner.

She called up Sylvia to talk it over.

"So why are you worried?" Sylvia asked, puzzled. "Though it's true, I've never seen you in anything but blue jeans!"

"Well, I'll be so exposed in that stuff. Have you ever seen a disco outfit? It's skin tight, it's like being naked only covered."

"Naked but covered?" Sylvia sniffed; she did not like lapses in logic.

"You know. Exposed. Like saying, 'Here I am, a sex object on display for your pleasure – no matter who you are, if you're a man. And if you're a woman, you're supposed to envy me."

"Because you look so good?"

"Well, in that particular way, yes, I guess so."

"Doesn't sound all that terrible to me," Sylvia opined.

"But to flaunt it? You're not supposed to do that, are you?

Weren't you brought up to think you should just be a nice girl and never try to look sexy? Besides, what if I try to look sexy and fail? Look ridiculous?"

"Sounds like two separate issues to me. Yes, I was brought up to think you shouldn't try to look sexy. Yeah, I know what you mean. Cheap girls do that. But now – I don't know, everyone does everything. So you want to look cheap?" Sylvia laughed. "But the other part – what if you should try and fail – that's different. Why are you so unselfconfident? You'll probably look fine – as good as anyone else."

"You're pretending," Louise countered. "You know just what I mean. What if I look like the spinster schoolteacher, dressed up in the town prostitute's clothes and trying to look sexy and all she looks like is ridiculous, and people laugh? That's what I mean."

"You think you're the spinster schoolteacher?" Sylvia screamed, giggling and snorting at the idea.

Louise waited for Sylvia to stop laughing. "All right, all right, I get it, Sylvia. But I have to wear really high heels, too. What if I fall over? That would be embarrassing, you have to admit that."

"Yeah, I know, and actually I'm giving you a hard time on this whole thing. I know just what you mean. But you shouldn't worry. You'll look fine. And I agree about high heels – I hate them. You can't walk in them, and I always feel so helpless and stupid. If you fall, well, maybe Philip will agree you should wear your running shoes!"

"Thanks a lot, Sylvia."

So she went down to a shop specializing in dance clothing, leotards, tights, plus absurd underwear of all sorts, owned by foreigners who ran the place like the ship in *Five Years before the*

Mast while oozing oily charm for customers. "Zis looks perfekt on you, darling – oh Zelda, come look, isn't zis perfekt?" while Louise shrank back behind the skimpy curtain of the dressing booth.

But it was fun, too. Growing up in the 1950s it had been ugly to be tall, thin, and small-breasted. Those were the days of the well-rounded sweater girl, who advanced through ads bearing two large sharpened missiles aimed exactly 90 degrees forward. Louise, uncertain whether to slouch down so that her small breasts and excessive height would go unnoticed, or whether to stand straight to show what little figure she had, had compromised by trying to be as invisible as possible. Now her shape was fashionable; she could try coming out of hiding.

Philip was delighted with her two outfits, and seemed undisturbed at all they revealed. Louise comforted herself with the thought that it was no worse than wearing a swimming suit. The heels, however, required a special kind of athleticism. It was impossible to walk more than two blocks in them, maximum. They were all right for dancing because disco was done on the balls of the feet. The shoes put her halfway between her usual prosaic flats and the ballet dancer's *en pointe*. With a little alcohol to dull the pain, she could dance the whole evening; but at the end she was too fashionably frail to get to the car. She had to be picked up afterwards at the dancehall door, as if she were an invalid – which, temporarily, she was.

Their first public appearance was at a place recommended by Mimi and Victor, who were already there when Philip and Louise arrived. Victor, who had never paid much attention to Louise, now came over and embraced her as she stood there in spike heels and both tits showing under the brilliant yellow Quiana. It was as if, she thought, he welcomed a new soul saved. He was resplendent as always, his perfect white silk shirt unbuttoned just far enough to show his perfectly tanned chest, set off by a deep turquoise pendant in a setting he had designed and made himself.

Louise and Philip stepped out on the dance floor. The music was good. She liked it. They started carefully, not wanting to look foolish, all dressed up fit to kill and in the public eye. But as they went on, they lost their self-consciousness. The music and the dancing took hold of them and they danced wonderfully, ecstatically. Philip seemed to swell and grow with energy: now he was some enormous bird, with his thin arched nose, furiously hopping in a mating dance; or then again, he was in the bullring, swirling a cape with masterful poise. Louise chose to overlook the fact that she was the cape, her full yellow silky skirt flowing around the two of them as Philip turned her this way and that. It was a reminder that in this dancing, the man still called all the shots. But it seemed harmless enough as they let the music and their now-practiced feet carry them along. Finally, out of breath, they had to stop and go back to the table with Mimi, Victor, and others from the disco class. To Louise's surprise, no one had noticed them dance. Their ecstasy had been private, though given spice by the sense of eyes watching.

Dancing entered the list of their favorite weekend entertainments, and once a month or so they would "go public," Louise in female drag and Philip in fine silken shirt and black pants, briefly part of a glamorous alien world, looking for those times when everything disappeared except the rhythm of their dancing together.

* * *

L ouise decided to return to martial arts class. It was her third
     bout with them. She had always dropped out when it came
time to dive towards the floor in the "forward roll," throwing
herself head-first over a rope held waist high, or over three or
more fellow students crouched on the floor like so many barrels.
She could too easily picture her body hurtling through those long
spaces, her supporting arm failing to be in the right place, and her
head cracking on the floor, breaking like a raw egg, neck snapped
as the rest of her body crashed in on top. As her head flashed this
picture like an emergency warning out to the extremities, every
limb cooperated, bringing Louise to a safe standstill.

But as long as she remained a beginner, she could still practice
the throws. Need it be said that 99% of the class was male? Mostly
they gave a good satisfying thud as their bodies hit the mat – just
where Louise had thrown them. Of course they got their turns to
throw her, so her conscience was clear: all good, clean, well-
regulated sport. It was like a kind of dancing, she thought – but
she got to call the shots as often as the men did.

Class began with forty minutes of calisthenics followed by an
hour and a half of throws, the whole calculated to leave even a
twenty-year-old jock limp as a sweaty t-shirt. Louise, not being
twenty any longer and never having been a jock, found all this
tiring. When she tried to keep up her running schedule as well,
she found herself so stiff she could barely shuffle. Still, she forced
herself along, afraid that if she stopped running, she would later
have to start at the very beginning again, one or two laps at the
track.

About a week before Thanksgiving, she phoned up Sylvia.

"You sound terrible, Louise, what's wrong? You sick?" Sylvia demanded.

"Yeah, I've got the flu or something. Mostly I just feel in a daze, and have a fever of about 101 all the time."

"Weren't you doing an awful lot, martial arts and running and seeing Philip and working and painting and god knows what else?"

"Something like that," Louise admitted. "And you left out something else neat."

"You don't sound too pleased."

"No – I guess not. I don't know. I just missed my period, and I never do that. I mean, it might be early or late, but it always comes. Do you think it might be just that I've been doing too much? It could be a very sensible economy move on the part of my ovaries, to save energy and not produce an egg at all this month. I could sympathize. But I don't know."

"Phew. You said you're going back to your parents' for Thanksgiving. I guess you wouldn't talk to them about this."

"Definitely not. We'll all be on good behavior, trying to paper things over. They'd probably disown me."

"Right. Not good. When will you know . . .?"

"Not until I get back. That was the first doctor's appointment I could make. I won't be gone long enough for it to matter. But I wonder about this fever. If I am pregnant, this fever comes at just the wrong time, when all the kid's basic cells are forming. It could be retarded or something. I mean, it's really a critical time for the fetus. Or so Philip has told me at other times."

"Have you told Philip?"

"No. I want to be sure."

"So what will you do if you are?"

"It depends a lot on Philip. I could go either way, except this fever business is a strike against keeping it. Frankly, I can't imagine Philip would really want it, since he can't even face living with me yet, let alone have a child. But on the other hand, one of his favorite corny lines is about loving to see me swell up like a watermelon etcetera. And then I have this fantasy about keeping it and raising it by myself, taking it to work with me, having it with me down at my apartment, and then Philip would learn to love it so much that he'd have to want it."

"Unhh, you serious about that?"

"Well, no, I guess it's just a fantasy. Really, it will all depend on whether Philip wants it or not. And how serious he thinks this fever is."

"Hmmm, you've got a lot to think about over Thanksgiving! But maybe it will all turn out to be a false alarm. You'll let me know as soon as you know, won't you?"

So Louise played the good daughter during her week back home in the Midwest, refusing alcohol just in case, watching anxiously all the while for the blood which did not come, the sign that everything might be all right.

When she got back and had the test, it came out positive: she was pregnant. She could hardly believe it. After all the years in which she had taken chances and never gotten caught, she had come to think she was not fertile. When she spoke to Philip, his answer came back with no hesitation: she must have an abortion.

She knew this was right. They were not ready for a child; it would be too hard. She had been keeping the door of possibility open, and now, with a sense of relief at not having to hold that weight back, she let go and the door slammed shut. She had not allowed herself to feel that other being, sucking her life juices as if at an inner breast, her quiet companion, her flesh forming a new being. And if she had insisted on going through with the pregnancy, what would have been? Perhaps Philip, feeling prematurely remarried, cutting himself off from her just when she would need him most; her own hurt and anger; accusations; maybe even separation. And the child? Not wanted enough to compensate for the difficulties it might cause, crowding out her painting, absorbing all her life energies, and forever obscuring her relationship with Philip. And what if a damaged child at that, retarded or deformed by her fever? There was too much likelihood of double or triple unhappiness. The decision was hard, but clear.

She thought of how this had come about, how she had found herself pregnant. It wasn't only that she had come to believe herself infertile. It was also the dream of union that she and Philip shared: they wanted to be submerged, to let the life-force move through them and overwhelm their defenses. Without quite thinking it through, she had stopped using her diaphragm, and Philip had not objected. Never again, she vowed, would she be so foolish. *Wuthering Heights*, Heathcliff and Catherine, elemental forces raging untamed on the moor – that, she thought, smiling at the bathos, was life without contraceptives. It was a story they could not, would not, live.

* * *

E ven in the seven weeks of its existence, the invisible egg made trouble. Always when Louise woke up with Philip, she would edge close to him, giving him the extra body heat she generated in the morning, almost teasing him with it because she knew he loved it so. As usual, then, she edged over, and he sleepily pulled her head up on his shoulder and held her close.

"Hold me tight," she whispered. "I'm feeling scared."

She didn't have to say what of. The same thing was on Philip's mind.

"You'll be all right, Lou," he said, holding her more tightly.

"Terrifying," she said. She really was rather frightened; and it also seemed like a legitimate time to regress a little and get some babying herself.

Philip loosened his hold and turned partly away. "Don't – don't scare me Lou, I can't stand it. What if I should lose you? I don't know what I'd do. And if I had to blame myself besides – it's on my mind all the time." He stared off into the gray spaces on the other side of the bed.

"Damn!" she exclaimed, "I'm the one who has to have the abortion, not you! I'm worried!"

"I know, I know," he groaned, "if only it were me, if only you didn't have to go through this. If only I could do it instead – it's terrible! Let's not talk about it any more – it's too hard." And he leaped out of bed, leaving her to not very cozy visions of hospitals and faceless people in white, armed with sharp instruments; a place where she would lose consciousness and perhaps not regain it; but a place also where her future could be given back to her. She kicked around in the covers awhile, and finally got up too.

After all, she reminded herself, the physical risk was less in every sense than if she carried the fetus to term.

She headed for the bathroom, where Philip was already showering. It would be warm and moist, and she could admire his pale freckled skin with the water glistening on it.

"Mmm," she said appreciatively as she went in, eyeing him behind the shower curtain.

"Hah!" he said. "Bullshit. You haven't been interested in me since you got pregnant. At first I thought you'd found another lover. You're a totally different person, Borgstrum, did you realize that? I never thought I'd get horny as long as I knew you – you always wanted it as much as I did. But now! Those new hormones have turned you off. I couldn't stand it if you went on this way. I'd have to call in some dancing girls or something. Your whole personality has changed."

"It's true," she said, "though I didn't realize you noticed so much. I thought I'd cleverly managed to conceal it from you! But it's very peaceful in a way, very calm, very collected. I find I'm not as restless. Don't even want to paint as much as before. I can't seem to get worked up about much of anything. Pleasant, but kind of boring, too."

"Well, now you know what it's like to be normal," he said. "Most people are like that. You and I are just weird, that's all."

"Speak for yourself," she said, flipping a towel at him.

"Oh, Ms. Self-Sufficiency!" he roared, splashing water at her. "Wait a few weeks, Borgstrum, we'll see!"

It was a month before she felt herself again. She and Philip never discussed the being they had summoned up and then dismissed from their world, never speculated about it. It was one of the roads not taken, a mystery with an untouched veil of sadness, and that was all.

* * *

E arly in December, Philip called Louise from work.

"Lou, something exciting is up. Apparently there's going to be a mass singing of the *Messiah* with the San Francisco Symphony, hundreds and hundreds of people, ordinary people, singing the whole score together with the orchestra. I'm getting tickets. You want to go?"

"You mean I would get to sing too?" she asked.

"Yes, everybody, all levels of singers. Of course I know the music now, after practicing it with the university chorus, and you know it too, from helping me on the piano. Imagine being in this big hall, singing it with all those people – and a first-rate orchestra! It'll probably be an annual thing, it's so good, and we'll be doing it the first time 'round. You'll have to come."

She smiled. "Well, I guess I will have to – it sounds exciting all right."

"Now listen, Lou, this is a nighttime concert in the city – no blue jeans this time. We're all going to dress up, okay?"

"We're all? Who else is going?"

"Some people from work – mainly Rachel and Bill. It was Rachel who first told me it was happening. It's this Friday. I'll pick you up at seven, okay?"

"Okay," she answered, thinking that it would not matter much who went along; the music would be so great a pleasure that the rest was secondary.

When Philip picked her up, he did not comment on her slacks and shirt. She guessed that she was not elegant enough for him, but she felt she was dressed up enough for a Friday night. The slacks were her good ones, well pressed, and the shirt was good-looking too. She wore her good boots, handsome leather, though they had flat heels; and her old leather jacket, her best. The evening was cool and drizzly, around 40 degrees, and she wondered with a little malice how Rachel would dress in this kind of weather.

When they arrived at the Opera House, Louise found to her surprise that she was under-dressed after all. For the most part, people were gotten up quite formally. They had enough time before the concert began to have a drink in the downstairs area. She knew Philip would be disappointed that they could not make a good entrance, coming down the stairs, a natural mark for the eyes of the people already there. Well, she didn't look *bad* she thought to herself; just less dressed-up than most. Still, she felt chagrined.

As they moved out into the crowd with their wineglasses, Louise heard a shrill voice to one side:

"Pheelup! Pheelup! We air here!"

Rachel was wearing a tight black sequined dress, with stiletto heels. Her long blond hair still almost covered her face on both sides, the large eyes, heavily lined with mascara, peering out behind the curtains of hair with a sharp inquisitiveness at odds with the rest of her appearance.

"Rachel! Look at you!" Philip exclaimed, delighted.

The two of them began a long banter, occasionally joined by Bill, but mostly observed in silence by Louise, who could not seem to find a place to enter in. People nearby glanced their way with curiosity; Philip grew more and more animated.

At last the lights flickered. With hundreds of others, most carrying a copy of the score, they filed into one of the balconies. And the music began. The orchestral parts were magnificent, and it seemed to Louise that the choral parts were hardly less than that. Untrained in singing, she herself could carry only the top part, the "melody"; but all around her she heard people singing, accurately, the difficult parts, the altos and baritones and of course, at her side, Philip singing the tenor. It might be amateur night, but many were educated amateurs. The music carried them all away, and at the end people could not stop applauding – did not want to drop back again into their ordinary worlds. She and Philip glanced at each other as they clapped, exuberant. Still humming, they went down the marble staircases, gradually descending into a less ecstatic mood, but carrying as much of the music with them as they could.

In the foyer they met Rachel, Bill, and a woman introduced as Pat Malloy, who had come by herself. Since they were all parked at the same lot, the five of them walked out together. Rachel engaged Philip in talk again; again Louise tried to enter, and found herself blocked. Giving up, she turned to Pat.

"You came by yourself?" she asked.

"Yes," Pat replied, brushing strands of light brown hair from her face. "I'm not going out with anyone in particular right now, and I wanted to come."

Interested by this straightforward answer, Louise looked at Pat more carefully. She had a round soft face, homely and yet attractive. Then Louise remembered, and smiled; it had been Pat who had brought cookies to Philip's house one Saturday, just "passing by" with them, though she lived on the other side of the bay. Louise remembered being amused by this evidence of Philip's attractiveness, and remembered that Pat had given her a few slightly hostile glances, evidently hoping that Louise would disappear. But Louise hadn't worried that Philip would be too attracted to Pat; their own relationship was too strong. And besides, Pat didn't seem to have the physical attributes that Philip always said he demanded: she was not tall, not very good-looking, and she didn't dress well. So she was still hanging around Philip – but seemingly not in a predatory way. She seemed as content talking to Louise as she would have been talking to Philip.

"Where do you work?" Louise asked.

"The Environmental Alliance," she replied. "I'm in charge of the international acid rain program, and it's heating up right now. All of a sudden, some countries are beginning to admit there's a problem. It's a real change, and we want to take advantage of the new momentum."

Louise stared. She had not imagined that Pat was doing anything so interesting – something she herself might have liked to do.

"How did you ever get into that?" she asked. "It sounds wonderful – work where you can actually do something worth doing."

"Well, I was in grad school at U.C. Berkeley, and then I had a sort of financial crisis – essentially I was broke, so I took this secretarial thing at the Alliance, and then I just sort of stayed on. It's gotten too interesting to leave – and so here I still am."

"Hey, what air you two talking about? It must be verry deep,"

Rachel shrieked at them, annoyed that they seemed happily engaged in a conversation apart from hers.

"Just talking about work," Louise replied briefly. Turning back to Pat, she continued, "But you're obviously not a secretary anymore. This sounds like a really responsible job."

"It is – though I still do my own typing." Pat looked off at the car lights as they gleamed through the light rain that was now falling. "I don't know what it would be like to have a secretary myself! Nice, I suppose."

Louise smiled, hearing the unspoken question mark: should one woman do another woman's "shitwork" – that is, "woman's work" – while the other woman moved into new realms of power?

"I was at U.C. myself a few years ago. I got my Ph.D. in 1976. When were you there?" Louise asked.

Now it was Pat who looked at her with curiosity. "Let's see," she began, but was cut off by Philip.

"Here's our car, Lou," he called out.

He came over to where she and Pat stood.

"Are you going back to work, Pat?" he asked.

She smiled, smoothing back her hair again. "No, I think it's too late tonight, and besides, after that music, I don't think I could concentrate again for a while."

"It's the Irish in you, kid," Philip teased. "Too excitable."

"Probably," she replied, looking at him. Then, smiling at them all, she waved and walked off by herself. Louise noted with pleasure that she walked easily, in boots with flat heels.

"Look, Philip," Louise said, unable to resist, "look at those nice boots!"

Philip, following her eyes, laughed, putting his arm around her. "All right, Lou, all right! Have it your way!" Soon they were on their way home.

* * *

Christmas was coming up soon. All of the house people would be gone, so she and Philip and Jo-Jo would have the place to themselves.

Starting way back in late summer, Louise had begun to puzzle about what to give Philip for Christmas. Now that the house was shared, he had enough spending money, and it was difficult to think of anything he had not already bought for himself. She did remember, though, how impressed Philip had been by something he had seen years ago: a life-size dummy, amusingly gotten up, sitting in a chair in someone's living room. To Philip it had seemed the height of sophistication. He had talked about it in the first months of their relationship, and again a few times when they discussed the furnishing of his new house. Then the subject had faded from view because he didn't have time to look for such a thing – if it could be found at all; and in the meantime, Louise's paintings filled the wall space and livened the rooms.

Although not sure how to do it, Louise decided to make a big dummy for Philip's Christmas present. Trying out and discarding ideas, she finally decided to make a life-size cotton stuffed doll. Life-size gradually came to mean Louise's size, and of course it would be female.

Before she had a face, she had a name: Rosie. Almost from conception on, she was full of life, kicking and bucking on Louise's sewing machine. While Louise stitched down her sides, or shaped an arm or hand, Rosie was knocking the curtains down with one waving leg, or swinging around to box Louise lightly on the head. Rosie gradually acquired a mass of orange yarn hair, and an idiotically happy, serene smile. Louise finished her in the month between Thanksgiving and Christmas – not long after she had recovered from her abortion. It seemed that she had managed to have a daughter, after all.

From the Salvation Army store Rosie got a neon pink bikini top to cover her flat chest, a pair of blue shorts, and for winter wear an orange dress, matching her hair. On Christmas Eve Louise folded Rosie over double, wrapped her in a sheet, tied her in a ribbon with a big bow, and put her under the tree. The mystery of it fascinated Jo-Jo, who gave her cautious pokes and looked puzzled. Philip was more restrained, but he too was curious.

"What is it," he said, "a big pillow? Or three cubic yards of cotton with one bowl hidden at the center?"

"Open it up and see," Louise challenged.

Instantly the ribbon was cut, the sheet fell to the floor, and Rosie unfolded herself.

"My god!" Philip cried, holding her up, "I can't believe it!"

"Her name is Rosie," Louise said, beaming.

"Rosie, Rosie, you sweet thing," Philip crooned, holding her obscenely close and dancing around the room.

"Careful!" Louise said. "She's very young! I don't want my daughter corrupted!" Philip began to run his hands over her.

"Philip! Your own daughter!"

"My daughter?" he grinned. "So you wanted to give me a daughter? Mmm, Rosie, you and I can have a lot of fun when

Louise isn't around. I'll teach you all kinds of things. I like them young and innocent. Red hair, too. I bet you have a bit of the Irish in you. You wild thing, you. And tall – I like them tall."

"She's very quiet," Louise said. "Self-amusing. Good listener. Always in a good mood. The perfect daughter."

Jo-Jo had sat watching Philip play with Rosie, and now he came over, hesitantly, giggling at this doll twice his own size. Philip held out her hand to Jo-Jo, and screeched in a high falsetto, "Hello Jo-Jo, I'm your new sister." Jo-Jo collapsed in hysterical laughter before this grinning creature.

"Jo-Jo, maybe you should look in the basement. I heard a kind of noise about fifteen minutes ago, and it could be Santa Claus has left something for you down there," Philip told him.

Jo-Jo looked wonderingly at his father and left the room slowly, apparently not sure whether he was being sent out so the adults could talk freely, or because there really was something down there in the basement.

"There's one other thing about Rosie you should know, Philip," Louise said, lifting Rosie's shorts a little to reveal a small red felt heart at the clitoris.

"Rosie! I don't know if I'll be able to handle you," Philip said. He arranged her on the sofa, and stood back to see how she looked. "Where should she go? Down here? No, I want her upstairs – in the bedroom," and he leered melodramatically. "Don't worry, I'll take care of her. She can sit on one of the window seats and look out at the view. You'll like it with me, Rosie."

He sat down and took Rosie in his arms. "Now I never have to be alone. She'll keep me company when you're not here."

"That was my hope. And Rosie," Louise admonished, shaking

a finger at her, "be sure to kick out any other women who come in up there, in Philip's bedroom."

"Oh-ho," Philip said. "I see. Well, Rosie, you'll just have to do nice things for me when Louise isn't here. You'll have to make up for the way your mother neglects me."

"What?" Louise cried out. Before she could go on, however, there was a shriek from the basement below.

"He's found it," Philip said. "Let's go down and watch."

They clattered down the narrow basement stairs to find Jo-Jo, who was tenderly stroking his new bicycle as if it were a living animal. He turned to Philip: "Is this really for me?"

"I guess so," Philip said. "It has your name on it. Looks as if Santa left it for you. It's yours, I'm sure. Though I think the wire basket is from Louise – she had a special talk with Santa."

Jo-Jo turned again to his bicycle, lost in shy admiration of its glory.

In the chilly basement, Louise and Philip drew closer to one another, watching Jo-Jo, their arms around one another's waists.

* * *

After dinner, Jo-Jo went to bed, exhausted and ecstatic. Philip and Louise brought Rosie up to the bedroom with them, making her comfortable on the south-facing window seat, where she looked out over the gridworked lights of Oakland and the distant glitter of San Francisco.

Philip flicked on the TV while Louise arranged the big pillows on the bed, so they could watch comfortably propped up. Soon they were lying side by side, watching the tube.

"Dumb, dumb," Louise said, watching.

"Clint Eastwood? He's great! You haven't seen this one? Just wait, Lou, just wait. Here," and he opened up a giant package of M&Ms, "these will make you feel better."

"Not bad," she granted, settling back. Then in another moment she felt impatient again.

"Tough, so tough," she said. "No woman would ever want to get near a bundle of barbed wire like that."

"Clint Eastwood? Women open their legs when he walks in the room."

"Oh! Disgusting!" she shrieked, poking him. Then she leaped off the bed and went into the hall; an enormous rumble followed, and then she came running back in, laughing.

"I just told the ghost something," she giggled, climbing back onto the bed.

He looked at her in disbelief. "What do you mean, told the ghost something? You just let out the most enormous fart I ever heard! How did I ever wind up with a woman like you? Gross, Borgstrum, gross!"

"You're just jealous," she challenged.

That was all he needed. He ran out into the hall and let out a huge bellowing fart.

In a moment she was out in the hall again. Lifting her nightgown, she roared, "Take that, you ghost!" filling the hall with gas.

Philip was doubled up on the bed. "Watch out Clint Eastwood, shake in your boots, Louise Borgstrum'll get you if you don't watch out! Even John Wayne's afraid of her!"

Louise fell on the bed, laughing. Philip ran out into the hall. "Okay you ghost, this is for you!" and he let out another resounding fart. "That'll keep him at a respectful distance!"

He threw himself down on the bed by Louise; both were laughing too hard to talk. Finally Louise got up and closed the hall door. "It stinks out there," she said. "Poor ghost."

"Have some more M&Ms, kid," Philip offered her the bag, "just in case the ghost gets rambunctious, I don't want you to be unarmed!"

"Don't worry," she said, taking him in her arms, "I'll protect you – if you can stand it!"

"Come on, lie down, Lou, I like it that way."

Soon they were making love. Not until they had finished could they lie peacefully side by side on the bed. It was still impossible for them to lie that close without desire, as strong as when they first met.

"Comfortable as two hot turds," he commented, as they lay there watching what was left of the Clint Eastwood.

"How did I find such a poet?"

"Admit it, you love it."

* * *

They woke up, warm together under the covers in the cool room. Philip lay curled up with his back to her, so she fit herself into his curve, putting her arms around his middle and pulling him in close. He groaned with pleasure at being warmly held.

"This is awful," he muttered.

"Awful?"

"I'm getting too dependent on you."

"Sounds all right to me. Why not? It's not as if I were going to desert you, or betray you or something."

"I don't like being dependent."

"But how is it possible to love without being dependent?" she asked. "If you love someone, you need that person. Love is a form of dependency."

"I don't like it. I need you more than you need me."

"What makes you so sure?"

"You're happy down there in your studio, damn you. You ride off on your bicycle and I can just see how you like to go off. And I miss you when you're gone. I don't think you miss me."

She pulled him back so she could look into his face. "Of course I miss you. But tell me, do you miss me when you're having a beer with Hugh and Jim?"

"No, no, we're talking and kidding around."

"And when you're working in the lab, do you miss me then?"

"Well no, I'm working then."

"Well? It's the same when I'm seeing Sylvia, or when I'm painting."

He considered that for a moment, then pulled her onto his chest.

"Just remember that I'm the boss."

"WHAT?"

"I'm the boss; I'm the man, I'm the boss. Just obey me and everything will be fine."

"Ha!" she cried, "Never! Oh, I wish I could remember the lines from Chaucer – when mastery comes, love flies out the window – or something. Anyway, the idea is clear."

She paused a moment, considering. "You sort of lead in bed; it seems to be the way of things. But you mustn't confuse what happens in bed with what happens out of bed. You know – I'm my own person. But it's nothing to worry about, is it?"

"I want you to obey me," he said again, joking, but sounding half serious and commanding, and half plaintive.

"No, no, it isn't healthy," she said, kissing him on the cheek. "I love you and I like to do things for you freely because that's my pleasure. But obedience – no, that's something else entirely." She bit him on the chin, scratching her teeth on his stubble. "Besides, you'd get bored." She tried biting his ear instead; it was softer.

"Ouch!" he said, rolling the two of them over so he was on top. "Now you'll get it, Borgstrum!"

"I hope so. Listen, you, I love you, isn't that enough?"

She pulled him down close, and they resolved it in the old way.

* * *

It seemed as if every spring had marked some big event. The first spring, April Fool's Day, appropriately, they had met. The second spring Philip had bought the house, and established a new life. Now as the third spring approached, a possible new event presented itself. Philip had to go to an April conference in Vienna, and then a June one in Tokyo. Instead of going so far and returning to Berkeley each time, why not start in England and then keep going eastward, around the world to Tokyo? And he wanted Louise to go with him.

"I can't afford to pay for both of us, Lou, so you'd have to mostly pay your own way. But we can get those 'around the world in 80 days' cheapo tickets, and that would be the main expense. It will be another big thing in our history together," Philip said. He wanted them to have a history, a long series of things they had experienced in common, the braiding of two separate strands. Because they had failed to meet at the beginning, before either one had any adult history, Philip thought they had to make up for lost time.

Louise's boss, kind and understanding, agreed that she could be absent for three months, as long as she promised to work as many extra hours as needed when she returned. And somehow, in the course of conversation, without formally saying so, Philip and Louise agreed that she would sublet her apartment not only while they were gone, but for three months beforehand. That way she could save six months' worth of rent, helping greatly with her trip finances. Neither Louise nor Philip quite came out with this proposal, was responsible for it. She would begin living with Philip now, and when they returned, Louise could move right back into her apartment. Once again they could enjoy living together, have a little taste of the forbidden paradise, with seemingly no strings attached.

But the prelude to their trip was not entirely promising. Philip had a lot of work to do first: writing long grant proposals, which would determine whether or not his work would be funded over the next few years; writing the papers he would give in Vienna and Tokyo; continuing to run new experiments and plan what his lab technicians would do in his three-month absence; organizing the house so it could run smoothly without him; and getting ready for the trip itself. He drove himself until his body rebelled, and he had fierce backaches that refused to go away.

Jo-Jo, aware that his father was going far away for a long time, began to misbehave. He threw a hardball in the basement and broke the only light fixture, which Philip then had to repair the

day before leaving for London with Louise. Distraught, Philip
rushed to install a replacement fixture, insisting that Louise help
him.

"But I've allotted just enough time to do everything I have to
do," she protested.

"Why should I have to do everything?" he roared. She did not
reply that he made it clear the house was his, and in no way hers.
But it was also true that she was freeloading now, not paying rent,
though she did as much cooking and housework as the other
house members.

"Okay. What can I do?" she asked. It didn't seem to her that
there was much room for helping. Philip stood under the low
ceiling trying to make a screw go up into the light fixture. All that
could be used was one screwdriver.

"Make sure the other screws don't get lost." In fact he had
already misplaced them. Angry and in a hurry, Philip could not
get the screw in. Louise could not find the other screws. She felt
her time slipping away as Philip tried and tried, unsuccessfully.

"Maybe I could do it," she suggested, anxiously knowing this
was tactless, but thinking she saw a possible method of getting the
screw in. Philip did not reply. There was a tense silence for a few
minutes.

"Can't you find a flashlight?" he snapped. "I can't see what
I'm doing in this half-light. What the hell did you do with the
other screws? Why don't you help me?"

Louise stood by his side, chained by feelings of obligation and
duty, completely useless, wasting her time, and wondering whether she could stand to travel with Philip. They would be alone
together, entirely dependent on one another for company, for

almost three months. Suddenly she dreaded it.

At last the fixture was in, and Louise was released to finish her errands. Finally she had done everything but pack, which she began hurriedly, eager to get to bed on time. The next day would be hard, traveling almost from daybreak, and arriving in London with jet lag. She did not want to go into it already tired out.

She was checking things off her list when Philip came into the bedroom. Her heart sank when she saw his face.

"Have you seen my passport?" he asked.

There followed hours of frantic searching: at the house, at his office, in his car. This was the one thing he had to have; almost anything else could be duplicated one way or the other. Finally, after sifting through every possible place, Philip located his passport. He had stowed it away for safety in the pocket of the suit jacket he would wear the next day. Late at night, the adrenaline still flowing, they fell into bed, unable to sleep for a long time. Morning came far too quickly.

"I'm sorry, Lou," he said as they rode in the bus to the airport. "It was such a dumb thing to do."

"Well, I have to admit that you're right," she answered, merciless.

"Don't be mean – it could happen to you, too," he pleaded.

"Oh yes, it's true. Maybe it's even one of the things I like about you. I know you're really smart, but still you do these things – I identify, it makes me feel better."

"You don't feel so dumb when you see me?" he asked.

"Something like that."

"Oh Lou," he sighed, pressing lightly against her.

"I have something for our flight today." She opened her purse to show a bagful of special brownies.

He gasped. "You're going to take those to London, through customs there? It's dangerous, Lou."

"Well, I thought maybe we could eat them now, for breakfast. That way customs will never know, and we'll sleep the whole way and be in great shape when we get to London."

"Incredible!" he said, pulling the baggie out of her purse and digging in hungrily.

By the time they passed over Seattle they were flying higher than the plane. Refreshing themselves with the last big crumbs as they passed over the pole, they arrived in London free of visible contraband, and totally stoned. Of the two of them, Louise was slightly more sober because she had eaten slightly less; her drug of preference was alcohol rather than marijuana. But she was not feeling much pain as they floated out into the cold gray London streets, blundering along until they found the small hotel where they had reserved a room.

More painkiller might have been appropriate to their London stay. The weather was unseasonably cold: it rained, sleeted, even snowed. They could afford only inferior seats at the theater, and cheap restaurants. Philip got depressed; it was too much like his childhood, with all the old feelings of being deprived and on the outside of things. The main branch of the British Museum was closed for repairs. And the air everywhere in the city stank of industrial pollution. Grimy dust covered the buildings, the streets, their faces, gritted coldly on their teeth.

But what about Paris, their next stop – Paris in the spring? Paris in the early spring was not very different from London in the late winter, featuring the same cold, dirt, bad air, and high prices.

Each had different memories of Paris, Philip in particular. When he had been in Paris with Concha, many years earlier, prices were low and it had been possible to move with ease, do whatever pleased. Concha, fluent in French, had made friends on the Metro with a wealthy man from the south of France, who had invited them to his chateau. There Philip's knowledge of wines, along with his surprisingly good French, had won them the privilege of drinking 100-year-old burgundy at dinner, from the chateau's cellars. Philip had told the story, minus Concha, many times in Louise's presence.

Louise, however, did not meet any wealthy Frenchmen on the Metro. While she could read French fairly well, her spoken French was poor. When she met Philip's French friends from his previous visits, she did not transfix them with scintillating conversations, though they seemed to expect that she would. She ripped one of her contact lenses and had to revert to glasses. Philip gallantly insisted he liked the glasses, but she knew that they were not really becoming. It made her feel at a disadvantage, especially in comparison to the fabled Concha.

After Easter, the weather suddenly turned warm, and Louise realized that her boots and heavy sweater, along with the rather heavy gear for her contact lenses, were all now unnecessary. Accordingly, she located a carton and packaged them up for sending back home, eager to lighten her small baggage. Later on, she would probably have to carry her things, perhaps longish distances, and she wanted her bag to be as light as possible.

"You can't send stuff like that through the mail," Philip protested when she mentioned it to him.

"Oh yes, I did it when I was here before," she replied.

"They won't accept it. You can take my word for it," he said. "You'll just be wasting time for both of us. You'll take it there and they won't accept it and you'll have to take it back again and it'll take all day. I'll be damned if I'll spend my precious time in Paris doing something completely pointless."

She was silent for a moment, exasperated. Finally she said, "Listen, Philip, I've been here before, I've done this before, it won't take that long, and I don't want to be carrying heavy stuff for the rest of the trip that I won't need in the hot weather. And you don't have to go to the post office with me, after all. I can do it myself just fine. We have two days left here in Paris. Why don't I do it tomorrow morning, and then meet you someplace for lunch?"

"That won't work at all," he snapped. "You don't know how long it'll take, you could be late by hours. You're just forcing me to go with you on this damned errand!"

She looked at him angrily, wishing he would evaporate under the heat of her gaze. She did not want him there, she was tired of him, he wanted to lead all the time even when he knew less than she did, he was an impediment she would like to send back, surface mail, with her boots. And she would not give in.

Early the next morning, she and Philip walked, very silently, down long blank streets in search of the post office. The blocks seemed to go on and on, big public buildings without color or interest, no trees, not even many people on the street. The package was heavy and unwieldy, but she could not say so. Her fingers were aching when at last they arrived and got into line. It was ten or fifteen minutes before they got to the clerk, who informed them that they were at the wrong office: there was a special office for sending packages overseas, several metro stops away.

Philip smiled a hard, quick smile, glancing at Louise.

"But I *can* send it," she said. "It's just that our hotel manager sent us to the wrong post office."

"You better not talk about it anymore. Let's just try to get this thing over with. Here," and he snatched the carton from her. She could not refuse; her fingers were about to give out.

As they sat together on the Metro, his now-abhorred body close to hers, he muttered, "What a great way to be spending a day in Paris! You really screwed it up, didn't you? Just remember, I've earned a lot of credits by going through this, and I'll take them, believe you me. You can't ruin my trip this way."

Her thoughts were in confusion. Could she stand to go on with him? Wouldn't it be better just to finish this trip by herself? But the thought made her feel desolate. It would not be much fun to go alone to India, Nepal, Thailand, Japan, Hawaii. It would be bleak. But could she bear Philip's company? Anger and fear alternated like lightning flashes in her head.

Looking up, she was startled to find the Frenchman in the seat opposite regarding her with curious, detached speculation, as if he were at the movies. She struggled to bring her face into control, maintaining silence towards Philip. There was nothing, absolutely nothing she wanted to say to him.

There was not much pleasure for either of them in the rest of their Paris stay. When they got to Germany, they quarreled again, this time over the question of which restaurant to go to. Louise felt despairing. Would this supposedly wonderful trip end in their complete separation? Did she really love Philip after all? She could hardly bear to look at him these days.

Then, in the German countryside, they visited a research lab that did work related to Philip's. A car and driver came to pick them up. Philip knew the men at the lab, and they knew Philip. They treated him with friendly respect. Suddenly the two of them were lifted out of their tiny two-person world, out of the antagonistic roles in which they were stuck. It was no longer appropriate to go around behind spike-studded shields. They relaxed a little; and when they were alone together, they no longer fought.

Soon afterwards at the conference in Vienna, Philip was again in his element. Louise remembered that he was a well-known scientist. It was a side of him which she usually forgot. Mostly he was just Philip, her warm companion in bed and voluble presence at the dinner table, or lately, the irritable and irritating person who wanted her to do all the same things he did, even if she wanted to do something else, and even though he did not seem to enjoy her presence. Now, remembering that he had a respected place in the world, he began to relax; and Louise began to like him better, though she could not tell if this was because she was impressed, or simply because his mood had changed. She could not help wondering if their egos had been so vulnerable that the disappointments of the trip had seemed to them like reflections on their own worth. She had certainly been feeling diminished and guessed that Philip had been feeling the same way. Later she saw this European part of the trip as a sort of preparation for later events, something like the way veal steaks are prepared by being pounded with a mallet until tender, before being put in the frying pan.

* * *

Their next stop was India, and they arrived already sick, sick from something they had caught in England, or eaten in France, or failed to do in Germany. Philip was the sicker of the two, and collapsed in the airport at Delhi, after a long and rough airplane ride. They found him a place to lie down in the muggy pre-dawn heat, a couch in a restroom that seemed not to have been cleaned since Kipling's time. Louise took care of business for the two of them, not entirely sorry to prove her competence, and to take care of Philip.

They had arrived in Asia at the beginning of the hot season. It was 114 degrees in the shade. They could drink eighteen cups of liquid in a day, and barely have to urinate; it all came out their pores. The heat rolled over them, pressed the stuffing out of them.

Philip gradually got better, but still suffered more from the heat than Louise did, almost fainting in the hot afternoons while she could still function, albeit slowly. An awareness was growing in her that things could change, and it might be she who would need taking care of next time.

In this more truly foreign world, there were no memories for either of them, no past to compete against or measure up to. Whatever they did, they were outsiders. Everything became simpler. Dutiful tourists, they took a train to Agra, to see the Taj Mahal. To their surprise, they were overwhelmed by its beauty. They saw it in every light, even after dark when it glowed quietly, looming out of the hot Indian night, the sounds of music and of pressing multitudes of people drifting across the kempt and well-fenced grounds.

"What a memorial!" Philip exclaimed, as he and Louise looked at it from the far entrance. "This thing was built by some big ruler whose wife died, very young. They really loved each other. He mourned for three years, and wouldn't even speak to anyone all that time. Building this was his cure – or at least he could live after that. I want to see the palace across the river where he lived – the red fort."

Louise nodded. As so often, she had read the same brochure as Philip; but she had learned to stop saying "I know, I know," in impatient response.

The red fort was an enormous building of red stone, dusty and hot. They paid the small admission fee and entered in. Like so many minor tourist attractions in this hot season, it seemed to be deserted.

Wandering from room to room, they quickly realized that they were in a maze. Each room had several exits, leading into dark corridors with several identical staircases which led into identical rooms with several identical exits. It would be easy to choose a wrong exit, just once, and become completely lost.

Some rooms had great three-sided windows looking out across the river, and they came into these rooms always with a feeling of surprise and pleasure at the opening-up of the walls, and the sense of light and fresh air. Louise stood for a time before one of these windows, letting Philip go on by himself while she gazed across the water at the Taj Mahal, gleaming, pale, a vision of cool order in the shimmering afternoon heat.

A memorial, she thought. That suggested that he believed his wife was irretrievably gone. Different from the lure put together by Euphony, for a spirit imagined as existing on after death, unchanged, and with plenty of leisure to attend séances on earth. Maybe that was why Euphony seemed so happy: After all, though she had complete run of things, she was also never alone. Her dead husband, like God, could be around at all times, witnessing each action and thought with love, blessing and validating her life. Louise smiled to herself, and turned away from the window. She had no idea where Philip was. But somehow that did not seem important. No matter how lost in the maze, surely they would find each other again – they always had.

Before her in the recesses of the room were three dark doorways. Choosing one at random, she slipped into the shadowy corridor, exploring.

* * *

As she and Philip walked back to their hotel room, they were quiet. The constant heat, pouring into them, was tiring, as were the ceaseless soft sounds of voices and radio music, beating into their skulls. A scent of hot straw and dust permeated everything. India was gradually sucking them into itself, and digesting them along with the millions of its own people. They were coming to feel less important, somehow, two motes in a sea of sand. The feeling was relaxing, but also rather frightening.

Back in their hotel room they stood at the window, watching workers build another hotel across the way. There was no machinery used, and no metal except what went into the concrete blocks as reinforcing rods. The only wood was the scaffolding, which was clearly designed to be used again and again. Everything was done by hand. Looking around their own room, they realized that the ten-story building in which they now stood had been made the same way. But they were safe – weren't they? Aloof in their air-conditioned room, their well-nourished bodies still intact, they stood behind the discreet shades and watched those other human bodies labor under the hot sun.

* * *

Wanting to keep the distinction between themselves and India clear, they tried to get first-class train tickets to the border of Nepal. Unfortunately, they learned, they could get only second-class tickets for the first part of their trip; and as for purchasing a continuous ticket for the whole trip, it was impossible. In India, they gradually learned, one does not plan that far ahead.

Thus it was with second-class tickets in their hands that they stood on the stone railroad platform at Agra. It was late at night. They were surrounded by people dressed in white and holding various unidentifiable bundles – their life's possessions? – and when the train arrived and opened its doors, the two of them were carried in on a great wave of people, fighting for their second-class sleeping places. The less strong were pushed off into corners as the shouting crowd swarmed through, like a river below a broken dam. Finally they were settled into their places, separated by sex, each to sleep on a bare wooden plank, one of three on each wall, with just room enough to slide in. They had begun their real immersion in India.

Sleeping and waking, the hours were interminable. The train crawled slowly through a landscape which did not change: flat, monotonous, and hot. But they were still safe, in a sense. As long as they did not get left behind at some unnamed stop or station, they could not themselves become one of those children carrying eighty-pound packs on a bowed back, or one of the women sitting in the stations picking lice from another's hair, or one of the men in the baking fields, squatting to relieve himself in full view, his body perhaps weakened by a constant diarrhea. They would not have to live in a world where electricity – to say nothing of radio, TV, or movies – was rare; where evening was lit by a small cooking fire, or not at all; and where it seemed no one had known anything different since the beginning of time – if indeed time ever did begin or could ever end here.

They could see neither beginnings nor endings, from the bland horizon to the melting-together of day and night. That was what made their trip across India so long, and why it changed them both without their quite agreeing to the change. Lone travelers from another world, they looked at each other to remember who they thought they were, and to reassure themselves that they might return to that old impossible existence, where there were real beds with sheets on them, and TVs and movies and choice of clothes and even meat, whenever they wanted it, and clean water coming out of the tap. They could not pretend they had deserved their luck; too many of the people they met were intelligent, sensitive, warm, and often very beautiful – and nearly always very thin.

Slow hour after hour passed. The train swayed gently through the heat, stopping every fifteen minutes or so to pick up and let off passengers. Sometimes they stopped at towns, but often it was at some spot in the countryside, where a cluster of people stood by the tracks, waiting for them. People came and went in the compartment – now first-class – occupied by Louise and Philip. Some spoke English, especially at first; but as they traveled farther, fewer spoke their language. Station signs stopped being bilingual. When they got off at stations to get tea, small children looked open-mouthed and with some fright at them both, but especially at Louise – a tall blue-eyed woman in slacks. Home was more and more distant. They seemed lost in some vast desert of time, and of poverty.

They grew desperately eager to reach the border. Finally, they were to change trains at a relatively large town. It was the last connection they had to make. Unfortunately, however, the electricity was out, and everything had come to a halt. They sat on the stone railroad platform in utter darkness, wondering what creatures, insect, rat, or human, might be creeping towards them. At one end of the platform there were fires built, people cooking and selling tea, gesticulating, their baggy costumes lit fantastically by the flames. There were occasional liquid sounds breaking the silence, as someone urinated off the platform onto the tracks; and occasional murmurs in the darkness. Then groups of two or three men began to flit past them, quickly, sometimes on one side, sometimes on the other.

"Watch out, Louise!" Philip muttered. His ghetto upbringing made him aware long before Louise would have perceived danger signals. "They're up to something."

They were certainly the only foreigners on the platform, and that alone marked them as likely hits. They were bound to have something of value on them, in a land where a living wage for a family of six might be eighty cents a day. It would be easy to attack and get away quickly in the complete absence of lighting. They gathered up their things and moved, very close together, towards the flickering fires at the platform's end.

Hour after hour they waited. They were a mere two hours' journey from the border town, Raxaul. So close to deliverance! And meantime stuck forever in the eighteenth, or perhaps the thirteenth, century. Small groups of men still flitted past, like bats swooping in the darkness, seeming to be stopped only by the faint light of the embers. It grew long past midnight.

Finally a train pulled in. Louise and Philip gathered up their belongings – suddenly surprisingly heavy – and rushed to find a railroad agent who might understand their destination's name. This was not easy, given that they had long since passed the point where English could be taken for granted as the lingua franca. The official they found seemed to have a glimmer of comprehension in his eyes as they put their questions to him. They pointed to the name, Raxaul, on the map. Would the train take them there? The answer was yes, and no. They could not understand. Finally they just got on and hoped. They could not bear to wait any longer – days and nights? – on that stone platform. In the dark they sat behind the barred train windows and watched dawn come. Hours passed, as the train rattled slowly, slowly across the flat and parched land. Many more than two hours had gone by. It was fully light, and the familiar heat began to grow as if day – every day – was a slow journey across a vast hot griddle, cooler on the edges, burning at the center. They were well on their way once again to this center when Philip, shaking his head, went to find a conductor, an official, someone who could tell them where they were, and where they were going. When he finally returned he was half in despair.

"It goes to Raxaul, I think – but it takes eighteen hours! And we have to change trains again, in some big city that's coming up."

It was almost unbearable, except that it had to be borne. There was no getting off this train, or going back. They had to find their way going forward, and survive.

At the big city they changed train stations as well as trains. They picked their way through the crowds of travelers and the small families that seemed to live in public buildings, and the lone ones who had come there to die, in out of the sun and dust. Philip and Louise rushed by them, half sprinting, to find the right train to take them away.

This time they were lucky. They got on, and in early evening they arrived at one of the dirtiest towns in the world: Raxaul. With misgivings they ate in a filthy place, the restaurant in their hotel, the best in town. Louise thought of Persephone, fated to stay in Hades because she ate a single pomegranate seed there.

Early the next morning it was cool; they were already higher in altitude, and the day's bus ride would take them still farther up, into the Himalayan foothills where Kathmandu lay. Her bag safely on the bus, Louise looked at her watch: fifteen minutes before departure time. She had eaten nothing that day, and it would take six or seven hours on the bus to reach Kathmandu. Looking down the dirt road, she saw a shop open – a sort of counter across a front door, looking into a kitchen. Inside was a primitive stove, a broken-down woman, and two small children. Louise gestured towards the stove, where a large amount of rice was cooking. Soon she had a plate of it in her hand. She ate hungrily with her fingers, not trusting the dirty-looking fork she had been given. As she ate she tried to forget the sight of the woman casually hawking up and spitting on the kitchen's dirt floor, while dishing out the rice.

As she stood eating, Philip came up to her, looking angry.

"What are you doing?" he exclaimed. "The bus is going to leave in a few minutes. For god's sake put that stuff down and get on!"

She looked at her watch. "By my reckoning we have seven minutes left. I'll be done in about three minutes. Just hang on. Or if you're too worried, go get on. I'll be there in plenty of time." She glanced towards the bus, about fifty yards away from them.

Philip looked at his watch. "My watch says we have about three minutes. Goddamn it, Lou, drop that stuff!"

"But nobody else is getting on yet," she pointed out, taking another mouthful of hot rice. Actually there were a few people already on the bus, but most stood about in the small dirt loading area. As far as she could see, no one was in a hurry.

Philip's voice rose. "I'm not going without you, dammit, you know I can't! Put that down!" he shouted.

"A few more bites," she said. "Relax!"

With that he pulled the metal plate from her hand, and slammed it down on the kitchen-counter, while the woman inside looked on with a detached curiosity. Turning back, Philip took Louise's wrist, grabbing it hard, pulling her towards the bus. Without thinking, she stepped in front of him and broke his hold with a judo move. The move, which she had practiced countless times in class, came to her automatically; she was both frightened and angry.

For a moment they stood facing each other. Then he marched off to the bus. Louise paused a moment, rolling her shirt sleeve down over the red mark on her wrist, and followed. As she got on the bus, she could hardly believe what had happened. Never had Philip touched her in any threatening way. Always before she had felt safe with him.

He had saved the window seat for her: a gesture of reconciliation? She took it in silence. The bus was about half full, and in a few minutes the driver got on and started the motor. It coughed a few times, and died. The driver tried again; again failure. Outside the window Louise noticed a group of about ten young boys, barefoot and in rags. The driver waved at them and they disappeared behind the bus. A moment later Louise could feel the bus move a little. They were being pushed! Involuntarily she glanced at Philip. They had come so far; surely they would not have to repeat the unbearable train journey back to Delhi. Philip's eyes met hers, equally fearful. She looked out the window. They were moving now, very slowly, down the main street, which had remnants of paving on it. On either side were ramshackle huts and houses built of stone and wood, the same color as the road and the people, all covered with a film of dirt. Poverty here, where it was cooler, seemed almost more depressing than it had been in the extreme heat of the plains. Off to one side there was a line of people and pack animals, including a small elephant. But this did not charm Louise. The only thing that interested her right now was the thought of getting out, escape.

Behind the bus the young boys, with their frail-looking bodies, still pushed, shouting to one another as they went. The driver turned over the motor. They were coasting now quite rapidly, but she could see that the road turned uphill a short distance ahead. The motor coughed, coughed, coughed again and then caught. It was running; perhaps they would make it.

Slowly the bus chugged out of town, up into the hills. Louise looked out, and thought. The man at her side was no stranger. She had always known there was violent anger in him, and that it could come out someday at her. But pride in her automatic judo response partly balanced out her anger and chagrin at Philip's attempt to impose his will on her in this high-handed public display. Because she could take care of herself physically, she did not feel compromised. And she also understood that he was desperately afraid, as was she, of somehow getting stuck here, falling ill, subsiding into the dust and filth and poverty, losing their former privileged identities as if they had been dreams, or previous incarnations.

By the time the bus reached the outskirts of Kathmandu, they were both aware of a new weakness, and a feeling of unrest in their guts. They did not have the strength for the luxury of staying angry at each other. Their only thought now was to find a decent yet affordable place to stay.

In the following days they found that, while they had escaped to Kathmandu, they had not succeeded in leaving India behind. Both became sick, dog-sick, Louise worse than Philip. This time he took care of her, doing what had to be done while she lay in bed, weak and frightened. Every time she thought of where they had just been, her stomach clenched; her whole system was trying to throw off that experience of unending poverty and misery, and human patience and labor and love and sensitivity subsisting through it all. She literally could not stomach it.

As Louise gradually got well enough to walk, they tried to see something of Kathmandu. Most of their attention, however, had to go to their bodies, trying to contain their stomachs and bowels.

They had little energy left over for Kathmandu, or for one another. Both showed their most irritating traits, unable to hide or transform them. Philip was bossy, know-it-all; Louise was whiny, stubborn, and too easily hurt. Each had clear moments of wishing to be without the other; but they knew, too, that they needed each other more than at any other time. Not for love, now – there wasn't much of that feeling in the air – but simply for survival. Need alone made each tolerate the intolerable other.

Health gradually returned. By the time they left Tokyo they could eat normally again, though their old clothes no longer fit their trimmed-down bodies. They had lost a lot – everything they had to spare. Anger and hurt receded into the past; but Louise wondered if they would ever love one another with quite the same wholehearted acceptance and abandon.

They could not undo their trip into Hades. Not because it was 114 degrees in the shade. It was that survival could be more important than love, and that survival was important only to the individual, to the one craving an identity and a name, staking out a claim to ownership of one cubic inch of time. It was that people, like themselves in all but opportunity, could be lost there, completely lost, and it did not matter. It was that they themselves could have been lost, and only they would have known. And in being lost, maybe they too would have forgotten. And it would not matter at all. Life in its pain and beauty would go right on without them, and no roll call at the end.

* * *

They reached Hawaii with a sense of relief; at last they were back on terra firma, the USA, where they more or less knew the rules and were at home. Their old innocent selves were permanently gone; India had purged them of those. Still, they would surely reconnect to some extent with the old, more optimistic personae, the ones who believed in the reality and importance of beings called "Philip" and "Louise."

For a few days they stayed in a small touristy town where a friend of Philip's had a sailboat they could sleep on, free. In the evenings they ate and drank to excess, dancing wildly afterwards, working off anger and frustration and disillusion. After a while they went south and tried body-surfing, risking themselves on the crests of waves, throwing themselves in time and time again, breathless with the game, trying to be washed clean.

On the last night they returned to their rented room as usual. While Philip brought things in from the rental car, Louise got out a good supply of beer and cheese and crackers, laid it out on the little table, and sat down.

"All set, Philip," she called out.

But as he approached, he suddenly froze.

"Don't move, Lou," he said sternly.

She looked out of the corner of her eye at the wall next to her, and there, about one foot away, was a spider as big as her fist. Or perhaps as big as Philip's fist, she thought.

"God, what a monster!" Philip said with respect. He was looking around the room for something to kill it with, but could see nothing that was the right size and weight.

The spider lifted one or two hairy legs, as if thinking about moving on.

"I'll have to try it with my bare hand," Philip said, his voice sounding breathless. "Don't move, Lou."

He came up slowly beside her, lifted his arm high, and came down swiftly, with his full strength behind the blow.

"Ow!" he shouted. "Damn!" He was dancing around the room, holding his bruised fist.

Louise looked at the floor, but there was no spider body.

"Did you get it?" she asked.

"No, no, dammit!" Philip replied, obviously still in pain.

"Oh Philip," she laughed, getting up, "your poor hand!"

He smiled wryly at her as she took his hand, still balled up in a fist, and held it.

"Guess I was so scared, I missed," he said. "Here I was going to rescue you and everything. And now that spider's loose somewhere in this room. It probably thinks it owns the place. It's probably mad. It'll probably come bite us when we're asleep and all helpless. God! I can't sleep in this room!"

"Worse than ghosts!" she laughed. "Don't worry, it's probably more scared than we are – though it's practically as big as we are."

"Yeah, it could eat both of us the way we are now, all skin and bones from India. We'd just be the hors d'oeuvres."

"Well," she said, "we'd better stick together tonight."

When they went to bed that night, they did lie close together, almost as they would have before the trip. Louise pulled Philip's back into her belly, trying to be comforted into sleep. But she was aware, in another compartment of her mind, that the spider was still out there, somewhere in the dark, sharing the room with them.

* * *

W hen they got home, the house was nearly empty. Ilona and Jonathan had gone back to England for the summer. Martha had some money from her mother, and was buying a small house in Oakland; she and Gloria were moving out. Kathleen and Willy were the only regular housepersons left. It was hard to resist the conclusion that Louise should continue to live with Philip, at least for the two remaining months of the summer. She could continue to sublet her old apartment, and because she would be paying rent to stay in Martha's former room, she could have a legitimate and quiet space of her own. She and Philip did not talk about what they would do in the fall, when students – a pool of prospective renters – returned. They were, without admitting it, particularly eager to be together after the experiences of their long trip. Perhaps they could recapture some of the old closeness simply by living under the same roof, in the secure familiarity of Philip's house.

At first everything seemed easy. After a few weeks, however, Louise began to notice that Philip was leaping out of bed in the morning, uncharacteristically cold and quiet. Yet he did not say anything.

"What's going on, Philip?" she finally asked one morning, before he had managed to escape from the intimacy of bed.

"Ouch!" he cried sharply, as she rolled over onto his chest.

"What?" she asked, very surprised. She had rolled onto him this way so many times, countless times. "Did I hurt you some-how?"

"Yes! You must have dug your elbow right into my clavicle, right here," and he fingered gently the place where his collarbones came together. "Don't be so careless!"

"Hmmph, it's strange. I'm sorry – I didn't mean to," she went on, still uncertain how she could possibly have hurt him.

"It's all right, Borgstrum, just try to be more careful, will you? Were you going to tell me something?"

She frowned, thinking how to begin. "Is it my imagination, Philip, or are you strangely quiet these days? I don't feel as if I'm getting very much of you."

"Well, maybe," he replied. "Maybe I feel too married, with you here all the time. Maybe it's too soon for this, I don't know. Maybe it's too much like Concha. Did I tell you she's getting married? I mean really married, to this guy she's been seeing for the last year. He's rich and famous, so I guess she's getting what she wanted. Much better than with me."

He tossed impatiently under the covers. "Anyway, I don't want to be like Concha. She hasn't learned anything. I want to grow, I want to learn how to be independent before I make any new commitment. And I just feel too married right now. Every time I wake up, you're here. It's not that I don't love you. I don't know. Be patient. Maybe it will go away."

But other problems were brewing. From the window of Louise's room she could see the hot tub Philip had built two years ago. He was now busy planning a new, larger project: a deck, framed around the hot tub.

"It will be outdoor living space," he said excitedly. "It'll be like adding a whole new room to the house – you'll see."

Louise was a little skeptical. Building a deck was very low on her list of priorities. Painting was very high. She was looking forward to a quiet summer with a space of her own to work in.

Philip, however, was completely absorbed in this new project.

"I'll take what's left of my vacation time," he said, "half a day at a time. I'll go to work in the morning, and then spend the afternoons on the deck."

It was extremely time-consuming. The plans alone took a few weeks; then there was the buying of lumber and other supplies, and getting them up the long stairs from the street to the house. And after that came the measuring, cutting, leveling, and building.

To her dismay, she found that Philip wanted her with him at every step, and tacitly assumed that like him, she would go to her job every morning and use every afternoon to help him build. She fought it. She wanted her hard-won painting time. Besides, it was one thing to be the master builder, the one with the dream and the plan, who commanded at every step. It was something else to be the helper, standing in the sun hour after hour, occasionally being useful, available to be told, impatiently, what to do – down to how the most miserable little nail ought to be driven in.

Meanwhile, Kathleen was seldom to be seen. They had the house almost entirely to themselves: Philip and Louise and Jo-Jo and Willy. Which is to say that Louise had responsibility for Jo-Jo, Willy, and everything connected with the indoors functioning of the house, since Philip felt he was doing all the house-related work he could or should handle, in building the deck. Louise found that in addition to her half-time job on campus, she was doing all the shopping, cooking, and cleaning, plus child-tending. Painting time was reduced proportionately.

One Saturday afternoon Louise had fixed their favorite hot-dog and melted cheese lunch. Philip had been working in the hot sun all morning, while Louise had cared for Jo-Jo and gone shopping for the things they liked on a weekend: good steak at one shop; produce at another; chocolate dessert at another; Sunday breakfast croissants at another; milk and other staples at still another. It was pleasant enough, but it had taken the first half of the day. Now she looked forward to a few hours of painting in the afternoon.

Philip put down his can of beer and wiped his forehead.

"God it's hot out there." He paused. "Can't you help me just a little bit? I've been working out there for a couple of weeks now and you haven't even offered – except to help carry lumber up, I'll admit that. But that's all." His voice began to rise. "You haven't done anything but here you are living in the house. I've been taking off work, using up my vacation time, I'm out there every weekend sweating and you aren't doing anything. It isn't fair – it isn't right! Are you even my friend? What are you doing here? I'd like to know that, what are you doing here?"

She flushed. "I do pay rent," she began. "The other renters aren't helping either. It's your house, and your deck. I've tried to keep my hands off everything here. I understood why you wanted to have your own private empire, after feeling so ripped off by Concha, and I know it isn't my house and I don't have any share in it." She was half surprised to hear the hurt and anger in her words; she had prided herself on her ability not to be greedy. But she went on, pushed to self-justify.

"And after the deck there'll be other projects – they're endless. You want to shingle the whole house with redwood, and build a fence, and paint the trim, and solarize, and clear out the back yard and cart dirt from back there up to the front yard and dig terraces and – and it just keeps going on. So I'd give up painting for a few months now, and then it would be for just a few months more and a few months more, and so on and on. I do feel guilty when I see you out there working, but –"

"How can you say this isn't your house too?" he broke in. "Aren't you living here? Don't you think your being here is different from the other people's being here? Why are you always thinking in terms of mine and yours? Aren't we trying to share a life?"

He had hit a painful spot. She feared a tendency in herself to keep a narrow debit-credit sheet in her relationships, a too-careful marking of boundaries between mine and thine, with an emphasis on mine. She felt ashamed.

"Well yes," she said hesitantly, "I do think we are trying to share a life. But it's not all that straightforward. It's not as if I wasn't doing anything. Any shopping, cooking or cleaning that gets done around here, I do – plus babysitting the kids at all kinds of odd hours."

"Well that's your fault," he snapped. "Tell Kathleen she has to do her share. You shouldn't have to be doing everything. Well – I'm tired of this whole thing. It's clear you don't want to help me. Go and paint if that's what you want to do. I can't force you to do anything, that's clear! Just get out of my way!" and he headed out the back door.

"Wait a minute!" she said, on the verge of tears. "It's not fair! I didn't even want a deck! Why should I have to build it? It's not that I don't care about you!"

"Oh hell," he said gruffly, pausing in the doorway. "Don't worry about it." Another pause.

"I'm not that mad anymore. I guess we're both right. That's why it's so hard. It's true it's my project, not yours. Maybe it was unreasonable of me to expect you to help me."

She stood there a moment, still torn by the conflicting feelings: that she should help him; and that she should not have to give up her painting time. So she painted away in her upstairs room, playing her favorite records to block out the sounds of Philip's construction just below. She had begun working in water-color about a year earlier, and was finally beginning to get results. Her feelings were like unwillingly braided snakes, writhing and hissing with pent-up energy, unable to disentangle: anger, guilt, longing for freedom, longing for secure love and a nest. And yet the watercolors were light, unencumbered plant forms, fresh, simple, clear. She didn't know where they came from; it seemed a miracle to watch them emerge.

* * *

The Italian actor Marcello Mastroianni never struts. With hangdog grace, he enters his house after a long "business" trip on which he's actually played revolutionary politico, while enjoying plenty of casual sex on the side. He's a free man, and one hundred percent in charge at home, where his pale asexual wife has gradually become an invalid. But when the political game backfires, he must pretend to die – which in a sense he does, as he is confined to an apartment which he dares not leave, and from whose window he can see perfectly into his old house. Thus he can watch every day as his wife, believing herself to be a widow, gets out of bed, takes over the real business, and with the lessons of marriage inscribed on her brain, becomes completely untam-able. No one is going to trap her into another lifetime confined in the upstairs bedroom. Every day the husband gets to watch this transformation, and particularly, of course, the sexual delights enjoyed by his once-frigid wife. It is hard to dislike him, but all the same, clearly it serves him right.

The next morning Louise and Philip sat on the sunny, almost-completed deck, having breakfast.

"You know, Philip, there's something I'd like to talk about," she began, hesitant. "That movie started me thinking."

Philip did not let her go on. "Yes, that movie! You still have your lease on your apartment, don't you? You only sublet it?"

"Yes," she answered, "yes, and I've been thinking, Philip, would it be too awful if I moved back there? I'd still want to spend a lot of time with you, at least as much as before. But the situation here right now isn't good for me, really."

"You don't mind?" he said, obviously incredulous and relieved. "You know I still love you. I just feel too married this way. It's too soon. And I don't know – I still have to get over a lot of stereotype stuff. Part of me wants you in the kitchen all the time, cooking the meals, and serving me, all that old shit. But you're too independent, I understand that. It's just not working out. I'm not getting what I need, and I feel trapped. Can you understand? Is it all right?"

Louise nodded, though her initial relief was turning into something else. Had she and Philip seen the same film? She could never be the servant-wife Philip was describing. For her the movie said that the wife, deprived of agency and identity, withers away. And the husband, shut up in a house he can't leave, is reduced to mere envious voyeur. Louise, in returning to her apartment, would be released from Philip's expectation that her time and energy should mostly be devoted to him; her own life would be returning to her, shaped by her. Yet she would still love him, be glad to help him. For Philip, though, the movie had seemingly meant release from a stifling emotional bondage, into a life of complete sexual freedom. And offhand, Louise didn't see anything in that fantasy about "dancing girls" devotedly cooking meals or being continually on-call for house construction projects.

She paused a long moment, looking at the deck, aware of its sweet wood smell – the smell of guilt and resentment, for her. "Yes, it's all right."

Two days after Louise's move back into her old apartment, Philip had to go to England for a conference. He was to be gone nearly fifteen days.

* * *

Soon after Philip's departure, Louise invited Sylvia over for tea. Entering the small apartment, Sylvia looked around appreciatively.

"Wow," she said, "the view's fantastic. Not like my place out in the Valley. I mean, I'm glad, really glad, to have gotten this job, it's getting me started. But the Valley! It's like being in exile."

"Exile, hmmm?" Louise said, sitting down opposite Sylvia at the table by the window. "I think I know something about that."

Sylvia looked surprised. "What do you mean? You don't miss being at Philip's house do you? I thought you were so eager to move out!"

"I was, I was," Louise said, pouring the herb tea she had prepared. "And it was just wonderful to come back here and feel so free, and not feel guilty just because I wasn't doing everything Philip wanted or the house needed. But –" She hesitated. She could hardly believe, herself, how she felt. "You know he went to England a few days ago, and I'm really having trouble. I feel as if he's disappeared from the face of the earth, as if I'll never see him again. As if moving out was like saying the relationship was over, we couldn't be together, that the whole thing is a failure. As if I'll never see him again," she repeated.

"But he's coming back," Sylvia objected. "In two weeks, right?"

"Yes," Louise replied, smiling shakily. "I know. But somehow I can't believe that. Before Philip left I had this vision of our relationship just going on, forever I guess, with us living separately but getting together all the time and standing by each other in crises and all that. And then someday, in five or ten years, both of us earning more money and feeling more sure of our independence – eventually we would live together in his house, without other people around to complicate things – and sort of live happily ever after. Because we do still love each other, even after all this stuff lately. But now –"

"Seems to me," Sylvia said, "as if underneath you aren't that sure about the relationship. Otherwise, why would you be so worried now? But I guess you still love Philip."

Louise nodded.

"Sooo," Sylvia went on, "you love him but you aren't sure it'll work? You think what he wants and you want are, like, not compatible?"

"Maybe," Louise granted. "But after everything we've had together – I can't imagine living without Philip. The thought is just too painful."

"Hmmm," Sylvia said a little plaintively, "I thought you used to be more independent?"

"Maybe. I never felt this way before, as if I might never see him again. All we went through on that trip – and then not being able to live together. And now he's gone. Subconsciously I guess the message is that we've lost everything."

"So if it's that bad, why don't you just go back and do everything the way Philip wants, just like an old-fashioned wife? Then you can be together!" Sylvia smiled.

"I know, I can't. I keep thinking of Milton's Satan, in *Paradise Lost*, when he gets kicked out of heaven. He says, 'Better to reign in Hell than serve in Heaven.' I have to agree. I just can't give up everything. And yet it's terrible right now, with Philip gone –" Louise closed her eyes, shaking her head.

"Well look," Sylvia said. "Philip's coming back. He still loves you, right?"

Louise nodded. "I do think so."

"So why make trouble for yourself? And forget *Paradise Lost*."

"Yes, I know. But maybe the myth of romantic love in that course I taught, maybe it's like the myth of paradise. We have these overwhelming feelings of love, and it's so good and we want it to last peacefully forever and ever, but things keep happening and interfering and we want to do different things and we get mad at each other and yet –"

"And yet you still love each other," Sylvia finished her sentence for her. "Don't take this wrong," she said, reaching over and taking Louise's hand, "but I can't believe how hard you're making everything! Forget all this theory. I mean, you have Philip, you have your independence, you love each other – what else do you want?"

Louise could not help laughing, though some inadvertent tears squeezed out of her eyes at the same time.

"Oh, Sylvia," she sighed.

* * *

P hilip did indeed return to Berkeley. He arrived with presents in his suitcase, including a variety of "sexual aids." Louise longed to go to bed with Philip, to reunite, to be assured of his existence, to feel close to him again.

Instead she got mechanical toys. They seemed designed to return appetite to the jaded. They were also, she thought, surprised at this return of her German philosophy studies, ways for the will to objectify itself, to manipulate a dormant, disinterested body. Body and spirit were separated, strangers, as she and Philip now seemed to be. He had brought these things to be translators between the two of them. Yet not long before, they had been speaking directly.

The second night was no better. For the first time in their years together, neither one of them had any sexual desire for the other. Everything seemed false and artificial.

On the third day they met on campus, at Philip's suggestion. It was a warm, lovely afternoon that made her think of earlier days when they had come up to campus after their subterranean lunches. Everything had been so much simpler then, when it seemed that only external circumstance held them apart.

They walked a while, talking aimlessly, politely, boringly. Neither of them was engaged in the conversation. The words were like representatives they sent out to do their work for them, while their real selves were busy elsewhere.

"Want to sit on the grass for a minute?" Philip suggested, pointing to a shady spot close to the men's Faculty Club, where he had stayed when he first left Concha.

"Louise," he began, "there's something I have to tell you. At first I thought I wouldn't have to, but I know you know."

Her brows pulled together, puzzled and fearful. "I don't know, Philip. I thought maybe it was just the strain of my moving out. It was so terrible for me while you were gone – it seemed as if I had lost you forever. There was our trip – and then we had this bad thing, that we weren't happy living together, and then you went to England and suddenly it seemed as if you didn't exist anymore. You wouldn't believe what it was like. Or maybe you would. And I thought maybe that was the source of this strangeness between us now. I feel as if I haven't really seen you since you got back."

"I never could hide anything from you," he said. "There is something. But it's nothing for you to worry about – I want to tell you that before I begin. It's very important that you know that. Okay?"

"Okay," she said hesitantly, uncertain what she was agreeing to.

"Do you remember when I said, way back at the beginning, that I couldn't believe you were real? That you were a mirage, one of those beings that comes out of the woods at night and the man falls in love with her and thinks he's living a whole different life, and then she disappears back into the dark and he doesn't know any more what's real and what's a dream?"

Louise nodded, mute.

"When I was in London, it was sheer hell. You weren't there – it's like what you were saying – I felt as if you didn't exist anymore. God, I felt so alone! Like the last person in the universe. I felt as if I had lost everything. One night I went to a play, and Ilona and Jonathan were there, and they had this woman with them. At first I didn't pay much attention to her, I mean I wasn't attracted to her. She wasn't the type I usually like. She was short and plump and had brown hair, and she was even about five years older than me. Swiss. But we all had dinner together later and I realized I liked her – liked her a lot. I began to see her. For about five days, the whole time I was in London, we were together constantly. I guess – I fell in love with her. There were so many things about her. She had her own career, and was very well off – owned her own house in Switzerland. She had sophistication, she knew about wines, she had made it in the world. And then, she had an incredible story, a terrible life. She was the only one of her family to survive the German concentration camps." He paused. "Maybe that was why I fell in love with her. She's a wonderful person. You'd even like her."

She nodded, irritated. She probably would. Except for Concha, she liked most of the women Philip liked, though she would have ascribed different reasons for the liking.

"But I came back to you. I'm here. I don't know. Maybe I'll see her again some day. But it's over. We might write once in awhile. But she's in Switzerland, and you're here."

"Thanks," she said.

"I didn't have to tell you," he began.

She broke in. "If you hadn't, it would have been hard on the relationship – if that's what it is. It was either tell me or keep behaving like a zombie or the wonderful mechanical man."

Tears began coming out of her eyes. "It's one thing to be shaken up by the moving out and then the sudden separation. But to 'fall in love' – that's something else. It means giving yourself to this woman. It means –" she could hardly get the words out – "you thought at some level all the same things with her that you thought with me. Falling in love – that's a hope of forever, and it's exclusive. There is only that one other person then. How could you?"

She tried to control her tears. There were people occasionally going by on the path behind them. Maybe that was why Philip chose this semi-public place to speak out, she thought angrily. Coward.

"But I came back to you. Maybe it was just fantasy. I don't know if it could have lasted."

"Did you come back to me, or just to Berkeley and your job?"

"No, to you," he said.

"Well, you don't have to see me anymore," she said, mentally holding the hari-kari knife to her gut. "You're free. Maybe she'll come to Berkeley. In fact, it would be a lot better if she would. Maybe you wouldn't like her so much if you saw her every day and she became a real person. It's too hard to compete against this romantic fantasy woman, off in Switzerland."

"She's not coming here. Did I make a mistake in telling you? Remember we said we'd tell the other about anything important."

"You said that. You're the one who's felt this great need to play around."

"Can you say you haven't enjoyed the freedom sometimes too?"

Honesty silenced her. She had enjoyed some rather active window-shopping, though she had never actually gone out with anyone else.

Philip went on. "Can you accept this? It's over. And it's a tribute to how close I feel to you that I had to tell you."

She was silent, tears still running out of her eyes. She was desolated by the sense that he had been so loosely connected to her, that he could fly off to someone else so easily – that he was so weak, and that he had such faint trust in their love. Was their once-in-a-lifetime love really only one episode in an endless series of mere sexual infatuations?

"Please, don't make it too hard on me," he pleaded. Perhaps there was a shadow of a threat in that, too.

"Too hard? Do you expect me to listen calmly?"

"I know it's hard on you. But it's over. I'm here. Let's make the best of what we have."

A friend of his, whom Louise knew slightly, stepped over to them.

"Hi," she said cheerily. "What are you guys doing here?"

"Talking," Philip said in a neutral tone. She looked at them both. Although Louise's face was streaked with tears, the woman's expression did not change. Perhaps she really did not see. She wanted to talk about her new job.

"How are you doing?" Philip asked, drawing her on to talk.

"Okay. This commuting to Salt Lake is terrible." She smiled happily.

"The new job is worth it?"

"Yes, I guess so."

Louise stopped listening, concentrating instead on her own feelings. There was enormous hurt and shock. But there was also something else: she could not deny that once Philip had told her, she had felt a powerful sense of – relief. Why? Had she long expected this blow, and was it a relief to have the hanging sword finally descend? Or was it a relief to have the unreality broken, the estrangement of untruth which had engulfed them since Philip's return? The question distracted her, and when Philip had said goodbye to the intruder, Louise was calmer.

"Honey, you've got to forgive me. I felt as if you didn't exist anymore, as if you had left me forever and just disappeared. I was desperate. She was a wonderful person, but it's you I came back to."

Louise nodded, unable to speak, but no longer crying.

He saw the change.

"Come on, let's walk back to the house," he invited. "You don't have to forgive me all at once. I know it'll take time. Come on," he coaxed.

They rose from the damp grass, stained with its cold green. Half reluctantly, she allowed Philip to take her hand as they walked back uphill to the house, "with wandering steps and slow."

* * *

It was not that easy for Louise to forget; she found herself returning again and again to this center of pain. Meanwhile Philip, irritatingly, was busy. There was a new housemate moving in. There had been several attractive applicants for the spot left vacant by Louise, and it had been difficult for house members to choose. Finally, after repeated interviews, they had settled on a young graduate student in math. She was bright, pretty, and seemingly pleasant and responsible as well. Philip was disappointed to have had no men to choose from, but he had to admit also that it was easier for him with women.

"They're not territorial in the same way that men are," he said.

"You mean you think you can boss around the women more easily?" Louise prodded, curious.

"No, no, how can I think that after knowing you!"

"Mmm, very funny. Well, you did try to have it balanced, starting out with Bob. And of course there's still Jonathan."

"Yes – and he's not so easy either. Or he and Ilona, I should say. They're always so broke they don't want to spend any money on communal food. I don't want to live that way, and yet they don't like it if I go out and buy things or cook meals that cost something. Fish and pasta are okay, but once in a while I like a change. I can't stand the pettiness of counting every dime."

"Well, they really are poor right now. It's been a long time since you were that poor."

"That's just the thing! I'm not poor now, and I don't want to live that way. Sure, I remember what it was like not to have enough money for a beer – and I hate it. And I don't like it now if there's never any beer in the refrigerator, or any peanuts or anything extra at all. Besides, I told them before they moved in what they should expect to spend for food every month. They knew, and they said they could afford it. That's not right."

"It is a problem," she conceded, with perhaps a touch of schadenfreude, comfortably aware that, damn it, she had her own private apartment and could stock her refrigerator as she pleased. "It's too bad it would be so un-house-like to put aside a separate stash, with your name on it, bought out of your own private funds," she ventured.

"No, I don't like that at all. I want this to be like a shared home, not a rooming house. Well – I do have some peanuts in the bedroom bookcase."

When Jonathan and Ilona returned from England, they immediately approved of Jane, the new house member, and things seemed to return to the usual routine. Philip persuaded Ilona and Jonathan to spend a little more for food, and his own bookcase shelf grew crowded with nuts, M&M's, crackers, and a variety of liquors.

Meanwhile, Louise wrote a short story:

It was a calm afternoon, perhaps even too calm, though I was enjoying myself doing my work. It was quiet, though, I will say that, and maybe I was a little bored, doing the same thing I loved day after day. So when the doorbell rang, in the midst of this quietness, I was excited. I wasn't expecting anything.

I ran from my studio to the front door, patting my hair into order. But no one was at the front door. I closed the door and the bell rang again – ah, the back doorbell. But who would come that way? I rushed through the kitchen and there, behind the dimity curtain, I could make out a familiar face. I opened the door.

"Unhap!" I said, "What are you doing here? It's been a long time."

"Yes, I know," he said, in that low-pitched unconfident way he has, that always disarms me. "Yes," he said, "but you're always home to me, aren't you?" and he moved forward a bit, putting one pale bony elbow inside the door frame.

"Well, of course," I answered, "come on in. What's your news?" though in fact I wasn't entirely enthusiastic about seeing old Unhap. It's true that one's neurotic friends are often the most interesting – but they can also be difficult, difficult.

"Oh," he said, finding his place at the table, "nothing all that new. It's just that nothing ever really works out over the long run, you know?" And he thrust his yellow face out over his folded hands, propping himself with his elbows on the table. "I mean, look at you, one divorce, and Rolf one divorce – at least you two didn't make the mistake of marrying. I mean, who can you think of who's happy in a couple? Really, I mean, who can you think of?"

"Well," I answered carefully, "why all this emphasis on married couples? It's quite possible for an individual to be happy – and for two reasonably happy individuals to get together. Why not?"

"Why not," Unhap groaned, "why not? But who does, Mary, who does? And then you know what it's like alone, you're just a dried prune rattling in a big tin box, all alone, no one cares if you live or die, no one to tell your thoughts to, to eat pizza with and have a beer with and go do different things with and have real sex with and be warm next to you at night. That's why I feel so sorry for you, really I do."

"But what do you mean?" I said, somewhat irritated. "You know Rolf and I get along very well. VERY well," I added firmly.

"Aw come on Mary. You and I know better – we know Rolf is restless being tied to one woman. And before you he always liked more glamorous types, too. You aren't exactly a fashion page, you know. And don't you think it's tiresome, the way you're always moralizing about how high heels cripple women and hair sprays get in your lungs and all that? Rolf likes that stuff on women – you know that. And what about you? You hate being told what to do. After all, you ran your life very well before Rolf came along to tell you when to blow your nose and what kind of conversation you should have with your friends and telling tall tales to blow up his ego and all those things – I know you hate all that stuff, don't you? I'm so sorry for you, Mary."

He clasped my hands across the table.

"But Unhap," I said, looking away, "there are always ways that people irritate each other. And I get so much with Rolf – the good far outweighs the bad."

"Mary, Mary," he said, caressing my hands and moving around the table to sit beside me, "you know Rolf can't stand the way you always have opinions on everything. You do always think you're right, now, don't you? Admit it," he whispered, kissing my hair. "Admit it. You know he's going to leave you, don't you? Sooner or later – when you're a little more wrinkled, a little less quick on your feet – come on . . ." His breath was warm on my face. Then we were kissing and I knew I wanted him. Like conspirators we ran to the basement bedroom, where the sun wouldn't come in and spoil our fun.

Unhap has a big member, of which he is very vain, and I loved unwrapping him from his clothes. We stretched out together, our bodies both warm, skin-sensitive. And yet, after a long foreplay, I still couldn't come. It was terrible, hovering on the brink, keyed up like a spring, and no relief. Unhap is super conscientious and he rubbed me and rubbed me until my skin was sore and red and still I couldn't come. It was awful, and he kept whispering, "I'm so sorry for you, Mary, really, what can I do?" and rubbing away at the poor chafed skin.

This could have gone on indefinitely – I couldn't end it; my skin might have disappeared and left horrible flayed flesh and I might have bled to death into the cushions except that then we heard footsteps overhead.

"Oh," I said, "it's Rolf! Quick, get dressed, hide – no, get out – quick!" and I rushed on my clothes and smoothed my hair and ran upstairs.

"Hi Rolf," I said as calmly as possible, though the sight of him was awful just then; my body was still coiled around that unsatisfied wanting, and the sight of this man whom I loved and would probably lose was like a cut into my gut.

"Hey, Mary, what's wrong?" Rolf came over and looked me closely in the eye, concerned, his hand on my shoulder.

"Oh, just worrying about my work, a little down," I lied, and my tension was flowing out of me into his arm. I could see it discharge like electricity in the air behind his head. "So what happened about the theater tickets?"

And under Rolf's voice I listened for the sounds of my treasonous lover, leaving by one secret door or another. There was certainly some shuffling around downstairs, but then gradually it got quiet again and I was able to focus properly on Rolf.

So, I suppose old Unhap did leave – but I'm not entirely sure. This house is a big one. He could still be hiding out somewhere. It's like having roaches. You go down in the morning into the kitchen, there's a calm early sun smoothing over the clean surfaces, everything is in order from the night before, you make your coffee and sit down at the table. You take the lid off the lovely blue and white sugar bowl, and suddenly, there it is, crouching brown and ugly among the clean fresh cubes.

* * *

P hilip found a new outlet for his energies: training for a marathon that was coming up the following spring, in eight months. That was approximately long enough to train properly, he estimated. Louise was still running every weekday after work, and it seemed logical enough to start extending her runs, to keep up with Philip and run the marathon with him. Jonathan was interested, also, and the three of them began to go to the shorter races scheduled locally on weekends.

Philip was pleased to have Jonathan along. "I'm still looking for more men friends," he said one morning as he and Louise lay in bed. "Hugh is a loyal friend when you need something – an extra hand for moving a piece of furniture, say – but he's too flaky. I can never depend on him. If I call him for lunch and he says yes, he may not ever show up. He does that too often. It depends on whether he can find someone more prestigious for lunch. That's bad enough, but he doesn't even call to let me know he's not coming. I'm cultivating some other men, like Jim, for instance, the one who teaches chemistry. But it's not as easy as you might think. Most men don't really seem to have male friends. They have wives and family and their job. It's hard to find men who are interesting and have something to say and – I don't know – have some warmth, and can open up. I'm still jealous of you with your women friends. I know that Sylvia has gone off to the boonies for that teaching job, but you still have Deirdre and that woman painter you like so much – Masha – and these people you have lunch with at work. Maybe something will develop between Jonathan and me. We'll see. I don't like to be too dependent on you."

"Well," she said, turning her back into his side, "you seem to be doing all right that way."

"Come on, Lou, you know I'm still here for you," he answered, curling around her warmly. She felt his body, almost like a temptation she needed to resist – a temptation not of sex, but of a love which she was still almost afraid to believe in.

* * *

Yet gradually she was returning to herself. That was what it felt like: not so much a forgetting of Philip's weakness in London, but rather, simply, a return of her belief in herself and her own life. Her half-time job was easy now; she knew what to do and there were no anxious questions. Her German-born boss – "David" now – suggested, in a kind grandfatherly way, that sometime they should have a beer together and address each other as "du," the way friends would. And at home, painting was going well; the more time she put into it, the more it thrived.

She was having coffee with Masha at the Café Med, when a good-looking man moved over to their table, hailing Masha as an old friend. Soon all three were in a spirited conversation. He had interesting ideas. Moreover, when Louise talked, she felt pleasantly heard. She found she liked this man – Harry Davis. They went to dinner together. Then they went to his house for a drink.

He had a roommate so they went to his bedroom for privacy. They sat on his bed and talked. The room was untidy and not very clean. Louise thought it would be distasteful to walk barefoot across that floor. He earned a living doing photography, and wanted to make movies. He had wanted to for years. He was 44 and Louise thought perhaps he would want to for many more years before he stopped talking about it and moved to other topics – possibly, how certain persons or certain government policies or certain bad luck had prevented his realizing his genius for the cinema.

Yet he was more like her, she thought, than Philip. She too, without Philip, was merely an aspiring artist, living poor, with little likelihood of financial success or fame, on the edges of things and deliberately choosing that place. It was such people who gave Berkeley its particular flavor: people choosing art or intellect or a certain non-materialistic quality of life. Money and success might or might not come, but these were secondary, and not worth sacrificing your life for. Maybe they were even rather suspect: too much success could easily corrupt, make spiritually lazy and dishonest. And there was also the question of how success had been acquired. Had anything important been taken from someone else? There was general agreement that having more, in general, was not fair or just. The possibility that anyone could actually envy the rich and powerful was not much discussed, in Louise's experience.

At the moment Harry was working on a book, based on various women friends' sexual fantasies. He had carefully recorded each interview, and Louise sat awhile on Harry's bed as they listened to several. After each interview he had recorded his ideas about what the woman wanted, and – possibly different – what he thought she actually needed. Soon Harry's warm body came closer to Louise's in the cold and cluttered room. Wouldn't she like to participate in his book?

A little bit tempting. She was not too involved here, she was safe. She could have a nice warm sexual time and confide her most inane inconsequential thoughts and still be considered interesting.

But a sense was growing in her, like the feeling of being too full after dinner. She didn't want any more. She didn't want to cross the dirty floor with her feet bare. She didn't want to become a case study. She didn't want the clutter. Giving Harry a quick apologetic kiss, she leapt off the bed and took off. Outside in the cool night air, freedom and her bicycle were waiting for her. And Philip too, whatever that meant.

* * *

It was a Thursday night, and she was working with particular gusto. Finally, exhausted and satisfied, she went to bed. At two in the morning, the phone rang. She found it easily, the room being, as always, bright from the powerful parking lot lights outside her window. She thought it must be a wrong number – as much as she could think at all through her interrupted dreams.

"Hello?" she mumbled crossly.

"Louise. It's me. God, baby, I just was in a terrible car accident. I'm okay – not really hurt, just shaken up, but it was close. The car is totaled. You almost lost me tonight."

She suppressed the answer which came immediately to mind: So what else is new? "Really?" she said out loud.

"I was coming home from one of the disco classes in San Francisco. I had just stopped at an intersection, and this car came barreling along. I couldn't believe it when I saw him start coming right at me, fifty miles an hour. I guess my foot released the clutch, or maybe I did it on purpose, I don't know, but my car went forward a few inches before he hit. His car hit squarely just two inches behind my head. He kept going. I'd had my seat belt on but I found myself on my hands and knees beside the car, outside it. He'd popped the whole car open like a can."

"Good grief," she said, moved in spite of herself. "Are you really all right?"

"Yes, I think so. Maybe I'll go have my back looked at tomorrow just to be sure, but I think I'm okay. I'm really shaken up. Suddenly I could have died. It's already changed me. It's putting things in perspective, about what's important. I wish you were here. I'm at home now. They have the guy. He was drunk. He almost killed me but it's only a misdemeanor. Can you believe it? He had no insurance and no money, and he was allowed to be out there driving. He's free. He could go out and do it again and kill someone tomorrow night. He would have driven onto the freeway going the wrong direction after hitting me – that's where he was headed – but then his car died before he could go on. Can you believe it?" he repeated.

She did not reply. She knew he wanted her to come up to the house and be with him, but she was still too angry. She couldn't make it that easy for him, to turn her on and off like a light switch.

Philip did not seem to notice her silence; his words poured out at her. "I'll be all right. Go back to bed now, and I'll try to get some sleep too. I'll probably take a sleeping pill – and I'll see you tomorrow night. I just had to talk to you. I love you, babe. Goodnight."

"Goodnight," she whispered softly into the receiver. Then, closing the door on her feelings, she went back to bed, and slept.

* * *

Philip was all right, though the doctor insisted he have full x-rays of his spine just to be sure. It seemed as if the accident really had changed him, though she was slow to believe it.

"Home seems more important to me now," he said one Sunday evening as they were finishing off dinner and the pitcher of beer at Pedro's. "And a quiet life. The idea of chasing after dancing girls doesn't seem very appealing now. Not that I ever actually did it, once we were together; but I used to want the freedom to do it if I wanted to. I think I'm closer to settling down now than I have been in these three years we've known each other. I think I could be very happy, just doing my research, singing in the university chorus, and being with you. I begin to see now what's really important to me instead of what was just some story about what you're supposed to want if you're a man. I'm feeling so lucky to be alive, and with you. And my work is going really well."

He had recently been given a tenured position as Senior Scientist, an honor at his relatively young age. It partly made up to him the bitterness of having been denied tenure as a professor; and while he had enjoyed teaching, research was his love. Louise could not help feeling they were entering a new period of calm and happiness. Carefully, as she might have entered a very hot bath, she allowed herself to feel this new warmth, bit by bit immersing herself in it.

She leaned back in her chair, allowing Philip to refill her beer mug.

"Something weird is happening in the house, though," he said. "It started with Jane not doing her share of the house chores. Just as you'd think, everything that Ilona signed up to do got done, on time, and really well. If she says she's going to wash the front windows, they really sparkle. If Kathleen says she'll do something, well, maybe a week or two later she'll do part of it, or do something else like carve a pumpkin for the front steps on Halloween. At least it's a contribution to the house, though she is still sort of a slacker. But Jane – she thinks it's pure meanness on my part if she's expected to do anything at all. After all, she's a poor over-worked graduate student, right? And her time is so valuable – more valuable than any of ours, apparently. And she's so poor, she can't afford the luxury, as she calls it, of decent food. So she gets together with Ilona and Jonathan and they kvetch about money and Ilona feels sorry for poor little Jane and they all look at me as I were some kind of monster.

"Jonathan gets on his Berkeley high horse and says I should do more than the others because I own the house and they're paying rent to help me own it, so I get all the benefit. It's a kind of mushy Marxism. What he really means is he wants things reversed: *he* would like to own the house. God! I pay more than all of them combined each month, including taxes and insurance plus the mortgage. And I have all the responsibility. And I put extras in all the time, like the new food processor, and the new fireplace screen, and they all benefit from it. But I'm to blame for everything!"

"What about Kathleen? Is she part of this?" Louise asked.

"No, thank god, she isn't taking sides as far as I can tell. It's Jane who's the trouble-maker. If she doesn't shape up she's got to go. She's poisoning the whole group."

Louise poured him some beer from the pitcher.

"What about the running? Are you still running with Jonathan?"

"Not as much. He pushes himself too hard and keeps getting injuries. He always has to be ahead, but he hasn't trained long enough for that. I don't try to compete. I run against the clock, and according to the schedule I've set up. But Jonathan – he's younger, and more insecure. He's still trying to prove something. He pulled a muscle so badly that he hasn't been able to run for the whole past week."

Philip leaned forward now, his elbows on the table. "Sometimes I think of changing the house, turning the back half into a separate apartment. I could get about the same amount of income from that as I do from house-sharing."

"I guess this shared house isn't too much like a second family," Louise commented in a carefully neutral tone.

"It's awful, at least right now. I'll wait and see. It wouldn't be until next summer, but I'm thinking about it."

Louise nodded. "I can imagine – you'd get rid of the hassles and still have the income."

"More space for you then," Philip smiled.

"Maybe."

Philip took her hand across the table. As so often, she could feel a warmth radiating from him – not an actual physical warmth, but some psychological equivalent.

"Well, it's too early to think about now," he conceded, "but I'm changing, Lou, I'm really changing." He put his other warm hand around hers. "We have time. I want us to have . . ." He didn't finish his sentence.

She squeezed his hands without replying. Like Philip, she could not bring herself to put her hopes into words, and there was no need for it. They both knew.

"I'm glad you're coming home with me tonight," he went on. "You won't believe this, but it's hard to face the other people there by myself."

When they walked into the house, Jonathan, Ilona, and Jane were at the dining room table. Conversation ceased as Philip and Louise went by. No one looked up or greeted them.

"You see what I mean?" Philip asked grimly as they got upstairs. "And this is my own house."

"I think maybe you should try talking to Ilona. She likes an underdog. If you let her know how it feels from your side, she might try to change things. Right now she's all full of sympathy for poor Jonathan with his money problems, and for poor Jane because you think she should do her fair share of house work. But if you could make Ilona feel a little sorry for you, she might shift the balance some."

"Easily said," Philip commented irritably.

"It's true, easy to give advice. But it might be worth trying."

"You've got tomato sauce on your face," Philip pointed out, and turned on the TV.

* * *

It was some weeks later that Louise got a phone call from her mother. Her mother's voice was small and weak. "Louise, this morning Daddy died. He died in his sleep."

Louise sat down on the floor, clutching the phone. "I'll be home right away, Mother," she said. "Today."

Within a few hours she had gotten a plane ticket home. When she knew the departure time, she phoned Philip.

"Do you want me to go back with you?" he asked. "If you need me to, I will, Lou."

"Oh," she said, her voice surprising her by its shakiness, "I think I'll be all right. And maybe it would be a good thing to be alone with Mother and my sister." She paused, trying to think. "But I will be at your house to pick up some things there, and then I'll need a ride to the airport. Can you meet me at the house at two o'clock?" She realized that she could count on him; she did not even have to ask.

The house was empty when she got there, and after finishing her packing, she played the piano softly, thinking of her father. A little before two o'clock, Philip came in. Without a word, he folded her in his arms.

"I told you I'd be here when your parents died," he said, stroking her hair. "I'll be here when your mother goes, too. I know how terrible that will be for you. You'll never have to face it alone the way I did. And if you change your mind about being by yourself back there, phone me up and I'll come to be with you."

He held her for several minutes while she cried. She felt almost safe in that warm circle.

But back at her parents' house, things were different. Her father's death had opened the door to all kinds of demons, restless angry remnants of the past, who now dominated the household. Ellen, Louise's older sister, had arrived first, and had quickly managed to take over their mother, who was cast as the weak, helpless, but honored parent. Louise, on the other hand, was cast as the ne'er-do-well who deserved no voice in the proceedings.

Grief could not be expressed in Ellen's presence; her pointedly fixed smile denied the possibility of such self-indulgence. Their mother acquiesced in these scripts, and had her own going at the same time.

The second night that Louise was home, her mother came up to her in the hallway as both were going to bed. "I'm so sorry you don't have anyone," she said. "And you don't have a home." She kissed Louise on the cheek.

"But I do have someone, Mother – Philip. Just because we aren't married doesn't mean we don't love each other."

She did not acknowledge Louise's words. "You have no home, no place to put things if I should die," she went on. "And you seem to be wasting your life out there in California. You have so many talents, dear, and it seems as if you aren't using them."

"But I am – I'm painting. And I'm not bad at it and I intend to get better."

"Well, it seems as if you're just throwing your life away. Your sister feels the same way – she says so all the time. Why don't you get a full-time job, doing anything? If only you had a home, darling, some security."

Louise was unsure where to begin. "I'm fine, Mother. And Philip and I love each other, we really do. And painting is my life, it's what I want. I'm really all right."

"Good night, dear," she said, kissing Louise's other cheek.

Louise began to feel alone. Her mother's and sister's faces seemed barely to register her presence. Neither of her allies was there: not Philip, and not her father, whose favorite she had been; his big easy chair sat empty in the living room, facing the blank TV set.

As the interminable week went on, family friends helped them avoid their feelings by taking them out for nearly every lunch and dinner. Conversations were intelligent, kind, and neutral. If someone inadvertently asked Louise what she did in Berkeley, the answer always led to the end of the conversation, with a polite smile and "Oh, a half-time secretary and, did you say, a painter? How nice!" In a dream she lived through the week, able to breathe only when she left the house for a run by the snowy lake, surprised to find her legs still strong beneath her.

* * *

Returning to Berkeley, she knew that Philip would be there to meet her at the airport. And how she needed him, almost as if to confirm her existence. She rushed off the plane. The crowd of passengers surged into the crowd of welcomers; all dispersed down the hallways; and Louise stood alone in the great cold lobby. Philip was not there.

She stifled the panic in her heart, and rushed to the luggage claim area. Maybe he had come late and gone there. No Philip, though she combed the crowds. Back to the gate where the plane had unloaded. Still no Philip.

Something inside of her turned. Of course he had not come. As her mother had suggested, he did not really care. They were not together. He hardly existed, even though he had phoned her several times during the week at home. She was alone. Steeling herself, she investigated the return limousine service and picked up her suitcase. She would find her way out somehow; but her eyes were hazed over with tears.

Suddenly the door inside her turned again. Surely Philip would come, had intended to come. She phoned the house and got Ilona. "I'm sure he left for the airport to pick you up. I don't know how long ago. Maybe 45 minutes?"

Louise wavered between the strangeness of the past week, that separate world insisting her world did not – and should not – exist; and the sense that Philip did love her, that their love, however battered, was real and strong.

A voice, half incoherent with static, came over the loud-speaker system: "Louise Borgstrum, pick up a white telephone." She felt like Alice in Wonderland. Obediently she picked up the first white telephone. It was Philip.

"Thank god I found you," he said. "I phoned the airport this morning and they told me your plane would be delayed an hour."

"No, it even came in early I think," she said, trying to keep her voice from quavering.

"Meet me at the Northwest ticket counter," Philip com-manded.

Soon they were driving home in Philip's old green VW, while she told him about the past week. He was surprised: he had expected to hear about her father. But her father had slipped away from her, lost in the power struggles of the living.

"Well, Lou," he said, trying to comfort her, "they're both very far away. You can forget them."

She smiled at the simplicity of this. "Well, at least I don't ever have to see both of them at the same time again. I can see Mother when she's not tempted by my sister into being a mindless prude who pretends not to know what consenting adults do together in bed; and I can see my sister when she's not competing with me for ownership – as she sees it – of Mother. And Mother –" she paused, almost unable to say something so painful, "Mother kept insisting that you didn't exist, that there was nothing between us, and then when you weren't there just now, it was sort of as if –"

"Lou!" Philip exclaimed. "You mustn't doubt me! Don't you know how much you mean to me?" He turned to look at her so long that she began to be afraid they would crash into someone; her eyes darted to the highway but then back, where Philip's eyes, intensely green, held her. Then he grabbed her hand and returned his gaze to driving the car, shaking his head.

"Lou, Lou," he said, "don't you know?"

* * *

There was a possibility that Louise might get a small house of her own. The family lawyer had suggested that her mother might want to give her sister and her each a large sum of money now to avoid inheritance taxes later. The possibility was exciting; it seemed Louise's only chance ever to have a place of her own, because house prices were rising so quickly that in a year or two it would be impossible for an ordinary person to afford one.

"So you might get a place of your own, Lou," Philip smiled. "Lady of the manor! I bet you'd change, you'd get even more impossible. I suppose then I'd have to start spending as much time at your house as you do at mine. What a pain!"

"You'd be surprised what a nuisance it is," she replied truthfully.

"So now you have to decide what kind of dream house you want," Philip continued, more seriously. They both knew she would not be able to afford anything very fancy, but it would be a beginning, a foothold in a quickly-moving real estate market; and it would be a kind of security she had not had before.

"I'll figure out what I would need and write Mother," she said. "She's out visiting Ellen right now –" she broke off at Philip's quizzical look. "Yes, Ellen pressed her hard to come stay with her for a while. I offered too, but as Mother pointed out, it's easier for her to stay right in the house with Ellen and Swede and the children. And she says she's going mostly to see the children. It's the last year they'll all be at home together, before the two oldest ones go off to college. At least, that's the rationale. Don't ask me. I should think it would be good for her to be around people, a whole household. I can't imagine that Ellen would try to turn her against me or anything."

"Maybe," Philip answered in a doubtful tone. Louise knew he was remembering a day spent with Ellen a year or so earlier, when Ellen's arrogance and condescension had made Philip vow never to spend another moment with her.

When Louise had figured out what she thought she would need, she wrote a long letter to her mother, describing the advantages and assuring her at the same time that she would understand if her mother preferred not to make the gift.

The following Sunday her mother phoned.

"I got your letter, dear. You know, I just don't feel I can give up so much money. It just wouldn't leave enough for me to live on."

"Oh, don't worry, Mother," Louise answered, eager to reassure her, and feeling rather guilty, greedy, for even having proposed it. "That's fine. I just thought when the lawyer suggested it, I should speak up and check it out with you, and do it in the six months' time the law would allow for such a gift. But of course I certainly don't want you to feel pinched, in any way. So that's just fine. I won't mention it again."

Her mother went on, a bit doggedly. "Well you know, even if I could afford it I don't think Daddy would have wanted me to do it. You know he didn't want to give you girls as big a birthday present as usual last year and the year before because of what your sister said – that she doesn't need it, the way she and Swede earn so much – and we felt you didn't deserve it because you weren't working hard enough, and after all that education, too." She went on with local news about the weather and the neighbors. Louise was too dumbfounded to interrupt. Her mother closed with protestations of love.

The next week her mother phoned again. Louise had spent much of the week in silent debate with her, but had ended by not wanting to confront her too aggressively. After all, her father's death had upset her mother's whole life, and it was understandable if she was less than rational.

"Mother," she began carefully, "I don't have any problem with your deciding not to fund a house for me. The only thing that bothers me is this business about my not being 'deserving.' After all, I've been self-supporting since I left home, including all through graduate school, and I haven't done anything shameful that I'm aware of. Of course Philip and I are not married, but millions of people have close relationships these days without benefit of law."

"Oh, I didn't say you were not deserving, darling. It was only Daddy. You know he didn't understand why you would want to paint when you could be a teacher. But I don't see why you don't get a full-time job – at anything, even being a secretary."

"I work half time to support myself, Mother, and the rest of the time I'm working at painting. There's nothing wrong with that."

"Well, when I was studying at the Art Institute in Chicago, I saw that artists usually have terrible lives, even when they're good. And most of them aren't, you know."

"So I should do what you did? Give up art, get married, and have children?"

"Not necessarily. But I certainly don't see why you can't work eight hours a day."

Louise began to dread her mother's phone calls, and sometimes avoided them by being out on weekends, or even unplugging the phone. When she went running, her legs carrying her along the wooded trails, she saw nothing. Her mind was filled with replies to her mother, the things she could not bring herself to say.

Philip's reaction was merciless: he was too angry at the grief Louise's mother was causing her. "Don't argue with her, Lou. You can never win. You'll never convince her. Don't waste time thinking about her." Then he softened, remembering, perhaps, that she had felt close to her mother before. "Wait it out. She's been under terrible stress. Maybe she'll come around. And you aren't alone, you know. Have I told you lately that I love you?" He put his arms around her, pulling her in to his warmth.

* * *

L ate one night at Philip's house, after sleeping a few hours, Louise had a strange dream. She had – in her dream – gone to the bathroom down the hall, and had sat down on the toilet. As she sat there, two or three old men came walking in. They seemed to be from another time, perhaps fifty or more years ago. They were "gentlemen," used to bossing others and having the run of things. They had walked in on her by accident, but seemed threatening nonetheless. Alarmed, she used a weapon she guessed would work.

"How could you just walk in on a woman this way!" she exclaimed with indignation. "Have you no sense of decency at all?" The old men, looking confused, turned awkwardly out into the hall again.

Still uneasy, however, she woke up. Philip was not beside her in the bed. She got up and went out into the hall. Philip was in Jo-Jo's room, tucking him into bed, stroking his forehead and evidently comforting him.

Philip waited to talk until they got back into their own bedroom, and had closed the door. "You won't believe this, Lou," he said excitedly, "the most terrifying thing just happened. I was lying there sleeping and this old man, dressed in old-fashioned clothes, stood over me. I looked at him for a minute and then he reached down and started to put his hands around my throat. He was trying to kill me. There's absolutely no doubt of that. But I fought him off – I fought him off with every bit of strength I had. When he saw I wasn't going to give in, he gave up – I guess he left – I don't know. I just lay there a minute afterwards, catching my breath. By then I was wide awake, so I got up and went down the hall to the bathroom to take a pee, and passing Jo-Jo's room, I saw that he had his lights on. So I went in and there he was, hiding in his bed, holding a knife, scared to death and ready to defend himself. He said an old man opened his bedroom door and seemed to be looking for someone. I don't know how he got out of bed and turned on the lights but he's terrified. He thought he could fight off the old man with the knife. What a kid! But I think maybe he'll have to sleep in here with us tonight."

"Wait, Philip, I have something too."

"You too?" he said, his eyes opening wide.

After the dreams, the house was quieter. There were no more intrusions from the past, no more mysterious rustlings or strange presences. The house was no longer haunted, as if the ghost from that earlier time had done as much as he dared – or perhaps accomplished all he wanted – and departed, leaving them in seeming peace.

* * *

It was only a week later that Philip phoned Louise at her place – an unusual thing for him to do, because he prided himself on not asking her for contact on nights when they were supposed to be independent.

"Well kid, brace yourself," he said. "I think it's the end of the shared house. I still can't believe it. You know Jonathan has been under a lot of pressure lately in his work, but this – there's no excuse for it. It's too much for him that I have the house, that my job is secure, and that I have you. Oh, and the food thing again. He can't dictate to me who I can have in the house and what I can and can't eat. And he's got Ilona and Jane on his side again. It's not workable. They have to go. All of them, so I can just make a separate apartment to rent out, in the back of the house. My wonderful shared house," he added ruefully.

"It is sad," Louise said. "It was a good experiment. And it did work for awhile."

"Yes – a while," Philip said a bit wistfully. "And I won't have the house back for a while. It'll take a few months for everyone to find a new place."

"Well, at the beginning, when you first bought the house, you said you'd like to have a place all your own."

She could hear the amusement in Philip's voice. "Independence, Lou! Handed to me on a platter!"

* * *

They were spending more and more of their time running. Louise had never returned to the martial arts after her illness and abortion the previous year; she had been too exhausted. Now she was building herself up in a single field, organizing her energy carefully to be fit for the marathon in May. They were continually tired, but their distances and times improved. The winter rains, with the dirt trails turned to mud, did not stop them. It was cool and private then, running along the wooded trails through mists and bad weather that kept most people at home. Running gradually took over their lives. Three or four days of the week, Louise put her spare time into running. Much of the rest of the time she felt tired, or had errands to do. Painting got squeezed, though she could still keep up a basic momentum. Meanwhile she and Philip enjoyed the necessity of eating more. Louise also drank more at dinner time, as the wine seemed even more delicious than usual with the food. Philip, however, had a different reaction.

"I've gotten so healthy," he boasted, "that I don't even like to drink as much as I used to. It just doesn't taste good anymore." Louise felt a little gross in comparison, drinking a second or even third glass of wine at nearly every dinner. Formerly it had been the other way around: Philip would order a whole bottle of wine at dinners out; she would drink one glassful, and the bottle would be empty when they left.

She didn't worry about Philip's new disinterest in wine, because he was doing so well with the running. He had gone far beyond her in speed and distances covered, and both were running to places they'd previously thought could be reached only by car, or maybe by bicycle on an ambitious day. It changed their idea of distances, and gave them a feeling of power.

* * *

The marathon was set in the redwoods, about two hundred miles north of San Francisco. They figured that even if they had to walk part of the course, it would at least be beautiful.

Louise was nervous, and did not feel very well. Her stomach was giving her trouble.

"Do you feel run down, Lou?" Philip asked jocularly.

"Ho-ho. Too appropriate, I'm afraid. The eight months of training seems to have been fine for you, but not quite enough for me. I could have used another two or even three months."

"Could be, could be. You've been running forty-five miles a week?"

"Yes. It's not fair – you've been running sixty and you feel fine!"

Philip was silent, obviously trying to find a reason for the discrepancy. Sex difference was not a reason he would accept, and Louise didn't like to challenge his gallant assumption that they were equal physically as well as intellectually.

"You've just got a touch of a cold," he reasoned. "By next week, when we actually run the marathon, you'll probably be feeling good again."

They packed their best running gear, choosing as carefully as if they were to make their debut before the Queen. They went up a day early, to attend a series of classes at the local community college. There they watched films of people making running shoes, showing the stress that running exerted on feet and skeleton. A remarkably elastic woman told them they should all spend at least two hours a day stretching. And a physician assured them that they would never die of anything, except maybe cancer, the one thing a marathon had not yet been shown to prevent. In the evening there was a communal spaghetti feed, to stoke up on carbohydrates.

Afterwards they went back to their motel, a small musty cabin set amongst the redwoods.

"Shall we see what's on TV?" Philip suggested.

"How about just going to bed? Though I don't know if I can sleep. I'm too keyed up."

"Why don't you come over here?" Philip leered from bed. "I know how to make you sleep."

"What? Before the marathon? Use up your vital juices? Not to mention mine." Her stomach was grinding uneasily, though she did not feel actually sick.

"Come on," Philip said, grinning, "I'll keep you warm all night, I promise."

"And not take all the covers?" she asked suspiciously, coming closer.

"Aha!" Philip grabbed her robe and pulled her into bed.

* * *

M orning came. She could not avoid it. They had to run. In the chilly room, lit by a dim light bulb, they pulled on their shorts and t-shirts and super-padded running shoes. She was nervous, her mouth dry, her stomach tight. Philip was all happy business, planning the day.

"Let's go, let's go," he said, standing at the door while Louise tried to decide whether or not to take her windbreaker.

"You won't need that," he decided for her. "Let's go."

The race was to be on a 26.2 mile stretch of old highway, winding through the enormous trees and following a small river for the last six miles. Louise tried to calm herself with the thought that it would, as they'd thought, be beautiful, and a fine place even to walk, if that should prove necessary. They arranged to meet at the car afterward, since of course Philip would come in before her. But she might see him on the last six miles, where the path doubled back and the slower ones would see the faster ones coming from the opposite direction.

Her race was fairly predictable. The first eighteen miles were fine, though she still felt dragged-out, as she had felt for several weeks before. But after mile eighteen she began to feel queasy. A chance running companion talked about travels in India and Nepal. She evoked the scent of hot straw, dust, the people, the people everywhere, sweating under the sun. Louise talked about their long journey across that continent, and the fear of sinking into it as into a hot mud bath that would weigh them down, trap them, decay them. The more they talked of India, the more anxious her body became. Pretty soon her bowels forced her to start making detours into the woods, and her companion finally ran on ahead. Louise grew feverish and felt truly sick. There was no choice: she had to alternate walking and running in order to finish at all. She looked at the trees and river, trying to appreciate them, reassuring herself that she was here, not in India. Nearly everyone else in the race ran past her. She had seen Philip an hour or so earlier, running in the opposite direction, going fast, but his face showing a degree of pain she had never seen there before. Still, he had waved cheerily.

She managed to run across the finish line. She did it in obscurity, since most people had already left. She picked up her t-shirt and her official time: five hours and eleven minutes, a long time to be pushing her body so hard. But she did not feel terrible. Her fever soon went away, and all she felt was some stiffness. She began to feel pretty good. After all, she had done it.

Philip found her at the car, sitting on the ground, drinking water.

"I almost qualified for the Boston!" he said, excited. "How do you feel, Lou? I waited and waited for you at the finish line and finally went to get some orange juice. Are you all right?"

"Fine – but I did terribly. Five hours and eleven minutes!"

"Not bad at all. Just think, how many people could even crawl 26.2 miles? Come on, let's go back and shower and get into some clothes."

They were high for hours, discussing their performances, wondering if they would ever want to do it again. They headed towards the coast for a few days of vacation, and checked in at a rather luxurious motel. They spent the evening drinking vegetable juices, eating – they were down some twenty-six hundred calories, they figured – and watching TV. Finally winding down, they opened the windows, to hear the ocean waves crashing in the near distance, and breathe the fresh ocean air.

But Louise could not sleep: she itched. It was not poison oak nor poison ivy. She knew what they looked like too well. Whatever it was, she had picked it up when she had had to squat in the woods, relieving her body of anxiety and India. Perhaps it was a herbicide sprayed into the forests, or some kind of insect bite. Whatever it was, she itched and swelled and was shortly in such agony that she filled the bathtub with ice water and lay in it most of the night, replenishing it with cold water as her body heated it up.

She could not help but disturb Philip, since the bathroom gave directly on the room where he lay, trying to sleep. But he did not complain, though sleep was what they both most badly needed after their exertion. At dawn he drove her into the nearest town with a hospital, for emergency treatment.

"Don't worry," he said, "I'll take care of you."

It must have been a long vacation for him, she later thought. They had perfect weather, unseasonably warm for the coast. Spring flowers were out, and there were few other tourists as they walked along the bluffs or down on the beaches or through brilliantly green fields. But she was drugged during the daytime, and at night still resorted to the bath of icy water, the pain of being cold less than the agony of itching. Philip put up with it all, stoic; and she felt, through the haze of antihistamines, the warm security of his love.

Perhaps because of this lack of rest when they so needed it, they were both quite tired when they returned home. They dragged around, and pampered their uncooperative stomachs and heavy bodies. This state continued on, week after week. Louise did not worry, but to her surprise, Philip did.

"I feel there's something seriously the matter with me," he said about a month after the marathon, in June. They were lying warmly in bed in the morning, as usual, fifteen or twenty minutes before they had to get up, enjoying the closeness of the time together. "I have an appointment today at Kaiser," he went on. Kaiser was their health maintenance organization, where they could get every kind of medical treatment.

"What do you think it is?"

"I don't know. Maybe hepatitis. Or maybe some intestinal parasite we picked up in India. But I lean towards hepatitis. Where have we eaten in the past two months?"

"Mostly at home, except for the spaghetti feed at the marathon," she answered, rolling over and propping herself up on one elbow so she could look down into his face. She stroked his cheek as they talked, following the high curve of the cheekbone down along the soft edge of his face to the slight dent in the middle of his chin.

"That's a likely place," he mused, "at a mass feeding like that where things can't be controlled very easily."

"I don't feel that anything is seriously the matter with me," she said, "but still it might turn out to be a help to me too if you should turn out to have a parasite or even hepatitis, since whatever you have, I probably have too, since our symptoms are pretty much the same."

He nodded, partly absorbed in the stroking, partly absorbed in his thoughts.

But he did not have a parasite that the doctors could find. His liver did not seem to be functioning quite normally, but it was not hepatitis.

The liver worried her a little. Not long ago, someone in her office at work, a thirty-six-year-old man, had found he had liver cancer, and had died within two or three months of the discovery. But it was unlikely that Philip could have anything so serious. Still, he maintained his conviction that something important was wrong with him, and kept going back to Kaiser.

Though she was not well, either, Louise did not want to bother. In the small amount of time she had free, she enrolled in an accounting course, a desperate ploy to advance out of the secretarial ranks into something with more future and better pay – perhaps the administrative assistant series of jobs, a whole new ladder to climb in the university structure, and one where there were half-time positions available from time to time.

The feeling that she might somehow break out of the secretarial slot in which she seemed stuck, and the feeling that she was gradually getting back into painting after months of spending all her extra energies on running, made her happy. Still, she could not help but worry about Philip. As she gradually regained her appetite, Philip seemed to lose his, and with it, his strength.

Nonetheless, he plunged into the conversion of the house into two separate units. Jonathan and Ilona had found another house to rent in May, and had moved, taking Jane with them. Louise and Philip laughed a little vindictively at the prospect of Jonathan trying to be in charge – at long last – with Jane as part of the household. He would soon discover that he had taken with him a zero, a sinkhole for household energies. Kathleen moved in with her boyfriend, taking little Willy with her; and Philip had the house to himself.

This was expensive, but temporary, while Philip got the new apartment ready. Louise watched him with some surprise. He seemed ready to be on his own, master in his own house at last, without the support of an imitation family to prove that his house was actually a home. He did like to have her with him more often now, but on the other hand, he did not seem eager to have her move in. Maybe he really was achieving the independence he had been working towards for such a long time.

* * *

Philip's health seemed to improve. Perhaps it was sheer will power, as he had something he wanted terribly much to do. All year long he had enjoyed singing in the university chorus. Now he had enrolled in a special summer workshop given by a famous choral director. There were to be almost daily rehearsals, with attention to each individual singer, and at the end of a few weeks' intensive work they would perform the Bach *B Minor Mass*.

"You should hear this music, Lou!" he exclaimed. "I can't believe how beautiful it is. And I've learned so much in the past year. Maybe this fall I can even get into the Oakland Symphony chorus. Would you come all the way to Oakland to hear me sing?"

"Looks as if it will be San Francisco first," she returned.

Rehearsals and the final Bach performance were all to be held in the city.

Philip arranged to take some afternoons off from work. He was accustomed to fitting all kinds of things into his day, and with his former high energy he had always been able to carry it off. Now, however, he had to budget his strength.

After a week or two of rehearsals, he began to have trouble with his back.

"It must be from standing so long," he said. "It's awfully tiring. Hour after hour. And that's a long trip in the car every day, too."

"Maybe it's just the combination of tiredness and tension," she suggested. "Remember the terrible backache you got the week before we left for around the world? You were trying to finish all those grant proposals at the same time that you had to organize yourself for the trip – including the talks you had to give in Vienna and Tokyo. You were in agony, as I recall."

"Maybe it is like that," he said, though he did not seem very convinced.

His pain grew worse and worse, but he fought it off. Between bouts of rehearsal he found a place where he could lie down. He skipped some rehearsals, and he took some extra time off from work. Finally came the first night of performance.

Louise met him afterwards. He was ashen-pale, but exultant. "Quick, let's go downstairs where I can lie down," he said urgently. He rushed her though the crowd.

"We weren't that good," he said critically, "but I don't care. What a piece of music! Did you hear the beginning?" and he sang it again, *sotto voce*.

He sang again the following night, and then dropped out,

although a second piece of music was planned. He had run out of strength. No amount of desire or will power would have been enough to carry him through another series of rehearsals and performances.

"If I rest now," he said, "I can get into more singing in the fall. I think this is going to be my new hobby. Or more than a hobby. And we'll sing the *Messiah* again at Christmas. What a wonderful thing to look forward to!"

All the while he continued having tests done at Kaiser. It seemed they were beginning to run out of new hypotheses and new tests, but Philip persisted, repeating his sense that something serious was wrong with him.

* * *

It was the Fourth of July, and they had decided to watch the fireworks from the upstairs bedroom. With its views out over the whole bay, they would see the displays from Berkeley, San Francisco, and Marin County. But Philip lay in bed, while Louise hovered by the window, watching.

"Oh, Philip, they've begun. It's wonderful! Come watch."

He did not move. "I can't, Louise. I'm very sick. I feel that I'm dying."

"Philip, no!" she exclaimed, going to the bed and running her fingers along his face. He had had nothing but a few glasses of orange and cranberry juice that day.

Then she jumped up and went to the window, wanting to see the fireworks rise from the dusky city and explode in the sky. She wanted so much for Philip to enjoy it with her. The Fourth had been one of their special celebrations. Now Philip lay in bed, inexplicably, and said that he was dying.

"Shall I call the doctor?" she asked anxiously.

"I don't know, Lou," he groaned. "Let's wait a little while. I don't know what's wrong with me. I think I'm dying," he repeated.

Louise alternated between the bed and the fireworks, pulled from one to the other. At last, when all the fireworks were over and the sky was quiet again, Louise turned her full attention to Philip. She felt divided between fear, and exasperated disbelief. If only she could get him to eat something!

"I think I'll have some ice cream," she said. "We have some of your favorite coffee kind down there. Do you think you might like some too?"

"Maybe," he said doubtfully. "If you're going to have some, I'll try a little. Just a little," he warned.

She gave him a fair portion, and he was able to eat it. Soon they were both asleep.

In the following days, he seemed to rally a little. She bought him lots of the things he was able to eat. That meant junk food, mostly: soft cinnamon doughnuts, white bread, and slightly more nutritious ice cream and fruit drinks. He was able to continue going to Kaiser for more tests, and to keep working on the conversion of the house into a duplex, although he could not do much at a time.

* * *

It was mid-July when Philip phoned her at her apartment, where she was cramming for an accounting exam she had to take in an hour or so.

"Where are you, Lou? Are you standing or sitting down?"

"Standing. Why?"

"Better sit down. I have something to tell you."

"What? What could it be?"

"I have cancer."

"What?" She hung on the telephone with both hands. "No, that's impossible."

"I know, but they did a bone marrow test in the middle of my chest, you know that spot that hurt so much when you leaned on it one morning? And there are wild cells. They had to come from some organ. Now they just have to figure out where they came from."

"What does it mean?" she asked, sitting down on the floor.

"I don't know. If I'm lucky, it might be Hodgkin's disease. That and a few others they can cure now. If I'm unlucky, it's the pancreas or the liver or – god knows what."

"Oh Philip," she breathed, resisting the information.

"I know. It doesn't seem possible."

"And you ran such a good marathon."

"Yes, and I must have had it then. But remember those back x-rays I had done before Christmas, when that car hit me? They didn't show anything wrong, so it's spread very fast, and just since then. Maybe being in such good shape for the marathon even spread it faster – my circulation is so good. I don't know."

"I want to be with you tonight, even though it's not on our schedule. I can skip this accounting exam, or take it later. Would you like me to come up now?"

"No, I'll be all right, babe. Take the exam. When will you be up?"

"It'll be about three hours before I'm there. Are you sure you're okay?"

"I'll be all right. I know you're coming. I do need you tonight."

"I'll be there."

In an instant the world had been altered for her. She threw her books into her bicycle basket and rushed to class. No one there knew. Everyone was wrapped up in the moment, in the exam. Or were they? Who else there had a secret at home, or within themselves? Who else sat there balancing accounts on a safe piece of paper while, at home, deer ran loose in the garden, ravening hope down to the bare rootstock?

* * *

They went almost immediately to bed – not for sex, now, but to lie as close as possible together, under the covers, huddling for safety.

Philip was too wound up to lie quietly, however; his mind was running on the possibilities. "It all depends on which kind it is, Lou. All I have to do is survive a few years. By then maybe one of these new experimental therapies will be working, or I can get a few more years from one, until another is improved. We'll see."

He held her more tightly. "But if I die, I want to do it at home, not in the hospital."

She nodded, half-smiling at his jocular tone, but serious. He was kidding only in manner.

"With lots of candles, you know . . ."

"An organ playing, maybe? People on their knees around the bedside?"

"Yes, that sounds right. Especially the candles. And at home. Do you mind?"

"Of course not. I'd want the same thing." Strange to speak of wanting. It suggested an acceptance she did not have, refused to have.

"You know my mother died in the hospital. Did I ever tell you about that?"

"Not in detail."

"She didn't actually die of cancer. It happens a lot: the pain got so bad that she actually died of morphine. She had to have it. The dose was so large that all the body processes just stopped."

He paused. "That's the thing about morphine. They don't start you on it until they've given up hope, because they have to keep increasing the dose as the pain gets worse, until the drug is a threat in itself. Or maybe not a threat, really, more like a godsend way of ending. If they ever put me on morphine, you'll know –"

She wrapped her arm around his head, stroking his face with her hand. He accepted this tacit statement that they were still in the present; this worst future should not be invoked. Holding one another close, they fell asleep without making love. Philip's body was too much in question now.

* * *

Philip had to spend much of the next day at Kaiser, having tests done. Louise went to work, and then went to the house, to be there when Philip would arrive home.

She met him at the door, and when he saw her, his face relaxed a little. They kissed and she put her arm around him as they walked upstairs. He was clearly exhausted.

"I have to lie down awhile, Lou, and rest. Want to keep me company?"

She nodded. They went into the back bedroom, which was a particularly quiet, serene room, and lay down together. She could not relax, however, and find a comfortable niche next to Philip's newly-strange body. She was rigid with fear, sadness, and something else: anger.

When Philip put his arms around her, he pulled his head back a little, to look into her face.

"Let it out, Lou, let it out. Come on." He pulled her into his arms.

"It's not fair!" she exclaimed. "You can't do this to me!"

Philip smiled a painful smile. "Want to hit me? Here," and he offered his upper arm.

"Damn! Damn!" she cried, hitting the arm he had bared. "I hate you! You can't do this to me!"

"I know, I know," he groaned, lying back. She fell onto him and they cried together, loudly, past shame. When the tears had finished and they lay resting, feeling their nearness to each other, she raised her head.

"Philip, I swore I'd never do this, but – I have a question – a proposal." She hesitated. "Would you like to get married?"

He smiled, his face still wet from tears. "Lou, you want to get married? I'm honored. Honored! But why? Don't you think I'm going to live?"

She was startled by the directness – and astuteness – of the question.

"Well, I don't know what's going to happen. But" – the words were mangled by sobs that wanted to rise like hiccups – "if you should die, I'll be damned if I'm going to refer to you as my dear departed friend. That doesn't express the relationship at all. 'Husband' is the closest word for what you are to me, or it's the only word most people would understand."

"Well," he mused, "it might be better for inheritance too."

She had not thought of that, but as soon as he said it, she saw that it was true.

"But won't it change our relationship?" Philip asked.

"You think we'll instantly turn into stereotypes, little servant wife and big master husband?" she kidded him.

"Well, maybe it doesn't matter now if we do," he said.

She opened her eyes wide. "What do you mean! But we won't. I don't think we could even if we wanted to."

"I'm not so sure about that – though maybe my real fear is that you could turn out like Concha. Maybe marriage would ruin this wonderful thing we have. I always thought the only reason for us to get married would be to have a child. Do you want to have a child?"

"No, I don't," she answered firmly. "And neither did you, before."

"Things were different then." He paused, then grabbed her more tightly. "Oh Lou, of course I want to marry you. I always thought we would eventually, but I didn't want it this way. Now you're not sure whether it's just the pressure of this awful situation, or our love. But you know how much I love you, don't you? God, I love you so much."

"I know, I've always known." She pressed her face against his shoulder, shutting her eyes. She could not tell him, just now, how much she loved him; whenever this seemed to be most obviously required, she was unable to say it, no matter how much she felt it. She had to trust that Philip knew.

"Listen, babe, I have to go back to Kaiser tomorrow for another lab report. Why don't you come with me, and we'll get blood tests started for getting married? We can talk about this child decision in the meantime. It takes a long time to get all this stuff done, blood tests, VD tests, waiting period."

The child question had taken her completely by surprise, since Philip had been so adamantly against it when she was pregnant. Of course it was understandable: a form of immortality. But she could not make another complete about-face on this enormous question. She had used up all her flexibility the last time, leaving behind her unrealistic fantasy.

They got the blood tests the next day, though Philip was barely able to do it. Leaning heavily on Louise, he staggered from room to room at Kaiser, as they filled out forms, left their blood samples, and finally labored back out to the car.

* * *

The next Monday Philip was scheduled to have a biopsy performed on his prostate gland, which had come to seem the most likely source of his cancer, after tests of other possible sites had turned out negative.

Over the weekend his back pains spread and intensified. When Monday came, he was running a fever; the biopsy would be impossible for that day, at least.

"Take me in to the hospital anyway," Philip said as Louise stood by his bed with the thermometer. "I'm too sick, they have to do something."

"Where shall I take you? Emergency? Shall I call the doctor first?"

"What? I don't know, Lou . . ." he trailed off, confused. Then opening his eyes again, he half shouted, "I can't think, I'm in too much pain, just get me there. You have to take charge now, Lou, I can't. Just help me, all right?" He shut his eyes again, conscious only of the pain.

Half in a panic herself, Louise helped Philip into her car, and drove him to the Emergency door of the hospital. Standing at the admissions window there, facing a nurse who, she knew, would want to turn Philip away if she doubted the seriousness of his condition, she blurted out, galled by the lack of the proper word for their relationship, "My friend here is very sick, he has cancer, he has to be let in, he feels as if he's dying."

The nurse looked critically at Philip, slumped in a nearby chair.

"Who's his doctor?" she asked.

Louise gave the name.

About ten minutes later, they took Philip into the Emergency ward, where they put him on a hard little table divided uncomfortably into sections, and about a foot too short for his six feet three inches. Every fifteen or twenty minutes Louise got up and searched in the halls for a nurse or doctor, someone who could tell them that a regular bed would soon be ready, that Philip had not been forgotten. Finally, after several hours, she found a nurse who could pause long enough to bring in a longer, softer table for Philp to lie on, and a much-needed blanket. They waited a few more hours. Both dozed, Louise leaning on Philip's bed, Philip under his blanket. It was nearly ten o'clock at night. They had been there around six hours. The nurse reappeared, saying a bed would be ready for Philip in half an hour.

"You'd better go home, babe," he whispered to her. "I'll be all right now, and there's nothing more you can do. Go home and get some rest."

She felt that he was right. She tucked the blanket in around him once more, kissed him, stroked his face, and left. She was exhausted, and had to rest. She felt as if she were embarking on a second marathon, one she had to finish. She could not lose all her strength here at the very beginning. There was no telling how long the course might be.

* * *

She phoned in the morning, from the echoingly empty house. Philip was resting. So she went to work and then went to the hospital in the afternoon. He was in an attractive room on the ninth floor, with a view out over Oakland and the southern part of the bay. He was pale and weak, but at last he was comfortable.

"Hi Lover," he said, in the soft voice of sickness. "I'm so glad to see you. Sit down here by me."

"How are you feeling, babe?" she asked. These words – lover, babe – had come into their vocabulary gradually. They were ways of reaching out, caressing the other, less strenuous and somehow less sugary than repeating "I love you" each time, but having the same sense.

"Not too well. I lay in that room until two in the morning. That nurse probably saved my life. He kept me warm, and brought me some juice to drink, and kept checking on the bed until they got it ready for me. He could have just let me lie there. They were terribly busy last night in Emergency. He finally brought a doctor in and they gave me an intravenous feeding – I was so dehydrated. They tell me this morning that I almost died last night."

"Oh Philip." She shook her head, trying to take it in. And she had gone home to sleep. It was the first of her many failures.

She forced her chair into the narrow space between bed and wall, trying to get closer to him now. "What are they going to do, Philip?"

"They can't take a biopsy – I'm too sick. So they're just going to gamble that it is the prostate and start me on the hormone tonight. I get my first pills around dinner time."

"Hormone?" she asked.

"DES. It's a female hormone." His face contracted. "I don't know all the side effects. I don't know what it'll do to me." He paused for a moment, and then went on. "Well, kid, we've been father and daughter and mother and son and brother and sister and lovers together. Now we can be sisters, too!"

They smiled, but their eyes met, too knowing, above their smiling mouths.

"As long as I get to keep you, I don't care what the terms are," she replied, taking his pale freckled hand.

"Well, Lou, if I die now, at least I die when our love is at its height. Maybe that's a lucky thing. There's no chance for anything to ever come between us, or make us doubt what we have together."

She shook her head, almost irritated, though she knew he wanted to reassure her, set her up for life, as it were, with this legacy of having loved and been loved, completely, definitively, as if it could be taken care of once and for all.

"I want you alive. I'll take my chances on the future with you," she replied.

"If the DES works, it might not be so bad. Compared to other cancer therapies it's very benign – really the easiest one there is. Just a pill, and it doesn't make you sick or hate your life and want to die the way chemotherapy does, or radiation sickness. So it could be worse."

"Sounds good," she said. "I'd love to see you eating again."

He nodded.

They sat there for a long time, not able to make small talk to cover over what was happening. They were together, and they were waiting. Philip drifted off to sleep.

Louise looked at his face, so precious, apart from her in the hospital bed. She could not hold back the tears, crying silently so no one would notice.

Philip woke, opening his eyes on her face.

"I know," he said. "I feel the same way."

He looked around. The other patient in the room was sound asleep, or unconscious – it was impossible to say which; and no nurses were there. Philip shifted over in the narrow bed.

"Here. I don't like being all alone in here. Can you get in too? Just lie on top of the blankets, right here by me. Would you like to?"

She nodded, and took off her shoes. A moment later they were lying warmly side by side, holding hands. She fell asleep instantly, still exhausted by the previous night's vigil and by the tears – those she had not shed as well as those she had. She was partly aware that nurses were coming and going in the room, but they did not disturb them. Philip slept too. For this short while, once again, they gave one another peace.

* * *

It was several days before they knew whether the DES was going to stop Philip's cancer. Every morning Louise phoned him, and then went to work. After work, a dinner sandwich in her purse, she went to the hospital to be with him until seven or eight o'clock. Then she went back to Philip's house, working for a few hours on the house conversion, finishing up the sheet-rocking, putting screws every foot or so into the steel supports. After the fear and tedious confinement in the hospital room, the physical work was a godsend, and she went at it furiously. She felt as if she was working to protect Philip: not from the disease – over that she had no control – but from want, from the specter of unmet mortgage payments, not enough money for food, while Philip, perhaps, lay too sick to help himself.

In only a few days, Philip was well enough to wisecrack to her, "So you're going home to screw, are you? Can't stop you, Borgstrum!" The drug had worked quickly. Monday night Philip had nearly died; on Friday he was able to go home.

It was only a week or so until his August birthday: he would be forty. "I'd like to have a big party," he said. "Invite all my friends, the real friends, the people I see all the time. You know, Hugh, Jim, Rachel and Bill, the lab technicians – all those people. We'll have to have it early. I get tired by evening time, and when I get tired now, I'm really tired. People may not understand that. It's different from the way a normal person gets tired."

The party was a larger version of their regular Saturday night routine. Philip charcoal-broiled the steaks; Louise baked potatoes and made a salad. Philip circulated among people cheerily, sometimes joking, but taking out more time than usual for long quiet conversations. Hugh and Louise orchestrated the food – something Philip would ordinarily have wanted to do – and everyone except Philip ate heartily. The food was good, but it was too rich for him now. He could not eat the steak, nor drink the wine – his two favorite things. At nine in the evening the guests were still there, but Philip was too tired to stay up. His goodnight was a wave of the wand. The party, though it seemed to be going well, melted like a mirage. The desire to celebrate was strong, but hard to maintain over the consciousness that another birthday might not come. People fled home where life seemed more secure.

The day after his birthday, Philip entered a short notation into his runner's log and calendar, with the exclamation mark he always used: "Have TERMINAL cancer!" That was all.

* * *

P hilip began to research his disease.
    "I want to find out everything I can," he said one morning as they were lying together in bed, listening to the campanile bells from campus. "I don't want to be passive and just go see the doctor and do whatever he says."

    "Well, it's very close to your own field, isn't it?" Louise observed.

    "Close enough for me to be able to understand what's going on and what the decisions are based on. As far as I can see, I'm already one of the lucky ones. DES only works for a certain percentage of men. You know what they used to do? Cut off the man's balls. God! I don't know whether it would be worth living. Well, I guess you choose life no matter what, if it is anything like a normal life, being able to eat and walk and work. But to have your sex taken away completely –" He paused for a moment and then went on.

"The doctor says DES sometimes takes away the sex, but not always. He was trying to be delicate and not make a statement, but I got the impression that I don't have to lose it. God, I hope not."

Louise thought back. "I remember when my father had some prostate problem – not cancer, but he did have an operation – they said that if he kept having sex he wouldn't lose it."

Philip laughed. "I'm not well enough yet, babe! Though maybe . . ." He groaned as he moved. "I still hurt too much, I think. It's distracting. But it's getting better all the time. Watch out! You're not safe yet!"

She only smiled in response, afraid to say anything and strike a false note – of forced hope, or premature discouragement.

"But you know that prostate cancer is much different in a young man. It's almost like an entirely different disease. Most old men get it if they live long enough, but hardly any of them die of it. It doesn't go very fast when you're old. But in a younger man it goes like wildfire. It must have with me, when you consider that in May I ran a good marathon and felt great, and now in August I almost died – would have died, if it hadn't been for the DES.

"The DES works by turning off the prostate cells. And it stops working at some point. That's the question: When? I feel sure there must be more than one way of doing it, so that when the DES stops working we could try something else. Maybe take something that goes only to those cells, and load it with something to kill them. Because the cells keep their identity as prostate cells even when they start growing in the bone. They're screwed up: they think they're growing prostates there. As long as they keep that identity there should be some way of reaching them. When they lose that identity, then you have to go to something more general. But I'd never consider chemotherapy. Why go through something that makes you wish you were dead, sicker than you were before, just to get a few days of survival until you have to go through it again? I wouldn't do it. And I'll never be a vegetable, just to survive. I'd much rather die."

He turned to her fiercely. "You understand that, don't you? That I'd rather die?"

She nodded. She was not sure what her own choice would be, but understood that for Philip, death would be preferable. But she did not want to think about it at all. It was too hard. She would have to respect his freedom to choose death, if that was what he wanted; but she could not see herself helping him to die. That seemed unbearable, impossible. But the thought of Philip, with his enormous energies and delight in life, lying in bed "like a vegetable," was also impossible.

* * *

Exactly one Friday after he had been released from the hospital, Philip came to pick up Louise at her apartment. He had a noticeable limp.

Louise looked at him questioningly, half afraid to ask.

"Don't worry, it's nothing, just a leg-pull. I was such an ass. You won't believe it. I went running."

Her eyes opened wide.

"Yes, I know, but I couldn't resist. It's everything I love, being out there on the trail, moving, and I was feeling so good! And all of a sudden I got this incredible pain. I had to limp home. It took forever. So I got worried and called the doctor's office, and told the nurse what happened. She just laughed. She says this happens to all the patients with my disease, they start taking the pills and they feel so good again and they all go out and wreck themselves doing something they always loved – golf, swimming, running – stuff like that. So I guess it's nothing unusual. I'm just supposed to go easy."

Louise laughed, relieved at the talk of "usual" and "happens to all the patients." It made Philip's cancer seem more within the range of the normal and hence, by some unexamined implication, within the range of continuing life.

She shook her head. "Running!" It was all she could say.

"I feel great, Lou. The drug is really working."

She remained silent, still unable to speak.

Philip went on. "There's no telling how long it will keep on working. It could be one year – or maybe even five years. But I'd like to take a little trip soon, within a month or so, while I know I can do it and enjoy it. I've been looking at a book about country inns out in the foothills. What do you think?"

"Wonderful," she said. "Just what we can both use." She meant it. Here in Berkeley it seemed as if all the old things they liked and had done together were contaminated by this new presence, the cancer. She realized now that each pleasure had carried with it a tacit promise that it would be repeated. They had loved their routines – the Saturday night steaks, the Sunday night dinners at Pedro's, the bicycle trips over the Golden Gate Bridge into Sausalito – partly because each repetition strengthened their sense that the past would go on into the future, that they would be doing these things together forever. In their elaborate dances on the themes of independence and closeness, moving apart and coming together, the routines had been the invariable forms they could always be sure of. Now these same forms made them afraid: soon it could be the last time. Nothing was assured, absolutely nothing. It would be a relief to go away from Berkeley.

* * *

Meantime, Philip continued to work on the apartment conversion at the back of the house. Louise worked with him, whenever he would allow it, and friends came in to help with some of the difficult electrical and plumbing questions. But Philip did most of it himself, pushing himself on through fatigue and depression. It had to be done.

He finished it in the middle of September, just in time for the beginning of fall term at the university. When two young students rented it, a great stone fell off Philip's back. There would be no financial crisis; he could make the mortgage, insurance, and tax payments without having to share his own space with strangers.

Philip's health continued to improve, bringing them slowly, slowly, back into something like hope. By the time of their vacation in October, he was able to do all the things he usually would have done. As they went from inn to inn, it seemed almost like a normal vacation. It was not until Yosemite that Philip cut through the veneer of normalcy. They were laboring up one of the trails out of the canyon, the hot still air an extra weight on their bodies. They had been walking in silence a while when Philip suddenly asked, "Do you ever wonder what happens after death?"

"Um, I used to," she replied, taken by surprise. "I've sort of given up on it because I could never work out a system that seemed right. I do think that if there is existence after death, we must drop the things that keep us apart from one another here: pimples and bad grammar or different table manners or degrees of intelligence or experiences that have marked people or distorted them in some way. But maybe then personality and identity fall away too, and I don't want that. I want to be reunited with particular people, not just be absorbed into some big happy glob. So in the end I don't know. I'm more or less waiting to see."

Philip considered for a moment. "Would you be too alienated, Lou, if I went back to the Church?"

She took a big breath. "The church! You mean the Catholic Church?"

"Yes. I've been thinking about it a lot lately. You know I agree with you about the way the Church deals with women's issues. But there's a lot I miss. I was very religious as a boy, and young man too. Did you know that? I was an altar boy and the whole works. When I went to college I went to mass every Sunday, sometimes twice a week – until I took that course in college where they taught us the history of religions and I lost it. But now – I might go back, Lou."

"Wow," was all she could say at first.

"When I try to think about these things, I always wind up thinking in terms of what I learned from the Church. You could say it's just an arbitrary arrangement of basic things, but to me it's familiar, it's comforting. Not the politics of the Church, but the ritual and certain beliefs about the afterlife, even just the Latin and the mass and confession."

She considered. "Maybe," she said a little doubtfully.

"I'm sure there is something after death, Lou. I'm absolutely positive. The Church may not have the right idea of what it is, but it's something. And the Church gives me a way of dealing with it."

They paused by the side of the trail, looking back into the canyon. On the opposite side they could see people climbing the sheer rock walls, three or four little dots of color swaying precariously. As they watched, one lost his grip and fell about fifteen feet, caught sharply by his safety rope. He began to climb slowly up again, to the place where he had fallen.

"It seems incredible that people voluntarily risk their lives that way," Louise commented.

Philip did not answer, and they watched a while in silence. But no one fell again, and it got less interesting. They stood up and went on. A few days later, on the morning of their departure, Philip insisted that he and Louise explore the hotel, and decide which rooms they would ask for on their next visit there.

* * *

Once back home, Philip began a carefully worked out counter-assault on the cancer. He began to run longer distances, slowly and carefully working up to several miles at a time. In his log he recorded each day's run, a sort of temperature-taking on his health. He gained weight: another triumph, fifteen pounds' worth. And yet his body was constantly threatening to fail. His left leg continued to be weaker than the right; the x-rays had shown that the cancer had concentrated in the left groin and femur, the bone from hip to knee. He had back pains, also, which came, went away, and then returned. It was hard to attribute them merely to tension.

Meantime, Louise, looking inside her head, had discovered some unexpected inhabitants. Grief, fear, anguish: these were not surprising. But there were other feelings, less easy to admit to. Philip had talked to the lawyer already. If Philip died, the house would go to Louise, in trust until she died, when it would go to Jo-Jo. For so long she had scrupulously refused to allow herself to think of the house as in any way hers; but now she might own it. No one could tell her what to do with any of it. If she chose, she could set up her painting easel in the living room, as Philip had teasingly suggested long ago. Looking around the house, with its beautiful light and spaces, she felt overcome by her desire for it, to have it entirely for her own.

Her time, too, would be entirely hers. She could paint many hours every day, even with the half-time job. She could go visit a friend in southern California and be gone for a week or two – something she had hesitated to do so far, because Philip protested bitterly if she was gone even two or three days. She could go hiking in the Sierras. Her time would be entirely her own because, she realized, her heart shrinking, no one would be wanting her company all the time; there would be no one there, loving, enveloping, devouring her.

In England, unable to believe their love was strong enough to last, losing faith almost in Louise's existence, Philip had moment-arily turned away from her, allowed himself to love another woman. But Louise felt she was almost wishing Philip away in

fantasy: she was trading his life for more free time and for possession of his house. Yet she did love Philip. These contradictions
obsessed her to such an extent that she hardly noticed how this
furious energy and tension resembled, and drew her away from,
the terrible fear for Philip's life.

* * *

H er mother decided to visit them for a few days. She was
going to visit other relatives in California, and it would
look strange not to visit her own daughter at the same time. And
maybe, Louise guessed, her mother might want to mend the
strained relationship that had developed between them. Maybe
she even wanted to get to know Philip. Still, Louise half dreaded
the visit.

But when she met her mother at the airport and saw her
expression, Louise realized that things had changed. Her mother
embraced her warmly – something she rarely did, having a mid-
western shyness of bodily contact, even with her own children.
As they walked through the long airport corridors, her mother
held Louise's arm close, looking up into her face with concern.
With enormous relief, Louise felt that her mother might be her
friend again. It had been less than a year since Louise's father had
died. Her mother, too aware of what Louise would suffer if Philip
died – the loneliness, the grieving, the hole in life's daily fabric –
and strong enough now to overlook the lesser question of sexual
morality, had arrived flying flags of peace. She was on Louise's
side.

During dinner back at the house, Louise watched her mother
and Philip nervously. It hardly seemed probable that they could

like each other. They began by being very polite. But gradually the three of them began to relax.

Perhaps testing the ground, Philip then proceeded to tell a string of jokes, most of his favorites, all off-color. Louise watched anxiously.

Her mother waited until Philip paused in the joke-telling, and then put down her wine glass, shaking her head.

"You remind me so much of Oliver," she said. "He used to love to tell jokes like that. He was wonderful at it too – just like you." Louise was surprised. She had never guessed that her father loved to tell jokes. Although she had felt so close to him, his social self had been completely hidden from her.

Philip managed to stay at the table through the whole meal, but then had to go lie down on the old velveteen couch in the living room. Louise and her mother cleared the dishes together, the accustomed activity bringing them still another step closer.

"What a darling person," her mother said. "No wonder you like him so much."

Louise shot her mother a look of agreement, and of gratitude. But she did not say much more. The painful rift she had felt between the two of them could not be so easily swept aside. She needed to talk to her mother, tell her how she had felt, open up those baffling months to the light so they could both look at it and clear it away.

The next day they all three went on one of Philip's favorite trips, taking the ferry boat across the bay between San Francisco and Sausalito. It was a bright clear late October day. Louise stood with her mother at the ferry landing, waiting while Philip parked the car. In the back of her mind, Louise worried that he would have to park so far away that the walk would exhaust him; but he had insisted on driving, on having everything appear to be normal.

The two women were quiet as they looked at the water and the docks and the heavy ropes that hung here and there in unreadable formations. It was time for her to speak, Louise thought, but she hardly knew where to begin. She had gone over the subject countless times in her mind until she had formed ruts, scripts that played over and over almost without her having to think. Her mother's actual presence, however, changed things. Always the script had been directed at a woman who was set against her, resenting, angry, wanting her to be less. But the woman with her now seemed none of these things. She would have to speak in a different way.

"Mother, I wonder if you realize how I've been feeling since the time Daddy died," she began. "I remember you telling me once how Grandmother said that of all three children, you least enjoyed traveling. I guess it seemed to imply you were the least adventurous, or maybe least sensitive to what was new – something like that. And that little remark hurt you so much you remembered it for years and years afterwards. But do you realize what you've said to me in the past months? You've said you didn't like my work life, my love life, or my painting. Does that leave anything over? What can I talk to you about? Food recipes? The weather? That's about all there is, because my life you've condemned. Thinking of how you reacted to that remark of your mother's, just about one little part of life, can you imagine how I might feel about what you've been saying to me?"

Her mother did not turn towards Louise. She continued to look out at the water, but her face changed. She was listening, taking it in. She did not reply. There was no self-justification, no apology, no arguing. Philip rejoined them, and the conversation turned. They got on the ferry and moved out onto the open water. Louise knew that she had been heard, and trusted her mother to respond from her best self, the one that subsisted beneath the turmoil and pain from her father's death.

By the time Mrs. Borgstrum left, Philip was calling her "Mother," and she called him "Philip," not "Dr. Brett." Love had overcome the ghosts; at least momentarily the angry disappointed voices from the past were stilled.

* * *

Philip's leg appeared to heal, and he did not physically need Louise's presence in the house any longer. She returned to her apartment, back on the old schedule of visits. He was especially determined not to call her in now, ask her to stay extra nights, when it might seem motivated by raw need for someone – anyone – rather than by love for her. Still, she did stay with him more often. And he began to throw out hints.

"I had a bad night last night, when you weren't here." Or, "You can't imagine how hard it is, sometimes, when the thoughts come in the middle of the night, and you're all alone."

She tried to leave it up to him, because she feared seeming patronizing, as if she thought him unable to care for himself. But her instinct was to be with him, another presence in the house.

The decision to move back in with Philip was reached just as the earlier decision to move out had been: spontaneously, by both of them at the same moment. Once they had spoken, they slammed together like two strong magnets, released. A few weeks later, Louise moved in, this time burning her bridges behind her – giving up rather than subletting her cheap bay view apartment.

She set up her painting easel in the basement. But it was hard to get a good painting schedule established, with the holidays coming on. And it was more important than ever to Philip that they celebrate well. They had to have a celebration at Thanksgiving as well as at Christmas.

"Remember how we did it last year?" Philip said. "The turkey, and stuffing, and potatoes or wild rice, and cranberry, and candied squash, and a green vegetable, and boiled onions, and maybe rolls, oh and of course relishes, and three pies – mincemeat, apple, and pumpkin – with whipped cream."

Louise rolled her eyes

Philip looked startled for a brief moment, and then recovered. "Oh I know, Lou, I wouldn't expect you to do all that. I forgot that I might not be able to help all that much. But turkey? We could buy the stuffing and the cranberry . . ." His voice trailed off uncertainly.

"Oh Philip," Louise cried out, taking his hand, "of course we can figure it out. It won't be hard. Who would you want to have?"

"Well, Hugh. Now that he and Hannah have split up, I guess he'll want his new girlfriend to come. She's nice, you'll like her. She's Chinese. Hugh can't stop talking about how beautiful she is. The funny thing is, she looks exactly like Hannah, small and dark and skinny with long black hair. And brainy, of course. And then Tanaka, my first teacher, I told you about. He's here alone, since his wife and children went back to Japan last month. He's a wonderful man. Who else?"

"Deirdre is the only other one I can think of. Sylvia's still in Modesto. So it can be a more quiet Thanksgiving. I think I might like it that way, actually," Louise answered.

Philip nodded. "Yes, I don't know how well I'll last. These days I nearly always have to rest at the end of dinner. So just a few good friends will be the best. They won't mind."

Deirdre brought the relishes, and Louise simply bought the pies and the extras. It was not too hard. Thanksgiving was good, and people talked quietly, without the desperate forced party-mood of Philip's birthday. Once again they had successfully repeated the past.

* * *

Not long afterwards, Deirdre phoned. "Louise, on Friday I'm driving up to Shasta. Want to come? We can hike on Friday and Saturday and then drive back in time for dinner on Saturday, so you won't have to be away from Philip very long. Can he manage Friday dinner without you?"

"Oh yes, I think so. It would probably be good for us both – and I love the idea of some hiking."

"You know the sacred trail? It leads to the mystic rocks. We can hike up and meditate there. We can send Philip healing messages from the spirit of the mountain."

Louise gave a quiet sigh. There had been a lot of advice for Philip's health, from the acquaintance who came rushing up to Louise in the supermarket, saying that if Philip would just switch to a macrobiotic diet he would be cured, to the suggestion that the cancer was Philip's fault because he had bad thoughts. But it didn't matter here. Whatever the spirit of Shasta was, they might as well try sending some of it to Philip while they enjoyed the hiking.

When she told Philip, his first reaction was doubt; Louise could see he was uncertain, now, about being alone. "I don't know, Lou," he said, fingering the string of reddish-brown beads at his neck. "Hmm. Well, maybe I could still cook. Chicken. Rice. Maybe I'll invite someone. Maybe even Pat." He looked off in the distance, as if planning.

"Really?" Louise said. "Pat Malloy?" She hadn't thought of Pat for a long time. "Hmmm, well," she ended, not knowing what else to say. Over the next few days she put it out of her mind.

But the day before the Shasta trip, Deirdre phoned. "Oh Louise, George phoned, his car broke down and he needs me to drive him somewhere. Do you mind if we postpone our trip?"

That was fine for Louise, but when she told Philip, he was clearly disappointed. "You mean you're going to be home? I thought this was going to be my night off, I mean –"

Louise interrupted. "'Night off'? I'm not a job! What were you planning with Pat?"

Philip waved a hand as if swatting a languid fly. "You know what I mean. Pat's not expecting you either. And it's too late to call her now and tell her."

So Pat arrived, clad in form-fitting black trousers and a pale ivory-pink silk shirt. Louise played gracious hostess while Pat shimmered in the living room, sending out sexual messages, Louise thought, in vain.

* * *

They lay in bed, enjoying the warmth, delaying the moment of getting up for work.

"I can feel it invading my body, you know that, Lou?"

"What invading?" she asked anxiously. She thought he must mean the cancer.

"The female hormone. It's changing me. It's like one of those pipe-spirits in the Castaneda books. It's an invasion."

"What's it like?"

"Well, it's softer, less driving. At first I thought – I'm sorry about this, but I thought it would affect my ability to concentrate, that I wouldn't be able to work as well. But that hasn't happened. In a way it's the opposite, because I've lost that terrible sex drive I used to have. It wasn't just direct wanting to fuck women all the time. It was more subtle than that. It was a constant distraction, always being aware of who was around, what she looked like, always operating at a low level of consciousness but always there. It took a lot of my energy and attention, much more than I realized. It's kind of nice to be without that. I suppose this is the way most people are. Not you – but the way you were when you were pregnant."

He grinned at her, mockingly. "That's how the world's work gets done, Lou – not by sex-crazed maniacs but by people who are calm and just go to work, go home, eat, watch TV and repeat the same thing every day. Sex once a month is enough for lots of people."

"But not for you even now," she pointed out, moving her hand over him.

"That's true," he said, peering under the covers. "It just doesn't want to go down. But it's harder to come now. It's really frustrating. I feel like it but there's no release, except just a little bit, and in waves instead of all at once. It's not very satisfying, really."

"Well, don't give up. It may be that practice makes perfect. Like what they said to my father after his prostate operation."

"Self-interest," he cried, "self-interest! Well, come here then and let's see. At least I can do something for you."

* * *

The following weekend was gray, cold, and misty. Time dragged. They needed a distraction. Late on Sunday afternoon, desperate to get out, they decided to take a walk across campus to Cody's Books, a favorite spot. They put on their jackets and started out. As they proceeded, Philip began more and more to lean on Louise.

"My left leg is hurting me. I don't think I can make it without leaning on you. Is it too much for you?"

"No, it's okay," she answered. It would be too demoralizing if they had to turn back, unable to reach this chosen destination; and she longed to be in a place full of interesting books, interesting people, bright lights, life.

"You're going too fast, Louise," Philip grumbled.

They slowed down. It was hard to talk. Philip was involved in the effort of walking, and Louise had no thoughts in her head. They lurched silently through the damp evening.

When they had gotten about halfway across campus, Philip came to a halt. "It's too far, Lou, I can't make it."

Healthy herself, and still accustomed to long distances in running, it was hard for her to imagine being that tired. "Let's sit down over here for a minute," she suggested, hoping Philip might get a second wind.

"This isn't good," Philip commented as he eased heavily onto the cold concrete bench. "I shouldn't be this tired. Don't move," he commanded, as she shifted a little, "I need to lean on you."

They sat silently a few moments, looking at the bell tower which rose over the middle of campus, gray in the cold gray fog. Louise was conscious of a stiffness beginning in her lower back, her body protesting Philip's heavy weight.

Her thoughts turned vaguely to the future. She could not help it: she wanted to live. If some deity had materialized there out of the mist, and offered her the chance to accompany Philip over the threshold of death, even into an assured future life, she would not have accepted. Alcestis, offering to die instead of her husband, was completely beyond her. She could not, would not die. Desire for life was in her like the sweetness in the apple, inseparable from her being.

Philip moved fretfully on the bench. "Come on, Lou, help me up, will you? It's too cold out here. I have to get back to the house."

They labored slowly up the hill home, uncomforted.

* * *

Christmas was coming up. Louise was finding it painful to think about presents, because this forced into consciousness her uncertainty as to what Philip would be able to use, and for how long. She avoided things connected with running, or singing, or wine. Still she bought things – everything she could think of, far more than she would usually have thought appropriate. What if it was her last chance?

Their unspoken project now was to keep up a sense of normalcy, of things going on as usual in spite of the gradual small changes in Philip's ability to do things. One evening in mid-December, Louise, Philip and Jo-Jo were finishing dinner. Louise was doing nearly all the cooking now, as Philip could not manage it because of fatigue, and the fear of losing appetite from handling the food. She had made one of their favorite desserts, a crunchy brown-sugar apple concoction. Philip had been shifting about on his chair all through dinner. As Louise finished her sausage and potato, always the last one, Philip suddenly got up from the table.

"I have to go lie down, Lou. Don't worry, I just have some arm pains. It should get better if I lie flat on the rug. I've been working it out."

With that he rushed into the living room, propelled by pain. Louise put down her fork and followed him in, watching as he quickly – and carefully – lowered himself onto the rug, flat on his back. She sat down close by him. "It's all right, Lou," he said. Their eyes met, knowing too much, afraid, tears running down their faces. They could not escape.

Jo-Jo got up and approached them, unsure what was going on, or whether there was a place for him in it.

Philip saw him. "Come here, Joseph, come sit by me. It's just some arm pain, but it will go away."

Jo-Jo nodded, still a little uncertain, and sat down close to his father.

"That's right, you can help me while Louise gets dessert. Can you rub this arm? Not so hard – that's right, that's right."

Jo-Jo worked seriously at his task. Philip's face was absorbed and tense, listening to the pain and waiting to see if its intensity would diminish. Seeing the two of them together, Louise went out to the kitchen to get dessert, wondering if anyone would want to eat it, feeling inadequate. Apple dessert would not do anything for Philip's pain.

She put the dishes on the table. "Dessert," she called out. Jo-Jo came running. Philip remained on the rug.

"I'll have some later, Lou," he called. His face still had the look of absorption in some other world.

She and Jo-Jo ate dessert. Louise's portion tasted good, and she felt guilty. How could she enjoy something while Philip lay on the floor, thrown down by pain?

Philip called in, "Don't worry, you two, the pain's getting better. Joseph gave me a good rub. I haven't got room for dessert anyway."

* * *

Finally Philip consulted the doctor about his arm pains. He had new x-rays taken. They showed a collapsed disk in his upper vertebrae, near the base of the neck. It was a bad sign: the cancer had eaten out the core. He was given a foam neck brace of the sort used by whiplash victims. It held the vertebrae in place, and prevented the bones from pressing on the nerves to his arms. To put it on, Philip had to take off the bead necklace Louise had given him four years earlier. Until now he had never taken it off, but he could not wear the neck brace and the necklace at the same time. Carefully he put the necklace on the shelf at the head of the bed, out in view. Wearing his white plastic muff, now, the pains grew less intense, more bearable. He would start radiation treatment to the upper vertebrae after Christmas.

One morning Philip turned to her in bed, pulling her in to him as close as he could without pain. "Lou, I'm so sorry it's turning out this way. I'd thought maybe we would still have some years. I thought maybe I'd get a reprieve. I'd wanted us to get married when it would be clear that I wanted you for yourself, not just because I might need help. I mean I wanted to have achieved my independence first, and have proved it. Now I don't know if I'll get the chance. You just have to trust that I do love you. It's not just need. I've never loved anyone this way. You know that, don't you?"

She nodded. "I do know. It's the same for me."

"Well," he said, a little embarrassed, "Louise Borgstrum, will you marry me? I'm proposing."

"Yes!" she said, and kissed him on the mouth. "Philip Brett, I would love to marry you."

It was so simple. This time Philip did not mention children. This formal union was too important to be hedged with conditions.

"Our old blood tests have expired," he said. "We'll go get new ones in a week or two."

He turned suddenly on his elbow. "Wait! What's that?"

He reached to the shelf at the head of the bed and turned up the volume on the clock radio, which had just gone on. It was Handel's *Messiah*, and they were playing the tenor part which Louise had helped Philip with long ago, she playing the piano while he sang. They both knew this section by heart: "Ev'ry valley shall be exalted, and ev'ry mountain and hill made low, the crooked straight, and the rough places plain."

Holding one another close, they listened to the music, with its happy promise that life would be tailored to human desire. In their own way they had believed that, believed they could make things happen simply by the power of their desire. Now they knew otherwise, but the music went right on in its self-enclosed perfection, proud, exultant, with its beauty pulling them in again to its make-believe. Listening, Louise felt the skin of her face and skull grow taut with pain, pulling the lips back from her teeth in a sort of grimace. After a few minutes, Philip slowly reached up and turned the radio off.

"I can't take any more of that," he said, falling back into bed limply. "That music is unbearable right now."

* * *

One evening as Louise was making dinner, Philip came in. She was not surprised; he often came in around six o'clock to prepare his vitamin C. This time, however, he hovered about the sink counter, as if indecisive.

"Hi, babe," he said quietly. She looked up. His face was stiff, though he tried to make it smile.

"Hmm," she said, "looks like the pre-dinner blues. Maybe you need a cracker." He did not respond. "I'll have one too," she went on, thinking he might feel insulted at the implication that he was getting cranky for lack of food, and she was not.

Philip still did not reply, but sat down at the kitchen table. Worried, Louise followed him and tried to see into his face.

"Are you all right?" she asked.

"I don't know," he said in a flat, expressionless tone. He paused for a minute, then went on. "I don't know if I'm all right."

He paused again. "I don't know if I can take it, that's all. It's too hard, it's too hard! Everything was just right – settling down with you, singing, the new promotion at the lab – and I'm young, Lou, I'm only forty, I'm too young!" He paused, his face stiff with resistance. "I can't stand it," he whispered, and bowed his head down to the table. "It's too hard, I'm going to kill myself. I can't stand this dying by inches. I'm going to kill myself."

"Philip, no!" Louise cried, sitting down next to him and putting her arm around him as strongly as she dared, afraid of hurting him. Feeling the light pressure of her arm, he put his hands to his face and cried loudly, helplessly, his body taut with resistance to the tears, to his illness, to the daily battle with his body's deterioration.

Louise sat by his side, almost hysterical with sadness and fear for Philip. Yet at the same time, incongruously, she was aware that dinner was waiting on the stove, cooked and hot, ready to be taken into the dining room and eaten.

"Come on," she said softly, "at least eat a little. Maybe it will help."

"Nothing can help me – can't you see I'm dying?" he burst out. Nonetheless he slowly stood up and went into the dining room.

Dinner was quiet. Louise did not know what to say. Her health excluded her from his ordeal and his consciousness. All she could do was to stroke the hand he had laid on the table between them.

That night he was able to tolerate, even to have pleasure in her curling around him, pulling his body into the curve of hers. She tried to recapture the feeling that her love for him was the most powerful thing in the universe, that it could move out through

Philip like electric waves, annihilating illness and holding him safe by her in the warm bed. Yet she felt his body gripped as if by an invisible undertow, pulling him inexorably away, out into a cold sea.

* * *

Louise's boss, David, too idealistically uninterested in political power, had gotten the shaft from the law school administration. His extra funding was taken to re-carpet some greedier professor's office, and in a few months he would have no money for a half-time secretary. Desperate, Louise took the first new halftime job that came along on campus, and found herself committed to working mornings at the law school and after-noons in computer science. This schedule was to last until February, the earliest she could conscientiously leave her law school professor and friend. Anyway, she might need the extra money. What would happen if Philip became unable to work? If he had to have some kind of services not provided by Kaiser? She did not know, really, what eventuality she was preparing for, but it seemed a good idea to have a little bit of extra money put aside.

On the surface, at least, it now seemed as if they were an ordinary family, families as they might have been when they themselves were growing up: an adult woman, an adult man, and, on weekdays at least, a child. Every morning while Philip slowly showered, shaved, and dressed, Louise got breakfast for herself and Jo-Jo. These were peaceful mornings in the sunlit kitchen; Jo-Jo seemed at last to fully relax with Louise, and in this simple way they connected. A strange thing, she thought, this gift coming now.

About the time they were through eating, Philip came in to the kitchen to get his vitamin C and breakfast cereal. Together he and Louise saw Jo-Jo off to school, with hugs and goodbye waves as he went down the brick stairs. Then the two of them walked the few blocks to campus, through a deep green tunnel of bushes and trees arching over them from either side of the walk. The December weather was sunny and mild. At Philip's lab they kissed, lingeringly, softly, goodbye, a temporary separation only, their eyes turning back to each other as they went their different ways.

Near the end of her four hours at the law school, Louise ate her sandwich, and then headed back across campus for the next four hours in computer science. Her new boss there had told her that the first months would be difficult, and he proved correct. Her head was full of disconnected words which meant nothing: requisitions and blanket numbers and the whole byzantine system by which the university made sure that money set aside for equipment purchases did not end up in the wrong person's pocket.

At five, exhausted, she made her way home. If she did not have to go to the grocery, there might be an hour before dinner for painting. More often, however, the cooking had to begin so that dinner could be ready before seven. It was later when she had to go to the grocery. On those days she labored up the stairs to the house, carrying the regular groceries plus perhaps thirty cans of V-8, tomato juice, and assorted other juices for Philip's gigantic twice-daily doses of vitamin C powder, which had to be mixed with something to be palatable.

When Louise entered the house, the veneer of normalcy evaporated. It was no longer a re-run of a TV script for middle-class America. Philip, pale and tired, lay waiting for her on the old green sofa in the living room, listening to music or the news. His fierce monologue of earlier times was now completely gone. He wanted to talk to *her*, hear her reactions, share with her whatever was on his mind – his readings on cancer, or a new experiment he was doing at the lab, or the news that another man at work had just discovered he had cancer, though a different kind from Philip's. And he wanted to hear about Louise's day, questioning her closely and shrewdly.

"Hi, honey," he called from the couch, his tenor voice a little uneven. "I'm so glad to see you. Come and sit down here a minute," and he moved himself towards the back of the couch, leaving a little shelf for Louise to sit by him.

"Just a minute," she called, rushing out for the rest of the groceries, which were sitting in the open car across the street, down the long flight of stairs. She felt wrenched. She wanted to sit close by Philip, warm under the lamplight, and hear what he was feeling and thinking, and tell him about her day. At the same time she had to get the groceries safely into the house and start dinner so it would not be served too late. Usually she wound up choosing to sit by Philip on the old couch, half caved in by the athletics of the children, comfortably worn.

To salve her conscience she said, "Why don't I just go and get things started, Philip? I'll be back in just a second."

"Just for a minute, Lou, just for a minute, come over and sit by me." His voice was seductive: not sexual, but vulnerable and wanting. "I won't keep you from making dinner," he added. Thirty or forty minutes later Louise pulled herself away to the kitchen. When dinner was ready, Philip was then a little cranky.

"It's really too late, Lou, it's hard to go to sleep when you've just eaten."

He nearly always had to leave the table before dessert, now, driven by his arm pains onto the living room rug, holding himself down as flat as he could get on his back or side. And always Louise made dessert, hoping to keep his weight up. She or Jo-Jo brought it into the living room for him, trying to pretend that everything was all right.

More and more often the pains would not go down. Philip dragged himself, groaning, up the stairs to bed. Jo-Jo and Louise rushed back and forth to the bathroom to put hot water on towels, to wrap around Philip's arms.

One night, after Louise had been working at her old and new jobs for a few weeks, Philip suggested that she go to the drugstore to get hot pads for him.

"Do you really think you have to have them?" she asked, balking, too tired. The effort of going down to the street, driving and parking, going from the quiet dark into the cold glare of the drug store, and returning, all seemed too much.

"No, no, babe, I really need them. I'm sure they'll help. I wish I'd thought of it before. Give me the phone. I'll call Jim. He won't mind going."

Guiltily she roused herself. "Oh no, it's all right, I can go." But as she said it, she sat down again at the foot of the bed.

Philip reached over and phoned Jim. In less than an hour Jim came in with two hot pads.

He was full of energy, and seemed delighted to have been called. Louise watched him with grateful amusement as he bustled around, making Philip feel cared for, safe. She guessed that Jim had no idea how grateful she was. For him it was a welcome chance to do something, a relief.

In mid-December, exhaustion caught up with Louise. Maybe some hypothetical other woman would have been able to do all she had set herself to do, but that didn't matter; she was running dangerously low on energy and the ability to cope. She had to quit her old job early, disloyal though it seemed. She arranged to leave after Christmas.

Meanwhile there were Christmas parties at work, and she went to them purposefully. She ate and drank – especially drank – and was noisy. She could see the steam escaping from under her hairline, depressurizing her head. At home she made a huge batch of eggnog, from scratch, just the way she liked it. These jars of eggnog were of course intended for Christmas presents, to Liz at the office, and for people who might drop by the house. In fact, however, Louise drank most of it herself, stoking up before dinner each night. It was mother's milk, the next best thing to the warm security of being held against a warm body asleep, in a good dream.

Then, a few days before Christmas, Philip talked to the doctor again. He had just had another battery of tests, and was to get the results. Louise dreaded asking Philip about them, as she came up the stairs to the house. He was too chronically tired, and in too much pain.

As usual, he was lying on the soft green couch. "Hi, Lou! Come here!" he called out.

She put a smile on her face, and sat down by him.

"Don't look so worried, kid, the news is good," he said, taking her hand. "My hemoglobin level is up! That means that my bone marrow cells are taking over from the cancer, there are more of them, and they're manufacturing good blood for me. Look," and he showed her a chart he had drawn up, "look at this projection. If I continue on the same curve, I'll be running again in a month or two! We can have a good Christmas, Lou, we can celebrate!"

They had Sylvia and Deirdre for Christmas, and a young mathematician, one of the men Philip had been cultivating for a friend before he got sick. The mood was precarious, almost too quiet. Louise was tired; Sylvia was disheartened by isolation in the small provincial town where she was teaching; and the mathematician was painfully shy. Usually Philip would have played host, directing with gusto; but now he was more the observer, passive and even slightly tuned out. It was Deirdre who pumped energy into the conversation, which flowed around Philip like a stream around a rock. Eventually Deirdre managed to draw everyone out and create a celebration, a sense of Christmas as it ought to be. Once again they had achieved a repetition, though without daring to ask if this one could ever happen again.

* * *

The day after Christmas, the doctor phoned again, with the delayed results of one last test. A critical chemical in Philip's blood had increased – not by much, but a little. The chemical was given off by active cancer cells, and the increase meant that somewhere in Philip's body there were cancer cells not being reached by the drug.

"It's like a death-knell," Philip said, sitting in deep dejection on the window seat where he had earlier sat so often, looking out at the view. Now his back was towards the window; he sat with his shoulders slumped, looking into the room. "All it takes is one cell, or one little pocket of cells, not being held back by the hormone pills. Those cells can just multiply and multiply and eventually kill me. God, we were so happy just yesterday! These ups and downs are terrible, it's like a kind of insanity, a rollercoaster. If only we could get off of it. I want to live days one by one and not be crazy with hoping, or in the pits of depression, ruining what time there is when every second is so precious."

He paused for a moment, looking inward; then shifting impatiently, went on. "If we only knew where the wild cells were, we could get them! I have a hunch they're either in the left leg bone, or the vertebrae at the top of my spine. If they're just in one spot, we could get them with radiation treatment. I'm going to tell Harry about it." Harry was the doctor's name. Philip had, as usual, moved quickly past the formalities with him, and established a warm connection.

But before the new medical questions came something else. It was not unconnected: they needed something to raise their spirits, something that affirmed hope and the future. Not a rollercoaster item, but something more solid, something that would not disappear with the next call from the doctor.

It was December 30, Louise's last day at the law school. Everything was quiet, since it was the holiday break. She sat at her desk, trying to put things into an order her kindly boss could follow.

The phone rang. It was Philip.

"Hi, Lou. Listen, I have an idea. How would you like to go on a little trip – tomorrow? Up to Nevada. You know what they have up there?"

"You want to gamble?" she fumbled, uncertain.

"Wouldn't you like to get married? We can do it there in an hour, without blood tests and waiting periods and separate trips to get a license and have the ceremony. And it's perfectly legal. How about it, Lou? Want to elope with me?"

"Oh my god," she replied. "Well – yes! Why not? What an idea! Elope! How exciting!"

"That's what I think!" he laughed. "And by doing it before the year ends, we'll even get tax advantages because you earn so little."

It was her turn to laugh. "Oh, so you want to marry me for the money?"

"Well, frankly it won't amount to much. But maybe enough to pay for the ring."

"Ring? Heavens. This sounds so real. Shall I get you a ring?"

"No, I don't like to wear one. It gets in the way."

"Of dancing girls?"

"Well, sure, and also working in the lab. So you're ready to take off tomorrow morning?"

"Um, well, um, yes, why not? But will you be all right to drive such a long way? It must be four or five hours to Nevada."

"Yes, babe, I can make it. But I think this is the time to do it. There's no point in waiting."

"I agree. We can sleep together tonight as usual, in sin of course, and then elope in the morning – with Jo-Jo along, presumably."

"Yes, he can be our witness and best man, I thought – or best child? I don't know."

The next morning the three of them packed their things into Philip's green Super-Beetle. He insisted on driving, and backed the car out of the garage. Suddenly he froze at the steering wheel.

"It's my arms. Wait!" and he leaped out of the car and lay flat on the sidewalk, his face pale, his mouth open and taut with unvoiced pain. "Oh god, I hope I can make it," he said through clenched jaws.

Jo-Jo and Louise stood by him, helplessly watching. It was about ten minutes before Philip could get to his feet, looking embarrassed. He did not want other people to know how bad the pain was, or how it forced him against his will to drop everything when it came.

"No one saw," Louise said. "No one walked by – just a few cars."

"All right, gang, let's go. Jo-Jo, get into the car, pronto!" They all got in and began the long drive to Nevada.

The county seat was at Carson City, where they arrived late in the afternoon. Since it was early New Year's Eve, the only place that was open and carried jewelry was Penney's. They had a small assortment of gold wedding bands, and Louise chose a narrow one with a slight design of oblique lines, very simple. Then they rushed off to the courthouse, and thence to the judge's.

The witnesses were across the street in the bar, beginning their New Year's celebrations, but one was hauled back to stand beside Jo-Jo, in the back office with the tinselly Christmas decorations, and watch with disinterest as Louise and Philip exchanged vows.

"Do you, Philip Brett, take this woman to be your lawful wedded wife, to love and to cherish, through sickness and through health, 'til death do you part?"

Philip looked at her briefly, his green eyes intense. "I do."

"And do you, Louise Borgstrum, take this man to be your

lawful wedded husband, to love and to cherish, through sickness and through health, 'til death do you part?"

The man could have no idea what these words meant to them. They were already in sickness, and too close to death. Yet these marriage vows seemed like a lifeline thrown between her, safely on shore, and Philip, the swimmer caught in the undertow. They were linked. Surely it was more impossible, now, that they could be separated.

Jo-Jo looked on with mild curiosity, and signed his name well.

As they walked out into the street, they became elated. They had done it. But even Louise was exhausted, and she did not have to ask how Philip felt. They raced in the car back to the motel, where they had a set of two rooms, one for Jo-Jo, and one for the two of them. When they got there, Philip fell immediately onto the bed, too tired to eat yet. Jo-Jo was tired, too, and a little cranky, so Louise went by herself to find a liquor store. They needed some champagne to celebrate.

When she got back to the room, Philip was feeling better – or he pretended to be; she could not tell for sure. Jo-Jo was still resting in his room. They opened the bottle and poured out big glassfuls for themselves, and a small one for Jo-Jo.

Louise sat with Philip on the double bed, which she would share with him tonight legally, for the first time.

"My husband," she said. "It's strange – I feel so much closer to you. I hadn't thought that was possible, but it's true. I didn't know the ceremony would make any real difference. But it's as if we've given ourselves to each other in an open, formal kind of way, publicly acknowledged what we are to one another. Do you feel different?"

"No, I feel the same as always, but I can sense that it's different for you, and it makes me so happy we did it. My wife," he said softly. "Oh-oh, no crying, Lou."

"Jo-Jo!" he called. "Come on and toast our marriage with us."

Jo-Jo came in and looked at them, shy, and still a little irritable. "Here, Jo-Jo, you'll like this," Philip said, handing him the small glass.

"To the woman I love – my wife," Philip toasted, smiling at Louise.

"To the man I love – my husband," Louise replied, and immediately burst into tears.

"Drink, drink!" he said, clinking glasses with Jo-Jo and Louise. "You've just got low blood sugar. We'd better get you to dinner. How do you like champagne, Joseph?"

"I like it," he answered, smiling happily, his mood changed.

Philip poured him another half-glassful. "You'll sleep well tonight," he said.

They quickly finished off the champagne, and went downstairs. But Philip could eat only a bite or two before starting to nod off at the table. Jo-Jo was equally sleepy. Louise's stomach hurt, but she was hungry and ate as much as she could before Philip began to lean dangerously over the edge of his chair. She could not resist gathering up the remains of the steaks. They would make the basis of an easy meal at home. Then she got them all upstairs. A strange wedding dinner, she thought.

When Jo-Jo was safely in bed, they closed the door. Self-consciously Louise began to pull down the cover of their bed.

"Let me see that sexy nightgown from your girlfriend at the law school," Philip said. "You did bring it along, didn't you?"

"Yes, since you asked me to before, and because this is when Liz wanted me to wear it. Do you really want me to put it on? I'll just be taking it off again; it's too uncomfortable to actually sleep in. It cuts across the ribs."

"Yes, yes, I want to see it on you," Philip said, smiling his old lecherous smile.

So Louise went into the bathroom and put it on, trying to look as glamorous as she could after all the long day. The gown was becoming, a lovely odd shimmering shade of deep blue.

"I like that," Philip said appreciatively. "Come here, let me see you," he teased, pulling her down to him as soon as she came within reach.

"I'm afraid I'll start hurting if I move very much, so you'll have to do all the work. But you like to be on top anyway, I know. And get out your diaphragm! I'm still dangerous!"

But she could not relax, and, to her surprise, found she could not get very excited. She was afraid of hurting the bones around his pelvis, which she knew were riddled with cancer. The thought that under her weight one of those bones could collapse, like the disk in his spine, was agonizing. Yet she did not have the heart to tell Philip her fear.

Philip, aware that she was holding back, did not know why. After too long a time they finally fell back in the lumpy bed, exhausted, incomplete, and went to sleep.

* * *

In January, Philip began to receive radiation treatments to his neck, where the upper vertebrae had collapsed. Every morning for several weeks he went to the hospital and lay down in an enormous metal machine, like two halves of a huge rock that had been neatly split open. Technicians positioned him carefully between the two metal slabs, and wrote on his pale flesh with red and purple pens as if he were a piece of meat going to market; they were making sure that he would be irradiated only and exactly in the right places. Then, when he was correctly placed, the technicians left him alone in the room, closing the heavy doors behind them, and directed the machine to send its radiation into Philip's waiting body. Except for the occasional pain of being put into position, the treatments did not hurt; but they were frightening.

Nonetheless, Philip found a way of being enthusiastic about it. "The doctor tells me that the radiation treatment will make scar tissue form inside and around the vertebrae, and the whole thing will sort of fuse together. When it's done the spine will be strong again, and I can take off this damned collar." He had worn the white plastic muff-like collar steadily for months now, even at night. "I can hardly wait, I'll tell you. And I'm not getting enough radiation to make me sick. At the most, maybe just a little tired."

They were sitting in the upstairs bedroom, and his eyes went out over the view, eagerly. "I'm still planning on going skiing with you in February. You'll love it at Aspen, and I can show you all the trails and intermediate slopes, and maybe we can take in some of the night life. If I'm too tired to ski all day I can just sit around while you ski. I always meet people and I'd like that too. I just have to be very careful when I ski. The doctors told me that if I took a hard fall and hurt my neck, the spinal cord could be severed and I'd be paralyzed from the neck down."

Louise could feel her face drain of color. But it was Philip's back, his life. She did not reply. She would not patronize him, as if he were a child to be taken care of. Maybe he would change his mind. Otherwise they would go.

* * *

I t was Jo-Jo's weekend to stay with them. On Saturday he had one of his soccer games. Philip did not say anything about it, but Louise guessed that he would want to go.

Saturday arrived, cold and drizzly.

Jo-Jo came into the living room, where Louise and Philip sat.

"Dad, are you going to go?"

"Look at you," Philip replied. "You look good in that soccer outfit, you know that, Jo-Jo?"

Jo-Jo looked away shyly for a moment, then repeated, "You going to go, Dad? I promised you'd give a ride to one of the other kids on the team. He lives pretty near here."

"I think so, Joseph. I'll need to sit down today, but I can take that folding chair from the deck, and a blanket. I can manage."

"With crutches, too?" Louise asked anxiously.

"Yes, I'm not going to give up yet," Philip replied. "Come here, Joseph, come let me hug you for a minute. Did you know you're Daddy's favorite little boy?"

Jo-Jo went slowly over to Philip to give him a hug, as he had done countless times before, invited by the exact same words. This time, however, he put his arms around Philip carefully. At eight years, he was old enough to understand that even the pressure of his small body could give Philip pain.

"That's my boy," Philip said. "That felt good. Are you ready to go?"

"Yeah, it's time, too," Jo-Jo answered, his voice high and a little reproachful.

"All right, all right, let's go." Philip raised himself slowly from his chair, reaching for the crutches he kept at his side. His face was pale, but he kept going.

"May I come along and carry the chair and blanket for you?" Louise asked. "I made a dentist appointment for this morning, before I knew there would be a game today, but I could help you settle in on the field."

"Don't worry, Jo-Jo will help me, I'll be fine," Philip said, his back to her as he went into the hallway.

She watched him labor down the stairs on his crutches, Jo-Jo following with the folding chair and a blanket. The air was cold, and while the drizzle had let up for a minute, it was threatening to begin again any time. She shook her head. Philip would not give up; he was trying to make up to Joseph the years of fathering and love which he might miss.

* * *

Philip canceled the Aspen trip; deterioration continued. He was forced to give up his work at the lab – a huge loss, the work he had loved, work both meaningful and fascinating. At home, it became too difficult for him to sit up through dinner, and he began to eat in bed upstairs. His appetite was fickle, and Louise outdid herself trying to make food he might want to eat. While Philip lay upstairs, reading or watching the evening news on TV, she fussed in the kitchen.

One night he commented, "You know, Lou, I don't want very elaborate food. I'd rather you spent more time up here with me, and just had soup for dinner or something like that."

But she felt she had to cook. She wanted him to get vegetables and protein and whole grains – anything to give his body
strength to fight the cancer. And there was something else, too: it
was easier to be working downstairs in the kitchen than to sit,
helpless, by Philip's side, watching an insipid TV program. It was
too hard to be so confined and so useless, and to feel the time float
out from beneath her hands. So she cooked and cooked, trying to
turn out something that could sustain them both. Mostly,
however, she was the one who ate, guiltily, grossly, given to her
healthy appetite while Philip picked at his food, struggling to get
some of it down.

* * *

It was time for another check-up at the doctor's. When they got
to Kaiser, Louise commandeered a wheelchair, and got Philip
to the doctor's examining room. When he lay down on the long
metal table, Louise could not help thinking that his body had
become exquisitely beautiful. Somehow the loss of weight, or
perhaps the sickness itself, had refined his features and his body;
they looked sensitive and aware in a way that health, with its blunt
matter-of-fact assumptions, had not. Louise wondered if the
doctor noticed Philip's beauty. How could he help it? But he said
nothing.

While Philip slowly dressed, Louise followed Harry to his
office.

"The pain seems worse," she said. "Is there anything stronger
you could prescribe for him?"

He looked sharply at her for a moment, his pudgy face focused. "You are aware, are you not, Louise, that your husband's case is essentially hopeless? We may be able to prolong his life a little, but that's all. He may have a few months, or maybe if he's lucky a year or so."

She nodded, unable to speak. The telephone rang and the doctor busied himself with the call. She picked up a magazine and pretended to read it, trying to maintain a normal surface. She could not afford to break down, out here in the world; and Philip must not see. He knew his prognosis as well as anyone, but he lived on hope. So did she. They were battling the cancer not simply to eke out a maximum number of days for Philip, and not just on principle. They battled in case Philip might be one of the exceptions, one of the rare but seemingly documented cases of a serious cancer that goes into remission, or even, mysteriously, disappears. And if not that, perhaps at least they could keep Philip alive until a cure was found. Every week it seemed the newspaper announced some new promising approach.

She would not repeat the doctor's death sentence to Philip. As for the doctor, right now he was the enemy, and she would not give him the satisfaction of seeing her understand his words. She understood them secretly, in a locked room at the very pit of her consciousness. There, in the dark, they slowly ate like acid at the foundations.

* * *

New x-rays showed significant growth of the cancer in the groin and left leg. Philip was quickly scheduled for more radiation treatments. These would affect his general health more radically than the first set, because there was so great an area involved. It was very discouraging. The cancer was showing up in too many places, like a brush fire showering sparks over a whole town. It seemed impossible that all these fires could be put out in time. Soon Philip's left leg and entire groin were marked with indelible red ink lines, guides for placing him in the radiation machine. The trick would be to kill as many of the bad cells as possible without at the same time killing their host – Philip.

Every weekday morning Louise drove him to the hospital for his radiation treatments, going in to work late. Luckily her new employers were kind and understanding. As long as she worked four hours a day, they told her, it did not matter when she came in.

And everything took more time for Philip. Because it hurt to move his legs, it took a long time for him to get dressed. Slowly he eased himself down the stairs, hanging onto the banister. Slowly he moved through the house, out the door and down the long front steps. Both he and Louise thought of those steps with fear. It was too easy to imagine Philip losing his balance, falling, crashing down that long length of brick edges.

It was a triumph to get out to the curb and into the car, but even then he could not relax. Stopping, starting, curves – any sudden movement of the car was painful to him. Gradually Louise learned to drive more smoothly, though there was no way she could cushion Philip from the jolts caused by irregular paving. Her old Datsun translated each bump in the street into an equal bump to its passengers.

When they got to the hospital, the doctor in charge looked Philip over carefully.

"I think you're too sick to continue the groin treatments," he said. "You've had almost all of them – all but two. That's not bad. But the radiation is affecting too much other tissue. We'll get the leg today, and see abut the groin later."

Neither Philip nor Louise replied. Louise wheeled him out into the hall, her face set. Philip, too, was silent. It was another setback, in the midst of too much loss. Often it seemed better, more efficient, not to feel too much.

Near the end of February, Philip began to draw up schedules, figuring out how soon he would be through the radiation treatments on his leg. The first morning of the last week he was jubilant. "We're getting through it, babe," he grinned at breakfast. "The cells in the marrow of this leg and hip must be nearly all dead – especially the bad ones. They get it first because they multiply faster and that makes them more vulnerable to the radiation. I just have a feeling that the wild cells were in this leg. Maybe we'll have gotten them all!"

He looked down at his cereal in distaste. "I've just got to get through this week, that's all." With difficulty they made their way down the brick walkway, with a falsely cheery hello to Victor, their disco teacher and carpenter, who was out there working on the front fence. Victor smiled in return, but Louise could see the concern in his eyes. No one was fooled, but still appearances had been kept up, and with them, Philip's courage.

At the hospital, Louise wheeled him into the radiation department and went to get the newspaper he wanted. He insisted that she do this; he needed to keep up his connection with the world outside. There were always four or five other patients waiting there, lined up to take their turn between the two metal slabs of the radiation machine. They were various ages, though none quite as young as Philip. One had his nose partly eaten away, but the cancers of the others were invisible. Every day they greeted Philip eagerly, and he was glad to see them. They understood. They were the initiate. They were friendly to Louise, too, but carefully, as if from a distance. It was to Philip that their trust was turned.

As Louise came back with his newspaper, Philip shook his head. "I don't think I'm well enough to have any treatment today," he said in a low voice. "Where's the doctor they have here? Would you go find him?"

She rushed off to find him, looking from empty office to empty office. Two nurses joined her search. Finally they found out that the doctor, the only cancer specialist there, was doing surgery that morning and would not return for an hour or more.

Philip looked confused when she told him. "I have an appointment with Harry in half an hour. Kaiser is only ten minutes away, but –" He thought for a moment. "I guess we'd better go. It's terrible to miss a treatment, but I just don't think I can take it."

Still, they hesitated a moment longer, reluctant to forego the treatment when he was so close to the end of the series. Maybe the very last treatments really would kill the last lurking wild cells, and give Philip a reprieve on life.

"No! Let's go!" Philip finally said, impatient. "Quick! Out the emergency doors into the parking lot! I need to get out fast. Fast!" he repeated urgently. "Careful! Careful!" he said, anxious as Louise opened the doors around his wheelchair.

Seeing them go out the forbidden doors, one of the technicians came after them, but Louise's attention was on maneuvering the wheelchair, as the doors gave onto a very narrow sidewalk, bordered by a curb dropping down six or eight inches into the parking lot.

As the sun struck him, Philip lurched forward in his wheelchair, violently ill. He threw up, wracked, and as he leaned forward to avoid soiling himself, he pitched out of the chair, forward and down, falling helplessly over the curb into the parking lot, striking his back, hard, across one of the concrete bars placed at the front of each parking space.

"Philip!" Louise screamed, rushing over to him. The parking attendant and the two radiation therapists were by him almost as soon as she was. He lay on the pavement, his stomach still convulsing, but now with nothing left to bring up. They got paper towels and cleaned off Philip's shoes and the wheelchair. Everyone was kind; but Louise saw horror and disgust glimmer behind their helpfulness. The veil of good cheer and civilization had been torn; mortality and the body's ugly disintegration had intruded.

Though the two of them were half hysterical with dismay and fear, they managed to get to Kaiser, where Harry was expecting them. Philip's back hurt him, but it seemed that he had at least not broken it. He was not paralyzed. But they did not know what had happened, or what to expect now.

Louise rustled a wheelchair from an unobservant nurse and got Philip into Harry's office.

She and a nurse helped Philip undress so that Harry could examine him. Philip was still beautiful, though too thin now. His enormously high rib cage stuck out almost grotesquely, and the skin, which had shimmered pale milk-white before, now had a greenish tinge.

This time she could not hide from the doctor. Her entire face shook as Harry examined Philip and talked with them. It was pointless to try to hide any longer. Besides, Harry must have seen too many others like them; only to themselves were they unique.

Philip could do little more than lie on the hospital table, but he turned his head to the doctor. "I need stronger pain medicine, Harry, I can't sleep. I can't even rest. It's wearing me out. The two grains of codeine doesn't even touch it anymore. It's a deep pain, and steady. It doesn't go away. There's no rest from it. I can't take it anymore!"

"I'll get you something stronger, Philip," Harry nodded. "Will you just lie there for a minute? I'm going to give some prescriptions to Louise to take to the pharmacy downstairs."

She followed Harry out into the hall, waiting as he closed the door on Philip's examining room.

"He may have only a few weeks now," he said quietly. "I found more collapsed disks in his lower back. That means the cancer is progressing faster than we had thought. There's very little we can do now." He paused, to make sure she had taken it all in.

"Philip should take the pills I'm giving him for nausea, every three hours around the clock. He'll have a stronger pain pill, too, and this also should be taken every three hours."

She waited to go into the pharmacy until her face had stopped shaking. She must go like everyone into the pharmacy, wait in line in a windowless, airless room filled with the small rustling sounds of many people, coughing, sneezing, children complaining or crying, everyone looking tired and yellow under the yellow lights.

Finally, the prescriptions filled, she wheeled Philip back out to the car. He could barely hold himself upright. Louise did not like to think about how they would get him up the hill to the house, and then up to the second story, to bed. First they had to get to the house. She drove as fast as she dared.

When they got home, Victor was still there, working on the front fence. He did not need any prompting; it was enough to see Philip's face. "Come on, old guy," he said, half lifting Philip out of the car. "I'll give you a hand up the steps."

Philip grimaced, trying to acknowledge the help gracefully. "I need more than a hand, Victor. God, I'm glad you're here. I don't know what we would have done. I have to get into my bed. Can you get me up that far?"

"I think so," Victor said calmly. Philip was now so thin that Victor could have carried him, if necessary; but he did not say so. Slowly the two of them labored up the stairs, Louise following, watching anxiously.

Once he was in bed, he could not leave it. At night the alarm was set for every three hours. He had two alarm clocks set to go off within a minute of each other.

"This way I can be sure of not missing a pill," he said. "If I miss one I'm afraid the pain could get out of control. I'm sorry you have to wake up, Lou, but I need you. My head isn't too clear with all these drugs and I could make a mistake doing it alone."

"It's okay," she answered. "Don't worry, I go right back to sleep each time." It was true. It was like falling off a cliff into a black dreamless space where she lay completely inert and unconscious until the next wakening. She had never slept that way before. Although she did not feel worn by sleeplessness, she took extended sick leave from her new job. She could not work while Philip might die at any moment. And confined now to bed, he needed someone with him most of the time.

"I'm so sorry, Lou," he looked at her with wide eyes, hollowed by his inability to eat. "I didn't want you to have to do these things. I'm afraid you might come to hate me, or at least be too disgusted. I don't know how we'll handle the BMs. Maybe we should get a nurse."

"No, no, I'd rather do everything myself. I don't want some stranger with you. Don't worry. It's nothing, absolutely nothing." This was more or less true. What had to be done, would be done. They could figure out everything as it came along.

Philip looked doubtful, but he accepted her word. He too did not want a stranger; and he had no other choice but to accept Louise's help, even though it hurt him to need it this way.

* * *

Philip called his father, breaking a twenty-five-year silence between father and son. "I can't believe it," Philip said, as he lay in bed, staring up at the ceiling. "My father's finally gotten religion, and it's softened him. He wants to do the right thing. It's a little late –" he raised an eyebrow and gave a wistful smile. "But it's wonderful. I want to be reconciled with everyone. Maybe I'll even like Marge. I didn't before, but that was probably because it was too early for them to marry, just a month after my mother died. Guess I told you Marge was the nurse for my mother? It could be I didn't give her a chance. It seemed as if they could just barely wait for my mother to die. But I don't know – that doesn't seem as important now. But you –" he turned and looked directly at Louise – "wait at least six months, all right?"

"You don't have to worry," she said. She could not imagine taking anyone after Philip.

He laughed. "Don't worry, Lou, I know you too well. You'll find someone after me. But just don't rush it, just for the sake of my memory. Don't you think I know you? You need love, it's the way you are. I want you to be happy again. Don't pretend. I know you love me."

"I could never love anyone again the way I love you," she said, her voice weighted low with sadness. The love that had engulfed and consumed them, wrapped them as if in an ecstatic flame – no, this completion could happen only once. Yet she knew it was also true: there were other desirable men out there, not Philip, yet still offering something precious, and she would want one of them. In the conflict between the ideal – staying forever faithful to Philip's memory – and her feelings, she knew her feelings would win. It was one more way in which she was unable to protect him from death.

* * *

When Philip's father and stepmother arrived, Louise was surprised to find that she liked them – or almost liked them. It was hard to forget the hardness of the father, stubbornly set against his son for all those years, while Philip had tried again and again to reach across the father's well-defended barricade. Philip senior – Phil – had the same animal presence she knew in Philip, the high energy, maybe even some of the same intelligence, though less developed. But Phil senior arrived full of the desire to do the right thing – quickly, though, and then get on back home.

He had brought Philip a gift: the crucifix and beads belonging to Philip's mother. She had died with them in her hand. Philip immediately wound the beads around his hand, looking gratefully at his father. Philip had often told Louise how deeply his mother and father had loved each other – "like you and me" – and the crucifix was his father's most powerful memento. Giving it to Philip now was convincing proof that he wanted to repair the relationship at last, and be close to his son.

"Thank you," Philip whispered.

Phil did not speak, but took Philip's hand. With Marge, Louise watched in silence, thinking how easy this reconciliation appeared to be, and of all the years Philip had endured without it. Why did their parents forgive them only when Philip lay dying? Did they think he had expiated his sins now? Paid in full for being born with such a strong and happy spirit? For being different from them, and believing in different things?

Later on, when Jo-Jo came by, Marge took photos: Jo-Jo with Phil, Phil and Philip, Jo-Jo and Phil and Philip. Relationships confirmed, Phil and Marge left for southern California. Louise was glad to see them go. Except for Hugh or Jim, who did not need to be treated with company manners and knew their way around the house, visitors were only an extra burden.

* * *

A few days later, Philip asked Jo-Jo to come by and talk to him after school.

"Hiya, Jo-Jo," Philip said softly, as Jo-Jo came in.

Jo-Jo stood by Philip's bed, looking at him.

"Pull up a chair, Joseph. I'd like to talk to you for a minute."

Jo-Jo dragged Philip's heavy desk chair over to the side of the bed, and pulled himself up into it, trying to look adult.

"Give me your hand, Jo-Jo."

"Good. You know Daddy's very sick, right?"

Jo-Jo nodded.

"You know it doesn't have anything to do with you. I just got sick because I got sick, not because you ever got mad at me or anything like that. It's not your fault I'm sick, and I don't want to be sick, either. I don't like lying around in bed all day, believe me! I'm sorry I can't go to your soccer games any more. I just can't do it, I'm not strong enough. But I'd like to go. And I don't think I want you to stay overnight here in the house any more. It's not your fault, but I'm just not strong enough to see you very much. I can't see anyone very much, but I love you very, very much. Never forget that, Jo-Jo. Your Daddy loves you very, very much."

Jo-Jo nodded again, looking sulky and impatient.

"What's wrong, Jo-Jo?"

"Nothing. Can I go now, Dad?"

"What's wrong? Are you mad at me?"

"No, nothing," Jo-Jo replied, looking to one side. "It's just that I need to go now." He paused, then added hurriedly, "If you've said everything, I mean."

Philip looked at him.

"I can understand if you're mad at me, Jo-Jo. Maybe it seems to you as if I'm kind of unreliable, or as if I don't really care about you. But that's not true. When you get older you'll understand more, and I want you to remember just these few things until you do get a little older. Remember that it's not your fault, and that I love you. Okay?"

"Okay. Can I go now, Dad?"

"Yes, but come back and visit me as many afternoons as you can. It means a lot to me to see you."

"Okay. Bye, Dad," Jo-Jo said in a toneless voice.

"Bye, Jo-Jo." Philip tossed in the bed impatiently. He tossed all day, all night. In a short time he had worn a hole in a new sheet. Louise changed his pillows often, so they could dry out. He was constantly sweating, constantly thrashing. It was good to make peace with his family, but something more was needed.

* * *

He phoned the local Catholic Church, and arranged to have a priest come to hear confession and give him last rites – now called something less fearsome, but last rites all the same.

Louise made sure she was well occupied when the priest came. She did not want to meet him. Didn't he belong to the Catholic Church? Wasn't he against women? Didn't all these celibate males do everything they could to keep women pregnant and dependent? Didn't they fight contraception and the Equal Rights Amendment and keep women out of the Church's hierarchy? They were her enemy, and not just passively: they worked at it, hard.

When the priest arrived, she was making up dough for sweet rolls. Her own hands covered with flour, she did not have to touch this priest's hand in false friendship and gratitude; she was suitably soiled. She showed him the way upstairs, then went back to the kitchen, kneading the dough, throwing it down on the counter, thrusting the heels of her hands into it, picking it up and throwing it down again.

Upstairs the priest and Philip talked. The sweet rolls had begun to rise by the time the priest came down the stairs. She had been waiting for him to leave, compressed tight as a spring in the kitchen. He went out the front door by himself.

Instantly she went upstairs, to talk to Philip and find out what had happened. He looked at her calmly and lovingly as she came in. She had rarely seen him look so calm.

"He did everything," he said, "anointed my forehead with oil, everything. I am happy, Lou. Maybe for the first time in my life I am really at peace, with the Church, and my father, and somehow this acceptance. I'm off the rollercoaster. I can accept death."

She could not help crying, frustrated at her tears because she felt she understood. She could see that he was, in some new way, whole – though she could not quite accept the means by which this had been accomplished.

Ironically, having accepted death, Philip seemed to get better. He slept more easily, and began to eat more, too. Louise watched without saying anything, but she could not help beginning to hope again. Philip too began to look more pleased, more lively.

* * *

A week or so after the priest's visit, Louise entered Philip's room and found him tossing about angrily in bed.

"I just talked to Concha on the phone," he said. "I didn't want to get mad but I couldn't help it. She was pressing me about the will, and trying to act so sweet and lovey-dovey at the same time, it just stank and I called her on it."

"What did you say?" Louise asked, needing to know, wondering if she was any better than Concha. Her own desire for the house had not diminished.

"Well, I asked her why she hadn't shown any of this caring before and why she expected me to believe her or trust her after the way she betrayed me when we were together, and how she rubbed my face in it when she thought I was in her power, and a few other things like that."

"Wooph," Louise breathed. "A lot. How do you feel?"

"Not too good. I shouldn't get excited like that. It uses up too much energy. But I'll calm down. Maybe now anyway she'll quit calling. I don't like it. She's still trying to manipulate me, I see it more and more clearly."

By the end of the day Philip had in fact calmed down. Two days later, however, there was a letter from Concha in the mail.

"I can't believe it!" Philip shouted, his voice almost as strong as before the illness. "She tells me I have to change my will and do it the way she wants! She says there's a clause in the marriage settlement that gives her the power to make me do it. I can't believe the woman's nerve! She's already taken half – more than half – of everything I had, and now she wants to tell me what to do with what I have left. It's as if I haven't got anything. No running, no singing, no job. All I have left, the only power, is deciding what to do with these things I've collected – the life insurance money, and the house, and the retirement money I had to pay for so dearly in the divorce settlement."

Louise sat down in her chair by the bed.

"What does she want you to do?" She wanted to know the worst.

"She wants all the retirement, and all the insurance money. But she doesn't know how much there is – there's more insurance than she says in her letter. If she knew, she'd be after all of it. And the house should just go to you. Don't worry, Lou, she hasn't got a chance. It's all just a big bluff. She thinks because I'm dying I can't think straight. But I still have my head together, at least part of the time, not right after I take my pills, but an hour or so afterward. We'll have to settle it though, and make everything clear."

As Louise watched Philip it was hard to believe that he was really dying. Anger had roused all his latent strength.

"You sound so well right now. Maybe Concha will have inadvertently made you healthier by making you so mad!"

"No, no, it's not good," he said, turning away from her on the pillow. "It's exhausting."

The next day he called the lawyer. There was doubt, after all. The clause in the divorce agreement was ambiguous, and Concha might have a chance of breaking the will.

"I refuse to change it!" Philip shouted again. "You'll just have to fight her if she tries to go after everything, Lou. The worst that can happen is that she'll get more of the insurance money, but you can still manage on what's left plus the retirement."

Louise was not sure what to think. All she knew was that she did not want to lose the house, this castle on the hill, filled with memories of Philip, and a treasure more precious than anything she would ever have a chance to own again.

A week or so later, the university confirmed Concha's claim that the retirement would have to go to her – or nominally, to Jo-Jo. Philip could not leave it to Louise until they had been married a full year. It was March, and they had been married less than three months. It hardly seemed possible that Philip could live much longer. His eyes were clouded with anger and frustration as he told her.

"But don't worry, Lou, we'll get around her anyway! I'll live for nine more months just to frustrate her! It'll give me a real motivation." He tried to laugh, but was still too angry.

Louise tried to keep calm in front of Philip. She did not want him to know how terribly she wanted the house, how she had come to look at it as if it might be hers. Could Concha take the house too? At last, trying to downplay the strength of her desire and fear, she told him what was on her mind.

To her relief, he did not look appalled.

"Don't worry, she can't get everything, Lou. I'll leave the retirement to her, and you can have all the insurance. You'll be rich!" he smiled, amused at the thought. "You'll have to stop being a hippie after all. You'll have too much money!"

But Concha turned out to have a claim on the insurance money as well. At last, after several weeks of deliberating, the lawyer came up to the house with a new will. Concha got all the retirement and half the insurance. The house would go to Louise directly, instead of being in trust to Jo-Jo.

"She wins," Philip said softly when the lawyer and witnesses had left. "She wins again. But you'll still have plenty. You won't have any trouble keeping the house, and that's the important thing."

"It will be fine," she answered. "You're right – I can keep the house this way. And the lawyer says she's signed papers saying she won't try to go after any more. I feel a lot safer this way. The house is the important thing. It's so beautiful, and we've lived through so much here together."

Philip smiled at her with satisfaction. "And as long as you have the house, you can have Jo-Jo here too, just as much as before, half the time. I just wish you could get full custody. The less he has to see of Concha, the better. I don't want her warping his values, growing up thinking the only way to get along is to cut other people's throats. You'll be good for him."

Cold struck into her stomach.

"Philip," she faltered, "there's no way Concha will let me have Jo-Jo half-time. You know the courts would never take him from his biological mother, who's respectably remarried and well off, and let his new stepmother have him half-time. And I doubt that Jo-Jo would want it, either."

Philip looked at her. "You mean you don't want him," he accused.

She breathed deep. "No, I would like him. I would – especially if I could have him full time and raise him entirely myself. But that can't happen. Concha wouldn't let it. The law is on her side. But I will keep in touch with Jo-Jo, see him regularly, try to remind him that other worlds exist, with different values."

Philip turned his face away.

"Philip!" she said, coming close to the bedside.

"You mean I have to give up my son, too," he said in a low voice, his head still turned away from her.

She did not answer. After a moment she took his hand. It was still warm and strong-seeming, though thin. "I do love you," she said, putting her other hand along his cheek. But as she did so, he shrank back.

"Sorry," he muttered, "it's awful. The pain has gotten worse. These pills don't seem to do anything any more. You've got to call the doctor in the morning."

"Okay."

After a moment he said, "I'll get over it, Lou. But it's a hard blow, about Joseph."

They sat in silence a long while, his head still turned away, their hands clasped on the bedcover.

* * *

That night Philip felt he could not bear the pain, and yet there was no way he could prevent its coming. By morning he was in a frenzy, and Louise called the doctor as soon as the hospital offices were open.

"You'll have to come in here, Louise," Harry said. "I'm prescribing morphine. He'll need shots. You'll have to learn how to give them. A nurse in my office will show you how. Can you be here this morning?"

"In half an hour," she replied. She left immediately. Morphine. But she already knew that Philip was dying. Why was it so hard to face this new confirmation of it?

At the hospital she took notes, with the strained lucidity of fear, as the nurse explained what to do. She left with a set of small bottles containing the morphine solution, a box full of sterile needles, and a box of alcohol swabs to prepare Philip's skin. She was in a hurry to reach Philip with this relief; but reluctant, too, afraid of having to do this new thing.

When she entered the bedroom with the apparatus, she could see that Philip was feeling the same conflict. Carefully, self-consciously, aware that he was watching her, she filled the needle with morphine, shaking the air bubbles out, getting the alcohol swab ready. He bared his arm and offered it to her.

She looked at it: an intact-looking arm, Philip's arm, full of nerve endings, sensitive. She tentatively brought the needle up to it, hesitating.

"Come on, Lou, hurry, can you? You don't know how I feel," Philip said, impatient.

She pressed the needle against the freckled skin. It made a small dent, but did not puncture the skin. She pressed harder. Still it would not go through. Harder. Harder. At last it broke through and Louise forced the measured brown liquid into the flesh, where it raised a small bump.

"Do you feel anything?" she asked, carefully withdrawing the needle the way the nurse had shown her.

"Not yet. Give it a little while. How long is it supposed to take?"

"Only a few minutes. But that seems impossible. After all, it's only under the skin. They were very adamant about not getting it into a vein or anything."

It was just about three minutes.

"Aahh," Philip breathed. "It's working. Thank god."

He looked up at her. "I'm sorry I need it, Lou. It could change me. I don't know all the side effects. But I feel it. Not just the pain getting less, but in my head. I may be confused. I don't know."

He was quiet, withdrawing into the drug, and visibly relaxing as the pain receded.

But the lull did not last long. In half an hour he was restless again.

"It hurts, Lou. It's too much. I need more. Give me another shot – quick."

"So soon?" she asked. The doctor had not said anything about a second dose so soon after the first.

"Yes, yes, don't worry about it. I'd rather be dead than in so much pain, but you won't kill me with these one-milliliter amounts, it's not that much. Here, in the other arm," and he bared it up to the shoulder. "Two milliliters this time."

She filled the needle with two milliliters, shaking it carefully again to get the air bubbles out.

"Hurry, hurry, can't you?" he said sharply. "Please," he added more softly, "please try to hurry."

She gave him the shot. The needle went in more easily this time.

"Good, that was a good shot. You're getting good at this," he kidded her through the pain and the growing confusion of the drug.

After that he did not need another shot until it was scheduled, three hours later. For the night shots now, she had to wake up more thoroughly than before, bustling about the bed with alcohol swabs and needle and little bottles of morphine; but still she fell asleep again each time, into a blank trance, as if buried in warm earth.

* * *

Just when Louise began to feel that the relentless three-hour schedule was wearing her down dangerously, Hugh remembered hearing about an alternative to shots: a mixture that could be taken orally, called Brompton's Cocktail. It would be much easier, and less traumatic for both Philip and Louise. She promptly called Harry, who sounded a little nettled.

"Well yes, it exists. But why not continue with the shots?"

"They hurt," she replied, surprised at the question. Had the doctor really not thought of this elemental fact? In addition, Philip could take oral medicine himself. He would gain more control, and Louise might be partly released from the grinding three-hour schedule.

Soon they had a big brown bottle of Brompton's Cocktail. Louise measured it out into old spice bottles with good stoppers. A row of these, each holding one dose, stood lined up on the shelf above the bed every night, insurance and reassurance. Philip still needed an occasional shot for sudden pains, as it took Brompton's at least twenty minutes to work, compared to the three minutes or less for a shot; but the drinkable morphine gave them both relief.

Morphine did, however, have side effects. "It's disappointing, in a way," Philip commented dryly, after being on the morphine for a week or so. "At the very first I had some pretty interesting dreams – mostly of things that were all white, and very still and silent. But now all I get is sleepy and stupid, and something else: anxious, nervous. It makes me nervous. I'm afraid of things I didn't used to worry about."

"Oh," she replied, "it's the drug that's doing it! I'm so glad you told me. You've been questioning everything lately – do I have the right bottle, is the dishpan right here in case you feel sick to your stomach, is the chair too close to the bed –"

Philip shook his head. "Has it been that bad? But you know I'm sick," he said, a slight reproach in his tone. "But anyway," he went on, his eyes more sharply focused on her now, "while my head's clear enough, there's something I need to tell you. There's something in my papers, my stuff, something you'll probably find later. It's nothing. It's not important. It has nothing to do with you and me, okay?"

She was startled. What could there be to hide at this point? Something financial? But that seemed settled. Looking at Philip, though, she could not doubt what he was saying. Whatever it was, it wasn't important.

She nodded. "Okay, I won't worry about it."

Philip continued to look at her intently for a moment, as if to make sure Louise really meant it. "Good," he said, "good." He lay back for a moment, thinking. "What about Marge? What did she say when she called?"

His stepmother had begun phoning every few days from southern California, offering her long experience in caring for cancer patients.

"I asked her if there were foods you might be able to eat without getting sick at the sight or smell or even just the thought of them. She recommended oatmeal, and orange juice that's still left frozen, and an artificial drink that's supposed to be high in nutrients and calories. It's really worrying how few calories we get into you each day."

"That's good," Philip said, his voice fainter now, tired from the conversation. "But what I think I want more than anything is a real hospital bed, with sides on it so I can't fall out. I get so restless and with this drug I don't always know what I'm doing. What if I fell out of bed? In the middle of the night? Could you get me back in? Besides, the pain –" and he looked away from her quickly.

"It sounds like a good idea – let's do it," she answered. They had already had a few crises when Philip had still been able to get

up to go the bathroom but hadn't been able to get back into bed
by himself. Even though he had helped by pushing and pulling
himself, they had barely been able to do it together.

The next day she began to phone around. It turned out that
Kaiser would arrange for a hospital bed, through the American
Cancer Society. They would put it in the living room, where
Philip would feel less isolated, and where there was enough space
for such a big bed. It would have bars on the sides to prevent falls,
and a motorized back which Philip could raise and lower at will.

When the bed was in place, and Louise had put fresh sheets
on it, two ambulance men came to the house to carry Philip down
the stairs.

"Careful!" Philip warned, eyeing them anxiously as they
stood by his upstairs bedside.

They did not reply to him. "Should we take him on the
carrier?" one asked the other.

"No, the stairs are too narrow. We'll just pick him up. I'll take
the head and shoulders and you take him under the knees."

Philip nodded, trying to take part in this decision about
himself.

"One-two-three-up!" The two men scooped up Philip's body.
"Careful now!" They moved into the hall and down the stairs.

Philip did not say a word. Only Louise saw his expression as
the two ambulance men picked him up and moved out into the
afternoon sunlight of the hallway. Out of that face, the staring
eyes, the skin pulled tight over the high cheekbones, she heard a
silent scream vibrate through the house. The pain had broken
through the morphine, a giant wave sweeping over the carefully-
erected dike.

That night she decided to sleep in the dining room. With Philip right there in the living room, it would be close enough that she could hear him call out if he needed anything; not quite as good as being in the same bed with him, but still close.

At eleven o'clock she lay down on Jo-Jo's mattress, which she had dragged downstairs. But it turned out to be a solid mass of lumps. How had Jo-Jo ever been able to sleep on it? She eased herself into a valley between the biggest lumps, and turned her back to the living room, where Philip kept the lights on. He was not sleepy, and in fact suffered from insomnia. Partly it was being in bed all day, partly the drug, and partly his fear: he knew that people often died between midnight and dawn, and he did not want to be taken unawares.

She heard a loud motor sound; it was Philip going up and down in his bed, raising and lowering the back. Confined within the bars on the bed, able only to toss from side to side, the back-adjuster was a last piece of power. The sound went on and on; she pictured him riding the bed, restless, anxious, drugged. She could not sleep. Finally she crept into the living room.

"Babe, I'm going to sleep upstairs. But I'll leave the living room door open and the bedroom door open so I'll hear you if you call. And your pain medicine is all measured out there on the table beside you."

"You can't sleep down here, huh? I'm sorry – I guess I am noisy. Will you be down at two?"

"For the next morphine dose? Can't you take it by yourself? It's all measured out, and I can set the alarm here," she said, made blunt by desire for uninterrupted sleep.

He looked vague. "I don't think so. I get confused. I'm afraid I might not know what I'm doing. I might not remember to take it or I might take too much or not set the clock right for the next dose. This drug makes me confused," he repeated, waving one hand disconnectedly towards the medicine bottles.

She nodded. "Yes, I can see. Well," she hesitated, reluctant to commit herself, "okay, I'll set my alarm upstairs and be down at two. I'll make sure the five a.m. dose is ready, so you can take it at five, and then I'll be here again for the eight o'clock one. Good night, babe," and she kissed him on the cheek. He looked a little hurt and offered his mouth. She had avoided that because lately a thickish white film had started to form over his teeth. For some reason she could not bring herself to deal with it. Philip did not seem aware of it. Guiltily she bent down and kissed him on the mouth. There, as on his cheek, he tasted bitter to her; it was a smell on his skin, a salt, an acid, something new. She thought of it as the taste of the cancer. She did not like it on her lips.

He smiled. "Night, babe. See you. Sleep well. I'll be all right down here."

She trudged up the stairs, thinking. Perhaps it was foolish of her to go down at two each morning. In theory Philip could take his own medicine then, and re-set the alarm. The doctor seemed to think this was plausible too. Philip could make a mistake – take both the two o'clock and the five o'clock doses at once, for instance, or forget to set the alarm and wake up in pain; but these would not kill him. She could not, however, allow even the possibility of these things. Everything had to be done exactly right, to maximize hope and minimize pain. There was reason on her side, but it was also a sort of ritual dance she was performing against death. Superstitiously, she felt that if she did anything poorly, it might be just enough to break the spell and let death in.

* * *

In spite of the fears, Philip's condition had clearly stabilized. And Louise had to get back to her job. It was almost April; she had been on sick leave for over two weeks. She had better save her remaining sick leave and vacation: there was no telling.

But somehow the mornings, when she would be working, would have to be covered. She phoned Kaiser. Only the grapevine had whispered that there were visiting nurses available. No one at Kaiser had ever breathed a word about this service, though it should have been obvious to the doctors that she and Philip might be needing it.

But once she had found it, it proved generous. Not only would a nurse come to the house as often as needed; a nurse's aide could also be sent, to give Philip a sponge bath, change the sheets and do anything else of a practical nature. The nurse was free; the nurse's aide cost only a few dollars for each visit. They would come out three mornings a week. That left Tuesday and Thursday to be taken care of. Who? What?

When the nurse came out, she asked him. "It has to be someone responsible, and with a good heart," she said. The nurse smiled. He was a young man, about thirty, with a round open face, and an easy manner. Louise found herself speaking freely with him.

"I know, it sounds corny, but that's what I want: responsible, with a good heart. How can I advertise for that?" And how, she thought to herself, weed out the cold-hearted incompetents who would faint at the sight of a big BM welling up around Philip's body? Or who might touch Philip carelessly, cause him pain, and by the carelessness make him feel less than fully human?

"I'll ask around for you," he promised, going out the door. "There may be someone unofficially available – I'll see what I can find out. But don't depend on me. I don't know what I can find. I can only try."

She shut the door behind him, and sat down in the hallway, trying to think. They could pay, though not well. Money. Of course – poor graduate students! It would be a perfect job for one of them. Philip didn't need constant tending, only constant proximity to someone who could help if needed. Before leaving for work, Louise could set up the morning's eleven o'clock morphine, give Philip whatever he could eat for breakfast, clean up the BM. The helper could spend most of the morning reading. Make tea and toast. Sit on the comfortable old green couch, in the morning sunlight.

She called Deirdre, who had nursed her own mother through six months of severe illness. Deirdre was clear: she would stay for two weeks, long enough for Louise to find someone who could stay on for a longer time. Deirdre was not shocked by a body out of polite control. She was soft-spoken, kind, and competent. Philip felt safe and comforted in her presence, even when she sat silently reading on the couch behind him. She refused pay, even though Louise knew Deirdre was usually short of money.

And the nurse came back with the name of a woman, Beverly, who would stay with Philip on Tuesdays and Thursdays. When Beverly arrived, she turned out to be a pretty Black woman just about Louise's age, capable and full of warmth. The gods were with them. Philip was delighted.

"Beverly," he smiled his old flirtatious smile, "tell me, what's your sign? You've got to be a fire sign."

"You mean my astrological sign?" She laughed. "I don't know. I don't hold much with that stuff. I was born April 12. So what does that make me?"

"Aries!" Philip crowed. "I knew it! You're just like Louise – your fellow Aries. I'm a Leo."

"But of course," Louise kidded him, "Philip doesn't really believe in astrology."

"The hell I don't!" he cried. "It works! I knew Beverly was an Aries, it fits perfectly."

"And you are a perfect Leo," Louise admitted.

Beverly laughed again. She didn't mind their Berkeley brand of nuttiness. Louise knew she was leaving Philip in good hands. And sure enough, Beverly did kind, thoughtful things – things that Louise had left undone, she noted guiltily: cleaning Philip's teeth, shaving him, understanding that these things made him feel more civilized, more a part of the living world, and lifted his spirits.

The nurse's aide turned out to be another gift from the gods. That was the way Louise thought about her; she needed something or someone to thank. "The heavens" could so easily have been less kind and sent lesser persons their way. The aide was a small solidly-built woman of Thai origin, who entered rooms, as she did everything, with a burst of determined energy. "Life hard," she said, standing squarely on her feet, bouncing a little. "I come to this country alone, I don't know language, know anything, it hard. I making it. Now I help you. You going to get better, sir, you going to get better! Remember that!" and with strong hands she washed him from head to toe, changed the sheets, massaged his legs, all the while clearing the air by the waves of energy she sent out.

With a feeling of security about the situation at home, Louise returned to her job. But it was no isle of serenity. Her only enemy in the entire building had been asked to fill in for her while she was out with Philip. Joanne's job was similar to Louise's, and she had been doing it long enough to understand the complicated equipment-purchasing process. There had been a decision to standardize procedures, and Joanne was to institute these standard procedures in Louise's books while she was gone. Looking over Louise's desk, Joanne had announced that it was a mess, that nothing could be found on it, that orders were getting lost, that Louise was terrible.

Louise had to admit that her desk was messy; she had left too abruptly to put it in order. She felt sure she hadn't lost any orders, but by the time she got back, Joanne had changed the books so that it was impossible to prove anything. Her boss called her in for a private interview. Was her job too hard? After all, she had had to start it from scratch, without a desk, paper, forms, and most of all without someone nearby to ask questions of. An hour of advice from a woman in another building had helped, but Louise had not known enough at the time to follow the advice well.

And it was true, her mind was not entirely on the job. When she walked down the halls, what she noticed most were the tables set out there for student papers; their sturdy wooden legs created safe shelters, and she longed to throw herself beneath one and sleep. Everything looked like a place to sleep, to rest, to lay her head down and forget just for a while. She had noticed another good spot behind the copy machine. She knew all the good spots. Not that she ever did it. She kept awake and tried hard to sort out all the orders. She never wasted a minute; but often she felt confused. Since she had been told that she would feel that way, that the job was hard to learn, even that she would be useless for months, she had not worried too much. There were plenty of other things to think about at home.

Earlier, Louise had come to dislike Joanne because she was rude without cause, high-handed, superior. Now Joanne sat in Louise's own office, in her own chair, haughtily telling her what to do in her own job. And Joanne wanted Louise to fail, had made her boss distrust her, made her appear a failure, slandered her – all gratuitously.

More than anything, Joanne loved paperwork, especially if it could be categorized as an order and she could put her name to it. She collected a whole array of rubber stamps with which to slam her papers. Never mind that the stamps obliterated much of the information on the forms. She sent out memos right and left – every time she farted, Louise thought maliciously. She did not know how long she could stand this tutelage.

Rescue came unexpectedly: Joanne decided to leave in order to get married. It was hard for Louise to imagine Joanne loving anyone, or that there could exist someone who would actually choose to live with her. Nonetheless, she did formally attach herself to some unfortunate person, leaving Louise once more in possession of her office, her chair, and her newly-ordered records. After a few weeks her boss seemed to relax and trust her once more, and her job became bearable, and even, as she gathered confidence and experience, pleasurable. The people around her she liked, liked exceptionally well. As for the people she had to deal with over the phone, they were fine too. They were, after all, sales people, paid to be pleasant. She even began to like one of the rubber stamps acquired by Joanne, the big heavy one saying "COMPLETE." She filled books with finished orders, her accomplishments. The world at work had a welcome face of rationality, going by the clock, running on rules and schedules, with small regular rewards.

The world at home, however, was out of time; it was spatially defined, Philip lying in the center of the living room, the hours a circle around him, marked off at regular three-hour intervals, always the same, day and night and day. There were no accomplishments there, nothing that could be labeled "complete." It was a world colored by pain and fear and lassitude and moments of intense closeness. Louise could not tell which was sane, and which insane, although her confusion in crossing the boundaries made her think the labels must fit: one of them must be insane. Or perhaps the insanity lay in the fact that neither world knew of the other. A few people at work were aware of Philip's illness, but most of the time work proceeded – as it had to – as if health and continuation were the norm. At home, all her love was confined between the bars of a hospital bed, in a body which had ceased to obey the usual rules. Here health, continuation and a future seemed unlikely, and best not thought about. And oblivion was not possible.

* * *

One afternoon, as Louise sat quietly by Philip, she asked him hesitantly, "Do you still love me?"

Philip looked at her so directly, with such concentration, that she could feel no doubt as to his answer.

"Unutterably," he said.

The gift was so incommensurate with her ability to receive it that she was only half pleasant to Philip the rest of the day. Why was that? She could only hope that Philip understood; more, that it might even slightly amuse him. It was not unlikely. She had grown accustomed to having her foibles received with love. It was evening before she could behave naturally with him again, all the while holding the precious gift close, as she might have held Philip's own self through the night in better times.

* * *

It had been weeks since the radiation treatments, and Philip seemed to be gaining strength. His appetite grew better, and his mind clearer. He began to want visitors again, and whenever Louise left the house in the afternoon for a hasty walk or on errands, she left the front door unlocked so that friends could come in. Jo-Jo was a regular visitor, and there was a steady stream of others.

They were most welcome, yet Louise dreaded them. Each was to feel welcomed, and be encouraged to return. Conscientiously she offered them wine or beer or tea, hoping to be turned down. Her camel's back had gotten thin and easily broken, by less than a straw. To those who actually took their empty glass or beer can out to the kitchen, she was ridiculously grateful. Those who left things to be straightened up, she hated – hated. There was just too much to be done, all the time: urine bottles to be emptied, blankets on or off, food to be offered, the TV to be changed, the long cleaning-up after a BM, the phone, relentlessly ringing, demanding an answer – a constant stream of things, each small on its own, together almost overwhelming. And always there was the three-hour morphine schedule to be watched and obeyed, night and day.

One afternoon a co-worker of Philip's came by with flowers. Louise had just dropped full-length on the sofa, exhausted. The friend walked into the living room, already miffed that no one had met her at the door.

"Oh, thank you very much," Philip said in a weak voice. "I'm sorry I can't visit with you right now, Sally, I'm so tired, but it was nice of you to come by."

Sally glared at Louise.

"It was nice of you," Louise echoed, in a voice almost as weak as Philip's.

Sally continued to hold the flowers, obviously expecting Louise to rush over and take them and rush dutifully out to the kitchen and arrange them in some perfect container.

"Just put them on the table by Philip," Louise said. "I'll put them in water right away, don't worry."

Sally left the flowers and stomped out, angry that her act of charity had not gotten a proper reception. Louise did feel sorry – but not sorry enough to rise from her couch, to which she felt as connected as Gulliver, tied down by countless minute threads to the ground. And anyway, the flowers had to go in the hall. The scent repulsed Philip; it was too strong, even with daisies.

* * *

S he could feel herself wearing down. She tried to find a hospice, a place that would take Philip for a few days and allow her to rest. There was nothing, no place to go. She began to think she might get sick, or somehow fall apart. Just one night's uninterrupted sleep. A little space, a little respite. She had endured well up to now, she was proud of herself; but she had reached a breaking point.

She phoned up Hugh. After all, he was supposed to be Philip's best friend. She asked him point-blank, desperately: could he come over the next evening and take care of Philip through the night?

"Sure," he said, "I can't come until ten or eleven, but that's okay, isn't it? Where should I sleep?"

"You can take the big front bedroom. If you leave the door to it open, and all the doors open downstairs, you'll be able to hear Philip when he calls."

"Sounds fine to me," he said.

She hung up, shaking her head with relief. How easy it had been! And she slept well, though she heard Hugh going up and down the stairs during the night, answering Philip's calls.

In the morning he was exhausted. "How do you do it, Louise?" he asked. "It was incredible. I must have gone down there five times." He left, gray from lack of sleep. Watching him go down the stairs, she felt satisfied. It wasn't just the sleep she had needed; she realized that she had called him for a witness. She had been feeling terribly lonely because there was no one who knew what it was like – not even Philip, whose consciousness was no longer entirely his own.

* * *

In calling around looking for a hospice, she had stumbled on something else: an organization called Shanti. They would send trained volunteers to see close friends and relatives of someone terminally ill. Each volunteer had had personal experience with death – that of someone they loved, or a close brush of their own. Shanti would also send someone to talk with Philip. Tentatively she asked him; the answer was no. He still did not want that kind of help. Or rather, he was relying on the Church to provide it. He called the local priest every few days, though the priest was beginning to resist making so many house calls. Philip was angry about it, but could not bring himself to request something openly called "help" or worse, "therapy."

For a long time, she herself had been reluctant to ask for help, but after asking Hugh and getting exactly what she needed, she decided to call Shanti. Soon afterward, Carole appeared on her doorstep. She looked like a slightly tough gnome: short, stocky, homely, a bit of challenge in her brown eyes. Not the usual image of the ministering angel. But for an hour she gave herself to Louise, listening to the thoughts she had not been able to tell anyone else, terrible thoughts, not the acceptable ones of grief and depression.

Louise told Carole a story she had heard long ago, about someone who had bought a bus ticket to L.A. and disappeared, simply walking out of a whole life. She could never do such a thing to Philip; the desolation of it was unthinkable. But as a guilty fantasy, the bus to L.A. made occasional appearances in her mind; it was something like the vacations granted by alcohol or marijuana, a safe escape, one that allowed return. Carole heard the bus story; she heard about Louise's love for the house and her greed for it; about her impatience with the daily ordeal of the illness; and she heard about the occasional wish, mostly suppressed but all the more troublesome because Louise could not admit it, that Philip would either get well, or die, but not linger on – this even though he himself rarely complained about his state. Although he had earlier said he would rather die than be confined in bed like a vegetable, now in his weakness he clung to life tenaciously, and it was her role to help him do so. It was bad enough that she could want something like the house, that presupposed Philip's death; it was unbearable that in any way she could want his death directly. Carole listened calmly, nodding. She was not horrified, though she felt with Louise's horror and sadness.

"You've told me so much," she said, "I know how much you also love him. No wonder. He's still a very attractive man."

Louise was amazed that she had seen this, in the weak and wasted person who had smiled at her from the hospital bed. But Louise knew it, too: it was in his eyes, and even now, in his body. The waves of flamey, flickery energy still came off him, though reduced almost to the level of reflections of light, shimmering on a wall.

She loaded Carole down with everything, shamelessly. Carole promised to come once a week for the purpose, like the garbage collector. And like an angel of mercy, giving something like absolution and forgiveness, allowing Louise to live with herself and freeing again her love for Philip, and the meaning of what their life together had become – this strange marriage – although she did not fully understand until a few weeks later.

* * *

S uddenly, in mid-April, Philip was able to do without morphine. She called up Harry. "You can just go cold turkey, Louise. I think he'll be all right. Obviously give him a dose any time he wants it. But if he doesn't want it, why that's a blessing. I don't think he'll have any severe withdrawal symptoms. He probably hasn't gotten addicted. When someone is in that much pain, it seems as if the pain uses up the morphine – something like that. It's not the way he would be if he'd been taking it for pleasure, believe me."

Harry proved to be right. Philip's only reaction to quitting the morphine was a slight cough or yawn, involuntary but not very disturbing. Gradually his mind cleared. The only impediment to his intelligence, now, was his weakness. It kept him from following a train of thought very far; but all of the essential Philip was there again.

* * *

O ld friends of Philip's from back east came to town, a couple, he an academic, she the enthusiastic organizer and orchestrator of their rather hectic life. They had always been fond of Philip, with his utter lack of stuffy self-importance. They came to see Philip almost every day while they were in Berkeley. At first they had the inability of the healthy to imagine so much, and so deep, exhaustion. As they realized Philip's state, however, Louise could see a sadness. It was hard for them to do anything for him: their books lay on the table beside him, barely touched. The extravagant flowers had to go in the hallway.

One afternoon when Emma stopped by, Philip asked if she could help Louise move the bed. This was something Louise had done once and then not repeated, because he had almost immediately wanted it back in the old position. Moving the bed meant moving two tables, some chairs, pivoting the old green couch around, and rearranging a complex tangle of electric and telephone wires. The bed itself was extremely heavy and hard to move.

Louise was sunk on the couch, exhausted, and in a bad mood. Every month or so, it seemed, her spirit rose in an angry rebellion. She wanted to be free, to take a long walk, to paint, to listen to music, to see friends – all things that had become more or less impossible. And yet it wasn't Philip's fault and she couldn't be angry with him; so she sat there, refusing, refusing. She was not inclined to be helpful. She was not inclined to move Philip's bed. She was "in a pet" – which, she thought with rue and irritation, must come from the word "petty," because there was a mean pettiness, close to malice, in her just then.

Emma, however, leaped to her feet at Philip's question.

"Sure, we can move it! Just tell us where you want it." She was instantly everywhere, moving furniture back, unlocking the bed's wheels, untangling wires, leaning hard against the bed to get it moving. It took the two women together – one enthusiastic, and one reluctant and ill-natured but pushing anyway – to move Philip a few feet from where he had been. It took several moves to find a position he liked, but when they had found it, he was delighted.

"Oh, now I can see out the side window. It's beautiful! Look at that tree – it's bloomed and I didn't even know it!"

Louise's shame was deep; but she still felt irritated at the extra work.

"And I can still see the TV. Thank you Emma, thank you Louise, this is wonderful."

"Wouldn't you like a remote control switch for the TV?" Emma asked. Again Louise felt angry. Remote controls were so new that Louise had never seen one, and it would take research to locate and several hours, perhaps, to go and get it.

"Oh, yes, it would be wonderful," Philip answered in the simple childlike way he had grown into as he got weaker. "But wouldn't it be hard to find?"

"No! Nothing easier!" Emma said decisively. "I'll bring you one tomorrow."

Relief. *She* would bring him a remote control. Louise was enormously grateful – and also angry again, at being so shown up. Why was Emma so knowledgeable and tactful and able and ener-getic, and she, Louise, was just a sort of irritable blob? And was this the love she had for Philip – so wavering and variable? How could she want to withhold things from him?

Emma gave Philip a great deal in the short time she was there. The simple change in position was a tremendous pleasure to him. He had seen life from exactly the same angle since February; it was late April now. The remote control allowed him to have TV whenever he wanted, whether or not Louise or anyone else was there. Along with his switch for raising and lowering the bed back, it was a way of exercising physical power. Now he had two of these instead of just one. It reminded Louise of what she had come to accept and almost, in a sense, lose sight of: the terrible shrinking of Philip's world.

* * *

One afternoon she noticed that Philip was scratching himself under the covers.

"Itchy?" she asked.

"Yes, I don't know what it is. My penis itches, and it feels sort of sore at the same time."

"Do you think we should worry?"

"Maybe it wouldn't hurt if you phoned the advice nurse at the hospital. Do you mind, babe?"

The advice nurse suggested rubbing with witch hazel, so Louise went out and got some. It did not help much, though. Late in the afternoon, Philip suddenly figured it out.

"Lou, Lou, take a look at the pee bottle. Is there anything in it?" They always kept a plastic bottle by the bedside, for Philip to pee into.

"It's almost empty, Philip," she said, puzzled. "I haven't emptied it since before going to work this morning. Didn't the nurse empty it?"

"No, no – that's it. I must have some sort of bladder or urinary tract problem. And look," he said, pulling the covers down, "see how my belly is swollen."

It did stick up from the emaciated body, oddly taut and round. Yet Louise realized suddenly that the whole bottom part of the bed was wet with urine, under the covers. Philip had not noticed it.

"Call Harry right away," Philip said. "This could be serious."

The doctor on duty ordered Philip to come in to the hospital immediately. In half an hour, an ambulance arrived and two men carried Philip out on a stretcher. This time, the nerves in his legs dead, he did not feel pain; he was able to almost enjoy getting outside, the trip down the stairs, even the novelty of the ambulance. It was at least a change.

At the hospital they decided to put a catheter – a narrow plastic tube – up Philip's urinary canal. It would have to remain in place for a week, at least.

Louise could not look when the nurse inserted the catheter. It seemed such a cruelly painful thing to do. But Philip smiled.

"That wasn't bad at all," he said. They were all relieved. An enormous amount of urine flowed from the tube into a waiting receptacle.

"Look," said the nurse. "This would have given you real trouble if you'd waited much longer."

They forgot to think about why the tube had not hurt Philip. His nerves were no longer able to tell him much about anything happening below the waist. Once again, his world had shrunk.

The tubing remained. He had lost control of both excretory functions, now. This embarrassed him briefly, but he soon accepted it. He had gotten used to accepting things.

At the same time, he began to be determinedly optimistic. This was a change. Back in March, when he had received last rites, he had thought he would die soon. Now, weeks later, he talked only of when he would get up, when he would walk, when his strength would return. It seemed to Louise that the upward swing, as he had gotten over his radiation sickness, had leveled out, and that there was perhaps a downward turn now. But everything was so gradual that she could not feel absolutely sure. So she smiled and nodded when he talked about his recovery, never contradicting. Yet something important to her was being lost: honesty.

She could not tell Philip that the nurse and doctor were giving him only a limited time to live – a year at most, and probably much less. But they had been wrong in March, after all. Maybe they were wrong again. Once again the illness divided them from one another. How could she tell the person she loved to give up all hope? Perhaps hope could mobilize his resistance, give him time, even save him.

Underneath, however, Philip knew as well as Louise. Every morning, particularly, he was deeply depressed. Beverly reported that he lay silently weeping for hours on end. Perhaps the hope was only a pretense for Louise, but she thought it was more than that.

One day Philip took her hand. "I have to tell you, Lou, sometimes I'm not so good, sometimes I have bad thoughts. For instance it occurs to me that maybe my pains went away because the cancer has blocked the nerves in my lower spine. Sometimes I think these thoughts. But I get over them." He looked at her, with his direct green eyes. "Don't cry, babe. We have to keep hoping. Don't let the bad thoughts win."

She nodded, and rushed out to the kitchen, where she could let out that batch of tears. When she returned, they were both calm again, at least on the surface. And without quite realizing it, Louise slipped back a little into hope. Philip was usually right about important things; why not this also?

* * *

On weekdays, Louise walked to and from work in a sort of trance. She felt with sharp ecstasy the warm air on her skin, the sun, the smells of plants blooming in the still-damp earth. To be alive – she had never been so aware of it, so in love with it. She felt like crying from the beauty of it. And there was no one she could share it with. She could not tell Philip; it would only make him sad. And the people at work would be startled. As for her women friends, she seemed to have lost contact with them. Sylvia was still off in the Valley, teaching. Deirdre also was teaching, a new course on feminism and peace that took up most of her energies. Besides, Louise could not talk about the things on her mind without crying. It seemed too great a burden to lay on friends, time after time; and she could no longer take much interest in the lives of other people. The other world, the world of the healthy, seemed too remote.

* * *

Philip was often in and out of the Emergency Ward at the hospital now. Louise got used to following the ambulance in her car, waiting in Emergency, and, if they decided to keep Philip overnight, rushing home to take advantage of the chance to put fresh sheets on the bed and get a laundry done.

The hospital was good for serious treatments. It was not good, however, in lesser ways. Each time Philip went in, he came out with diarrhea – an exhausting ordeal for both of them. And in late April he returned from the hospital with the red spot on his back turned into a real bedsore, because no one had bothered to shift him in the bed or rub his sore spot – heavy work, conveniently overlooked.

At first, the sore was small. It looked like a gym burn, or a lightly skinned knee. Once that skin had been lost, however, the sore was hard to control. It gradually widened, from about the size of a quarter to a three-by-four-inch rectangle; and it deepened, turning from pink to red to a deep purple color. It was frightening to Louise to see it – like a gradually opening door on Philip's insides. The thrice-daily treatment involved turning Philip onto his stomach – carefully, to minimize the pain – using a sheet for leverage. Then came the washing, rubbing around the edges of the sore, and then an elaborate antiseptic ritual before bandaging again, or putting on a new patch of "artificial skin." When this was done, Louise gave his legs a workout, lifting, bending, and flexing them, so that if strength did miraculously return, he would be able to walk in spite of the months without movement. Philip got everyone he could to exercise his legs for him: not only Louise – increasingly reluctant – but the nurse and the nurse's aide, and even Jo-Jo. Philip still refused to consider any possibility other than recovery. Upstairs, Louise left his running shoes where he had left them, on the bathroom floor.

* * *

Of all the visitors, it was John, the nurse, who had become their closest friend. He could talk with them about the things that absorbed them, but that most people did not care to hear about: all the minute changes in Philip's body, what each one might mean, and what might be done to help. After a visit, Louise would often walk with John to the door or even down to the sidewalk where they could talk about things Louise wanted to know, but hated to ask in front of Philip. There was no one else who was both qualified to answer her questions, and sincerely interested as well. John's warmth and intelligence had won them both completely. They looked forward to each of his visits.

Now Kaiser, recognizing John's ability, had decided to promote him out of the ranks of those who dealt with people, into the ranks of those who dealt with paper in closed private offices. John and Harry insisted that John's replacement would be every bit as good as John. But the new nurse, Barbara, was only as intelligent as a person can be when no new information is allowed in. When Louise tried to tell her things about Philip's condition, she took it as a reproof, as if Louise was implying that she, the nurse, did not know her job. Oddly, though Barbara was deaf to Louise and Philip, she spoke to them in a nervous shout, so their ears rang.

Gradually they stopped telling her what they knew and thought, and when they disagreed or couldn't see a reason for what she told them to do, they simply didn't do it. There was no point in asking, and somehow it made them doubt Barbara's competence. They knew she wanted to do the right thing; she was trying; but they could not really like and trust her.

"Well," Philip said philosophically, "it's the old trick. Is the glass half empty or half full? We were so lucky to have John all this time. And it's really awful that he's gone."

Barbara had been unable to understand their worry about catheter emergencies on the weekends; she could not accept the idea that the best staff was absent then, nor did she understand Philip's reluctance to undergo the now exhausting ordeal of being taken by ambulance to the hospital. On Fridays they eyed each other apprehensively when it was time to empty the urine bag. Would it be empty? Or would it be empty on Saturday or Sunday?

One weekend, when the urine bag had stood empty since morning, Philip asked Louise to try calling nursing associations. To have a competent person come to them at home seemed well worth the out-of-pocket expense. They did not know which nursing associations would be good and trustworthy, but finally Louise located one which promised to send a nurse out, within the hour. An hour went by, then another and another. Philip's belly was distended and taut. At last, desperate, they called a distant friend of Philip's, a doctor who mainly did research now. He was out, but they left a message with his wife. In another hour, the nurse finally arrived from the agency. She was in sloppy casual clothes, and did not speak very good English. Her daughter came with her, a pudgy teenager with bad complexion and frightened eyes, who insisted on standing by herself in the hallway.

Louise explained the problem to the nurse.

"What," she exclaimed, "you don't have a new tubing? Nothing? No germless solution, no saline, no clamps, no means of injecting a solution? How can you think I can help? I vill leave, this is impossible."

"But I explained everything to the person who sent you out –"

"That doesn't matter. Ve must irrigate, okay, where is your stove?"

Louise could see the uncertainty on Philip's face, but he nodded. He had to try whatever was available. They had waited too long.

The woman – Louise had begun to wonder if she was really a nurse or not – stomped off into the kitchen. At that instant, the doorbell rang. It was Philip's doctor friend, Bob, necessary materials in hand, come to save the day. The woman left in a huff, angry to have been displaced, though she had not wanted to stay, either.

Bob loved being the hero, the rescuer, or at least he made them feel that he did, cleansing them of whatever guilt they might have suffered at calling him over on a Sunday evening. He stayed on for a glass of brandy, which he recommended for Philip, too.

"Great diuretic," he said. "Just drains out all that extra fluid."

Philip was amused and so, to Louise's amazement, he took some brandy and seemed to enjoy it. Ordinarily these days, it was all he could do to drink half a glass of ginger ale.

"Nice," Bob said, gesturing with his glass at one of Louise's paintings, hanging on the wall. "I see a leg there – see? A big leg coming down the middle. I like legs."

It was a painting of abstract plant forms, but Bob was too open and genial to be offensive.

"I'm a painter myself," he went on.

"Really?"

"Yes. When I was only a boy, maybe nine years old, I used to love to paint ships. They said I was amazingly good. Haven't done much since, though."

He settled back in his chair, happy at the thought that he had had more genius than there was time to develop. But it was impossible to be annoyed. Though he had some fifty years on his back, he was still essentially the much-loved, much-praised nine-year-old.

And he proved to be a generous friend. They had to call him over three times, always on Sunday evenings, to rescue Philip from the stress and anxiety of a trip to the hospital. Each time Bob came happily, as though they had invited him to a wonderful party it was a privilege to attend.

* * *

I n mid-May, in spite of all, somehow there was a new peace. When Louise came down in the morning, after a full night's uninterrupted rest, she looked forward to seeing Philip. He was very groggy then because of the sleeping pills he still took, plus the effect of a mood-elevating drug Harry had prescribed for Philip's uncontrollable crying. As Louise came into the living room, Philip heard her, and opening his eyelids, slid his eyes towards her, smiling softly.

Every morning this happened, day after day. It was as if he were making a large effort to be sure she knew she was greeted, even though he would rather have slept on. She got him some orange juice, and set out his pills for the morning, measuring everything carefully: two of this, four of that, ten of another. Now, instead of eating her breakfast out in the kitchen, alone, she took it into the living room to eat with Philip. They spoke very little. Speech was unnecessary. They were together, deeply and simply connected, looking out the window together at the distant mountains veiled in early morning gray.

She remembered what Philip had said six or seven months earlier: if he died then, it would be when their love was at its height, and that was something lucky. But now their love had become more perfect, perhaps as perfect as it could ever be. Without a future, and without an external life and all the things by which they defined themselves to the world – their work; their abilities and intelligence and education; energy or charm;

conversation and accomplishments; desire, and fear of not getting; posturing and games; satiety, excess, and the return of need again: apart from all these things now, they knew one another. They were off the rollercoaster. There was only eating and sleeping, sharing the time, sitting together, watching dumb movies whose plots they already knew, calm as eating honey toast, calm as Philip's eyes sliding beneath pale lids to greet her in the morning.

Not that physical pain, and fear of it, had left them. As the disease ate upwards into Philip's body, it had gradually become more and more painful for him to be moved at all. Now he would not let Barbara or the nurse's aide turn him over to treat his bedsores in the mornings, waiting instead until Louise got home to do it. She had so identified with his body that she could still move it without hurting him unbearably. In her own mind, she was his body. Occasionally in the shower, when she looked down at her legs, she was disconcerted to see that they were not the thin rods she had been massaging and exercising. She had a sense of wasting away herself. It was months since she had had time to go running; she felt stiff and weak in comparison with her former self. And yet she could see that she was, still, alive and well; she was not Philip. Another betrayal, and she put it out of her mind.

* * *

Sylvia came for one of her rare visits to Berkeley. Louise looked forward to her coming, although she wondered what Sylvia would think of Philip. When she had last seen him, he had looked more or less like his old self.

It was a sunny Saturday when Sylvia arrived at their front door; nearly all the days that spring began in a gentle mist and then cleared to perfect sun.

"Hi," Sylvia said, looking up at Louise before rather shyly hugging her. "How're you doing?"

"Good to see you, Sylvia," Louise said emphatically returning the hug. She had forgotten how little Sylvia was. She looked even smaller than usual, almost slightly wizened.

"God, you don't know what it's like to come back here to civilization," she sighed, shaking her head. "But where's Philip? I'd like to see him first."

Louise took her into the living room. As always, Philip lay in his great barred bed, loosely wrapped in a hospital gown of faded blue flowers. Directly over the bed and within reach were his mother's crucifix and rosary beads, along with the bead necklace Louise had made for him years ago. At the foot of the bed, the TV was on. Philip's face bore a dark gray film of whiskers. Louise still had not learned to shave him; Beverly and the nurse's aide did that during the week. The stubbly hair made his face look even more haggard and gaunt than at other times. When he saw Sylvia he smiled, moving his bony hand slowly across the bed to the remote control switch that would turn off the TV.

"Sylvia," he greeted her.

"Hi, Philip," she said, standing a wary distance away from him. "How are you feeling?"

"Not bad," he answered. "And I have everything I want here." He waved vaguely at all the equipment surrounding him. "How are things out in the Valley?"

Sylvia wrinkled her face. "What can I say, it could be worse. I have air conditioning, otherwise it'd be unbearable."

They exchanged a few more polite words, Sylvia all the while standing far from the bed, her body carefully held in, as if cancer were contagious as the flu. A few minutes later she was in the kitchen with Louise. They closed the door, ostensibly so as not to disturb Philip, but also for privacy.

Sylvia shook her head several times. "That's not Philip," she said, "that's not Philip."

Louise was taken aback. "What? What do you mean?"

"That person in there – it's just not Philip anymore, he's gone."

"But –" Louise hesitated, uncertain how to answer something so terribly mistaken, "to me – and to other people, too – it is. I'd say it's even more Philip than before. I feel as if the essence of Philip is there, here, with all the surface distractions separated out, taken off."

"I'm sorry, he's just so changed," Sylvia said in a petulant tone. "Maybe I just can't see it. I'm so tired, so tired of teaching, and being out there in that godforsaken place where they think a New York Jew is like –" she rolled her eyes, looking for a simile. "They make these bad jokes to me, about Jewish princesses, stuff like that, trying to show how sophisticated they are, and all it shows is how uncomfortable they are. The highest praise one teacher can give another is 'Oh, she's a good Christian,' as if that was the only way you could be a decent person. They don't know how to talk to me. And to tell the truth, I don't know how to talk to them. All they talk about is money, and their dogs, and – what else – oh yes, they'll talk about their cars. God! I don't want to talk about their dogs – oh yeah, some of them have kids too. Well, don't listen to me, I'm just tired. So tell me about Philip."

"He's terribly weak, but in some ways it doesn't seem that bad. He still has a lot of pain, but only if someone moves him, not when he's just lying there quietly. So he's off the morphine, his mind is clear. I feel as if I have the complete Philip here now. In some ways it's lovely. Almost, I'd almost say we're more together now, closer than we've ever been. There isn't anything else for either of us now, except just to live from day to day and be together."

Sylvia frowned. "You mean you never get out? Don't you do anything? You still go to work, don't you?"

"Yes, but that's about all – except go to the grocery. Oh yes, and I'm hanging a show of watercolors pretty soon. Masha arranged that for me. But I haven't done any painting for months. There just hasn't been time. It's amazing. And I hardly ever see anyone, except for Philip, of course. But the funny thing is that it seems very lovely, very peaceful. And what Philip and I have has never been so strong, even though we don't talk all that much. He's too weak to talk very much. But there's no need." She shut her eyes for a moment, thinking about it. "We've never been so close."

"Well, he really needs you, I mean you're all he has now, practically. You're like his mother or something. So you don't have anything else either? And you're perfectly happy? This is the perfect relationship?"

"I guess so, Sylvia." Louise smiled.

"So you're everything to each other and the rest of life is nothing? Don't you think it's unhealthy?"

Louise shrugged. "Healthy, unhealthy – who cares? This is the way it is. It's an incredible gift. It just happened, that's all. It came with the sickness. We finally figured out that everything is so simple. So simple, so good. Precious."

Sylvia leaned forward, peering at Louise critically. "Is there something wrong with you? You seem so, I don't know, you don't wave your hands around when you talk, and your voice seems kind of strange, like flat. Are you all right?"

"You really can tell a difference? That's amazing. I took one of Philip's tranquilizer pills last night so I could sleep. The doctor said it would be okay. But that was something like fifteen hours ago, and I only took half a pill."

"Ha!" Sylvia cried. "So you aren't yourself! I could tell! You're not the real Louise! It makes you strange. Usually there's so much life in you, but today you're like a zombie or something."

"Well, I feel the same. My head feels clear, maybe clearer than if I hadn't taken the pill. Sometimes I need something, that's all. The pressure is too constant, it's too wearing. I need these little vacations. But I feel perfectly present. It hasn't changed me, except maybe in these external things you talk about, the gestures and all that. It makes my body feel very quiet, and sort of restful."

Sylvia shook her head. "I have to say, with that in there," and she gestured towards the door behind which Philip lay, "I'd need something too."

"How about some tea, Sylvia?" Louise asked in exasperation, getting up from the table. "Tell me more about life in the Valley."

"Death in the Valley you mean," Sylvia groaned. Then, quickly, "Oh, god, how could I say that!"

"What?" Louise asked, puzzled.

"Death in the Valley! How could I say that? You must think I'm terrible."

"You think the word 'death' would bother me?" Louise asked, incredulous. She had not imagined that Sylvia could seem so alien to her, so obtuse. She began to estimate the amount of time it would take if she heated water, made tea, allowed it to steep, and then the amount of time it would take to drink it. Too long. She would rather be with Philip, sitting quietly, or doing some small thing for him, bringing him ginger ale, rearranging him in the bed, any of the countless small things that needed doing.

"Oh, don't heat water, Louise. I really can't stay that long," Sylvia said, standing up. "I hope you don't mind. I'm staying with Harvey while I'm here in Berkeley, and I promised I'd meet him when he gets off work today. We're going to visit his parents."

"Sounds exciting," Louise commented, smiling.

"I know," Sylvia said, as she walked back into the living room. "But I like them – maybe better than Harvey!"

Turning into the living room, she stood once again several safe feet away from Philip's bed. "Goodbye, Philip," she said.

"Bye," he said, without expression. Louise guessed that he, too, was irritated by Sylvia's fear of the sickness.

Neither woman offered to hug the other as they parted at the front door. With relief Louise turned away, back to Philip.

* * *

One Sunday night in early June, Philip seemed suddenly much weaker. He refused to let her turn him to treat his back and the deepening bedsore.

"It hurts too much," he said. "Don't bother. I don't want to be moved." He said it in a definite tone of voice that showed he meant it. Reluctantly, she nodded. She hated to think of the bedsore going untreated, and his back perhaps opening into further sores because she had not been able to massage it enough.

But Philip's mind was clear; it was his decision.

When she came down the next morning, Philip was different, changed. She had taken the day off from work in order to hang the watercolor show in downtown Berkeley, with the help of Masha. She was determined to do it. For weeks she had been matting and framing the paintings on the dining room table. Philip had taken part from the adjoining living room, as much as he could, admiring each one as it was done, commiserating when her hand slipped and ruined a mat board, commenting on which ones he liked best. He wanted her to hang the show, too. But he hardly seemed capable of being left alone today, even for a short time. Usually when Philip was to be alone before the nurse or the aide came, Louise put the telephone in the bed with him so that he could phone someone if he got lonely or needed help. Today it seemed as if the receiver might be too heavy for him, and she was not sure that he could remember any numbers, either. Still, she did not hesitate long. Philip had seemed worse before, and then rallied. Surely, she told herself, she could do this one single thing. The nurse and the aide would be visiting in the course of the morning. After breakfast, Louise kissed Philip goodbye as usual, and left. She and Masha hung the show and then had lunch together, sitting outdoors at a cafe table, in the warm sun. She had not had a chance to do such a thing in many months.

When she returned home, there was a note from the nurse, Barbara, saying sternly that Philip was now too ill to be left alone, even for an hour, even for fifteen minutes. Louise felt anger rise in her as she read the note. What did Barbara know about what Louise had been doing, how much she needed to be out of the house, just this once, out on her own for a few hours in freedom?

Easy to say, that she should never ever leave. Her anger was fueled by the sense that probably she should not, in fact, have left Philip alone. Well, she would stay with him now, but go to work the next morning as usual. Beverly was scheduled to be with him then, and he would be safe. Probably he would be better again tomorrow. She did not want to fear, to despair, and then turn around again into hope, wrenching herself each time there was a change. That was the rollercoaster, the useless exhausting projection into the future. She wanted to stay where she was, one thing at a time.

But that night she had trouble sleeping. After lying awake for a while, she realized that she could hear Philip breathing. It was a labored breathing, long hoarse breaths pulled in, heavily pushed out again. After a while she put on her robe and went down to sit in the dark by Philip's bed.

"Philip!" she whispered. "Are you all right?"

"What?" he asked. Then he spoke confusedly. She could not make out most of his words, which seemed as if broken up in pieces and reassembled according to some private pattern.

For several hours she sat in the chair, leaning on the bedrails, watching and listening. The thought came into her mind, so clear that she did not question it: in the morning she would phone her mother and ask her to come. Mrs. Borgstrum had offered many times, but Louise had not wanted to turn her into a second nurse for Philip. It would have been too hard and confining for her, with no one but Louise to turn to for company, cut off from her world back in Minnesota.

Louise did not know if Philip was dying now. She did not even ask that question. She had asked it too many times before, agonized over it too often. All she knew now was that she could not bear it alone anymore. No matter how long it went on, she wanted her mother by her. She could go home whenever she wanted to; Louise would not try to hold her. But she needed her now.

Finally, exhausted, she dragged Jo-Jo's old mattress out from under the dining room table. "Philip," she said, leaning close over him, trying to point her voice in such a way that it would slide past the shifting shapes of his confusion, into the receding center where his consciousness still survived. "I'm going to sleep right here, right by your side, on Jo-Jo's old mattress and a good warm sleeping bag. I'll be right by your side," she repeated. "I won't leave you."

"Really?" he mumbled. "That's wonderful." His voice trailed off into incomprehensible words, and then he resumed his hoarse breathing. Louise lay down on the floor by his side, and as she settled in, getting warm again in the down bag, Philip's breathing quieted, returning to normal. They both slept soundly until morning.

* * *

As soon as she was up, Louise phoned her mother. Even though it was already nine a.m. back in Minneapolis, her mother promised to be in Berkeley by that evening. Louise called Beverly, too, suggesting that since Philip was so ill, Louise would stay home with him after all, so Beverly need not come. But Beverly insisted on coming for at least a short while. Perhaps she wanted to say goodbye to Philip. The two of them had liked each other exceptionally well. Then she phoned in to work and told them she would not be in that day. And last she phoned Harry, describing Philip's condition.

"He's dying, Louise. Don't disturb him by trying to move him or forcing him to eat."

"Water? I feel as if he must be terribly thirsty. He's breathing with his mouth wide open. And his eyes are open, but he doesn't seem to see."

"Don't give him water unless he asks for it. The kindest thing is to let him go peacefully, to stay unconscious. Let the process go on."

She could not bear to sit with him, holding his hand, the way she had seen it done in movies. Somehow this dying seemed to her a private thing. To insist on her presence with him, to try to go with him to the edge, seemed akin to a kind of irritating flirtation, promising what would, at the last minute, be withheld. Still, she was not sure. Was it right to leave him alone now? Did he need her presence, the reassuring pressure of her hand on his? There was no way of telling. But it seemed cleaner, somehow, to leave him alone, as Harry had suggested, to let him handle it without distractions. The independence he had striven for with so much difficulty, he now achieved willy-nilly. Surely he knew how much she loved him; but in spite of that he had to die alone. Maybe it was her own weakness. She could not bear to sit by his side, hour after hour, listening to that painful breathing, watching the open sightless eyes, the open unconscious mouth. So she busied herself with small household tasks, passing often through the room where he lay, where his body struggled on, breath after labored breath.

It was a revelation to her to see how this physical body, like an independent entity, apart from the mind or spirit, simply refused to stop. It had achieved this life, this complex and beautiful form, and it wanted to keep going. Each breath seemed a labored miracle, yet breath after breath was achieved, hour after hour. Entropy had recently become a fashionable subject, but the will to form, and persistence of form, seemed to her now incredibly powerful.

Early in the afternoon the nurse came by on her regular visit. As usual she did not give Louise a chance to say anything, marching into the living room with her boxes of bandages and balm, her brown curls bouncing off her shoulders.

"Hello, Philip!" she shouted, even more loudly than usual, leaning down over him to deliver the noise more effectively.

"Ohhmn," Philip mumbled, and his eyelids fluttered as his eyes tried to focus.

"How are you today?" the nurse shouted into his face again.

Philip said something unintelligible to both the nurse and Louise. But he had spoken. He could still hear, and he was trying to take part in their world, though he looked bewildered.

The nurse continued shouting, trying to wake Philip up as if he were only sleepy, and Philip continued trying to reply. The only word Louise could make out was "hospital."

She closed her eyes, a brief exit from what was happening. There was nothing they could do for him at the hospital. Harry had made that clear. And this was the death Philip had chosen for himself when his mind was his own: death at home, with Louise there, and not in the cold impersonality of the hospital. She had not filled the room with candles; the drama they had joked about was missing. But the essence, the quiet dying in his own living room, he could have. She felt that she should hew to this earlier wish of his, and ignore this plea now for a salvation which did not exist. But the refusal tore at her. He wanted to go to the hospital, and she had to ignore this cry for help.

"What did the doctor say?" the nurse shouted, now in Louise's direction.

"He says Philip is dying, and that we should just leave him alone, not try to force things on him."

"Oh! Then there's not much point in all these things – and I'd just gotten a new kind of ointment for his bedsore! Well, goodbye and good luck, Louise." The nurse looked sympathetically at her, but Louise could not muster much of a response. She found Barbara too jarring. It was a relief to see her go. Then it was just Philip and herself again, alone in the house.

* * *

By 8:30 that night, Mrs. Borgstrum had arrived, driven in from the airport by Jim. She stood with Louise for a long moment by the bars of Philip's bed, where he lay with his eyes wide open, seeing nothing. They talked as if he was completely unconscious; and yet Louise wondered whether he could still hear, and if he knew that her mother was there. If he did, she thought, it would surely comfort him.

Late in the evening Louise and her mother went into the kitchen, to get a glass of sherry. They talked, and even joked a little over their Lutheran guilt in drinking. As they came back into the living room, Louise was talking. It was wonderful to have someone to talk to, and she found her voice rising on the tide of pent-up energies.

Her mother suddenly held up her hand, hushing Louise, listening intently. The room was silent. Then there was the sound of a slow breath, very slow; and then a long pause. They went over and stood by Philip's bed together. Another breath came, but just a little one, almost a sigh, gentle, without a struggle. This time the silence did not end.

Louise stood with her mother, hanging over Philip's hospital bed, shocked.

"Philip!" she screamed. "Goddamn you! How could you leave me?"

Even as the words left her mouth, she thought they sounded forced, contrived. She did not know what she really wanted to say. But she also believed that if Philip was able to hear her words, he would understand. He might, once again, even be a little amused.

"Louise!" her mother said, horrified. Louise could feel her mother's body recoil from hers. She was not supposed to be angry at Philip for dying; or maybe it was wrong to shout at a dead man.

They were silent then together, looking at Philip. His eyes were still open, as they had been all day. Louise made no effort to shut them. She did not want them shut.

Surprised at her ability to still function, surprised to find herself still alive, on the other side of this chasm, she called the mortuary. They offered to come immediately for Philip's body, but she asked them to wait until morning. Philip must not be rushed out of sight, like something suddenly become worthless. With her mother in the house with her, she would be all right even with Philip lying, dead, downstairs.

She phoned Hugh and Jim, who came over immediately. It seemed they had been waiting together at Hugh's house, only half a block away. They walked into the living room and looked a long moment at Philip's body. Their faces registered disbelief, perhaps remembering the old Philip, incandescent with life, and unable to associate that memory with this wasted corpse. Rather quickly they retreated to the hallway, leaving Mrs. Borgstrum to sit by herself with Philip.

There on the hallway bench with Louise between them, the two men cried, hunched together; and then, their tears stopped up, they let Louise cry for them awhile.

Finally lifting her head and looking back into the living room, she asked, "Do you think we could have him stuffed?" She was half serious. How could she allow Philip to disappear entirely?

"Oh god, I don't think so," Hugh replied.

After awhile the two men left. There was nothing for them to do. Louise went back to the living room, where her mother waited patiently with Philip.

"I think maybe we should go to bed now," her mother suggested.

Louise nodded. "Yes. Why don't you go on up? I'll be up in a minute."

"Are you sure you want to?" her mother asked.

"Yes, I'll be all right."

As her mother went slowly up the stairs, Louise sat down again by Philip. He lay there so alone. She reached out and stroked his forehead, as she had done countless times. But it was no longer Philip. The forehead was hard and cold, like stone or plaster of Paris. It was not him. This body was not Philip; it was totally distinct from the person she had loved. Amazing that she had made such a mistake, almost worshiping his beauty and the energy he gave out in luminous waves. The body was a sham. The eyes, unlit, were blank. Yes, it was Philip. But in a more important sense, it was not. Well, she thought, maybe the energy had been him; maybe the beauty that had informed that body had been him; she was not sure. All she knew was that the body was here, but Philip was absent. Slowly she took her own body up to bed, where she slept the old dark dreamless sleep.

In the morning the morticians came. They told her to leave until they had taken Philip away, but she came back from the kitchen in time to see him going on a stretcher, down the steep front stairs. She had seen the ambulance men take him down that way countless times before. But this time, dark green cloth was drawn over his entire form. There seemed to be almost no body left. The cancer, with its invisible claws, had eaten him away.

* * *

In the following days, with her mother's help, Louise began to clean up what was left, the detritus of a life. First the machinery of illness: the wheelchair and the mechanical lift which he had used briefly; the hospital bed; and pans and pills and cleaning cloths and tissue boxes and displaced furniture. When they were done working, the room came to look normal – that is, as if no one had suffered and died in it. A week later she went to pick up Philip's ashes. She did not want the remains of him to lie in a strange place. In a daze she drove with her mother to the mortuary. Could she really do this, and live through it? Pick up the remains as if they were laundry from the cleaners?

The funeral director, dressed in an ostentatiously tasteful suit, avoided staring at her; he appeared to be a kind man. He did not change expression as he handed her the box, about one foot by one foot, in which Philip's long body now lay. It weighed about the same as a five-pound sack of potatoes. She carried it across the asphalt parking lot and put it in the back of the car. Her mother remained silent. Louise wondered if she had picked up her father's ashes this way too. At home, she stowed the package by the front door. The ashes would fertilize the spot on the front hill, where Philp had loved to linger on his chaise lounge, looking at the bay and the mountains and ocean far beyond.

Meantime, Rachel arranged the wake, with perfect competence after all, making sure that everyone was called, everything coordinated. On a warm June evening, friends filled the house, talking in soft voices, sipping drinks, remembering Philip. Louise moved about in a haze, filling glasses, listening to parts of conversations. She wished Philip were there to hear all the praise, and to know that he did have some true friends. Maybe he was there – but she couldn't find him, sense him.

Louise's mother stayed on long enough to be sure Louise was all right, and then went back to her own empty house. It was time to do the final house-cleaning. And there was something Louise was looking for.

Upstairs in the front bedroom, she began to go through the piles of things that, in their stuttering way, told Philip's story. There was the old copy of his dissertation; photos of his parents when they were young; photos of Philip at his wedding to Concha, where in his boyish eagerness he looked so handsome and so vulnerable. And finally she found it, a single page folded over:

Dear Philip,
It's useless to continue. My love will always be with you.
– Pat

"Continue?" Louise thought. Continue what? The letter was dated about three months before Philip's death. At that point he was completely confined to his hospital bed. But before? How much before? She pictured Philip, too weak to actively have sex, lying under Pat as she opened her legs and milked him like a vampire, sucking out his last vitality.

A lurid fantasy. She leaned back in her chair, thinking. Philip had told her this note was not important, yet he had deliberately left it for her to read. So she would hear it from him, and not from some malicious gossip? But also a confession, a sharing.

If he had recovered and lived on, what might have been? Death had given them what life might have taken: a strange kind of perfection. Now time's slow inexorable current was bearing her away, each day leaving in its wake a fine shower of ash, detritus that might gradually obscure Philip from her. And she would move on too, in spite of everything, she would return to light, color, painting. Maybe, after enough days, she would forget what Philip looked like, forget the sound of his voice, the rush of her blood in his presence.

Yet, closing her eyes, Philip's presence came in on her, warm, strong, undeniable. Impatiently she ripped the letter in half and threw it in the wastebasket. Somewhere in the labyrinth, beside an ancient river, Philip would surely be waiting for her.

ACKNOWLEDGEMENTS

In 1981, very shortly after "Philip" (Jack Burki) died, I wrote down everything I could remember about him while it was still fresh in memory. For this, I really needed a computer – which I couldn't afford. Bob Kridle, my boss and friend in computer science at U.C. Berkeley, solved my problem: I got a cheap "dumb" computer, and Bob connected it to the giant computers on campus. This gave me a copy capable of being revised for the forty years it took me to get brave enough to say everything. After many moves, however, and surrounded by my re-writes, I was unable to find the core original version. Bob generously came to the rescue again with a clean original-version copy, and this has been my basis for the final writing.

I've had enormously helpful readers. The first and most important reader was Joan Kip, tactful friend and gifted writer (*A Different Woman: The View from Ninety*). Joan persuaded me to cut some of the more sentimental parts, and to ask more carefully what really belonged to the story. Georgiana Davidson was also a generous reader, annotating the text page by page with her usual sharp – and kind – insights. Roger Freeburg, too, was a very knowledgeable reader. Later, Susan Hanley told me what she and her husband, Kozo Yamamura, had learned about the publishing world as they published their several books. Sherrill Jaffe also supplied essential information about mainstream publishing, and it was Sherrill who led me to Kate Winter, essential preparer of books, from copyediting to layout to book cover to general professional advice about publishing.

In 2022, Carol Urzi read the second-to-last version and gave me the necessary nudge, telling me it was worth finishing. About the same time, a painter friend, Diane Rusnak, remarked that she had always been "married to painting." This comment reminded me again: everything must hinge on the question of what is most important. When at last I felt the book was finished, Sid Gershgoren, whose editorial and artistic acumen I greatly trust, gave the necessary warm reassurance.